A SMALL TOWN ON THE PLANET CALLED HEAVEN

NOVELS BY COLIN ALEXANDER

LEIF THE LUCKY (AND RELATED BOOKS)

Starman's Saga: The Long Strange Journey of Leif the Lucky
Murder Under Another Sun
The Lucky Starman
A Planet of Wrath and Tears
The Secret of the Martian Girl
A Small Town on the Planet Called Heaven (related)

THE INTERSTELLAR REACH

Complicated: The Interstellar Life and Times of Saoirse Kenneally
The Case of the Princess and the Interstellar Bounty Hunter

OTHER SCIENCE FICTION AND FANTASY

Princess of Shadows: The Girl Who Would Be King
Accidental Warrior: The Unlikely Tale of Bloody Hal
My Life: An Ex-Quarterback's Adventures in the Galactic Empire

MYSTERIES

Lady of Ice and Fire
God's Adamantine Fate

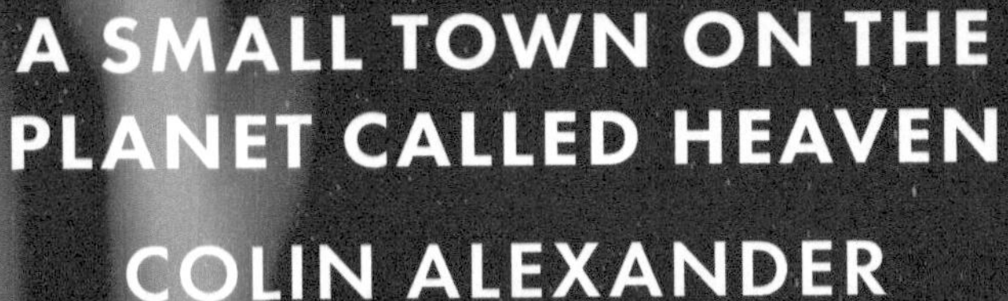

A SMALL TOWN ON THE PLANET CALLED HEAVEN

COLIN ALEXANDER

A SMALL TOWN ON THE PLANET CALLED HEAVEN

Copyright © 2026 by Colin Alexander

ISBN: 979-8-9905853-3-1 (ebook)
979-8-9905853-4-8 (paperback)

Cover art by Alejandro Colucci
Interior formatting by Mariska Maas (Rubre Art)

®

BRICKS AND STONES WILL HIDE THE BONES
BEFORE YOUR WORDS CAN HURT ME™
www.afictionado.com

For Cello, the reason I write

AUTHOR'S NOTE

This story takes place on the planet called Heaven in the fictional universe of Leif the Lucky. This is the same setting that was used for the book *Murder Under Another Sun*, but it is now twenty years after Leif departed for Earth at the end of that story. The settlers who remained on Heaven have grown older and their children are now reaching adulthood. This is their story.

For those who are interested, Thorny's name is derived from the Icelandic name Þórný. In the story, it is written and pronounced as though it were US English for the reasons given by the character.

As a point of reference, the date on the opening page is given in both the Earth Frame of Reference (EFOR) years that are used throughout the Leif the Lucky books and in Heaven Years (HY). Otherwise, all dates correspond to the Heaven calendar, which retains the names of the months from Earth's calendar, but each month has thirty-five days. The seasonal markers (solstice, equinox) of Heaven's calendar also differ from Earth's.

HEAVEN

AD 2195, EFOR

HEAVEN YEAR (HY) 21

PART I

The mind is its own place, and in it self
Can make a Heav'n of Hell, a Hell of Heav'n.

John Milton, *Paradise Lost*

DECEMBER 24, HY 21

DANIJEL

DANIJEL PETROVIC DID NOT EXPECT TO TRIP OVER A DEAD BODY IN THE DARK.

It was an unseen, unknown mass that caught his foot and sent him pitching forward. He broke his fall with outstretched hands, which kept his face from smacking into the ground, but the pain in his wrists was a vivid reminder of why he had been taught not to land that way in those gymnastics sessions at the school. He cursed, flexed both wrists, and gave thanks that neither one seemed sprained or broken.

He sat up and strained his eyes in a futile attempt to figure out what had tripped him. The dark was nearly absolute in the early-morning hours with the winter solstice approaching. Even this close, he could not make out the object in front of him.

The town's hydroponics facility he'd been edging around was unlit. It sat on the far side of Perimeter Road, the road that circled Saint Peterstown, and its bulk blocked the few lights in the town that were behind it. Angel, the smallest of Heaven's three moons and the only one in the sky, was also on the far side of the hydroponics facility. The gathering clouds, in air moist enough and hot enough to be a sauna even at this hour, dimmed whatever light Angel did cast and obscured the stars above Heaven. Danijel had turned off his phone and its light to avoid being seen by those he thought might be here. The blackness around him swallowed all evidence of the world.

He froze where he sat, more afraid of being spotted than curious about whatever he'd tripped over. But the darkness was quiet. There were no voices, no lights, no movement that said he had been seen or heard. Well, no one else was supposed to be out at this hour.

In fact, he should not be here himself. He had gone out only because he had been awakened by a call from Regan Mulders, who was in his cohort of high-seniors at the residence school. She'd told him she had woken up and found that Thorny was not in the hab the two of them shared. She was concerned that Thorny had gone out looking for Dalton's group, who often hung out here.

Danijel did understand what Regan had implied, if not said directly. That particular group of his high-senior cohort often congregated here late at night, as though it were their private party area. They would smoke cannabis, drink what they called whiskey, and engage in some other activities, none of which they wanted known to Reality Busby, who ran the residence school, or to her cohort proctors.

It was also rumored that they had come up with a drug from somewhere in the town that had unusual properties, another reason for them to avoid detection by those in charge of the school. Thorny was not part of that group—of any group, for that matter—but if they were there, she might attempt to push her way in to try something different. Thorny was the one reason he was out here, where he was not supposed to be and where there would be trouble if he were found.

Staring into silent blackness answered no questions. He told himself no one else was around and scrabbled in one of the leg pockets of his cargo pants for his phone. The time it showed him, 4:03 a.m., brought to mind thoughts of another curse. He thumbed the light on and swept it around. In the beam was a body. That was what he had fallen over. It lay face down, the head on one arm, the other arm flung forward, the whole body giving the impression it had been dropped flat from the air.

Drunk? Stoned? Both? Enough for whoever it was not to wake up when Danijel fell over them? He discarded those ideas as fast as they came to him, leaving the increasing likelihood of an awful answer. He gasped and recoiled from the body. Was it Thorny? *No, that can't be.* He nerved himself and crawled back next to it. The hair was short, the body too big. This was not Thorny.

He squatted next to the body, got his hands underneath, and strained to hoist it. The body was heavy, stiffening in places but not yet rigid. He was able to flip it over.

He shone his light on the face. It was an unbreathing body, a dead face, one that lacked all expression beyond a hint of surprise. Fernando Vargas. He knew Fernando.

"Oh no." Fernando was not a friend of his, far from it. But still . . . At that moment, his phone buzzed. The call was from Dalton Watkins. Which was strange.

"Hey, Dani, are you out and about?"

Danijel clenched his teeth. To the extent that this group of smokers, drinkers, and rumored druggers had a leader, it was Dalton. Danijel considered him a loudmouthed bully and stayed as far away from the guy as possible in the tight confines of the school and town. "What makes you think that I am?"

"Kojo said you went out. Woke him up when you left. He came to see me."

Danijel managed to stifle his curse. He thought he had been quiet on the way out, but coordination had never been his specialty. Kojo Owusu was his habmate and had complained about it before, even though he had a separate room in the hab. Kojo was also one of Dalton's crowd, and they put up with him because his mother, Ibiana Owusu, was usually elected to the town council. Now she was vice-mayor again, so Kojo could be a valuable connection for them if they got into trouble.

The body cast a lumpy shadow in the light of Danijel's phone. Why did he even bother worrying about cursing? Or shouting, for that matter? The unreality of the situation brought his emotions bubbling up. "Goddammit! Fuck you! Do you realize Ferdy is dead out here? What the fuck was going on tonight? What were you all doing?"

"Calm down, Dani, calm down," Dalton said. "We weren't doing anything. What do you mean, Ferdy is dead?"

"Dead!" Danijel shouted into his phone. "As in 'not alive'! Not breathing!"

A silence followed that lasted long enough for Danijel to consider hurling his phone against the hexagonal panels that made up the wall of the hydroponics facility. They weren't doing anything? As if. A faint odor of cannabis smoke clung to the area. He swept his light across the ground. Scattered in the thin cover of what they called grass were multiple partly smoked cannabis joints and an empty bottle. Of course, those could have been from previous nights. The spot was policed irregularly if at all.

Dalton's voice returned. "Did you do anything with him?"

"What the fuck are you talking about? He's dead! I am not going to do anything with him. We need to call . . . somebody."

"Why don't you come over here first," Dalton said. "I'm in my hab. We can figure out who to call and what to do."

The phone clicked off. Danijel stared at it for an instant. Then he began to run with only his phone for light at first. He rounded the hydroponics building, crossed the Perimeter Road into Saint Peters-town, and then went up the Avenue of the Americas, one of the hard-packed dirt roads radiating from the center of town. Dark, silent habs lined the street on both sides like parallel rows of mausoleums. It could have been a town of the dead.

Fortunately, he did not have far to go; Saint Peterstown was not a big place. Still, running on Heaven could be an effort—the high concentration of carbon dioxide in the air played tricks with a human's mind. But those born to it, like Danijel, found it much easier than the original colonists from Earth did. He pushed himself and was panting when he arrived at the hab Dalton used, about two-thirds of the way up the road. It was the only hab with a light showing from inside.

The door slid open at the touch of his palm. The front room of the hab was crowded. Dalton was there, naturally, tall and thin with a pallid face under a shock of brown hair. His beard had not come in thick enough yet to hide his receding chin. Ethan Cappelletti, his habmate, was there as well, which made sense. Kojo was in the room also. Nervousness was writ on his face, his skin a shade lighter than his dark brown eyes. His hair, too, was a light brown, an indication of a Caucasian father. That father was never mentioned by either him or his mother. Although it was customary for boys to take their father's surname, as Danijel had, and girls to take their mother's, Kojo used Owusu, his mother's name.

As the hab door closed behind him, Danijel was struck by the rank odor of people crowded together and on edge that pervaded the room. Food containers and wrappers were scattered around various surfaces, suggesting a late-night meal or an earlier one not cleaned up.

He glanced at the rest of the occupants. Jaelen Cardale, a stocky boy, was mostly hidden behind Kojo. Three girls stood close together all the way in the back of the living area, near the kitchen: Marlena Huggins, Sonia Janasch, and Mischa Torres.

All of them were in the first cohort of the high-seniors, the oldest students in the residence school. They would turn eighteen in the New Year, as would Danijel. Tension showed on all of them even if it was most obvious on Kojo, who twisted his fingers together as he stood there.

"All of you." Danijel made it an accusation. "You were all out there. What happened?"

"We were not out there," Dalton said. "Get that through your thick head. How could Kojo have come to see me here after you woke him up if he was outside?"

It was too early and too confusing for Danijel's brain to process that and come up with a good response. The best he could say was, "You're telling me Ferdy went out there by himself for a smoke and a drink? That's bullshit."

"Actually"—Mischa gave Danijel a side-eye as she spoke—"I think he was going out there with Thorny, and not just for a smoke and a drink."

"Thorny hates Ferdy's guts." Danijel could feel his eyes go wide and knew his was a stricken face when Mischa laughed at him.

"I don't actually know," she said. "What I do know is that Thorny wouldn't know you from the battery on a rover."

"Fuck you," Danijel said. "And don't pretend you're her friends. Where is she?" He turned back to Dalton. As he did, he noticed a small backpack on the side table by a chair. A printed symbol, a vertical line with a semi-circle at its middle that could have been a miswritten *p*, adorned its back. "That's Thorny's pack, the one she keeps at school. What's it doing here?" Thorny never talked about what the symbol meant. Thorny never talked much to anyone, including him, but he knew it was her pack.

Dalton smirked. "We thought tonight might be a good time to see why she makes such a big deal about always having that pack in one particular spot, so we took it. But somehow, she got a thumb and eye lock to put on the main compartment. I'm not going to break it or cut into it, because she'd know somebody looked. She's too crazy to chance that. And as for where she is, we don't know and none of us care. What are we going to do about Ferdy?"

Danijel blinked. They were asking *him*? "I don't know. Call someone. Call Busby. She's Head of School."

"Call Unreality Busby?" Dalton struck a pose of mock horror. "Are you insane? Do you have any idea what that will set off? Probably a whole battery of psych testing."

"It's not like she isn't going to find out," Danijel said.

"She doesn't have to find out at four thirty in the morning" was Dalton's reply.

"And not from us," Ethan added.

Danijel threw his hands in the air. "Fine. Call the doc."

"Dr. Song is in Happy Valley," said Sonia. "She was yesterday, anyway, when I spoke with my family. But we can call Watanabe later. She's seeing people at the clinic in town."

"Later?" Danijel had the feeling none of the people in the room cared about Ferdy—and they were supposed to be his friends. "What do you mean 'later'? Ferdy is dead out there."

"He won't be any more dead in a couple of hours," Dalton said. "What's the point of waking Watanabe up now?"

"Fine." All of a sudden, Danijel no longer worried about what they would do or what story they would concoct. Fernando was dead, and none of them knew where Thorny was. Had anything happened to her? That was what Danijel Petrovic cared about. Before anyone could stop him, he grabbed the little pack from the table and ran out of the hab.

JING

THE FOUR-YEAR-OLD BOY SAT STOICALLY ON THE MAKESHIFT DIAGNOSTIC BED AS DR. Song Jing finished examining the flame-red undersides of his upper and lower eyelids.

"It itches. Awful. It feels like I've got a rock in there." Each hand tightly gripped the edge of the exam table as a way of ensuring that he was good and did not move.

"I'm sure it does," Jing said.

The boy's patience lasted long enough for her to recheck his eyes and point out the salient features of the inflammation to her son, Michael Olivares. Now nineteen years old and a year and a half out of residence school, he was taking his apprenticeship with her to become, eventually, a doctor. *Apprenticeship* was the best term the colony could come up with for training the next generation of specialists in everything, since after finishing residence school in the year they turned eighteen, the only way the colony's youth could receive further training was to study the training material from the databases and work with an expert currently doing the job.

"What's wrong with him?" Maeve O'Brien's voice was tired. Her whole body looked tired: her face drawn and weathered, her red hair shot through with gray. She appeared much older than her forty-four years.

Farming could do that to a person, Jing thought. Two decades of building a farm from nothing was hard work on a world where neither humans nor their plants and animals had evolved. Even with bot assistance, it was hard work, and it wore a person down no matter what Penny might say. Add in raising a family . . . Jing remembered Maeve as one of the eager, energetic twentysomething Pioneer Youth who knew nothing about doing hard work with their own hands because on Earth, none of them had done it. Maeve had learned—most of them had—but at a price.

Jing blinked and snapped her focus back to Maeve's question. "It's an allergic reaction, but it's a very severe type. I'll give you some eye drops and show you how to put them in. Make sure you don't miss any doses, and I need to know if he's not getting better in a week. If that happens, I'll need to see him at the clinic in Saint Peterstown to make sure we're not getting any permanent damage. I don't have the specialized equipment here."

"Saint Peterstown? That's a two-day trip unless we can catch on to a rover going up." Maeve's voice, dubious at first, firmed. "If you say it, we'll do it. We'll take him up when we go to the meeting. But why Sean? None of my older three had anything like this."

"I don't know. It's probably something growing down here in the valley we react to. Most of the older kids spent a lot of their early years up in the town, and not much grows around there. Which, of course, is why we need to be here. Otherwise, no farms." Jing knew those words would not be much comfort to Maeve, but that was the truth. No farms, not enough food. Thirty-four family farms were now in the valley, growing the Earth food the colony depended on. The hydroponics at Saint Peterstown could not support more than a third of the humans now on Heaven. Maybe not even that. And the supply of ReadyMeals that had come on the starships was long gone.

"Do I need shots today, Mama?"

"No," Michael answered for Jing even as Maeve looked to her. "This isn't something you get your shots for."

"I'm surprised we still need them," Maeve said. "We're the only humans on the planet. None of what you give those shots for is here at all, is it?"

"Mostly true." It was a good question, Jing thought. The mission plan the International Space Commission had assembled for the settlement of the planet specified that the childhood vaccinations would continue to be manufactured and given, yet there could be no reservoir of those diseases. Well, zoster would linger in the ones who had been born on Earth until the first generation all died, and it was possible that the bacterium that caused tetanus had established itself in the soil here. "I think the concern was that starships would keep bringing people from Earth and with them the risk of reintroducing the diseases." Of course, if a starship brought a disease to which they had no immunity, it probably would not be polio or mumps.

"Hasn't been a starship in twenty years," Maeve said. "Not since we came on the *Dauntless*."

"I don't know why the next one didn't come, and for all we know, one could be here next year. It's seventy-six light-years to Earth; we wouldn't know in advance." Jing's voice lacked conviction, but it was good enough for Maeve.

"If you say so, Doc."

.   .   .

After Maeve left with her son, Jing turned to Michael. "I want to see your note on Sean O'Brien before dinner. Look up 'vernal keratoconjunctivitis' in the database—that's the diagnosis—and write a summary of it. Finish with your assessment of my care plan compared to what your references recommend as the course of action."

"Yes, Ma." Before Michael could step away, Jing held up a hand to keep him. "One quick old mother's question, if you don't mind." To his quizzical expression, she said, "Why the long-sleeved shirt this morning? Do you feel okay?"

Michael gave her a sunny smile. "I'm fine, Ma. You worry too much. It's almost winter, and it's a bit cool in the morning with the sun not up yet."

Jing glanced to her right, where her implanted chip superimposed on her visual field the data it plucked from the network. The temperature read 81 degrees F. She returned the smile. For a child born on Heaven and accustomed to its frequent triple-digit temperatures throughout the year, this probably did feel chilly. "Okay. I get it. But where did you get this shirt? A new cotton shirt, never mind the long sleeves." She gave a gentle tug at one sleeve. "Don't tell me this somehow came out of your equal share."

"Melanie, who works with the cotton fiber, did it for me." Michael's grin broadened. "I think she likes me."

"Ah, a side deal. That's certainly against the rules."

"Oh, Ma, don't be such an old rule-follower. Everybody does it if they can. It's not like the equals take into account how much work we do."

Yes, I'm a rule-follower, Jing thought. *That's my nature.*

Michael left the front section of the hab, which had been converted into a waiting room and a patient care area, for the back unit, where one of the bedrooms had been subdivided to create a private office with database access. She did want to see Michael's final assessment of her care plan and hoped her son would have a strong critique. The references would say she should have referred the boy to an ophthalmologist. However, the closest ophthalmologist was seventy-six light-years away on Earth. Jing had trained in rural medicine, a field that had her see and care for many patients who would normally be referred to specialists. That was why she had been accepted as a starflight physician. She would do the best she could.

Jing sighed. She would have enough of a fight with the town council over using cell foundry resources to make more cyclosporine for the eye drops the allergy required. This was a rare illness on Earth, but she had already seen a few cases of it here, despite the small number of young children growing up in the valley in the current age cohorts. The original colonists were at the end of their childbearing years, and the first generation born on Heaven was only starting to have children. Her clinical antennae were telling her there would be more of these cases in years to come. They had better be prepared.

It was pleasanter to think about Michael; those thoughts brought pride. He was the son Jorge had wanted, but he was going to be the doctor she wanted rather than the computer jockey she knew Jorge had hoped for. Well, their daughter Aurora, now sixteen, seemed to have the skill with electronic systems. Maybe in the end, both she and Jorge would be satisfied. Which was a good thing because there would be no more children. Menopause had come years ago. Two was all they would have. At least that was replacement level, even if it did not reach the colony's goal of replacement-plus.

She let her hands rest on the examining bed, her eyes focused in the distance beyond the wall. Thinking that way made her feel old. She did not look old; she knew that. Save for a few crinkles by her eyes, her face was unlined. Her black hair was still glossy, with no trace of gray to be seen when she let it loose from the tight bun at the back of her head. Her muscles and joints told a different story, however. She was stiff in the morning when she rose from her bed, and sitting too long in a chair made her back groan when she stood up. She was tired, too—tired all the time, the way she had been during her residency training. She preferred to blame the fatigue not on her age but on Heaven's short day, a rotation period of only twenty-one Earth hours. Jorge, computer jockey and nerd extraordinaire, had reprogrammed their clocks so that the short day was still divided into the familiar twenty-four hours, but Jing always felt that she'd had either too little sleep or was not ready for bed, regardless of what the clock read. The Heaven-born had no such trouble. She wondered about their pineal glands as a way to divert herself from thinking that this, too, was a manifestation of age.

Growing old was not something you thought about when you joined an interstellar program, not with hibernation—hib, as they called it—and relativity to keep you young while the outside world aged. But Jorge had needed emergency abdominal surgery from a side effect of the hib on the flight out, and he had decided to stay with the colonists rather than risk a return flight to Earth. That left Jing with a choice: the stars or Jorge. She had chosen to stay with him and age at the same rate as the world around her. She had made that choice without hesitation.

Jing reined in her thoughts. Going down the road not taken, the one that ran back to Earth, was a bad path. She spent enough time counseling others about that very problem—the "remorsers" who could not or would not adjust to life on Heaven. She would check the waiting room. If no more patients had come in, she would find other work to keep her busy. But before she reached the door, a notification from her phone flashed on her projection field.

It was Yuki Watanabe, from the clinic in Saint Peterstown. Yuki had been trained as a nurse on Earth before she joined the Pioneer Youth group that came to Heaven on the *Dauntless*, the same ship Jing had flown on. Jing had trained Yuki and Norma, the one other young nurse in the colony, as medics. In Jing's opinion, Yuki was competent enough except for a tendency to give in to emotion in high-pressure situations.

Yuki's voice was high-pitched now, words firing out like water spurting from a hose under pressure as she recounted the short, sad story of Fernando Vargas. "What do I do?" Yuki demanded. "What do I do with him now?"

"The first thing you need to do is take a deep breath, hold it, then exhale slowly," Jing ordered. That was good advice to take herself. "Get his body temperature and pics of his skin, his whole body, and scan him as best you can. Get blood and urine samples for toxicology testing. We don't have a forensic lab here, but there is still a lot we can check. Then have some of his cohortmates help you put him in a body bag and move him into the cooler in the clinic. I will need to go up there and do a post as best I can, so we can try to figure out what happened."

Jing frowned as she worked out her plan. If the postmortem and toxicology testing did not give an answer, the situation would be difficult. The original colonists had an implanted chip, as she did, from when they lived on Earth, where virtually everyone had one. Those chips would keep a record of vital signs, cardiograms, and body chemistries that would assist—if not give the answer outright—in determining why this boy had died. But people born on Heaven had no implanted chips. They were no different from all the generations of humans before the mid-twenty-first century. Neither those chips nor the surgery to implant them was available on Heaven. She left Yuki a few more instructions, then clicked off. She needed to pack and would be on her way by the time the winter sun was above the horizon.

REALITY

ONE PERK—QUITE POSSIBLY THE ONLY REAL PERK—OF BEING HEAD OF SCHOOL WAS a private office on the first floor of the school building. It was a small office, but it had her name on a plaque next to the door: REALITY BUSBY. Inside, it was as spartan and utilitarian as an office in a bot-assembled building could be. It had a desk with a computer screen and inputs, as well as a desk chair that tilted back. Three cushionless chairs were arranged in a rank on the other side of the desk. A round conference table, big enough to have four plastic chairs around it, fit in a corner, leaving barely enough room for someone coming in through the door. Two frames for images sat on the desk, but they were blank.

Reality thought it was fine. The most important attribute of her office was that she could close the door and illuminate the DO NOT DISTURB sign. That allowed her to shut out kids, parents, staff, and essentially, the whole world. She needed that from time to time. The only problem with the arrangement was that it did not allow her to shut out the memories of what she had done in her arrogance two decades ago, memories that no one else would allow her to forget, even if she could.

This morning, she needed her staff in the office for a quick meeting occasioned by the news she had woken up to. Tiffany came in first. She handled the day care area, the youngest children whose parents would drop them off before going to their work. Tiffany had been in Reality's cohort of the Pioneer Youth when they arrived from Earth but never brought up that topic, for reasons Reality was sure she knew without asking. She had been a lifesaver for Reality in the early years of the colony, when it seemed that every couple on the planet was having children and the school was drowning in infants and toddlers needing care.

There had been little work for Tiffany over the past few years, however, and she had gotten out of the habit of working hard. Reality knew she would need to find at least one, and preferably two, of the current first cohort of high-seniors to take on day care work when they finished residence school, because the first two cohorts that had graduated were now eighteen and nineteen years old. Brought up on a doctrine of replacement-plus, they were partnering and would be having plenty of children. Soon. Reality pushed that issue aside as she greeted Tiffany. It was not the problem of the morning.

Gordon Durham-Pole and Poppy Merriwether, Reality's proctors, came in together after Tiffany had seated herself. Gordon's angular face was paler and more worried than usual while Poppy's features were rounder, with skin almost as dark as her curly, black hair, and were locked in a stern countenance. They had been in the first graduating cohort, meaning they were now nineteen years old and had been working for about a year and a half. It was their job to provide guidance and discipline for the students in their cohorts, to see that computer-based lessons were completed and tests taken, and that physical training was done when students were in residence at the school from fall equinox to spring equinox. They did not need to teach the lessons—that was what AI, computer books, and vids were for—but keeping the cohorts in order and at their tasks was plenty of work.

From spring until fall, the children would live with their parents, and Gordon and Poppy would make home visits to see that the schoolwork continued. Until those two had graduated and taken the jobs, Reality had been handling all ten cohorts herself, since Tiffany's skill set did not extend beyond toddlers. That had been an impossible job, one that she thought might kill her, an occurrence she believed would make quite a few people happy. But she had no time to dwell on that now either.

Reality intended to keep the meeting short. In a few terse sentences, she described what little she knew about Fernando's death. "I've already spoken with his parents. After we're done, I'll speak to his cohort of high-seniors. I want you to talk to your cohorts—individually or in groups, whatever they need."

"It's all over already," Gordon said. "The phone's been lighting up with messages for the last two hours. What do you expect us to tell them? What am I going to tell them? I'm responsible for the high-seniors, and that means Fernando."

"Don't go off the deep end on this," Reality said. "You can't monitor them like little kids. The whole point of the two years as high-seniors is for them to start taking responsibility for themselves."

"Well, they can't," Gordon said. "This group isn't ready. Fernando was a valley-jerk who got into trouble and hung around with trouble."

Reality could feel pressure building behind her eyes. She remembered being in the Pioneer Youth, not so many years older than these kids, heading off to the stars from an Earth that had done little to prepare them to take care of themselves. She also had all the memories of how badly she had handled that task. "Whatever happened was not your responsibility," she said. "The message I want you to convey is that we will sort this out, and if anyone knows anything, we need to hear it. Right now. Get this under control. All your senior cohorts."

In addition to the high-seniors, the sixteens and seventeens, Gordon had the low-seniors, the three cohorts of ages thirteen, fourteen, and fifteen.

"I've got the same mess on the phones with the juniors," Poppy said. "Everything from a sawtooth roo running loose outside the perimeter to a starship here to take over control, and a couple of those messages have aliens on the starship." Poppy had the low-juniors, the eights, nines, and tens, along with the high-juniors at eleven and twelve. "Pretty crazy, especially now that the young ones are in it."

"We'll get them under control," Gordon said.

Reality gave him a sharp look. He had picked up the line she wanted, but she did wonder if his mind was in the same place as hers.

"Some time and some talking, but we'll do it." Uncharacteristically, Poppy was quick to agree with her fellow proctor.

Reality grunted. The two of them agreeing on anything without an argument first was a rare event, but maybe the seriousness of the situation was enough to have them cooperating. Reality was happy to have one less issue to handle. "Let's take care of it" was all she said to end the meeting.

·　　·　　·

THE FIFTY-ONE STUDENTS OF THE CURRENT FIRST COHORT OF HIGH-SENIORS, THE SECOND largest cohort after the sixty-eight who had been born the year after the *Dauntless* left, filed slowly into the auditorium on the ground floor of the school building. Their body language and expressions reflected the confusion and worry in the wild messages that had been circulating.

Snippets of conversation made their way to where Reality sat in a chair at the back of the stage that was normally used for plays, music, and graduation.

"... what the fuck ..."

"... heard he was cold and stiff as a girder ..."

"... can't imagine ... what Unreality thinks she's gonna do ..."

Reality winced when that came to her ears. She hated the nickname the teens used when they thought she wasn't listening—or maybe they hoped she'd hear it. She hated it even more than the silent disdain and aversion she received from her generation of settlers. She knew where that came from, knew she had earned it with her misplaced pride, the crimes she had been part of, and the one she had been saved from committing. The kids, though ... They had been fine when they were all young, even though their numbers had made her work nonstop. The little ones were still fine. It was when they turned into teens that their wires crossed and their programs corrupted. She did not understand it; her training had been early childhood education.

The last of the students seated themselves. The auditorium went silent. For the first time in years with this cohort, all of them were quiet and focused on her. Well, forty-nine of them were. Two were missing.

Reality strode to the front of the stage. She was tall at five seven and still fit in her mid-forties, so she cut an impressive figure in her black pants and tan shirt manufactured from recycled textiles. She had allowed her dark hair to grow out when she reached her thirties; lazy curls now covered her ears and almost reached her collar. Some gray had appeared at the temples in the past year. Her skin, stretched taut over cheekbones and jaw, was pale with scattered freckles. Any softness of youth was gone. Her face was further marred by two scars where Dr. Song had removed skin cancers.

She surveyed the waiting students, uncertainty a stone settling in her chest. She kept her hands clasped behind her back to avoid spoiling her image by having them wave as she talked. Reality was not a leader, and she knew it. She had proved that twenty years ago.

"In case anyone does not know, Fernando Vargas died last night. He was found behind the hydroponics facility." She scanned the faces. No one looked surprised. The message grapevine was very efficient. "Right now, we do not know what happened. Dr. Song is coming up from the valley to do some tests. That should give us the answers, but it is going to take a few days. Over today and tomorrow, I am going to speak with each one of you individually in my office. If you receive a message to speak to me today, do not leave here until you have spoken to me. This will take all day." Not that there was anywhere to go she could not find them. In the whole wide world of Heaven, humans lived only in Saint Peterstown and Happy Valley. It was forty-two miles across barren plains to the valley. Which left the obvious question.

"Does anyone know where Thorny is?"

"Out for a walk, probably," came from the back row. A titter ran through the auditorium.

"That hasn't happened since last year." Reality tried focusing on one person at a time, but no one else had anything to say. *That figures.* Another conversation she would not enjoy was obviously waiting in the wings. "Dani, I'll see you first. The rest of you, keep busy until you get a message to see me."

Back in her office, she took her desk chair, leaving Danijel to sit across from her. He was a slender boy of average height, thin rather than athletic. Light brown hair matching his eyes fell across his forehead. The small cleft in his chin felt a razor only occasionally. She watched him fidget while she thought about what to say. Officially, Cam and Jess were Public Safety and should be doing this, but they were useless, and dammit, this was her school and her students.

"You were the one who found Fernando. Correct?" Danijel nodded. "You're the top student in the school, even if I include the previous two cohorts. You're going to apprentice in IT and engineering with

Jorge and also with your father when you graduate at summer solstice. What were you doing out there at four in the morning?"

A flush spread over Danijel's Mediterranean complexion. "I woke up. I had a bad feeling."

"A bad feeling." Reality sat upright, then leaned forward, elbows on her desk. "You mean like telepathy?"

"No, no." The flush deepened. "I don't know. But I did go out there and found Fernando. Nobody else was out."

"And what did you do then?"

"I spoke with Dalton and some others who Fernando . . . knows. They said they were going to call Practitioner Watanabe at the clinic, and—well, they did, but I guess that wasn't until later."

No matter how Reality asked the questions or how many times she asked them a little differently, Danijel's story did not change. She was certain he was lying about part of it, but she could get no further than that feeling. Danijel was the best student they had; he did not have a history of lying; he had never been a problem. She must have missed something, but she could not figure out what it was.

She saw Dalton Watkins next, and he was even less helpful. "I slept through the night. At least until Kojo woke me up. He said Dani had gone out and asked me if there was anything going on. I said if there was, we would have told him. So, he asked if I could check on Dani with him and I told him, you know, first things first. Let's just call him. So, I made the call." He managed to slouch backward in the hard plastic chair, a posture that conveyed both a lack of worry and boredom. "You can check the records on the hab doors, you know. They record every time the door opens for someone going in or out."

His expression, Reality thought, was dangerously close to a smirk. The hab doors had that feature because the habs were designed to also be used in environments that required an air lock to be attached. Reality knew that from long ago, and Dalton knew she knew that. "They'll pick up the ident, too, for anyone who's chipped in, but none of you have chips," she pointed out. "But, yes, the door to a hab will record when it opens and closes. That's why you and your friends use a window to go in and out at night when you're supposed to be in the hab." Having watched Dalton grow up, she believed that was the limit of his ingenuity. If humanity on Heaven had to depend on him, they would not last another generation.

The smirk became a bit of a smile. Back in the day when Reality had been a cohort leader in the Pioneer Youth, particularly once they were in Saint Peterstown, she would have found a way to erase both the smirk and the smile. She tried to make the memory dissolve. Memories like that were only reminders of how she had failed at being a leader. She did not need the distraction now.

Reality worked her way through Dalton's friend group but learned nothing. Kojo said he'd woken up when Dani went out and admitted going to see Dalton. The others all claimed they had not gone out that night—not because it was against the rules; they all readily admitted they went out often, but last night they had been tired. They'd all been asleep until Dalton woke them after he phoned Dani. At that point, they had joined Dalton in his hab because that was where Dani was going. No, they had not known Fernando went out. They had not known he intended to.

Reality was quite sure they were all lying. It was consistent with what she knew of their characters. She was equally certain they were working hard to keep her from seeing that they were laughing at her as they lied. Still, they stuck to their stories, and the conversations went nowhere.

The brief hours of daylight fled as Reality spoke with the other members of that cohort. All of them denied leaving their habs last night. She was inclined to believe those cohortmates. Everyone broke rules occasionally, but they did not hang around with Fernando, Dalton, or the other members of that group.

The last student of the cohort she was going to see that day was Regan Mulders, Thorny's habmate. Reality had been postponing this conversation in the hope that Thorny would appear first, the old joke about being late to one's own funeral being applicable to Thorny. The girl had not, however, turned up. She probably would miss her own funeral, Reality thought.

Reality did not ask if Regan had been out last night. As soon as Regan sat down, she asked the girl, "Where's Thorny?"

"I don't know," Regan said.

"Did she go out last night?"

"No."

Reality stood up and stared down at Regan from across the desk. "If she didn't go out last night, where was she this morning?"

"I . . . oh . . . I don't know." Regan was all but squirming under her gaze.

"Regan, is she dead also and we just haven't found her body yet?"

"No!" Regan went white. "Thorny doesn't tell me what she's doing. But I heard talk. That's why I was worried—and, yes, she wasn't in our hab. That's why I called Dani."

"Wait. You called Dani?"

"Yes. I didn't do anything to Thorny, and I'm sure Dani didn't either."

Regan practically wriggled in her seat when Reality asked what "talk" she had heard, but all she would say was that others had heard Thorny talk about doing something interesting. Reality tried to pin down who the "others" were and what was "interesting," but Regan managed to talk without being specific. Right then, Reality decided she needed to speak to Dani again. Why didn't Dani tell her that Regan had called him? She dismissed Regan and sent for Dani again, but was told that he'd left the school building after their conversation. He did not answer his phone.

Reality sat at her desk, thinking. What about Thorny?

If ever a child was aptly named, it was her. This was not the first time the girl had disappeared. Far from it. From the day she had arrived from Penny's farm for her first residence term, she would bolt from time to time, with only the explanation "I was angry" when she returned or was brought back. Usually, if she did not return on her own, it was a matter of geolocating her phone and going for her. Although, there had been enough times that Thorny had conveniently left her phone in her room, or dodged Reality or Tiffany when they went to bring her back. Those occasions led to her father, Vo Hiep, having to go get her.

Reality did not want to have this conversation with Hiep.

DANIJEL

DANIJEL PETROVIC WAS SCARCELY OUT OF REALITY'S OFFICE, THE COLD, CLAMMY sweat running down from his armpits, when his phone buzzed. It was a voice message from his father.

"I need to see you. Lab Unit."

His father never issued directives that way. The bluntness of it sent Danijel quickstepping out of the school building without sending a reply, ignoring students who tried to halt him to ask what Unreality had asked or said. In a grim part of his mind, he thought several of them wanted to know what he had said to Unreality, but he wasn't going to take time for that either. What did go through his mind over and over was the clumsy fib he had told Busby about why he went out. Regan had figured out something of his feelings for Thorny but had sworn to keep the secret when he confronted her. He was not going to discuss any part of that with Unreality Busby. But he should have made up a better lie.

The Lab Unit was on the other side of the Dining Hall, two buildings farther around Town Circle, the dirt road that made a small loop around the Community Dome in the center of town. One division of the structure held the testing equipment for which the building was named and also housed the main computer and network center for Saint Peterstown. Happy Valley had a subsidiary node; the original installation was in the Lab Unit.

The lab and computer part of the building was quiet, as usual. Few samples needed the specialty laboratory equipment these days. Jorge Olivares spent most of his time in the valley, while Everett Jones, the official IT head, was disinclined to stir out of his hab for the purpose of work. Jones claimed that anything that needed doing on a computer could be performed remotely.

Danijel's father was standing by an open office door, every inch of his posture signaling impatience. Miroslav Petrovic was one of those men who had not aged well. At forty-five, he looked a decade older. A stoop cut his height from the five eleven of his youth to less than five ten. Thinning hair could not hide the gleam of the overhead lights off his scalp. A small paunch was partly hidden by his stoop but contributed to the image of diminished capacity for physical labor. His coloring was more olive than Danijel's and his chin was rounded, without a cleft.

"Come in here."

Once Danijel was inside the office, Miroslav closed the door but did not sit down. "There is nobody here right now, but that does not mean it will stay that way," he said. "I've heard many things about what happened, most of it garbage, I am sure. But I have heard that you were somehow involved in it."

"I didn't do anything, Tata."

Miroslav sighed. "But you are involved, Danko. Your face hides nothing. Tell me. What is going on?"

Danijel wanted to sit; he wanted to collapse. He'd had no sleep since Regan's call. But his father was not sitting. He stood and told the story.

Miroslav sighed again when Danijel had finished. "Childish stupidity, I'm sure, and it ends in a tragedy. I will hope that is all it is. We do not need more bad times here. This world is hard enough." He scuffed the tip of one boot against the flooring and contemplated the streak it left. Then he raised his eyes back to his son. "When I was at the rover station this morning, before I heard about any of this, mind you, I noticed one of the rovers was not there. Someone took it, for some reason. Would that be associated with whatever stupidity has left a boy dead?"

"A rover is gone?" Danijel asked.

"I believe that's what I just said. I'm the chief engineer—or what we have that passes for one—and so I am in charge of the rovers and the autonomous bots. You know this. So, if I tell you someone has taken a rover, they have taken a rover. It is not as though we lock up rovers around here, but nobody takes one without signing it out. Do you know anything about this? Is there anything you have not told me?"

Danijel would not sit while his father was still standing, but he sagged against the closest wall. "No one has seen Thorny since last night."

"Thorny?" Miroslav's dark eyes bored into Danijel's. "That girl is trouble."

"Tata!"

"I know you like her. You always have, although I can't understand why." Miroslav's voice went quiet. "That does not change my opinion. You need to like with your head, not your balls."

"Tata!"

"Okay, okay. Let me show you something." Miroslav moved to the office desk. The computer screen there lit up at a touch. He tapped in a series of commands. "I am responsible for maintaining our vehicles. Not for where they go or who uses them. However." He swiveled the screen around so Danijel could see the display.

It showed a map of Saint Peterstown and the surrounding area. A red dot occupied a position near a small lake to the southwest of the town.

"The rovers automatically maintain contact with the town network when they are powered on. The transmission towers we put up in Heaven Years 2 and 3 give pretty good location detection in the vicinity of town. Again, you know this because I have helped teach you how all these systems work. Can you tell me if there is a connection between a dead boy here, Thorny being missing, and an exploratory rover out by Dead Lake?"

Danijel felt his heart sinking through his stomach. "The rover is out by Dead Lake now?"

"Maybe. That was its last position in the network. It could still be there now and powered off. Or it could have moved elsewhere up there. The terrain becomes irregular and can block the signal. We never put any antennas out there. I had thought to put out a query if anyone was working out there, but then I heard about the commotion at the school. What do you think?"

"I need to find Thorny!" Danijel tried to bolt from the office, but Miroslav put a hand on his shoulder. It was not a firm grip, but it stopped him.

"Bring back the rover," Miroslav said quietly. "We have only two functioning rovers at Saint Peterstown now. The other four are in the valley."

Danijel muttered an agreement and pushed on out the door. He did hear his father's last sentence as he left.

"I hope that damned girl appreciates your concern."

. . .

DANIJEL RAN DOWN THE SHORT STRETCH OF TOWN CIRCLE IN FRONT OF THE LAB UNIT and the Dining Hall, then turned onto the Avenue of the Americas, the one of the five roads radiating from Town Circle to the Perimeter Road that ran due south. He slowed his pace there because some people were outside and he did not want to attract attention.

He did look closely at each person he went near, trying to divine if they were studying him and wondering if his haste were connected to the tragedy of the past night—because everyone in Saint Peterstown knew everyone else on sight. It never occurred to him that his probing gaze might cause more questions than his haste.

Staring at people told him nothing, but it did make him notice the street and its buildings, a sight so familiar that he typically ignored it. On either side of the dirt avenue was a row of fifty identical habs. That is, they were identical in the sense of being composed of two one-story cubical structures joined together at a slight offset as if to give the hab a break from being a boring, rectangular prism. What saved them from complete uniformity was that each hab was a different garish color, varying from yellow to orange to blue and many other colors in between. The coloring was part of the construction material and should have glared out at passersby for all eternity, but the harsh weather of Heaven, with its searing heat, storms, and windblown dirt, had worn away the brightness. The habs were glum, standing on bare lots, each with a privacy screen curving from side to back that blocked the view of the dirt expanse separating the row of habs on this avenue from the identical one fronting the next avenue over. The bare dirt was a planned park that had never been planted with anything.

It occurred to Danijel that he had seen many images in the books he had read as a child, in which all different kinds of children grew up in all sorts of different communities on Earth. None of those towns had been as bleak or lifeless as Saint Peterstown.

As much as he was a townie, he thought it would be nice if he could move to Happy Valley, where the valley-folk had built individual houses that followed no pattern, and were actually *living* outside. His father would never be a farmer, however. He dismissed the idea with anger. His father did valuable work and so would he, even if neither of them received more than an equal share for it. And he had more important problems at the moment. He made a brief detour to his hab, where he picked up the backpack belonging to Thorny that he had taken from Dalton's place. He told himself that would be the sort of gesture she would appreciate.

The facility where rovers were maintained and charged stood across the Perimeter Road in the other direction from the hydroponics facility, past the intersection with the southern end of the Avenue of the Americas. The structure, with its rows of fixed charging stations, had been the last bit of construction in the town, completed shortly before the *Dauntless* left. Now it was even more forlorn than the road he had come down. Of fifteen stations that could be used, in addition to the photovoltaic cells in the skins of the rovers, to charge the rover batteries, only one was occupied. Saint Peterstown could have had ten rovers, but three had been disassembled, their batteries used as additional grafts to extend the range of other rovers and their parts salvaged for repairs. Another one was inside the station building, waiting to be taken down that road by his father.

Danijel often wondered about the five extra charging stations. Rover batteries could not be made in Saint Peterstown, although the vehicle's other parts could be printed and the chemicals for the photo-voltaic cells manufactured in the cell foundries. Five more rovers was an impossibility. So why the extra chargers? He wondered about that old puzzle every time he came down to the rover station. He had no time to dwell on it now. What mattered was the one rover that should have been there but was not.

His father had told him to bring back the exploratory rover. On foot, he could reach the location the computer screen had shown in the remaining daylight and drive the rover back. Of course, he would cover that ground much faster if he took the rover that was sitting here. Then he could slave the exploratory rover to this one and drive both of them back to Saint Peterstown.

Taking this rover offered another huge advantage: If the exploratory rover had moved, say into a gulley where it was out of contact, and if it had been shut off, he might not find it easily. Taking this rover would allow him to search more widely and save him from walking back in the dark if he could not find the missing one. Taking this rover would also let him search for Thorny. That did mean the town would have no rovers for the time he was gone, but he told himself that would not be a major problem. His father's final words had been tacit permission, of sorts, to search for Thorny. What if she was out there and needed help?

He hesitated only momentarily before pulling himself into the driver's seat of the lone rover in the lot. He made a quick check of the supplies kept in every rover in the event a breakdown forced someone to walk back from the wild: Earth food, epinephrine autoinjectors, the safety tester for Heaven plants and animals everyone called a Penny-counter, vitamins plus methionine—the one essential amino acid that did not occur in Heaven biota—and weapons consisting of a spear, a bow, and arrows. The incongruity of those weapons in the most technologically advanced rover an interstellar program could produce did not enter his mind. The battery was fully charged. His father had agreed he could search for Thorny. That was all that mattered. He started the motors.

JING

BEFORE LEAVING HER HOME, JING'S LAST STOP WAS A QUICK GOODBYE WITH HER husband. Jorge Olivares used a small room of brick that had been built as an office against the outside wall of their hab living quarters. They lacked the tools to punch a doorway through the hab wall without creating a major mess, so Jorge's small office had its own door to the outside. It meant he had to walk out of the hab to reach his office, but the arrangement also allowed Jing to use the front unit of their hab as a clinic.

The nighttime fog that swathed the valley in cotton sheets of gray and white during the winter was lifting and burning away under the rising sun by the time she was preparing to leave, although the residual mist still left a damp sheen on her face and bare arms.

It reminded her a little of San Francisco Bay—her adopted home on Earth—but those mists had been cool. This was more like being shrouded in the steam from a dishwasher being opened after finishing its cycle. The oncoming glare of the morning sun promised that the dampness on her skin would soon be replaced by sweat.

When Jing stepped through the office door and wiped the moisture from her face with the handkerchief she kept in her pocket for that purpose, Jorge was seated at a small table built out from one of the brick walls, tapping away at his phone.

"Jorge?"

He turned at the sound of her voice.

Jorge was a handsome man from Spain on Earth with angular features, a sharply pointed nose, and a red diamond tattooed on the pale skin of his right cheek. Full black eyebrows and hair made a sharp contrast with that skin. In years past, he had combed his hair straight back and used a variety of products to keep it carefully in place, but he had run out of those and given up on trying to maintain that appearance in Heaven's humidity. Now he cropped it short, only a little longer than a crew cut.

"Don't you have patients?"

"Just saw Maeve and her youngest, who asked to come in early. But I have to go up to Saint Peterstown."

"Today?" Surprise registered on her husband's face. "We have to go up for the annual meeting of the Demos on the thirty-fifth anyway. This will make two trips almost back-to-back."

"I haven't forgotten the meeting, although I still count the days wrong in my head. Why couldn't we have just added a month to make the calendar work, my darling nerd?"

Jorge smiled. "It wouldn't work that way, not without it being a very long extra month. Our new sun here has a bit more mass than Sol, but our orbit is wider, so our year is pretty much the same length as Earth's. It's the short days that we have to deal with. With thirty-five days in each month, we can keep our twelve months and seven days a week. But you didn't come by to complain again about the way I fixed the calendar. What's up?"

Quickly, Jing briefed him on Fernando's death as it had been related to her.

Jorge's face immediately went somber. "It's not the thistle poison, is it?" he asked. "It was twenty years ago, but that's been done."

"It doesn't sound like it. Nobody mentioned the signs you'd expect, but you can be sure I'll run the tests. Those bad memories should stay buried."

The thistle plants grew all across the part of Heaven humans occupied. What the plant secreted as a chemoattractant to Heaven wildlife, a way to help spread its seeds, was an irreversible cholinesterase inhibitor in terrestrial biology. For humans, it was equivalent to nerve gas.

"I can't believe anyone would be fool enough to monkey with that again. People would know it's the first thing everyone would think of." The first mayor of Saint Peterstown had been murdered with the thistle two decades before. She shook herself as if physically ridding herself of the memory of investigating it. "What are you working on?"

"A puzzle of my own, but not a deadly one." His grin came back. Jorge grinned a lot when Jing was around. She liked that. It spoke of the feelings between them that had deepened over their twenty years on Heaven. "Miroslav shot me a report earlier, wondering if there was a network glitch. One of the rovers went out, I guess, and something happened to it. It lost contact with the network. Miroslav is thinking the terrain is blocking the signal, but he wanted to make sure there's no problem in the system."

"And you think?"

Jorge rubbed the cheek with the tattoo. "Too abrupt for terrain. I would bet either a problem in the rover or the rover was shut down.

I'm asking Miro for the maintenance records. When you're up there, you might have a chat with him about staying on top of these systems. And you can see Aurora at the school. It wouldn't kill her to message more often."

"I will. Both." She stepped over to give Jorge a quick kiss. "Let me go get the horses ready."

.   .   .

"Hey, Doc, do you have a minute?" A rider coming up to the hab greeted Jing as soon as she was back outside. A young man swung off the horse's back and hustled over to her. "Can you look at this?" He held up his right forearm with a bloody bandage taped around it.

Jing used to joke that Heaven's rotation did not leave enough minutes in the day, but Jorge had fixed that, although the minutes were shorter. Despite her hurry to leave, Jing would always have a minute for a patient, even if she now found herself wishing for more energy to fill those minutes.

"What happened to you, Jordie?"

Jordan Longfellow was a tall white man, at eighteen a year younger than Michael, having graduated from the residence school at the end of the past school year. He had a mop of light brown hair to go with a beard that had started to grow out. "Was helping to put on an extension at Guillermo and Donna's farm. One of the concrete blocks broke when I was pushing it into place. I lost my balance, and my arm went across where it broke. Gave myself some scratches and one pretty good gash." His smile turned rueful. "Klaus bandaged it and told me to have you look at it, but it was late when we got done, and you know how far upriver they are from where I stay. I thought it would be fine. This morning it hurts, so I figured I would come over before I go to work so you can see it." He unwrapped the bandage and leaned his arm against the saddle for her to see.

"That's not what I call an exam table," Jing said, but went over anyway. She supplemented the growing daylight with the light from her phone. There was a good two-inch gouge in the underside of Jordie's forearm along with a pair of shallow scratches. The sides of the deeper cut were red.

"We're going to need to clean that out, and you're going to need to come inside. I'm not doing this against a horse in twilight."

"Can we glue the skin together or do I need stitches?" Jordie asked as he followed her into the clinic.

"Neither. Yesterday, I would have closed it, but at this point, we're going to let it heal open."

The waiting room was empty, and Michael was not in the clinic area. *Probably doing the work I told him to do. Quicker to do this myself.* Jing sat Jordie at an exam table and pulled out what she would need with the efficiency of long years of practice.

"You still doing daywork? I thought you wanted a farm of your own." Jing made it a point to know about the lives of her patients, which meant every human on Heaven.

"I do. Thing is, I want a partner first, a long-term one. Better yet, get married and be permanent. A farm is too much work solo. Meanwhile, I work the farms and learn everything I can. Guillermo and Donna have been really nice about teaching me. I'll cover at least one farm when people go up to the Demos 'cause my cohort can't vote until next year anyway. I still get the same equal share as anyone else, and that's enough for now."

"You might consider that you'll have a partner or a wife faster if they see you're industrious enough to start the farm. You know the valley-folk will help you set up."

While she dispensed advice that could have originated with her grandmother, she rigorously irrigated the wound and rebandaged it to her satisfaction. "I'll have Michael give you antibiotics to cover any infection from Earth bacteria off your skin or clothing. You wait for him. I've cleaned it out with sodium hypochlorite. It's a nearly ancient treatment, going back to the First World War on Earth, when we didn't have any antibiotics. It's really effective at killing Heaven bacteria." She tapped an index finger against her pursed lips. "Any cut like that, you should have it looked at right away. None of this tough Heaven-born mentality. We rarely get infected by Heaven bugs—our immune system takes them out quite well—but if you do get infected, none of our antibiotics will work. I don't want to be taking off an arm or leg to stop an infection because someone waited too long."

"Yes, Doc," said a suitably chastened Jordie.

.   .   .

AFTER THE CALL TO MICHAEL ABOUT ANTIBIOTICS FOR JORDIE, JING HEADED BACK outside to pull two horses from their stable for the trip. These were the Icelandic pony version of horses, a small, hardy breed that thrived in, or in spite of, the hothouse climate of Heaven with its high carbon dioxide level. Another correct prediction of Penny's, Jing reminded herself as she was saddling the one she would ride. The other would carry the panniers with supplies for her and both horses.

It was only a two-day journey on horseback to Saint Peterstown, but the Demos had made a law that any travel outside the human-settled areas required the traveler to be armed and to take food. Some of Heaven's wildlife was edible by humans and other Earth animals. The shellhound, a ubiquitous dim-witted reptile named for its distinctive shells and doglike legs, could be cooked and eaten, as could some of the vegetation, but none of it had vitamins or methionine. That made foraging in the wild for the horses impossible, even without the risk of them chomping on a thistle, which would kill a horse in the same disgusting way it would a human. Most of what the packhorse was carrying was food for the horses.

Jing leaned against the packhorse when she finished with her tasks. Every part of the loads felt heavier than they had the last time she had done this. How many more years would pass before she needed help? True, she could wait for a rover to be making the trip, but how many more years would the rovers run? Not forever. She did not want to think about that.

Instead, she went back to the stable, pulled out her weapons, and fastened them to the horse she would ride. A plastic bow, printed so that the draw weight exactly matched her capability, went into a sheath on the left. The effort with the saddle and the panniers reminded her to have her draw strength rechecked to see if she would need a new bow. She slung her quiver with twenty needle-tipped arrows over her back. The spear was eight feet of plastic topped with an eighteen-inch spike, which, with a quick twist of the handle, would extend out to seventeen and a half feet, similar to the ancient Macedonian sarissa, although much lighter. In its compact form, it slid into a holder on the right side of the saddle.

Jing tilted her head back to look up at the point of the spear as it glistened in the sunlight. It was unbreakable, wickedly sharp, and would penetrate any shield nature could devise. Its true lethality, though, was the poison that coated it and the arrow tips as well. The chemical blocked a sodium channel in nerve cells that was involved in pain transmission in humans, and it was, in fact, a useful pain medicine for people. Heaven physiology utilized sodium channels as well. In Heaven animals, this compound shut down nerve transmission and vascular pumping almost immediately, making it a lethal poison.

"Yin and yang, I suppose," she murmured to the horse. "This and the thistle. What's benign for Heaven is deadly to us, and what is safe for us is deadly here. The universe works through opposite connected parts, no matter what brings the parts together."

Philosophizing won't get your job done. She strapped on a conical hat that would have been immediately recognizable to her ancestors as a dǒulì. Then she swung onto her lead horse and set it cantering to the east along the broad, earthen West Valley Road.

Valley Road, both its east and west sections, had started out as a single track of rover tires pressed into the soft river-bottom dirt. Many trips of rovers and wagons had pounded the earth free of any of the Heaven vegetation people called grass. Frequent rains turned the bare ground to mud so that the rover trips that followed the rain scored deep ruts into it. The kiln of an atmosphere baked those ruts hard, sending rovers and horses to either side in search of smoother ground, only to have the process repeated over and over again. The result was a wide thoroughfare crisscrossed with ruts, grooves, and gouges that annoyed both rover drivers and horses. This was the vital commercial artery that connected the farms on the north bank of Happy River.

·   ·   ·

It would be a pleasant ride but for the oppression of the heat, which dredged up memories of Jing's worst days from childhood in Shanghai. To keep her mind away from thoughts of roasting, she focused on the smell of the valley. This was not the perfume of a spring day on the San Francisco Peninsula. Rather, what hit her nose was heavy and cloying. Still the smells were of life, even if a rancid shellhound carcass was part of it. It was so much better than the high plains around the town where the air was as sterile and uninteresting as a new petri dish.

At a bend in the river, Jing came to a large farmstead. The core of it was the same two-unit hab that she and Jorge had, this one purple. Multiple brick additions, with windows of glass panes, had been built around the original unit, and clearly at different times, so that the purple hab was engulfed in a maw of reddish brick. The front door now came out of one of the brick units, and a side door from the same unit led to a lanai circumscribed by a waist-high wall of bamboo.

Jing recognized the three people who were seated at a table in the shade the lanai provided, ceramic cups in front of them. One of them was Penny—never call her Penelope!—Panagiotidis, who, along with her husband, Vo Hiep, owned the farm, the first and largest one in Happy Valley. Next to her was her eldest daughter, Yong. Across from them sat Klaus Koch, a solidly built man with blond hair going gray who wore a shirt and pants that looked like new denim. He and his partner, Sonal Davis, also had a farm, but in addition to the farm, he produced brick, concrete, and glass. He had even started a small plant to make clothing from the bamboo Penny and others grew.

"Jing, come join us for a moment," Penny's high voice called out from the lanai.

Jing would not make it to Saint Peterstown before the next day whether she stopped or not. It was odd how the conception of "urgent" and "quickly" changed when the mode of transportation became a horse. She slid off her horse, tied the two of them to a post set there for that purpose, and walked onto the lanai.

"Glad to take a break with you, Penny." She grabbed an empty chair by the bamboo wall, pulled it over, pushed her hat back, and sat down with the other three. "How are you feeling? I should be seeing you in town for your first trimester ultrasound."

"Can it wait for the meeting of the Demos?" Penny asked. "I don't want to make an extra trip if I don't have to. And I'm feeling fine. A bit tired, maybe. That's all. How do I look to you?"

Jing smiled. A little. She recalled Penny as she had first met her on Earth for her physical before the starflight: twenty-two years old, scared of her own shadow, with a mind that fired off on a million tangents at once and a mouth that voiced whatever came to that mind. The Penny before her today was the same collection of skinny arms and legs bolted to a thin body.

To Jing's clinical eye, though, she had been brushed by an unseen eraser that left the nose even more prominent and put lines in her forehead and cheeks while turning her olive complexion a bit sallow, although the brown eyes were as bright and lively as ever. Her shirt bunched up loosely over narrow shoulders, and a broad-brimmed sun hat made from bamboo hung across her back from a strap at her neck.

"Yes, the ultrasound can wait, but I also want to do your monthly check, and I'll want some blood tests. The fact that you've had six pregnancies and deliveries without complication does not mean the seventh will be the same. We're all getting older. Including you."

"Thanks," Penny said. "It's only one more, and each one is so important. You know, when you consider the number of mature individuals we have and how restricted our range is on this planet, humans qualify as an endangered species here. We need to bring our numbers up because we're still only one bad event from real trouble. I mean, back on Earth, in America, gray wolves came back right from the brink of extinction, and we're not near that point, but every increase is important."

"Oh, Mom! Not the endangered species lecture again!" Laughter followed from Yong, now nineteen years old. She was of sturdier build than Penny, with high cheekbones, partially rounded eyes, and dark skin showing the contribution of her father's Vietnamese ancestry. She wore a T-shirt and loose pants of recycled textile with her pants tucked into high boots. A hat similar to Penny's, but of native reeds, hung on her back. "Sometimes I think you and Dad are planning to populate the world all on your own. And all of us came from only you two. You didn't even have one with somebody else for diversity." She laughed again.

Penny managed to look everywhere except at Klaus while demonstrating that she could blush bright red. "Yong, that's not . . . I mean . . . Hiep, I mean your father and I . . . well, we're a couple . . . I mean we're married."

"Yes, Mom, I know. I am your daughter. But that makes me a Heavener, and we're different. For one thing, we've all listened to the biodiversity lectures in school since the day we could recognize the word." More mirth tumbled out. "I'll have to check with everyone else, but the one you're carrying could be Heavener number four hundred. That's a milestone, you know!"

"This is not a race," Jing protested. "The last thing we need is a preemie." That was only one of the complications she did not need. With all the—albeit necessary—emphasis on increasing the population, she also feared dealing with early teenage pregnancy. So far, the combination of contraception and same-sex rooming until the end of residence school had spared her that.

The humor fled from Yong's face while Jing was thinking about what could go wrong in a pregnancy on a world where she was the most expert—the only—physician. "Austin and I still haven't been able to start one." She ran her hand across her belly. "We've been trying since we became partners, as soon as mandatory contraception stopped after graduation. We've talked about it. That maybe I need to try with somebody else. I mean, it will still be our child. It's just mixing in some other genes. Biodiversity."

Penny's face, if possible, became redder, but she managed a steady voice. "You could take an embryo from the bank, you know. That's a child too."

Yong turned to Jing. "Dr. Song, are those embryos still okay?"

"Yes, and they should be good for a few decades more. If you want one, I can schedule an implantation. Have to do that up in Saint Peterstown."

"Okay. I'll talk with Austin. Maybe if we're still nowhere in another couple of months, we'll do that."

"Ahem," said Klaus. "Maybe we should be offering the good doctor a drink of this amazing brew you've come up with, Penny, and not be burdening her with the survival of our species and our moral code." He pointed to a side table where two more ceramic cups and a pot stood ready.

"Brew?" Jing was dubious. Many of the farms were able to brew beer, enough to be included in equal shares and shipped up to the town, but she had a low tolerance for alcohol. Riding a horse tipsy was not what she wanted to do.

"Coffee!" burst out of Penny. "Heaven isn't the ideal climate for coffee—well, it isn't the ideal climate for anything but a sauna, and that's not my cultural heritage, although it has cured me of my fear of ticks when I'm outside which I had from growing up in Maine, but that's not the point, which is that I've been able to get the robusta trees to manage here, actually found a spot with better drainage and some shade as other trees grew in, and this year I've got coffee beans to grind and it's wicked good. Try a cup!"

Penny took the pot and one of the empty cups and poured out a stream of brown liquid for Jing.

Jing took a sip. It was very strong and very bitter. "God, that's fantastic! I haven't had coffee since the packs from the starships ran out years ago."

Yong made a face. "I have never understood why you chippers rave about this stuff, and now that I've tasted it, I really don't."

"Chippers. I've heard Michael use that term, although not when he knows Jorge or I can hear him," Jing said. "Is this new slang?"

"Heavener slang, and not so new," Yong said. "I'm not sure who started it, but it's because you folks have chips." She tapped an index finger against her head. "It's a little pretentious the way you call yourselves Originals, you know. So, this got going. I think we can leave coffee to the chippers."

"It's an acquired taste," Jing said.

"I can acquire a toe fungus from Heaven, too, but that doesn't mean I want to," Yong retorted.

Amid general laughter, Klaus cleared his throat to create a break he could speak into. "Can I take a minute to be serious? I came over and we were going to celebrate with coffee because I worked up the numbers from the dimensions Yong sent me. Number of bricks and glass panes for windows and concrete for a foundation."

"Austin and I are going to put up our own house and start a farm of our own!" Yong's voice rose with excitement. "We could get a hab unit under equal shares, but there's a waiting line for whatever may be left, and then another waiting line on transport priority, and we don't want a hab, anyway. We'll take some printed parts; we can't go completely outside equal shares, but we'll trade farm products for building supplies—"

"I'll offset a lot of it against everything you've done for me, Penny," Klaus managed to insert in the middle of Yong's stream of words.

"—and this is going to be a Heavener house for a Heavener family. It's time for humans to be part of Heaven, not intruders."

"Which means it's time for you to finally tell us where you're putting it. You've been very cryptic about the location ever since you told me what you and Austin were starting to plan." Pride and worry chased each other across Penny's face.

"We're going to have the first farm on the south bank of Happy River," Yong announced. Her eyes shone. "I've worked on the farm here practically since I was a toddler. Austin has worked on his parents' farm much the same. You've taught us what to look for in the land. I've got the perfect spot picked out. We've got to get all the thistle cleared, of course, but there isn't that much growth of it there. Austin did the plans for the house himself. We're going to do it!"

"How are you going to get everything across?" Penny asked. "I don't think the hauler rovers can cross the river—at least, I'd be worried about trying and losing one. And you'll be very separated from the rest of us."

"Austin's going to ask the Demos at the meeting to support building a bridge," Yong said. "If not, we'll build a raft. We can get Jordie Longfellow to help. Austin helped him out when Jordie was new in high-seniors. And as for being separated, Mom, you were twenty-two when you took a starship seventy-six light-years to have a farm, and then you told the Demos to get their asses out of Saint Peterstown and help farm Happy Valley. I've heard all the stories."

Penny's eyes went down to her hands and the blush returned.

"It's a generational thing, Penny," Klaus said. "The rising generation always wants to show their independence, and here, well, you're about the youngest of the Originals, the Pioneer Youth that came with us, and you're forty-three now. The oldest Heaveners, like Yong, are nineteen. There's nobody in between. That's one hell of a generation gap."

"It's more than that," Penny said softly. "Look, I know what I did and why I wasn't even speaking to my parents at that point, but that's another story, and we shouldn't go there. Yong's right, absolutely right, about moving someplace new. I can't let my feelings about separation get in the way. I'm sorry I sounded like I was trying to hold you back."

She laid a hand gently on Yong's arm. "I won't ever do that again. We're going to have to move out in an even bigger way. It's still a struggle here. Too many animals don't tolerate the climate. Our farming area is okay now, but as the population grows—and it has to—even the south bank won't be enough. And we are going to need metal deposits, which we haven't found in the valley at all. And other resources. We won't survive long-term if all we do is stay here."

Penny paused to finish her coffee, which let those last words sink in. Then she went for the pot and refilled her cup. "I've seen the images and data the two starships, *Dauntless* and *Daredevil*, left in the database. We're at seventy-one degrees south latitude, or Saint

Peterstown is. With the axial tilt of ten degrees, we're north of the polar circle, but the climate farther toward the south pole is more moderate; the images show dense green. I'll bet there's some remnant of the old polar forest left there."

Penny's words took Jing back to the bridge of the starship *Dauntless*, where she and the rest of the crew had stared at the images and data from the planet. Heaven had a single supercontinent stretching from the south pole to the high northern latitudes in one hemisphere. Some massive volcanic event in the north in the recent geological past had baked off part of the crust, leaving a sea of lava and volcanoes while flooding the atmosphere with carbon dioxide, wiping out most of the ozone, pounding the land with acid rain, and ruining the climate. The carbon dioxide was at 2100 ppm when they arrived, and God knows how high it had reached. The consequences had made most of the land uninhabitable and turned the seas into hot tubs. Most of the plants and animals had died out. Saint Peterstown had been built where it was as a compromise among being at a high enough latitude for the climate to be somewhat tolerable, with still enough daylight in the winter for solar power, and having a reasonable landing zone for the spaceplanes. Jing was reliving the discussion on the ship before she realized Penny had not stopped talking. Well, Penny rarely stopped.

"If I'm right," Penny was saying, "we could have wood for building, not like the dwarfed trees that are all we have here, and better land for farms. I know the polar winter is a big problem for photovoltaic systems—that's probably why the *Daredevil* crew never considered putting the town there—but we can manage getting there now. We need to send an expedition down there and explore it."

"Penny, that's what got you voted out as mayor the last time you brought it up," Jing said.

"I've been mayor three times. I don't want to be again." Penny's hands waved in time with her words. "That's not the point. The point is that we need to do it, and I will keep bringing it up until we do it. The point is that Yong is right about moving someplace new. Maybe"—she looked at Yong—"your sister, Thorny, will join you. This coming term is her last in residence school. Maybe this would be good for her."

"Mom, that's not a generation gap you're talking about. That's a species gap." Yong's eye roll said everything necessary about the likelihood of bridging that particular chasm.

"You know," Klaus said, "we've been so caught up in what we are doing that we haven't even asked Jing why she is headed for Saint Peterstown now. With a packhorse in tow, that must be where you're going."

Jing sighed. She preferred listening to an old family argument to discussing her news, but she had no choice. She told them she was headed to Saint Peterstown to do a postmortem on Fernando Vargas, and what had been a bright mood around the table darkened.

"We've had messages"—Penny's hand included Klaus and Yong with her—"from the twins. They are okay. From what else they say, there was some kind of accident with Fernando."

"It's all very confused," Klaus said. "I had a call from Sonal as well. She is in town, and what Penny said is about all she knew. We were talking about it before you came, but we had no idea what really happened. That is horrible about the Vargas boy. Did you say he was killed?"

"I did *not* say that." Jing put as much emphasis on the negative as she could. "I said he was found dead. That's all I really know right now."

"Then maybe this was some horrible accident, the way the kids' messages sounded," Penny said.

"Penny, Yong," Jing said, "Thorny is in Fernando's cohort at school. Did she tell you anything?"

"I doubt Thorny would message us if the sun went nova," Yong said. "Actually, that's not fair. If the sun went nova, by the time Thorny knew it, she wouldn't have time to message us. But, no, a message from Thorny is cosmically unlikely."

Jing braced herself for Penny to start again on the topic of how every individual was important for an endangered species, but Penny did not do that.

"You'll probably meet Hiep on the way," she said instead. "He has more of a relationship with Thorny, so if she had something to say, it might be to him. He left for town earlier because he had a call about some trouble up there that he needed to look into."

"Remorse cases?" Jing asked.

"Hiep didn't say. Only that it would be best if he went. Hopefully, it has nothing to do with Ajit Mistry."

Klaus leaned forward, intent on Penny. "That man is a perfect reason why we need you as mayor again. He's got such an inflated concept of his value, I'm surprised the world can contain it. Used to be there wasn't a chance in hell he'd get enough votes in the Demos, but with the political splintering that's going on, I'm no longer so sure."

"Heaveners in the valley won't go near him," Yong said. "All he talks about is that the town has to come first. I know townies, but he's ridiculous. That and all the equal share shit he talks about. Everybody should get the stuff they need, and everybody who can make the stuff should make it so the others can get it."

"Where have we heard that siren song before?" Klaus said.

"Karl Marx—" Penny started.

"That was a rhetorical question," Klaus said. "It's hard to ask people to work their asses off on production when they know that under equal shares, some jerk who barely works at all has the same shot at getting the stuff as they do. I ask myself the same question."

"See what Hiep has to say when you catch up with him," Penny suggested.

"If he left that much ahead of me, I doubt I'll see him," Jing said. "He'll push on as fast as he can."

"I think you will see him," Penny said. "I asked him to check the pasturage we're trying to have for horses at the way station hab, because what we call grass here has no methionine, like everything else, and it's not good nutritionally for the horses otherwise, and it's not grass, of course; it's phylogenetically more a primitive fern, which makes sense because grass didn't evolve on Earth until late in the dinosaur era and this planet is earlier evolutionarily, but the point is that we have to make sure our grass is coming through the dark days okay and the netting is intact and we don't have thistle in there. We don't have time for natural selection to teach horses about thistle, so we have to make sure it stays clean. And that the grass is okay. It's two different types of fescue grass, you know, which will stay green in cool weather—not that our winters are even that cool—and does well even in poor, acid soil, which is all we've got up there, but most people wouldn't think of using it, because you don't feed it to horses on Earth, but I thought we could do it here because the reason you can't use it on Earth is that it typically has a fungal infection that makes it bad for horses but on Heaven we can have the fescue grass without the fungus, which is important because fescue grass is a reasonable source of methionine, and I've always found it odd that there is no methionine in Heaven biota, I mean, they seem to use a couple of different amino acids in its place but we can't make use of those, we just piss them out, which means we have to stockpile methionine like vitamins in case we have a big problem with our Earth food crops. I mean, you can eat your fill of edible Heaven foods like shellhounds and some plants like aspergrass and you'll still essentially die of malnutrition with a full stomach, and horses need methionine same as humans and other Earth animals, so even if fescue grass isn't the best source of methionine, like maybe—"

The clang of Yong's spoon was loud against the cup in front of Penny. "Mom, your coffee is getting cold."

Penny gave an embarrassed smile and finally took a breath. "That's my daughter. Always subtle."

"What Mom won't say, in everything she does say, is that nobody except her would even have put this together. Maybe fescue grass from Earth will cover the high plains of Heaven. That's why the Demos keeps bringing you back as mayor. When they need someone to save their asses, they go back to you. If it's you or Mistry, I know it will be you." Pride rang in Yong's voice.

"I wouldn't say that," Penny said, "but the point for now is that I asked Hiep to check it, so he will overnight at the way station's hab. He is always careful with what he does. Talk to him about what happened to Fernando. He may also have heard something, whether from Thorny or someone else."

AJIT

His lunchtime gathering was breaking up, people drifting off as pollen blown by the wind to whatever their afternoon held for them. It was not a big crowd, six people in all, but small numbers gave him the opportunity for a more personal impression. It also somewhat mollified his wife, since the food he supplied—a meaningful draw—came from their equal shares. He was always one to stress that point when he spoke to groups. It showed he was on the same level as everyone else, and if his wife grumbled, that would be later. As it was, they were one person short: Chloe DiMasi had not come, despite multiple messages from her saying how important she believed it was for him to succeed. A final message, right before he was to start speaking, claimed she had a crisis at work, although how that could be more of a crisis than the town's survival was an interesting question. The crisis was more likely related to that lunacy at the residence school that had killed one of the kids and probably involved her delinquent son Dalton, although since the dead boy was from the valley, that did not make sense either. He decided to put the matter of her no-show in the category of a portion of food saved. There would be another time and another talk.

"Inspiring talk, Ajit, truly inspiring. I do think you are the person to lead this town. Those fucking would-be aristocrats in the valley—we should call them valley-crats—they'll make servants out of us townies if they can. Even if Jacoby doesn't resign the way you're saying he will, I'd consider putting you up to challenge him at the Demos meeting."

He regarded the speaker, Herschel Northrup. A Black man with a face as round as a full moon. American, by his speech, probably from the Southeast. Food engineer here. Northrup had come out on the *Daredevil* also, but he had been very closemouthed about who he was and what he had done on Earth that had propelled him from prison to the stars. He had maintained that attitude on Heaven for two decades, even though none of it could matter here.

"Thank you very much," Ajit said.

"If there's anything I can do to support you, let me know. I mean it." Northrup held out his hand.

Ajit shook it, felt his hand engulfed by a meaty paw at least twice as thick as his own. When Northrup walked away and left, Ajit flexed his fingers a few times and examined the hand to be sure it was okay. He was a slim man whose shoulders could be called broad only in comparison to his trim waist. His brown eyes could appear lazy, but they sharpened quickly when he sensed an opportunity developing. Under a narrow nose he wore a pencil-thin mustache that he carefully clipped every day, and his black hair was combed straight back over a dark brown face that showed little sign of age. He wore an obviously recycled T-shirt and shorts that hung at his knees, also of recycled textile. He would have preferred to wear a new cotton shirt and wide cotton pants, both fit to his frame. Those clothes hung in his closet because there was always a way to get what you wanted, but as with the food, for these meetings it was better to appear as one who made do with his equal share. Looking the part made it easier to inveigh against the damned valley aristocrats and support equal shares for all.

The last one to stop and shake his hand was Cam, one of the pair who formed the town's Office of Public Safety. Ajit exchanged polite words that meant little while sounding sincere. If the public safety of Saint Peterstown ever depended on Cam taking prompt and forceful action, the townies would not have a chance. However, Cam attended every one of Ajit's little get-togethers. He was devoted to the principle of equal shares, probably because if his share depended on the quality and quantity of his work, he would have nothing. That did not bother Ajit. He had arranged an occasional favor for Cam in the past, facts that he could remind Cam of from time to time. It would be worth seeing if there was a similar hook he could put into Chloe. All followers were useful, even if it was unclear at the moment what use they could have.

DANIJEL

DANIJEL DROVE THE ROVER HE HAD TAKEN AS FAST AS HE DARED TOWARD THE LAST signal position of the exploratory rover in the vicinity of Dead Lake. If he was honest with himself, he would have said that he was not driving very fast in absolute terms. He was far better at diagnosing and repairing the vehicles than driving them. He winced with every bounce of the rover off a rock or drop of a wheel into a rut, convinced that the wiring in a wheel motor would break or the steering would jam.

The urgency with which he drove was authentic, however, even if his speed was moderate. Sidelong looks at Thorny's backpack in the passenger seat reinforced his concern. *If she planned to run away, she would not have left that pack where Dalton could take it. And it is impossible to run away forever on Heaven.* Thorny ran off; Thorny came back, the same as the sun rose and fell. She would want her pack. Somehow, this was all tied together with Ferdy Vargas and something *very bad* that had happened.

He would find her. He would give her the pack, and she would be grateful. He would manage to *talk* to her.

His phone buzzed. It was Unreality Busby. He ignored it. A few minutes later, it buzzed again. Her again. He continued to ignore it. Danijel told himself that he was already in so much trouble that ignoring calls from Busby could not make it worse. More properly, he thought, it was better than answering the call and then not doing what she told him to do.

The distance to Dead Lake could be hiked in a few hours, so by rover it was a short drive, even driving carefully. The sun had hardly moved in the sky when he first caught a glimpse of the lake and the trees behind it. No other rover was in sight.

Danijel rechecked the position of the other rover's last signal. He rechecked his own position. He did not get things like this wrong, but his adrenaline was surging far more than it did on any exam, so he double-checked again. No error.

The ground was uneven in this area, so he drove in a wide circle in a case a freakish fold in the terrain was blocking the signal and hiding the rover. Nothing. He opened the window and yelled out for Thorny, then told himself that it was ridiculous to think she would be within earshot yet the rover undetectable. He drove back to his original terminus, the place of the other rover's last signal. It was only then that he saw what he should have noticed right away.

Ahead of him, in the direction of the slope up behind Dead Lake, rover tires had left a track through the dirt and thin ground cover. No one came to Dead Lake except for student trips when they were learning about the acidification and lack of oxygen in the water that made Dead Lake dead. Students walked. No one would have come here in a rover. Not recently. Except Thorny.

Thorny's rover had abruptly dropped off the network, but she had continued driving. Did she realize she was driving a malfunctioning rover? He looked up at the skies that had clouded over to a sheet of dull gray lead and sent a prayer that it not rain.

The tracks led into the trees. At first, they continued south up the slope but then curved west once they were above and behind the lake. Thorny had either been driving too fast for the conditions—she had to have been here in the dark—or she had not been paying close enough attention. Her rover had brushed past many trees, snapping branches and scattering twigs across the ground. Rovers had a clear coating as a shield over their photovoltaic skin, but it was thin. It was not armor. Danijel groaned at the thought of damage to the photovoltaic cells that charged the vehicle's battery. The organics that captured the light and put out the electricity could be produced by the cell foundries, and new photovoltaic cells could be printed, but replacing damaged cells was difficult and time-consuming work. Even worse, if enough cells were damaged, the charging of the rover's battery would be impaired.

The one advantage Thorny's rough passage through the trees gave to Danijel as the light dimmed and the tracks became harder to see was that the broken branches and debris could be followed as easily as if a woodsman had blazed a trail. Darkness came early at this time of year, but he continued in pursuit. The bigger problem was his lack of sleep.

When he reached the point when he had to rest, Danijel sent a message to his father that he would not be back that night. Then he reclined his seat to go to sleep. He would not return without Thorny.

JING

THE ROADS—PACKED DIRT, NOT PAVEMENT, AND MORE TRAIL THAN ROAD IN PLACES—that led to the farms of Happy Valley, whether East Valley Road in the direction of White Sands Bay or West Valley Road to the foot of Staircase Falls, all met at a single route for the climb up the cliffside of Happy Valley and then across the high plains to Saint Peterstown. It was marked, at the point on the valley floor where the other roads split off, by a green-and-white sign that read HEAVEN HIGHWAY 1.

The highway followed, for the most part, the route Hiep and Penny had taken along with the scout from the *Dauntless*, Leif Grettison, twenty years earlier on the first exploration of the valley. During the intervening years it had been converted into a modest dirt road, cleared, graded, and widened enough for a rover to pass a horse. Switchbacks had been dug into the side of the cliff at several points to keep the grade of ascent—or descent—to one that could be managed by a horse or a less-than-expert rover driver. Equally important was the addition of lights. At regular intervals, two-foot-high spikes had been driven into the ground with a low-wattage LED mounted on each. A small photovoltaic panel attached to the spike kept the battery charged. In the dark of the winter days, those lights were all that kept the road safely passable.

At the top of the valley wall, Jing rested her horses briefly. She looked back across the valley. The southern wall was indistinct in the haze. The wind had died down to little more than a light breath across her cheeks. It was not enough to lessen the baking heat of the late fall day; the high plains had no shade. Even lightly clad as she was, Jing felt sweat drip across her body. The horses would need to take a slow pace on the road. The only positive thing to be said for the day's weather was that the clouds that threatened rain reduced the direct heat on her skin, and, given the season, the sun was already low on the horizon. Once it was down, there would be some relief from the heat. The corollary to that, though, was that she would be traveling in the dark.

A light kick started her mount moving, the packhorse following. The only feature on the plains was a low hill. It was not much of a rise; it owed its prominence to the lack of anything else sticking up from the flat terrain. From the top of the hill rose the communications mast with its antennas that knitted Saint Peterstown and the farms of the valley together. It was a thin thread for that purpose, Jing thought.

Heaven Highway 1 ran in a straight line forty-two miles from the valley wall to the Perimeter Road of Saint Peterstown, far too long a distance to cover in a single ride, even if the temperature were more moderate. In recognition of the fact that the increasing number of people in the valley meant that not every trip could be by rover, and that the rovers would not last forever, the settlers had created a way station fifteen miles from the valley cliffs. That split the journey into two long but manageable rides on a horse.

At this time of year, reaching the rest stop still took longer than the daylight hours. Jing's horses were plodding along as the sky darkened. The breeze picked up again with the fall of dusk. It was not truly cool, but the change was enough to create the sensation of a cool drink in her mouth. Around her was silence. The fall of night on Heaven's plains was not accompanied by the chirping of birds or the buzzing of insect wings. Nothing flew in the air over the plains. No animals croaked or scuttled through the thin ground cover alongside the road. Jing carried weapons, but predator attacks on the plains above the valley had numbered less than the fingers of one hand in twenty years. The true menace of the planet lay not in the teeth of carnivores but in its sheer emptiness, which preyed on the mind. She found herself wishing, as she often did on these trips, for the need to slap a mosquito as it bit, simply to feel less alone. The extinction Heaven's volcanoes had imposed on its environment had been crushing.

As the sunlight fled the sky, the plains on either side of the road vanished into gloom. There was only the road that ran straight ahead, marked on either side by the soft glow of the LEDs, a runway to the horizon.

After a little less than eternity, a spark of yellow rose out of the darkness to the right of the lights that marked the edge of the road. Yes! That was the way station hab. It could not be anything else. She resisted the urge to quicken the pace. The horses were tired. It would not be fair to them. Her back and her rump would survive a little longer.

As she approached, more lights appeared, illuminating the exterior of a standard hab unit. Two more lights sat atop the gate in the fence. She led the horses through that gate into the pasture, removed their saddles and loads, and saw that they had water. Then she put on their feed bags. The grass of the pasture—fescue, as Penny had termed it—was fine for the horses, but with the moonlight cut down by the clouds, she did not think she could be 100 percent sure no Heaven thistle had gotten in. *I have to get past this fear*, she told herself. *What is the point of a pasture if we are too afraid to use it?* This was not the night for that argument. She arched her back and offered a theatrical moan to the stars above before she walked to the hab door.

The door slid open at the touch of her hand on the plate. Cool, dry air enveloped her as she stepped in. Bliss. Inside, one of the six field cots was occupied by a man lying on his side, head resting on a palm and propped by the elbow braced against the mattress. He was reading something on his phone. At her entrance, his eyes came up and he swung to a sitting position. Hiep.

His was a square face with heavy, dark eyebrows and narrow eyes. His skin was dark, not the burnt obsidian it would be in the summer, but still much darker than hers, save for the near-white scar on his upper left arm. The muscles of his arms were sharply defined. The T-shirt he wore was recycled textile, varying shades of gray shot through with bits of other colors, courtesy of the number of times the material had been through the recycler rather than any intent of a manufacturer. The shirt fit tightly; it could almost have been sprayed on, showing a broad chest that tapered to a narrow waist. His cargo pants, worn to the point of being ready for the recycler, had multiple bulging pockets. His boots were off, placed together and aligned next to his cot.

Jing fought the urge to step back, even though nothing in his face or posture was unwelcoming. It would not be right, nor fair to him. She saw him regularly in the valley, had seen him stand with ill-concealed anxiety as she delivered each of his six children, had seen him cradle each one of those infants with supreme gentleness. And yet. An ill-defined sense of menace clung to Hiep, a dark shadow wrapped tightly around him.

"I'm sorry if I'm interrupting," Jing managed to say.

"Nothing important. I was only reading a book." His voice was soft, a bit flat, as though he knew what her immediate emotional reaction had been even if she had not acted on it.

"What book?" She thought that was an innocuous question.

"Dickens. *A Tale of Two Cities*. I thought I had read all the Dickens in our library years ago, but I missed this one."

Jing peered at him. He was serious. "I would not have taken you for a fan of Dickens."

"I read all sorts of things," Hiep said. "In that way, I am like Penny, although she does not read fiction." He shrugged. "Penny messaged me that you were on the way and why. I have also heard from our children—the younger ones of residence school age, at least—and have been in touch with Reality."

That figures, Jing thought. "Have you learned anything about what happened?"

"Only that I am reasonably sure thistle is not involved. That is something. Reality said there was nothing to suggest a fight; no wounds. So, I will leave that for your examination. None of the children say they know anything, which is not surprising. Reality said that Thorny had taken off and was not answering calls. She has not answered mine, either. No one has seen her since before this happened."

"She ran away again? I thought she had stopped that."

"She had." Hiep paused as though weighing his words. "She has not done it since residence school started this year at the fall equinox, and there were only a couple of times last year. Not at all the way it was when you saw her about this."

Jing remembered a frustrated and fed up Reality looking for a quick answer to a recurrent problem. She remembered Hiep being unhappy at the doctor being involved. She didn't want to bring it up all over again, but said, "All I could get from Thorny then was that she would get angry, and when she was angry, she said it was a choice between hitting someone or running and you would be unhappy if she hit someone."

"She would usually return on her own the same day," Hiep said. "The times she did not, if Reality could not get her, I would go and find her. She would come back with me. And then she discovered the heavy bag in the gym."

Jing had heard about that from Reality. Thorny would run to the gym and whale away on the heavy bag. The frequency of running away had dropped off dramatically and continued to decline as she got older. It was both fortunate and remarkable that the heavy bag had held up over the years. "Something must have stressed her badly. Do you think it could be connected to whatever happened to Fernando?"

"When I reach town, I will find her, and we will talk. Thorny is not the most communicative of people, but we will talk. No matter what has happened."

Jing had the feeling she was treading on territory Hiep preferred to leave alone, but she felt she had no choice. "I know Thorny can be . . . difficult. I can help, you know."

"Difficult is relative." Hiep leaned back on the cot, braced on his elbows as if deliberately trying to make himself less threatening. "By the time I reached Thorny's age, I had been forced to leave my family and join Dragon Company. I had fought in battles, been exchanged to Sicarius, trained as an assassin, and completed my first mission as one. That training gave me my command of English and also taught me how to learn"—he moved his weight to one elbow and held out the phone with the book page showing—"so there are positives, but it was a problematic way to grow up."

Jing nodded. Hiep's personal history, both as a mercenary soldier and an assassin in the free companies that had plagued Earth during what people called the New Golden Age, was well known. That accounted for the threatening aura around him.

Hiep paused, as if considering how much more to say. "Thorny has difficulties relating to others, both inside and outside our family, which, you understand, is also true for both her parents. She is very smart, very much like Penny, and she has learned and learned quickly everything I have taught her. Of all six, she is the most like me, and I would say she is my favorite." Hiep smiled.

Jing was surprised at the revelation about Thorny. Hiep never discussed his feelings, as far as she knew. Maybe he did with Penny, but Penny, for all that she could talk nonstop on multiple topics at the same time if those topics had to do with plants, animals, farming, or science from geology to paleontology, never talked about anything Hiep said to her.

"You *are* worried Thorny is involved in whatever happened," Jing said at last.

"If I were not going to Saint Peterstown on other business, I would be going because of this. Thorny will talk to me." Hiep's eyes fastened on Jing's and did not move off. "That should answer your question."

It did. Hiep was concerned, but he would not say more or speculate. "I will let you know what I find on my exam." Which left the other issue. "Why are you going, then? What was the original reason? Penny was vague. Is it about remorsers? I would think that would need me more than you."

"I'm not sure why Ibiana asked me to come," Hiep said. "She said she would explain when I got there. It could be remorsers who won't work but still want their equal share and will see the Demos meeting as a chance to sell their votes. It could be others from the *Daredevil* with the same idea. You remember, other than the six of us from free companies, the *Daredevil* Originals were all criminals, notorious enough that they volunteered to come here in exchange for pardons and erasure from the databases, to spare their families. Not all of them are keen to work. but they are keen to keep their shares. Most of them are townies and so form a natural target for Mistry and his promises. Remorse may play a role in all of this, but so do votes."

"Some degree of remorse is pretty common for people—a natural reaction, even if it doesn't rise to what I've been calling remorse syndrome." In fact, Jing thought, it would be strange if people did not have some remorse over their choice to come as the years went by and the reasons for the choice faded while the harshness of their lives and their isolation stared them in the face every day.

"Do you feel it, you and Jorge?" Hiep sounded truly curious. "You were both starfolk, with very different expectations on Earth from the rest of us, yet you gave that up. Do you think about it?"

"Sometimes." She and Jorge had talked about it now and again over the years, usually on nights when sleep would not come. "It was not that much of a choice, though. Jorge might not have survived another flight in hib. He had to stay. The idea of waking from hib back at Earth knowing that Jorge had stayed and already lived out his life here . . . that was impossible for me. I have thought"—she rubbed at the side of her head—"that when another starship came and we met the starfolk, it might feel awkward, but that hasn't happened. I may be the only one here who is relieved there has never been another starship. What about you?" Her voice regained its strength. "Do you feel any remorse?"

"I have none." Hiep's answer was unhesitating, his voice calm. "Because I am here, I have Penny. We have our children. I could die tomorrow, and I would still have had them for the time I lived here. This is the best life I could ever have. I would die for Penny. I would kill for her; I *have* killed for her. The same is true for our children."

"You are a scary man, sometimes, Vo Hiep."

"That is only because you know the truth." Hiep's voice remained quiet. "You know who I am. More importantly, you know *what* I am. If you did not, what would you see? A man of modest size from a village in still-rural Vietnam. You might find it unusual that I speak US English without an accent, but that would not be enough to raise your suspicions. I would not appear dangerous." He turned his open palms upward while still leaning back on his elbows. Jing tried to see him without her knowledge of his past. It did not work.

"Tomorrow," Hiep continued, "it may be useful if the knowledge of what I have done can induce some fear. That is a form of persuasion that I lack the spoken eloquence to achieve with words. After my meeting, I will go to find Thorny, speak to her as the father she deserves, and bring her back to school. For tonight, you may wish to take a cot in the other half of the unit." With one hand he indicated a door in the rear wall of the hab that led to the second section of the unit. "Or I can move back there, if you prefer the front."

Jing let out a short laugh. "I think we are reverting to an older set of morals here. When we left Earth, no one would think twice about a man and a woman bunking in the same room, whether they did anything or not."

"We are not on Earth," Hiep said, "and never will be again."

Jing took a cot in the rear unit.

THORNY

THE SMALL ROVER BOUNCED OFF ROCKS AND LURCHED FROM SIDE TO SIDE ON THE uneven terrain as it careered wildly southwest after she left Saint Peterstown, roughly parallel to Dead Creek. The light of a single one of Heaven's moons gave only a vague idea of the ground the rover was flying over, but that speed would not have been safe even in broad daylight. The moonlight was, at least, sufficient to make out the steep banks of Dead Creek, with the creek itself, shrunken in a dry spell, invisible at the bottom of its channel. The viewscreen in the rover cabin with its night-vision capability showed more detail, but the gyrations of the rover made it an unstable view. It was only when the shimmering surface of Dead Lake came into view that she brought the vehicle to an abrupt stop, one that almost pitched her into the steering wheel chest-first.

For a minute, Thorny Panagiotidis sat shuddering, unable to release her hands from their death grip on the steering wheel, her breath coming in gasps. When she did free one hand, it went in an involuntary motion to her belt and the top of her pants. One fastening was still open, but her pants were up around her hips; everything else in place. She would not accept that conclusion until her fingers had explored twice and reported that she had, somehow, fastened the belt and her pants as she ran. She let out a long breath. *That* had not happened.

What had happened was bad enough. She did not want to remember it. What she could not stop remembering, though, was Ferdy with his hands where she didn't want them and his mouth on hers long after she was trying to say stop. She remembered breaking free and remembered the others shouting, but she did not want to remember the words they had been shouting. She did not want to hear them. It was better to recall only a dull roar that merged together. She remembered running, with her chest and brain on fire, until she reached the rover and driving off in it like a madwoman, although she didn't remember planning to take it.

Of course she hadn't stolen the rover, she told herself. The rovers belonged to the Demos, the people of Heaven, both Saint Peterstown and Happy Valley. Even if she had not reached nineteen and was still in residence school, not yet an official voting member of the Demos, she was still one of the people. *Technically*, therefore, she had not stolen the rover. She had merely taken it without permission. She knew other people would not appreciate the distinction. They never appreciated much, where she was concerned.

But she could drive a rover and mostly take one apart and then put it back together better than any of them. As good as or better than the so-called engineers, except for Miroslav Petrovic and Dani. And her father, of course. Her father had started teaching her to operate and work on a rover when she was nine, long before any child was allowed to drive a rover. A fine one for talking about obeying rules, her father was.

And what about her father? When she did not return, he would find her here. It had been a year since the last time, but he would come and bring her back. He always did. A sudden determination filled her.

Not this time. She was not going back this time. Nobody was going to find her this time.

If she was not going back, then what was she going to do? No idea. But there was one thing she needed to do first, no matter what else she did.

Thorny brought up the rover's main control screen. In the SEARCH entry, she tapped in a command sequence her father had taught her. The screen blanked and all the graphics disappeared, leaving nothing but a prompt in the upper left-hand corner.

Again, she recalled her father's instructions. She tapped in several lines of code, then hit ENTER. The screen blanked again. When it refreshed, a dialog box displayed.

NETWORK CONNECTION LOST

NETWORK AVAILABLE: ST. PETERSTOWN

She closed it, which brought back the original screen, this time with a blinking red dot by the network symbol. Exploratory rovers destined for new worlds were designed to stay in contact with their base. The connection was automatic; it did not have a shutoff. If there was a rule, or a lock, or a barrier, however, her father knew how to get around it. A fine one for following rules he was. Hiep was a good instructor; Thorny was an apt pupil.

Thorny drove into the wood of low trees on the slope behind Dead Lake, then turned right to pass south of the lake. She should have driven more slowly in the dark and among the trees, but she was always able to find a path through the trunks, and none of the branches was stout enough to do more than lash against the rover as it went past. The rover easily crossed a few dry channels leading to the lake from farther upslope. She was not going to waste any time on the lake. Nothing lived in it, swam across it, or flew above it. Much of the plains of Heaven north of Happy Valley were that way.

The sun rose while she was still among the trees. They were more widely spaced ahead of her, with no real undergrowth. She kept driving and cleared the last isolated trees at the edge of the wood. Ahead of her stretched a rolling grassy plain, similar to the one around Saint Peterstown. Far to the west, the land rose to a line of mountains that were perceptibly higher than when glimpsed from the town. To the left and south the land sloped downward, although the start of that slope was still some distance from where the rover stood.

Thorny had never been this far. The longest she had ever run away for had ended in the trees above Dead Lake, although she did not know how far she had gone that time because she had gotten lost, and by the time her father had found her, she was both hungry and scared, a set of facts she was loath to admit. She did not think any of the other settlers had been this far, seen this view. Images from the spaceplanes and the starships did not count, naturally. The idea of being the first gave her a tiny thrill.

She reached into a thigh pocket of her cargo pants and pulled out a small package made of carefully glued-together pieces of plastic, in which iridescent gray bands shimmered in the light. She slid a finger under a sealed flap to open it. Her phone dropped into her hand. She thumbed it on.

The phone gave no indication that it had received any messages or calls. The shielding had worked. Yes, her father had known what he was talking about. He never spoke unless he knew what he was talking about. Well, there was also plenty he knew that he never said, but that was a different issue. She checked the phone. No signal. Good. She shut the phone off and, with an automatic movement, stuck it in the rover's charger slot.

She was not going back, so she would go forward. She would see what was there, where the land began to slope down to the south. She ought to be west of the point where the Happy River went over Staircase Falls, although she had no idea how far. The rover had images taken by one of the spaceplane drones, so she could see the river where it went over the falls and Happy Valley beyond it, but the images antedated any of the farms. The problem was that she did not know where *she* was. It did not matter. She was going to explore.

From the rover's emergency food pack, she pulled a strip of jerky.

That would take care of her stomach for a while. She was not really hungry, anyway. The bigger problem was that she was tired, not having slept the entire night since she had been out behind the hydroponics with Fernando. If she went to sleep, though, she would waste the precious few hours of daylight granted to her at this time of year.

She tapped at the controls and turned the rover's log on. The rover could not talk to her, but she could talk to it. That would be enough to keep her awake as she drove across the plain. It would have to be enough.

For a while, she could not think of anything to say. It was not as though she had any brilliant insight into the nature of humanity, or how to make the settlement work better, or even how to make people like her, so she drove in silence. When she caught herself yawning, fighting to keep her eyes open, she decided she had to say something, no matter how banal.

"The problem starts, Rover," she began, "with my parents. Of course it does, because I am the problem and they made me, so it starts with them and it's their fault. That shouldn't be a surprise. I mean, if you cross a not-very-social genius with an assassin, you're likely to get a weird result.

"I mean, look at me, Rover." Thorny held her arms wide away from her body and off the steering, as if the rover could examine her. "I've got my mom's figure, which is to say, none. Have you ever seen a skinnier collection of arms and legs glued to a body with the shape of one of these dwarf tree trunks? I mean, yes, anatomically, I do have tits and hips, but it's not as if you can get more than a suggestion they exist when I have my clothes on, which is the only way anyone is seeing me. I did get my father's muscles, I'll grant that, but what good does that do except create a girl who can hoist a bundle of bamboo or a pallet of brick? I might as well be a bot." She held one hand in front of her face and clenched her fist so tightly the knuckles blanched. "Like a rock. That was what they called me when I first went to residence school at eight: Hands of Stone. Only good if I want to hit someone, and that's just more trouble for me to be in.

"And then there's my face, Rover. It's like my father's, but it's rounded off because I'm a girl, so it's like a plate with black hair on top.

And my cheeks are chubby! And the eyes aren't properly narrow, but they're not really round, either—they're kind of halfway, which is like the rest of me. I'm not all of anything. My skin is not dark enough to be dark, and not light enough to call white. What does that make me? Off-white? I mean, seriously, Rover. My mouth is too small, which is odd because it's way too loud when it talks, and I have no idea where that comes from.

"Rover, I'm a fucking mess."

After finishing the catalog of her physical shortcomings, Thorny fell silent. The log was voice-actuated when on, so she did not need to touch the controls. She kept driving. The land did begin to tilt down to the south, giving the impression that she had reached the lip of an enormous funnel. The sun, meanwhile, had passed its zenith and begun its descent. Her eyelids drooped.

"The other thing wrong with me, Rover, is my name." She was *not* going to fall asleep. She had enough problems to review with the rover to last until nightfall. "This is entirely my mom's doing. Entirely." She paused for effect but received no reaction from the rover. "Who names a girl Thorny? Well, there's a story. Of course. My mom was so taken with these people from the *Dauntless*, the woman pilot, Yang Yong, and the scout, Leif Grettison. Mom said if her first child was a boy he would be Leif, and a girl would be Yong. I suppose they did save our settlement. I've heard that story since I was a baby, but still . . . seriously, Rover. Anyway, Mom's first was a girl, so she got Yong. That's Yong Panagiotidis, our Little Miss Wonderful. So, Mom figures she'd name the next one Leif, but she got me and there's no way to make Leif work for a girl. She went through the database looking for an Icelandic girl's name and she came up with Thorny. I've checked, Rover; that is a real name. Mom even put it in the log with that strange first letter that looks like a *P* with an erection, which sounds like *th* in 'think'—which is what Mom is always doing, even if what she is thinking is a mystery—and the accents on the *O* and *Y*. I write it as Thorny, which is what everyone else including Mom does, and we all say it the way it looks in English, so I'm not exactly right even with my name. Mom said it was a good name because it took care of naming for Leif and thorns reminded her of plants, and anything that gets Mom started on plants is good for a long lecture. Naturally, she had the twins after that, so that gave her a Leif, but I'm still Thorny. As if that's not bad enough, Mom had to take care of her Greek heritage. She couldn't make Odysseus work for a girl either, but she did give me Odyssey. When I got older, she would say raising me was a thorny odyssey, which was funny, but not to me.

"Honestly, Rover, Mom's brain runs in high gear all the time, but not in the real world. What was she thinking? From the day I got to residence school, it was like the class chant: 'Thorny is horny! Thorny is horny!' So, I figured I'd get rid of Thorny and use Odyssey, but they turned that into Oddity, and you can guess where that went, Rover. I thought I would use my initials, TOP, and that would be good, but the boys started saying that I always wanted to be on top. I mean, I didn't even know what that *meant*." She slammed her hand on the steering wheel.

"So, that's me, Rover: Thorny Odyssey Panagiotidis taking you on a thorny odyssey to God knows where. I hope somebody finds you when this is over. You've been a good listener. Better than most."

The slope downward became more pronounced. The foothills of the western mountains rose higher to her right. The gray-white clouds floating overhead grew larger and denser. Rain was in the offing.

Thorny peered ahead. The land was a darker green down the slope, although that could have been a trick of the light. She slid the driver's window down. The air was warm but not stifling. She could shut off the interior air-conditioning, which would help her battery life, as the available daylight to recharge it through the photovoltaic cells in the skin of the rover was less with each day.

Thorny took out another strip of jerky and chewed on it mechanically. The two pieces of jerky were all she had eaten since dashing off in the rover, but her stomach did not want more. What was she going to do? No one would ever find her this far from Saint Peterstown, not even her father.

"I think I am going to die," she said. *That was a decision, wasn't it?*

She made that announcement to the rover not with any dramatic flair but as a simple statement of fact. "That will serve all of them right," she said. "The Demos will blame Unreality Busby for not running the school better. They'll blame all the assholes in my cohort for being the assholes they are and for the way they always treated me. My parents will blame themselves for making Yong the favorite and paying all the attention to the twins and the next two babies and the one that's coming. They're all going to be so damned sorry."

She checked herself, then stared past the white knuckles gripping the steering so hard she might wrench it free of the rover. She thought about all of that as she stared at the dying of the light over the slope in front of her.

What if, in fact, no one cared? What if they held a funeral at the small cemetery out east, toward the old spaceplane landing area where the Demos had buried the ones who died in the turmoil when the settlement was established, and then shook their heads, said it was sad, and went back to doing whatever they were doing? Maybe her parents would simply have an eighth and forget about Thorny, who couldn't get along and whom no one liked. Certainly, no one at school would give a shit unless the Demos actually voted to blame someone—and how likely was that?

Wait a minute. Maybe there was a boy in the cohort who would care. Regan had said that she'd heard from someone that Dani Petrovic was interested in her. Not that he had ever said more than two words to her that she could remember, but maybe he did, somehow, like her. He would be *devastated*. He would regret forever not having spoken to her or come within three feet of her when he had the chance. He would be devastated *forever*.

Thorny fell asleep against the steering wheel.

DECEMBER 25, HY 21

JING

THE DATE BROUGHT A WISTFUL SMILE TO JING'S LIPS WHEN SHE WOKE AND SAW the notification her chip placed on her projection field. It had the same effect every year. December 25 meant Christmas Day. However, this day on the Heaven calendar was nothing more than a day. It did not correspond to December 25, Christmas Day, on Earth. She supposed she could have the computer calculate what day on Heaven this year would be Christmas on Earth, but what was the point? It would not *feel* like Christmas. Heaven had nothing that resembled a pine tree for lights and decorations. Heaven would never have a white Christmas. True, the San Francisco Bay Area did not have white Christmases either, but it had been possible to travel from there to places that did—Yosemite, for example.

But this was a useless train of thought. She had work to do. From the sounds in the front unit of the way station hab, Hiep was already up and moving around. She hauled herself out of the bed and swiftly remade it to leave it neat.

In the dark early-morning hours, Hiep and Jing prepared for the remaining long ride into town. The muggy air of Heaven greeted them like a hot, wet towel thrown in their faces the moment they stepped through the hab door. Only an occasional star twinkled through a crack in the clouds above.

"I am sorry for the early start," Hiep said, "but the horses will do better before the temperature rises. We can be in town by midday."

"I am only hoping we will not be finishing this ride in the rain." Jing had her face turned to the heavens.

"It does not feel like it. Not now, at least," Hiep replied. "I think we will make it to town dry. I will still need to go for Thorny later, however, and that may be a different story."

Hiep busied himself with the saddling of both their horses and readying the packhorses, while Jing considered both his words and what he had left unsaid. Hiep was closed off this morning, more so than usual.

"She has not returned, and they have not been able to reach her," Jing said when they were mounted and headed out to the road. "You have not been able to reach her either."

"No." It was not until they had traversed some farther distance down Highway 1 that he added, "That was not too surprising. I did have a message from Reality that they tried to ping her phone without success. There are also other complications."

"With her phone? Could it be the battery?"

The state of their phone batteries had become a constant topic of conversation over the past year or two. Twenty years after landing, those batteries did not hold a charge nearly so well as they once had. Saint Peterstown had equipment to recondition them, but that did not bring them back to their original state. The slow decline of battery life had become a proxy for other concerns about the settlement's technological equipment.

"I think it is unlikely that the battery is the problem," Hiep said. "The children are issued phones from the settlement supply when they go to residence school. Granted, they are also twenty years old, but they have not gone through as many discharge-recharge cycles with reconditioning as ours have, and ours still work. People are too quick to blame problems on aging equipment. The more likely explanation for the lack of phone contact is that Thorny knows how to shield her phone, and she has probably done it.

"The first complication is that the small exploratory rover has been taken, and it is assumed Thorny took it. That, of course, creates speculation about her involvement with Fernando's death. The other complication is that Miroslav Petrovic's son took the other rover that was in town and has not come back either."

"Is he answering his phone?"

Hiep's laugh was close to a snort. "Yes. Last night he said he would find Thorny this morning and bring her and the other rover back."

"You do not sound confident."

"I am confident that I will need to bring both of them back. Those are the only two functional rovers in town right now. I have received several messages of unhappiness."

Jing considered that the burden would make almost anyone more than simply quiet, but then, Hiep was Hiep. No one knew what went on behind those eyes. Except Penny. "I do not envy you the day ahead of you."

"I will do what I need to do. You will have the question of a seventeen-year-old's death to solve, and the quicker we have an answer to that, the better it will be for everyone. So, I do not envy you your day either."

.   .   .

They split up at the Perimeter Road, Hiep to head for his mysterious meeting and then to track down his daughter; Jing to her clinic for a most unpleasant task.

The Avenue of the Americas, the road Jing took entering the town from the south, was one of five such roads that radiated from Town Circle to the Perimeter Road. In a clockwise direction, they were the Avenues of Europe, Australia, Africa, and Asia, all grandly named but no different from the dirt Avenue of the Americas on which she rode.

The rain had held off as Hiep had predicted, but the lowering clouds were now darkly pregnant with the promise of rain soon to come. The waterproof in her pack was breathable and weighed next to nothing, but the idea of putting more clothing over what she already wore was suffocating. Maybe the rain would wait until she was inside the clinic.

It occurred to Jing as she rode toward Town Circle that Saint Peterstown had not aged well. She remembered her first impression of the place, fresh from the spaceplane landing strip. It had been nearly a ghost town then—no people on the streets, no children's toys in front of the habs, not even voices raised in argument behind closed doors. That sensation was gone. A tricycle sat outside the door to one hab. A man and a woman walked together down the street, their pace slow enough that Jing's ponies, tired as they were, passed them by. Two sweaty children, maybe six years old, kicked a ball back and forth. The town showed evidence of life, and if there was not more, the lack could be pinned on the midday temperature in the low nineties, moderate for a late fall day, or on the coming storm.

The physical structure of the place was what revealed its aging. On her first long-ago day in town, Jing had been struck by the modernistic contrast of the buildings, all sharp lines and right angles and garish colors, set amid the dirt roads and empty plains of an alien world. Now those colors were muted, bleached out by the sun, the heat, and the storms. Where the lack of bushes, flowers, and trees had, in the past, been a mark of newness, today they were signs of neglect. Jing was sure Penny could have fixed that, would have come up with a way to plant decorative bushes and flowers to create a sense of well-kept homes, but Penny had been preoccupied with growing food and teaching those who would learn how to farm. Jing marked that as the correct choice even as she looked at the bare dirt between the habs on the Avenue of the Americas and the ones fronting the next avenue over.

Penny had neglected Saint Peterstown in her planning when she held the mayor's office. If she had not, they all would have starved. The townies, the ones who lived in the town, did not seem to care enough to keep up its appearance. So, here was Saint Peterstown, once a bride-to-be, left at the altar to become a spinster still wearing the now-threadbare gown she had expected to be married in, Dickens's Miss Havisham of another world.

If you don't stop this, you're going to turn into a remorser yourself.

Jing took her horses to Town Circle, the road that ran around the Community Dome, a large amphitheater the designers of the colony had provided at the center of town. The circular structure was roofed for protection against rain, using tall lattice supports of graphene and carbon nanotube struts that were open, presumably to reduce the amount of construction material that had to be hauled between stars. The open structure also allowed wind to blow through the dome, although in the summer that was not much help, since the wind was no more refreshing than a blast from a furnace. Under the roof were seats for a thousand people arranged in semicircular rows facing a dais. This was where meetings of the Demos—the people of the settlement—took place so they could vote in person, as a direct democracy, on the questions in front of them.

As she started to circle the dome, neighing and a distinctive odor announced her destination. She rode behind the dais, where sheets of plastic and metal had been used to erect a large stable. She always found the image of a ramshackle stable attached to a soaring dome that commemorated the founding of an interstellar colony to be loaded with irony. As a former star traveler who needed to ride a horse to town, she found herself shaking her head every time she saw it.

Still a bad train of thought. You need to snap out of this, Jing.

Jing left her horses to the care of Cam and Jess. Officially, the two of them were the public safety officers for Saint Peterstown, but they were not police. They had no power to arrest or interrogate anyone. They could investigate and mediate disputes and accusations among people, but no one thought they did any of that well at all. It was universally acknowledged that they did a far better job running the stable.

Jing's mind was on what Cam and Jess did not do as she walked from the stable to her clinic. This was a time when police and a detective would be useful, but the town had few actual laws or rules. For any significant issue, the Demos sat as prosecutors, judge, and jury, an arrangement that sometimes made up in inventiveness what it lacked in thoroughness and impartiality. There had been, for instance, the case of Timothy from the Pioneer Youth, whose amorous attentions were not appreciated by two women in HY 6. The Demos had voted that he had to walk naked around Town Circle five times a day at midday for a week, wearing a sign that read NOT MUCH TO LOOK AT, IS IT? The computer would dock one day from his equal share of food for every lap he missed. He had been tagged as Tiny Tim forever after that, and since it had been summer, Jing had treated some nasty sunburn.

What had originally been called only the Medical Unit, now the Song Medical Clinic, was on the Town Circle, a short walk from the stable. She allowed herself a sense of self-satisfaction every time she saw the hand-painted sign. Inside, in the blessedly cool air, Jing was met by Yuki Watanabe, the woman who had called her when Fernando was found. She was a short narrow-shouldered woman who wore her long black hair in a braid that fell halfway down her back. Jing had taken over her training with an eye to converting her to a general practitioner. Yuki had been a good pupil, but Jing and everyone else called her Practitioner Yuki, not doctor. She did not have the skill set to be an independent physician. Jing thought of her son, Michael, and wondered how long it would be before the community produced more physicians and how the role would be filled when she was gone. More bad thoughts, she told herself. Yuki did make a point of wearing one of the white coats that had, from the days on Earth, been the uniform of a doctor. The coat was no longer quite white, but it was original, never recycled.

"What have you got so far?" Jing asked. She needed to focus on her business.

"Nothing really." Yuki tapped at a screen. "This is what we have from the lab results. Toxicology is clean. None of the thistle cholinesterase inhibitor. No other poisons, at least none that we can test for."

Jing nodded. She had chipped in during the ride up the avenue to look at the results herself, but she allowed Yuki to run through them without breaking into the recital.

"Let's go have a look at him," Jing said when Yuki finished.

The tray holding the body of Fernando Vargas slid out of the cooler, then rose to become a table. The two of them opened the bag and removed it.

"He was found face down. Correct?" Yuki nodded in response to Jing's question. "And this was behind the hydroponics building?" Yuki nodded again.

"His face was on his arm. Yes?" Another nod in response. "That's bare, stony ground, so that's why his face isn't that messed up. But did he try to shield his face, or did he just land that way?"

"I don't know," Yuki said. "But how does something like this happen?"

"I wasn't saying you should know. I do want you to give me a differential," Jing ordered. "What are you thinking of?"

Yuki held up a fist and extended a finger with each comment. "Well, number one could be trauma. A blow to the head, or if he passed out for some reason and his head hit the ground hard when he went down. No, wait, his head was on his arm, so maybe not from the fall. I'm not sure."

Jing held up her hand. "You did not find anything when you examined him that would indicate head trauma, and you imaged him. Right?"

"Yes. You told me to do it." Yuki tapped at the screen.

Jing paged quickly through the scans of Fernando's body, both on the screen and with her chip projecting alternate views on her field. "Nothing," she said. "At least, no obvious fracture like a skull fracture. Doesn't rule out trauma, of course; just takes an easy answer away. Keep going."

"Massive heart attack or stroke. But he was only seventeen." Yuki shook her head. "I would take it out. Too unlikely. Heart arrhythmia, but again, he was seventeen and has no history of that. I looked at his records. Could it have been a seizure? There's sudden unexplained death in epilepsy, SUDEP, but he didn't have seizures that we know of. If he was one of us, we could tell, but he's a Heaven-born."

"Correct." Jing tapped at her lips with an index finger. "With one of us, we'd have all the physiology, vital signs, blood oxygen, and seizure activity from the chip. As it is, we might as well be back in the early twenty-first century. Did you consider an allergic reaction, anaphylaxis?"

Yuki looked stricken. "No. Should I have?"

Don't cringe, Yuki, Jing thought. Yuki needed a thicker skin. "Yes, I would include it because it is possible. Maybe I'm becoming, shall we say, hypersensitive because of the eye cases, but we had one in the valley four years ago and we still don't know what caused that."

"You saved her," Yuki said. "No one will forget that."

"I had a large dose of luck." In Jing's mind, she had been doing her job, and she had been lucky. "That's why epinephrine autoinjectors go in the rover kits and we drill the kids on it in residence school. Sometimes, I think we are allergic to this planet." She paused. "All right, we might as well get to it. I never had training in forensics, so let's put up some references and we'll both learn as we go. Put them up on the large screens, if you will. I find it distracting to have text on my field while I'm trying to focus on doing something with my hands. Never understood how some of the surgeons pull it off. Also, ask Norma to handle the waiting room if anyone needs to be seen." Norma Fulton had been the other nurse in the Pioneer Youth, and Jing had trained her the same way she'd trained Yuki.

When she opened up Fernando's body and began to point out parts of the anatomy she wanted Yuki to observe, she thought the younger woman was paling, if not actually turning green. Yuki did collect samples properly, but the unease came through in her voice. Jing wished Michael were with her, but someone had to be in the valley even if they were nothing more than an apprentice with only enough training to handle routine matters and know when to call for help. How could she bring his training—anyone's training—to the level of being an independent physician? Too many gloomy thoughts of the future had been crowding in of late. She needed to focus on her work.

When it was time for the head, the laser scalpel made short work of removing the scalp and opening the skull, at the cost of some odor of burning tissue and bone that made Jing fear again for Yuki's equanimity.

"Wait. Is there free blood here?" Yuki was pointing at the exposed brain, her queasiness momentarily forgotten. "Does that mean there was a brain injury?"

"It could. But some can also collect after death. Here, I'm sending you text from the reference I'm using." The chips made that process so easy, Jing barely thought about it as she sent it. It would be harder, would take more attention, to do this with Michael or any of the Heaven-born generation. She shook off the train of thought. "We need to check for any sign of a torn blood vessel, now and when the brain comes out to be fixed."

· · ·

Two hours later, Jing ripped off her gloves and flung them at the disposal container. Putting one weary foot in front of the other, she walked to the office at the back of the center, where she dropped into a chair. Yuki trailed her.

"What did we see?" Jing asked the younger woman, who was still standing in front of her desk.

"Not very much at all." Yuki pulled her braid across her shoulder, undid it, and then rebraided it as she spoke. "Only that blood in the head, and I don't think I missed a source, although I suppose I could have. And I don't think I missed anything else. That does say, I guess, no trauma and no allergic reaction. Airways were clear; no mucus plugging them up, no obvious swelling."

Jing leaned back in her chair. "I don't think there was head trauma, not from what we saw. I agree with your description of the airways, but that does not rule out allergy. Anaphylactic shock can happen so fast that you don't see any of those signs. We'll run the tryptase and the other markers for anaphylaxis and look at the slides. ISC sent all of the reagents because allergy is always something to think about. Still, those help only if we have a positive. If they're negative, it's still not an exclusion. As an old teacher of mine liked to say: 'Absence of evidence is not evidence of absence.'"

"Then what do you think now?" Yuki asked.

"I don't," Jing answered. "Sorry, that's not fair. Maybe I'm not good enough at this. Right now, I've got no obvious cause of death. Maybe we'll get something from the anaphylaxis tests. We'll have brain sections and slides after its properly fixed, but that's two weeks, and I'm not a neuropathologist, so even if there's something there, I may miss it." She slumped down in her chair. "That does not mean I want to sign this off by saying this is anaphylaxis but we don't know from what, or he had seizures we never knew about, and this is one of those unexplained deaths that, by fate, happened behind the hydroponics in the middle of the night when nobody was around. That's bullshit. No way. Somebody knows something." She gazed up at the ceiling as if in search of inspiration. "I can't even be sure exactly when he died. He was completely stiff when you got to him, right?"

"Yes. Even with help from some of the boys, getting him into the bag was a problem." From her expression, Yuki's stomach was not enjoying the memory.

Jing paid no attention. She was busy recalling the body temperature and pics of skin discoloration Yuki had obtained and then wrestling with the conversion of Earth hours to Heaven hours because, naturally, all her references had time intervals in Earth hours. "I'd guess he died between midnight and two in the morning. Again, if we had a chip download, we'd know exactly." Suddenly she snapped her fingers. "Wait. We don't use our phones for health data because of our chips, but maybe we can still get some information from his."

Yuki's eyes widened. "I never thought about his phone. I don't . . . I mean, I don't know where it is. I don't have it."

That was when the office door opened, and Norma stuck her head in. "Dr. Song? Can you come see Athena Markopoulos? She's pretty distressed and says it can't wait."

HIEP

Hiep stepped through the doorway into Ibiana Owusu's hab. The contrast between the dirt road outside, where he had tied his horse to a post rammed crookedly into the ground, and the air-conditioning, cushioned chairs, sofa, and computer screens of late twenty-first century living on

Earth did not bother him. Hiep had spent his childhood in a village with dirt roads, had fought in untouched jungle, and, as an assassin, had pursued some of his targets through ultramodern cities. He shrugged off ephemeral contrasts and focused his attention on the three people in the front room.

Ibiana was a given; this was her hab. She rose from a corner of the sofa, her arms spread out in a welcoming gesture. She was a stocky Black woman with tightly curled black hair who had gone thicker in the midsection with her entry into middle age. Hiep did not trust the smile on her face. That would have been true for most smiles and most faces.

His eyes moved immediately to the other two. Sonal Davis he knew well, as she and her partner, Klaus Koch, had the farm next to his and Penny's. She was a tiny woman who had remained slender as she aged. Her dark hair, long and braided now, a change from her days as one of the leaders of the Pioneer Youth, framed a light tan face bearing a cluster of small hearts tattooed on her right cheek. The worried expression on her face Hiep took for authentic. Sonal was good at managing social tensions and group dynamics, probably because she did let all of the social matters worry her.

The final occupant was Jacoby Grubb. He stood to the side, a few inches taller than Hiep, with a recycled T-shirt not loose enough to hide his paunch and denim pants that also revealed the color variation of textile gone through the recycler numerous times. He bit at a fingernail as Hiep's gaze fell on him. Jacoby was the current mayor of Saint Peterstown.

"I did not expect this group." Hiep's words bypassed Ibiana's greeting.

"I told you we had a problem we could use your help with," Ibiana said. She brought her hands down and smoothed her black cotton pants as though her offer of a hug hadn't been ignored. "In the old days, I'd offer you coffee to start, but I'm afraid we'll have to do without." She gave a weak laugh, a way of showing she knew her words were neither new nor funny.

"Penny has coffee beans now," Hiep said. "I'm sure we can have some brought up to the town."

"She does," Sonal confirmed at Ibiana's evident surprise. "She made a cup for me before I came up here. It's real. She said she could do it, I'd guess ten years ago, and she has. When she says she'll do something, she doesn't quit until it's done."

"We're not here to talk about coffee!" burst out of Jacoby. "Not even to compliment your wife, although I don't mind doing that, as you'll see. But all coffee will do is cause an argument over when coffee has to be included in equal shares, and that's just one more thing for Mistry to rile up the townies and remorsers with."

"I did not think this was about coffee or Penny." Hiep's eyes scanned from one to another. "Ibiana, you would be more comfortable sitting. Why don't we start over."

"Of course." Ibiana folded back into the corner of her couch. She put her hands in her lap, which gave them a place to be. Her smile disappeared. "So, to business. First, thank you for coming to see us. We know about Thorny, and I'm sure you need to look for her."

"I taught Thorny how to take care of herself," Hiep said. "Sometimes she needs to go off by herself to vent whatever is bothering her. Do not worry about it."

"As you say." Ibiana looked to Sonal and then to Jacoby. Neither of them spoke. "It starts from the same problem we have been having in town for years, but it is worse now. Mistry is using it to widen the split between town and valley."

"Everything is wearing out!" Jacoby shouted into the silence when Hiep did not respond. "It's not just things like coffee, like not being able to have coffee, or there never being a new vid to see, or any kind of event beyond the school art exhibit or the juniors putting on a butchered Shakespeare play, or nowhere to go that you haven't been every day for years. It's the stuff that's been going on for a couple of years but is getting worse, like the phones, or the batteries in the phones. They're not holding a charge well anymore, and the phones that are held in supply are reserved for the children as they grow up, but even they don't hold a charge as well as they should, so we recondition the batteries but they don't come back to what we remember.

"It's microwaves that break and we can't fix again. It's toilet paper that's too rough or that comes apart when you wipe. I hear about that as much as the phones! When the ISC told us about settling a new planet, they never mentioned problems with toilet paper—but I hear about that every other day! Now I've been told we're having trouble making the altrubber, and we need that for everything from tires to door seals. Name it, it's a problem, a thousand and one things that are wrong."

Ibiana broke in when Jacoby ran down as he exhausted his supply of air. "There's nothing that wasn't wrong last year or even the year before and the year before that. What's new is Ajit Mistry and the way he's using all of this. To the townies and remorsers, he blames the valley-boys and valley-girls for not making it a priority to fix the town. He says they see the townies as an underclass, inferior to them. To those frustrated by the phones, he blames the work-for-rewarders for reserving unused phones and keeping them out of equal shares. It's not only the remorse."

"There is nothing to do about the remorse," Hiep said. "People want their old lives, although they have forgotten what those old lives were, and they can't have them. What they think they remember is more fantasy than reality. It's worse for those living in town. Talk to Dr. Song."

"She's doing what she can," Sonal said, "but this situation is past treatment, particularly with Ajit stirring it up. We could have the cell foundries pump out nothing but antidepressants and it wouldn't be enough. I see it in some of my old Pioneer Youth, especially if they're townies. And like you said, some Originals off the *Daredevil* are the same, even if they were in jail with a bleak life in front of them on Earth."

"You know what the real problem is?" Sonal went on. "ISC promised a starship every three to five years to bring more settlers and new supplies. We could keep a modern town that way. But it hasn't happened. No ships since we came on the *Dauntless*, and that's twenty years ago. When equipment starts to fail . . . it makes people focus on that."

Hiep was not inclined to be sympathetic to people who should know better, but he thought he should find some sympathy for Sonal, who, as secretary on the town council, was having to deal with this litany of complaints. "This is not your doing, Sonal. Has it ever occurred to these people that ISC may have lied, or changed their minds, or decided not to send more ships at risk since they can't know yet that the colony is still in existence? The whole point of the starshot program was launch one mission after another to burn up money and resources that otherwise would have gone into national militaries. Not to make discoveries or put human civilization around other stars." He could tell from the shock he saw that they had never heard this. Well, he had never said it before.

"I heard it from Leif before he went back up to the *Dauntless*, and I think he knew. The ISC doesn't care if the colonies survive as long as they can keep launching missions and support the Treaties by using up budgets. Look who they sent here. All of us on the *Daredevil* were criminals of one kind or another, since you would view the six of us from free companies that way. Sonal, your Pioneer Youth were kids who believed the bullshit propaganda they were fed in school and were not good enough at what they wanted to do to succeed on Earth. So, we have criminals who mostly want to avoid honest work and Pioneers, who were willing to work but mostly didn't know how. I never expected other ships. Not really."

Jacoby flushed, avoiding Hiep's calm gaze. "Hey. We all work at one job or another because we have to. Well, most of us. Or many of us. That's not the point. I had Gradison and two others in my hab three days ago demanding that I guarantee the Demos will vote to pull down the transmission towers and use the components to build a transmitter to signal ISC on Earth that they need to send another ship."

"Did these people wake up stupid one morning?" The scorn in Hiep's question said it was not merely rhetorical. "We need to link the farms in the valley together and link them with the town here. But even if we did do what they want, it will take seventy-six years for the signal to reach Earth. They'll be dead by then. Even *Dauntless* and *Daredevil* won't get back to Earth for another fifty-six years—possibly fifty-five for *Daredevil*, but the difference hardly matters."

"Gradison clings to Ajit like a fungus," Ibiana said. "This is just another stir Ajit is giving the pot so he can make promises at the

Demos and take votes." She shook her head. "I do want to be fair to the people Ajit is manipulating. They're getting older; we all are. One of the *Daredevil* Originals needed a root canal last week. That's what the AI said based on their chip download, but Dr. Song was in the valley and neither Watanabe nor Fulton could manage it with the surgi-bot, so they had to pull the tooth. It's hard to blame them for listening to Ajit."

"I can blame them," Hiep said, "because they should see that all he will do is find scapegoats for them. In the end, he will change nothing except to make himself mayor if he can."

"What really matters, Vo Hiep, is that I can't do this anymore," Jacoby said. "I can't put up with the crap. Every day, it's something else. I won't do it anymore."

"What do you want from me?" Hiep's voice was soft, silky smooth. "Kill Ajit Mistry, or perhaps kill one of those who run with him as an example?" Into the sudden silence he added, "When I was one of the Sicarii, I did that on contract, but I will not do it for anyone here."

Jacoby's shudder was visible. "No, no, no. We are not looking for that."

"Then, I ask again, what do you want from me?"

"We want you to talk to Penny about being mayor again," Sonal said. "She will figure out a way to move forward, and she is probably the only one who can. And we need to not have Ajit as mayor."

"The last time Penny was mayor, she gave people a way to move forward. You will all remember how that ended." Hiep managed to fling a challenge without changing his tone at all. "I doubt she will be interested. Now, I need to see about Thorny."

"Just talk to her, Hiep," Sonal pleaded. "If you talk to her, she might listen. We need Penny."

·   ·   ·

As soon as Hiep was clear of Ibiana's hab, he sent a reply to the other message that he had received, one marked URGENT. "On my way now."

"We're waiting for you" was the immediate response.

We. That meant more than Ajit. That was what Hiep had expected. Had it been only Ajit wanting this conversation, they could have done it by phone. Of course, they could have had a multiparty conversation by phone, too, but Ajit would not want the phone conversations because he would want to read the eyes and body language of everyone involved. He would also want to ensure that Penny could not listen in. Ajit was like that.

On Earth, he had managed an exclusive casino at a very high-end address and parlayed that into online casinos in the global Community along with multiple other Community businesses. He had been very successful and very wealthy, with famous investors, until a hack and a document dump made public the fact that none of his businesses had any substance beyond the lines of code that made them appear on people's screens. Hiep found it surprising that Ajit had lasted long enough to board the starship *Daredevil*, and there was very little that surprised Hiep.

The address Ajit gave Hiep was on the Avenue of Asia, another one of the radiating spokes from Town Circle, and it was out toward the Perimeter Road where few people chose to live. Hiep did not keep to the roads, which would have required him to walk either centrally to Town Circle or out to the Perimeter Road, then around and up the other avenue. Instead, he walked one hab past Ibiana's and cut quickly between the habs, using the privacy screens to block him from the view of any occupants. From there, he traversed the open ground between the rows of habs lining each avenue. In the artist's conception of Saint Peterstown the colonists had been shown before leaving Earth, this area was a park with flowers, shrubs, and blossoming dogwood trees. In reality, it was bare dirt, broken up only by stones and a sprinkling of Heaven grass. Even if any of the townies had mustered enthusiasm for the work of planting flowers and shrubs, they would have withered and died in the wretched, acid soil of Heaven's high plains. Hiep had never expected a park.

The hab Ajit was using for this meeting was identical to Ibiana's save for its color, a sun-bleached brown. This was not where Ajit lived, but that did not mean much. There were plenty of empty habs for doing what you would not want to do in the living space you shared with others.

Hiep put his hand against the outline of a hand that was next to the door, which promptly slid open. Hab doors in Saint Peterstown were not equipped with locks. He stepped through, then took an immediate sideways step so that his back was to a wall while he made a quick survey of the interior. He did not sense a threat, nor did he have a reason to fear trouble. It was simply an automatic move.

The front room of the hab had all the usual furnishings that came with the units, but nothing of a personal touch to suggest anyone actually lived in it. Three men were present. Ajit was there, standing by a desk, his mustache precisely clipped and his hair combed straight back as always. His shirt and calf-length pants were of recycled textile. His sandals had the loose fit of remanufactured ones but had been kept in good condition. Oscar Gradison was there, too: white, thin, and balding, with his remaining gray hair grown long and pulled into a ponytail. His clothes could have been cleaner and his nails could have used trimming. He was seated on the room's couch. He would not put forth the effort to stand if he did not need to. Hiep had met both of them originally on the outbound trip on the *Daredevil*.

The third man in the room was much younger. Gordon Durham-Pole had been among the first babies born on Heaven. That put him in Yong's cohort at the residence school. Since graduating, he had been selected by Busby to be the proctor for the seniors. In casual conversations at the farm, Yong said she thought he was okay, if a little stuck on himself. She was willing to give him the benefit of the doubt—something Hiep rarely did, but he did believe Yong to be a decent judge of character. The twins, now in low-seniors, thought Gordon was too strict, which Hiep considered was good for them. Thorny did not like him, but Thorny liked hardly anyone. Hiep wondered what Gordon was doing in this meeting.

The air in the hab was clean, the air handling system inaudible. That told Hiep the importance Ajit placed on the conversation. Left to himself, Oscar would have filled the place with the reek of cannabis.

"What is the urgent matter, Ajit?"

Ajit smoothed his mustache on each side with a forefinger. "There is no need to be antagonistic, Hiep. This is a friendly meeting."

"I am not antagonistic. I am interested in what this is about. We are not friends."

"With the exception of Penny, you could say the same for any of the Originals from *Daredevil* or *Dauntless*."

Hiep said nothing. He waited.

"Fine," Ajit said. "The urgency is that the annual Demos meeting is approaching. I have heard that Jacoby is going to step down, which means a mayoral election."

"I am surprised," Hiep said. "Do you have any idea why?"

"No," said Ajit, "and any reason we hear might not be the real one anyway. What matters is that he is going to step down. I need to ask you about Penny. Do you know if she has plans to try for another term?"

"I would have no idea about that," Hiep said. "Why would you talk to me instead of asking her?"

Ajit sighed and smoothed down his mustaches once more. "Because she will listen to you. More than anyone else on the planet. Don't get me wrong. Penny did good work for us years ago. We all owe her a great deal. But you remember how her last term ended. Penny is—well, she is disruptive. We cannot afford the divisiveness, the arguments. Not now. We have important decisions to make. Decisions about supporting the town, Saint Peterstown, the center of our colony.

"People need to be assured that they will continue to receive their equal shares. People in town see Penny as too embedded in the valley, and after the last time, they fear that she's looking even beyond the valley. We cannot afford that. They also fear that she would change the equals. This is the key reason I have asked Gordon to be here. He is Heaven-born, and he knows the needs of the town, the concerns of the town, just as I do. Have I said that right, Gordon?"

"Yes, you have, Ajit. We need to maintain support for the town and improve it. We cannot pull that support away." Gordon folded his arms across his chest and thrust his chin forward.

"Gordon is a leader among the Heaven-born," Ajit said. "You know his work at the residence school, and many in his cohort and the following ones look up to him for leadership. I say this so that you know my feelings come not only from Originals and not only from *Daredevil*. We need everyone united behind the town and behind maintaining equal shares."

"That is a lot of words, Ajit. What do you want of me?"

Ajit straightened his stance. He was a little taller than Hiep, but that could have been said of most men. "As I said, Penny will listen to you. Tell her the situation if you wish, but if you could persuade her not to run for mayor, it would be for the best. If she could support someone from the town, even if that is me, she would be doing all of us on this planet a great service. I know you never ask for anything, but the town would certainly be generous if you can help."

"I need nothing I do not already have," Hiep said.

"But you will speak to her? You will let her know that people here feel it is a good time for someone else to step forward?"

"I will convey what you have told me." Hiep put no inflection into his statement. He did not see the need.

"Is there anything else I can say that you think would be important for Penny to know?" Ajit pressed. "Is there anything that you want done that any of us can help with?"

"I need to go over to the school regarding one of my children, and that will not be anything that you or anyone else can help with." Hiep tipped his head the slightest fraction of an inch forward. Then he was out the door before any of the other three in the room could move.

Ajit

Ajit stood silently where he was for a long minute after the door closed behind Hiep. Finally, he said, "I have known that man for over twenty years, and I do not know him."

"That man wouldn't take a bribe if it bent over in front of him and spread its cheeks," Oscar said. "Did you really expect to get anything from him?"

"Even without your customary graphic imagery, I would not have expected him to show his hand. Not here." Ajit felt his hand go back to his mustache and pulled it down. Too much of a habit was embarrassing to have people see. "The important thing is that he saw that Heaven-born will take our side." *My* side, he thought. "They will support the town and the equals. You did a good job, son." He nodded at Gordon. "The more of your group we can line up to support us, the better it will be. You could be a leader someday. I will need someone growing behind me. That could be you."

"Thank you." Gordon tipped his head in acknowledgment.

"I mean that." Ajit bestowed a smile on Gordon, then flicked his eyes at Oscar. Behind the smile and the glance, his mind was counting.

Of the remaining 191 Originals, 105 still lived in the town, nearly half of them from *Daredevil*. He could count on them, he was fairly sure. The valley had grown to eighty-six, but only sixty-eight owned the farms, the ones who, he told the townies, gave themselves airs like the old landed aristocracy of Earth. He had found that phrasing resonated. The other eighteen in the valley worked those farms and would be sensitive about equal shares.

If Penny actually backed him, the election was all but over. He would win. Even if all she did was remain on the sideline, that would probably be enough. If she opposed him, the votes of the Heaven-born, who would vote for the first time, would make the difference. Possibly, Gordon could pull enough of them to his side. If he could make any inroad in the valley, if anything gave him a lever to shift some of those damn aristocrats, that would make it a certainty. This was going to be his time. He had waited for it, had feared it might be beyond his reach, but now it was there for the taking. He would be the next leader, in a position of real respect, the one who dispensed favors and disfavors. This would be genuine, true, concrete, not the house of illusions—for all its money—he had built on Earth. He would be what his father, with all his sayings and parables, had told him he would never amount to. At last. He felt the warmth of that thought. It was ironic, he thought, that it had taken a white English poet to say the truth about being the ruler of Hell as opposed to a mere servant in Heaven, but he would enjoy it nevertheless.

He said only, "I wonder what Hiep will tell Penny? He is very protective of her, and the fiasco when she lost that last vote was . . . embarrassing."

"Yeah, we all know how protective he is—at least, we Originals know that." Oscar put one leg up on the couch. "We also know he can be violently protective. He would be a bad man to play poker with."

"I would not play poker with him," Ajit said. He reminded himself that he had been a damned good card counter as a young man, a thought that made him smile. "Not with a fair deck, anyway. But he may tell Penny to stay out of the election. It is possible, and that is all I wanted or expected from today. It is especially possible if she knows she cannot count on the Heaven-born for their votes. Do you understand your role in this, Gordon?"

"Yes, yes, I do," Gordon said quickly. "I need to be back at the school. Busby will be expecting me to be working."

GORDON

GORDON STORMED UP THE AVENUE TOWARD TOWN CIRCLE AS FAST AS HE COULD GO without breaking into a run. Through a clenched jaw, he muttered as he went, "You did a good job, son. You could be a leader someday. You understand your role. Fuck Ajit Mistry!"

The problem was that Ajit would be the next mayor. Following him, allying with him, was the way for a Heavener to move up. He knew that. He needed Mistry. For now. He did not have to like the taste it left in his mouth, however.

He ripped his phone out of the thigh pocket of his cargo pants with enough force to partially tear away the flap over the pocket. That triggered another curse. He would not be up for a replacement pair in his share for a while yet. For that moment only, he envied the old chippers, who did not need to actually handle their phones but could send a message by being chipped into the network. With savage jabs, he punched in his message and sent it on its way. Then he headed not to the school but to the Dining Hall. His senior students would be fine without him for a little longer. No matter what Unreality Busby might say, none of them would be paying attention to the AI-led coursework or, in fact, to him if he were giving directions. Not after yesterday's events. There was a conversation he needed to have. Away from the school.

·　　·　　·

THE DINING HALL WAS ONE OF THE FIVE LARGE STRUCTURES THAT FACED THE Community Dome across the Town Circle. The name itself was something of a misnomer. True, it contained a large open area with enough tables and chairs to easily accommodate the thousand people who had been envisioned as living within the Perimeter Road of Saint Peterstown. It was, however, much more than a place for communal meals. To call it Food Central might have been nearer the mark. This building was where the prepackaged foods and complete meals brought on the starships had been stored. The first residents of the town had come here to draw their food rations, either to heat and consume in the hall or take back to their habs. Those racks were long since empty, all the food brought from Earth exhausted. But that was far from the only intended purpose for the building.

The planners of Saint Peterstown had thought ahead to the growth of the settlement. They had envisioned farms spreading out from and surrounding the town. They had foreseen the agricultural produce of those farms—fruits, grains, legumes, and animal products—as being brought to the Dining Hall where they could be packed, stored, and distributed to the populace along with products from the hydroponics facility. They believed that the importance of the hydroponics would dwindle with time, as more and more farms were developed, unless there was some plant people wanted that could be grown only in the hydroponics. Eventually, the planners expected small towns built of local materials to spring up as the belt of farms expanded farther and farther from the center until the Dining Hall finally lost its central focus amid a widespread agricultural community.

It had not worked out that way, of course. The soil of the high plains around Saint Peterstown was too poor to support farms of Earth agriculture. Indeed, it barely supported a thin growth of native plants. Only the establishment of farms in the valley had kept the colony from starvation when the prepackaged food from Earth ran out. The hydroponics facility was not large enough to support the initial two hundred people without even considering the children or animals they would be raising. The result was that the food for the town came via the forty-two-mile umbilical cord of Heaven Highway 1, either by rover-pulled cart or, more often now, by horse-drawn cart. Instead of a cohesive, expanding circle radiating out from a central town, the colony more resembled two barbell weights held together by a slender thread.

Once the produce from the valley reached the Dining Hall, it was handled in a different manner than the long-gone planners had intended. All of it was categorized by type and amount, with the computer system assigning equal shares to every member of the community. People would identify themselves at checkpoints, by chip for Originals and by phone for Heaven-born, so that an attendant could make certain everyone received their equal share. The Dining Hall did have stalls where food engineers would make an omelet or cook a beef skewer from a person's food. This created a pleasant smell of cooking that permeated the building, but the place was neither a restaurant nor a bazaar. Each person received the share they were due. Nothing was for sale. There were no extras.

Gordon took a seat at a vacant table widely separated from any that were occupied. Given the number of people present set against the size of the building, that was not hard to do. When no one came to join him within a couple of minutes, he found one of his legs rocking on its foot, the knee bouncing up and down in an expression of both impatience and annoyance. It was a habit he both hated and found hard to control. Through the windows, he could see rain beginning to fall. That did not help his bouncing leg. To take his mind away from it in the hope it would stop, he focused on the people in the building, observing what they were doing.

He saw a woman he knew, a chipper townie—and in a town this size, whom did he not know?—pick up her share of food. An instant before she left the checkpoint, the attendant slipped another clear plastic bag with eggs into her pack. Gordon did not need to see the look that passed between them. Did the Dining Hall actually have more eggs than expected from the valley, or would one or more others receive a weak justification for why their share was short? If there was extra, why did this chipper—who he knew did nothing of significance—receive them? Had she, at some time, given that man a personal marker that was being redeemed by the eggs? Or was a payment for the eggs—and he could guess what that was—expected later? The amplitude of his bouncing knee only increased.

It was at that moment of maximum irritation that Poppy Merriwether, his counterpart with the juniors, chose to appear. She shrugged out of a waterproof that shed droplets of water across the floor and dropped into a chair opposite him.

"It's a good thing the building wasn't on fire," Gordon said.

"Spare me the dramatic urgency. Anyway, the rain would put it out. My juniors won't attend to tasks if you don't tell them what they have to do and see that they get started doing it. Both Fernando and Thorny have sibs, juniors and seniors, so it's all yakety-yak around them. And the fact is, your seniors are no better than the juniors; they're only better at hiding it. Now, what's the emergency?"

"Ajit fucking Mistry wanted me at this meeting he arranged with Vo Hiep. Piece-of-shit Gradison was there too." Gordon ran through what had been said at the meeting in a couple of sentences. "What he wanted me there for was to show Vo how the Heaveners would back him, like I'm an obedient little kid who does what the grown-ups tell him."

"I could say that's what you get for hanging around that asshole, trying to impress him, but I won't do that . . . although I guess I did." Poppy chuckled, which did nothing for Gordon's disposition. "So, he's afraid Old Lady Penny is going to try for mayor again?" She did sound surprised. "We were just into high-seniors at that Demos meeting the last time she got voted out. You were there. Best fucking entertainment show the town has ever had. I can't imagine she would even think about it."

"I don't care about Penny. Not in particular. It's Mistry. It's all these goddamn chippers. Don't you see?"

"See what?"

"It's arithmetic, Poppy." Gordon leaned toward her across the table and, with a supreme effort, stopped his leg from bouncing. "Do the math. They started with two hundred chippers combined off the *Daredevil* and the *Dauntless*. One way or another, nine of them got killed right at the start. That leaves one hundred ninety-one chippers. That's it. There will never be any more. The law is that once you're more than a year out of residence school, you are a voting member of the Demos. That means our cohort votes in this meeting. There are sixty-eight of us, already one-third the number of chippers. And there will be thirty-seven next year. The cohort after that, this year's seniormost, has another fifty-one. It's getting to be time for Heaveners to start running this place. We are the ones born here; we are the ones who will be living here. We are not the chippers' little kids anymore, to be ordered around as they please."

"We." Poppy drew the single syllable out into a long sound. "There is no *we*. In case you have suddenly lost your mind, Gordon, you're a townie-boy and I'm a valley-girl. I'm not saying I think any of these chippers know what they're doing, but *we*, town and valley, don't agree on how things should go, and *you* know that."

"On one thing, we agree," Gordon said.

"On what?" Suspicion tinged Poppy's voice and showed in her face.

"All Mistry talks about is equal share this, equal share that, equal share, equal share. Why should Gradison, who only gets off his ass to get another joint, get the same share as you do, when you work your ass off all day every day? Is that right? When there are new cotton shirts, why is it random who gets them when there aren't enough to go around—which is always—instead of who does the best work or the most important work? When did you get a new cotton shirt, or one of the shiny viscose ones?"

"I haven't." Poppy plucked at the recycled fabric she wore. "Which is why it's bullshit the way you townies keep saying valley-boys and -girls are holding back extra."

"That's not the point! Or it's only part of the point. If we had a merit rank, or even money like in the textbooks we study—but the lessons somehow don't apply here—if we had any of that, you could have a cotton shirt. And don't tell me about personal markers, because nobody will agree on what one is worth except the person you gave it to, and the computer won't recognize them at all."

Gordon went on to tell her about the surreptitious transfer of eggs he had seen before she arrived. "Is it right that he gets to fuck her because he gave her the eggs—and you know that's the other side of the deal—and is it right that somebody else isn't getting the eggs because she's fucking him? And don't tell me it's just a barter transaction."

"I would think that would be the excuse you would give me," Poppy shot back. She leaned forward herself so they were nearly face-to-face across the table. "I know the saying out of the books as well as you do. The value of any object is what a willing buyer pays a willing seller. But she's not willing, I'll bet. He's using a power position to compel that trade. If I'd seen it, I'd have done something."

"No, you wouldn't because nobody does. Yet."

Poppy waved her hand between them as if to push the problem aside. "Okay. What are you trying to say?"

"That Heaveners think like we do on this. It doesn't matter if you're a valley-girl or valley-boy or a townie. We believe our work is worth something, and those who work harder and better and produce more should have priority. We agree on that. Right?"

"Okay." Poppy leaned away against the back of her chair. "And what you're implying is that we'll soon reach the point where we Heaveners can vote in a mayor and town council that will change the system. Assuming that we don't break our skulls over everything we disagree on. And who are you seeing as the mayor? You?"

Gordon felt the blush in his cheeks and wished it weren't there. "It might be," he said. "I'm the one coming up with this, so maybe it is. But I'll tell you this. It's important enough to me that if it needs to be someone else so that we can do it, then I can be okay with that."

"Uh-huh." Poppy paused. "Why are you spilling all this to me? What do you want from me? We work together, sure, but it's not like we're close friends or anything like that."

"You're valley," Gordon said. "Talk to your valley friends. See what they think. Let it be your idea. Leave me out of it."

"I'll talk to some people," Poppy said. "I'll give you that. No promises, but I'll talk a bit. Now, with all your talk about working hard, don't you think we should go do it?"

Hiep

Hiep left the meeting with Ajit and walked to the school. He ignored the rain that started as he reached the building. He also ignored the people who stared at him when he entered it. His target was the personal storage area for the students, where each student had an open storage bin and a locked cabinet.

It took little more than a minute to go through Thorny's open storage. He did not find what he expected would be there. Her cabinet was locked by a standard thumb and eye key, easily handled by his tradecraft. He tapped on the screen, then chipped in and retrieved two files. Then he located the lock on the network. A second later, the lock clicked open. The cabinet was empty. Nothing there either.

REALITY

WHAT SHE WANTED TO DO MOST WAS TO BASH HER HEAD AGAINST THE TOP OF HER DESK. She had finished the impossible conversation—the follow-up one—with Guillermo Vargas and Donna Billingsly. She had made it through their conversation the previous day because her call came before the student grapevine had the news to fling—mostly as rumors—across the human community of Heaven, and what she had to say had stunned the two of them to the point where neither could say much.

Reality had been able to escape with a promise to call the next day when she would have more information to give them. Unfortunately, the next day was now, and all she could tell them was that their son, their second child but oldest boy, had died; that he had been out late at night and *something* had happened. That had not been satisfactory to either Vargas or Billingsly. Reality had to admit that it would not have been satisfactory to her, either, if she had been in their place, but the screams from the two of them still seemed to be bouncing off the walls of her office despite the fact that Fernando's death had not been, truly had not been, Reality's fault.

The only saving grace Reality could find in the situation was that Vargas and Billingsly had a farm in Happy Valley, and their farm was the second to the farthest west up the river toward the falls. It would be a minimum of three days before she would need to confront either one in person. Unless they convinced someone to give them priority for a rover trip, which was possible with the Demos meeting coming up. That would still take a day, maybe two, if she factored in the argument to get on the rover. Maybe she would have more satisfactory things to say by the time they arrived. Not that anything would be satisfactory, but perhaps there would be something to direct their ire to someone other than her.

The *other than her* brought Reality back to the fact that Dani had lied to her. That meant she needed to have a conversation with Miroslav, which would need to be face-to-face because Miroslav would not take her calls. He had not taken any from her for twenty years. He was unlikely to change now. She was putting that off, and intended to put it off as long as she could, but she would have to do it sooner or later because Dani's lies involved both Fernando, who was dead, and Thorny, who was missing.

Thorny not having returned on her own meant calling Hiep. Talking to Hiep was another conversation Reality preferred to avoid, even though conversations with him involved a minimum of words.

Reality sighed as she thought about conversations she did not want to have. It was another reminder of why she was not good enough to be a leader, not even of a bunch of children, most of whom she had known from the time she changed their diapers. Maybe this time Thorny would be easy to find and some of the conversations would become unnecessary. She suspected that was as likely as a starship from Earth making orbit tomorrow.

There was no harm in trying Thorny again. Miracles could happen. She chipped in and called Thorny's phone. Nothing but an automated answer. No surprise, really. She checked the network for Thorny's phone but didn't find it. As the Head of School, Reality had the rights on the network to ping any child's phone. She pinged Thorny's on the off-chance that this time it would at least be on and somewhere nearby. The phone did not return the ping. Turned off. She called Jorge Olivares and explained the situation, hoping for some magical solution.

"Yeah, there's a trick we can use." Jorge sounded far too cheerful for the circumstances, a techie with an opportunity to show off.

"Could you explain the trick?" Reality thought she kept that calm enough.

"Sure." More cheeriness. "The phones that were stocked for the colony are no different from the ones we used to buy on Earth. They all have an additional chip as an always-on detector. Even if the phone is shut off, that detector is on unless both the phone's battery and the battery for that extra chip are dead. On Earth, since the Phone Location Privacy Laws of 2073, pinging it requires upper-level police or security authority to use it—well, that depends on your country.

"Here, the protocol was disabled in the original setup of the system, but when we put up the additional antennas, I enabled it. Seemed like a good safety measure for us; the rover base stations can also trigger it. Fear not, stalwart Head of School, I can do it if you want."

Was there sarcasm in that last sentence? That was not Jorge's style, but when it came to her, she was so accustomed to hearing it that she automatically assumed that was the intent. "Please. If it's considered invasive or inappropriate, I'll explain to Hiep and Penny, or the town council if it comes to that, but let's do it." Reality entered Thorny's number.

"Okay, well that's odd," Jorge said less than a minute later.

"What is?"

"I've got nothing. No response at all."

"Both batteries are dead?" Reality asked.

"We've never had that happen here, not yet," Jorge said. "It will sooner or later, as the equipment ages, but I would expect it first with one of our phones that have been in use since we were on Earth."

A pause followed before Jorge spoke again. "She could, I suppose, be somewhere or have gone far enough that her phone doesn't have any signal. And there's one other possibility. Some of our electronic supplies were shipped in inert, secure packing. That blocks any signal coming through. It's meant to shield components prior to installation, but you could make a shield pouch for a phone. Kids can be ingenious when they want to conceal what they are doing. And . . . you might consider who her father is. I guarantee he would know about it."

"Thanks, Jorge."

Reality clicked off with a sense of defeat. Her world narrowed to the rear wall of her office, which is where her eyes had focused when she had swiveled her chair around during the call. Not only would she need to speak again with Hiep, but the conversation would have an additional dimension. She dreaded the thought that it might sound like she was accusing him.

A thunderclap that made the walls vibrate broke her reverie. She turned back to look over her desk. Hiep was standing in the doorway of her office. She had not heard him arrive, had not been aware of his presence while she had been speaking to Jorge. She startled, jerked upright in her chair, and told herself that he had not appeared out of the thunder. The breath she exhaled turned into a squeak.

"Sorry. You seemed lost in thought, and I did not want to interrupt."

Hiep came in to stand in front of her desk, which took only a few steps. He looked no different than he ever did, clad in a nondescript recycled T-shirt and cargo pants that were threadbare in places and had holes in other places, garb that anyone else would have tossed in the recycler and drawn whatever pair they received as part of their equal share. He was not a big man, not at all impressive unless one could see the muscles now hidden by his shirt, but his presence scared her as much as if he had truly been a ghost that materialized in front of her desk. Had he heard her side of the conversation with Jorge?

"We've had no contact from Thorny," Reality managed to say. "We are also unable to locate her phone."

"I see."

When Hiep stopped after two words, Reality decided she did not need to bring up the question of whether he had taught Thorny how to conceal her location. She was sure he knew what Thorny could have done.

"There was no incident with anyone?" Hiep asked. "No one saw her become angry, no one heard her say anything or saw her run off?"

"No. I have spoken with everyone in her cohort about that night, and no other student has said anything." She had not been specifically asking about Thorny, but the statement was true as far as it went.

"That is unusual," Hiep said. "For her to do this without something provoking it."

"Well, I mean, there was . . . you know, whatever happened with Fernando." Reality fumbled her words and stopped there. She did not want to mention what Regan had said: that she had called Dani about Thorny and was the one who had, in effect, sent him out to find Fernando. Regan's mother was a friend of Penny's. She did not want Hiep to head off and interrogate Regan, not when she did not have any other information.

Hiep did not ask anything further. He said only, "I see," and then he was gone.

HIEP

HE STOPPED BRIEFLY OUTSIDE THE ENTRANCE TO THE RESIDENCE SCHOOL, HIS EYES narrowed, his lips pressed together. The rain was falling steadily, but that was not what brought him to a halt. He did not care about getting wet. Thorny's pack was gone. Nothing had triggered her disappearance. This behavior was not consistent with Thorny's pattern. That led to an immediate decision. Simply going up to Dead Lake might not be adequate; he might need to make a more extensive search. That ruled out going on foot or horseback. He needed to see Miroslav about putting that recently decommissioned rover back into service, even if that delayed his start.

It was not hard to find Miroslav. He was chipped in at a hab on the Avenue of Europe not far from Town Circle. That sort of information—precise location rather than the flag showing the person was on the network—should have been held securely by the system. Hiep, however, had routines that would extract it even from far more secure systems than the Saint Peterstown one. Everyone in the settlement was the equivalent of a soft target, but Hiep reminded himself that he no longer had targets. Not unless it was his decision to make someone a target.

When he arrived, he found Miroslav seated on the dirt between the rear of the hab and its privacy screen, a flimsy pop-up tent shielding him, his seating area, and his work area inside the hab wall from the rain. The grille covering the outlet of the air handling system had been removed and was lying on the ground next to him. He held a circuit board in his hands.

"System problem?" Hiep asked as a way of introducing himself.

Miroslav looked up, then hastily stood up. Hiep's clothes were wet, and water dripped from his hair. Miroslav held the circuit board between the two of them as though it were a shield. "Won't cool. Which is a real problem here. The diagnostic AI identifies the part that has failed, provides the least expensive supplier along with catalog number and price, and tells me to replace it." Disgust entered his voice. "It does not account for the fact that next-day drone delivery from seventy-six light-years away will not happen. When I prompt the damned thing for a workaround without replacement, it tells me there is no documented method and it is forbidden to provide a speculative answer. I'll have to take apart the system in one of the empty habs and use the part from there, but then that hab will not function properly if someone wants it. Or these people will need to move to another hab."

Hiep saw the problem as a very different matter, not an equipment failure so much as an attitude. "They could keep the windows open. There is almost always a reasonable breeze up here, and with interior fans they could adapt to the heat. People who are dependent on technology are not the best choice for interstellar settlements."

Even with his stoop, Miroslav looked down at Hiep. He hesitated. Hiep's personal indifference to the weather was obvious. "You have said that before. But here we are, such as we are. What can I do for you?"

"There are no rovers at the station, but the system shows one as being very recently decommissioned. I would like it put back in service so I can use it to go for Thorny."

"Danko took the other rover," Miroslav said. "He'll get the first rover and, I would think, your daughter."

"Forgive me if I sound like I am doubting Dani, but he may not locate Thorny. That is something I need to do, and it is my assessment that I will need a rover. Now, can we put the other one back into service? I will count this as a great favor."

Miroslav stepped back and felt rain hit his back. He squinted, clearly weighing the adverse consequences of contradicting Hiep's assessment and disappointing him against the advantage of Hiep owing him a favor. "Some of the components for the rover's base station have already been sent to the valley, and I have already broken down some of the motors and battery system to use for salvage. It will take some days to make the rover serviceable at all, and it will be wasted effort if Danko is back with her tomorrow."

"I am not an engineer, as you are, but I have had experience in the field doing repairs on vehicles that have some similarity to these. I will be glad to work with you. Dani may be back tomorrow, but I do not think Thorny will be with him."

DALTON

THE HAB STANK OF EQUAL PARTS CANNABIS SMOKE, SWEAT, AND FEAR. THE GROUP from the first cohort of high-seniors milled around in the front room, dragging on their joints as though they could pull serenity from the burning leaf. On this night, the drug was not having its desired effect.

"It's going to be obvious we were smoking in here." Sonia's voice was plaintive. "If we put the air cleaner on high enough to clear all of this, it will be obvious we put the cleaner up, and it will be equally obvious why. Unreality is going to know."

"You think she doesn't know we take the cannabis and drink out back of the hydroponics?" Dalton snapped. He was pacing as he smoked, weaving among people and furniture. "And what is she going to do about it?" He stopped in front of Sonia to snarl the question in her face. "Make you clean the air filters with a toothbrush?" He resumed his pacing, waving an arm at each person he passed. "It's a stupid rule that you can't smoke or drink until you've finished residence school. And we're done anyway, come the equinox. March thirty-fifth and we're done. Out of here. I don't even care about the exams, and why should you? Take a job. Collect your equal share. Done and done."

"Fine for you," Sonia said. "My parents expect me to take a partner and start a farm. And Busby will tell my mother."

"You're still scared of your mother?" Kojo had more than a trace of sarcasm in his voice. Sonia's mother had moved from the town to the valley five years before, when she became the partner of a farmer. The townies had teased Sonia about her "forced conversion" ever since.

"Well, I know you're scared of yours." Sonia's attempt at a comeback raised a few laughs.

"Fuck Unreality," Dalton said. "Not that anyone would. I mean, all three of her kids were implants from embryo storage. I mean, could you imagine Unreality undressing? Being with her naked? Obviously not!" Dalton gave a harsh laugh. "Busby isn't going to do anything." He jabbed in Sonia's direction with the stub of his joint held between thumb and forefinger. "Anyway, this is my hab and Ethan's. If she does anything, it won't be to you. But she won't. It's stupid to have a rule you can't enforce. Anyway, she's got other things to worry about."

"And we don't?"

With those three words from Sonia, all the talk stopped. The only sound in the room came from the air filtration system. Each pair of eyes darted around the room, each person assessing the state of every other one present. The rain had stopped, but there was a reason the group had gathered in Dalton's hab that night, had not gone out to their usual spot behind the hydroponics, and it was not because the ground was wet. It was a reason none of them had mentioned. Something neither cannabis nor alcohol had managed to banish from their minds.

"What's going to happen about . . . him?" Sonia's voice quavered. She was chewing so incessantly on the inside of her lip that her jaw seemed to writhe.

"Not a goddamn thing is going to happen." Dalton thrust his head forward and glared at her.

"I don't know," Sonia said. "What if it's not just Busby asking questions? What if it's Dr. Song too? And what about Thorny?"

"Thorny's gone," Dalton said. "Maybe this time she will stay gone. Nothing to worry about."

"Dani went after her," Kojo said. "Took a rover. He could bring her back."

"Which means they both took rovers, which means they're both in deep shit if they get back." Dalton flung the roach to the floor as it burned down to his fingers.

"Yeah. But that father of hers is in town now," Jaelen said. "Saw him at the school. What if it's him asking questions?"

"I'm not afraid of Hiep," Dalton said.

"Then you're a fool," Jaelen shot back. "We need to know what we're going to do, what we're going to say."

"Listen to me, you idiots." Dalton took a deep breath. "We're not going to do anything. We are not going to say anything. We didn't do anything. We don't know anything about this."

"But Ferdy's phone—" Sonia began to say.

"I've got Ferdy's phone!" Dalton's voice cracked in mid-shout, and that only made him angrier. "I grabbed it when we had to help Watanabe with . . . you know. Dammit! I've got it and Watanabe didn't even notice—and it's not like Busby or anyone can get into his phone anyway, and none of you left any stupid messages on the system. Right?"

"Well . . ." Sonia started again.

"Goddamn all of you idiots! The phone is going in the recycler. We didn't do anything!" Dalton's shout was half scream. "We didn't." He struggled to keep control of his voice. "Did any of you lay a hand on Ferdy?" Six heads shook no. "Were any of you even within reach of Ferdy?" Another shake of the heads. "That's what I mean. None of us did anything. None of us were there. None of us need to say anything more than that. Got it?"

"But what if Thorny does come back?" Sonia asked. "She always runs away, and then she always comes back, one way or another."

"Get this through your head," Dalton said. "Thorny isn't going to say a goddamn thing. Because what could Thorny say? That it's all her goddamn fault?"

"She could talk about—"

"I don't think so." Dalton cut off Sonia. "It's all her goddamn fault, and she's not going to say that, so she's not going to say anything. And when we're asked, we weren't there, and there's nothing Thorny can say. It's all her fault anyway."

REALITY

IT WAS LONG PAST DINNERTIME AS WELL AS BEING DARK. REALITY WATCHED MIROSLAV wipe sweat off his forehead as he worked to reconnect the climate control system of the rover that had been chosen for cannibalization but now appeared to be going back into service.

"Hello."

He looked up. Reality knew she was backlit by the bright lights in the ceiling of the rover repair facility, leaving her face mostly in shadow. That was probably the most appropriate way for her to be seen.

Miroslav straightened up. "Why are you here?"

"I needed to speak to you, and you don't answer if I call or message."

"Not yours, I don't."

Reality balled her fists and clenched her teeth. She wanted to stomp her feet, but she restrained that emotion. What she could not hold back was the frustration that burst out in her words. "Goddammit, Miroslav! I have done everything I could do. I have worked my ass off here for twenty years! I am sorry for what happened, for what I did. Can we just have a normal conversation?"

Miroslav wiped his hands, one against the other. He squinted into the lights. "I am sure you're sorry. But your sorry doesn't take the scars off my back or the memories out of my mind. And, yes, you work, and people tolerate you, but that's about it. Nobody forgets what you were doing."

"I was far from the only one," Reality protested.

"You made yourself out to be one of the leaders. And you're the only one of them still alive." Miroslav looked toward the rover. "How much of twenty years ago do you want to talk about, or can we get to what brought you here tonight?"

Reality throttled the scream she wanted to let out. Screaming would do no good. It would not even make her feel better. "I need to talk to you about Dani."

"You are not going to talk to me about anything you think my son has done wrong. I won't take that from you, and you know it. You can talk to his mother, as you've always done."

Reality strode over to him and planted herself in front of Miroslav with her arms crossed over her chest. She hoped she was going to use the correct tone. There was a time she would have threatened him, or belittled him, but those times were over and were one of the reasons for the current situation.

"Dani lied to me," she said.

Miroslav backed up a step and shaded his eyes against the glare of the lights behind her. "Lied about what?"

"I questioned all the students in the first cohort of high-seniors about the night Fernando . . . died. Dani is the one who found him, but he said he went out because he had a feeling something was wrong. That's already weak, and he didn't look good saying it, but then Regan told me she called him about Thorny and that's why he went out. What's going on?"

"Shit." Miroslav looked for something to throw and settled for kicking a bucket by his feet that sent tools clattering across the floor. "What I know that I'll tell you is that Thorny took a rover out to Dead Lake. Danko went to bring the rover back. Of course, he went to bring Thorny back. That girl could be a house on fire and he'd run to her, and he thinks nobody knows that. Now are you enlightened?"

Reality decided to ignore the gibe. "And you're recommissioning this rover?" She pointed at his work area. "Because neither of the other two are back?"

"Because Hiep wants to use it. Ask him about it. If he'll answer you, that is."

"I'll do that," Reality said. "And, yes, he'll answer me, just like most other people do." *What they say to me is another issue*, she thought, but there was no need to go into that with Miroslav.

THORNY

THORNY WOKE TO THE SOUND OF RAIN SPLATTERING AGAINST THE WINDSHIELD. NOT discrete droplets that made a pattern across the plastic but a sheet of water that cascaded down from roof to hood. A rumble of distant thunder added to the drumming.

At some point while she slept, she had fallen away from the wheel and against the seat back with her head flopped over to one side. Muscles groaned in protest as she sat up straight. She brought a hand up to massage her neck, felt wetness on the cheek, and moved her hand to explore it. The rover had not leaked. It was drool.

I am disgusting. She had to go to the bathroom, too, but she was not about to step out into that downpour. The rover had no facility to meet her need. She would have to hold it. Rain on Heaven often came as a deluge. Usually it was brief, but some storms could last the whole day. The thought had her twitching in her seat. She was *not* going to go in her pants. It would all be much easier if she were dead.

That brought her back to her thoughts from before she had fallen asleep. That she was going to die. That it was her decision. She turned the concept over in her mind. Certainly, if she did not go back, she would die. Sooner or later. Humans had a tenuous grip on Heaven, as her mother kept reminding her and everyone else. How was she going to die?

Thorny looked out the side window. The rain was slackening even in the time she had been ruminating, and the dim gray light revealed the immediate area around the rover. Scattered amid the thin ground cover they all called grass, stalks and flowers of the thistle plant stuck up. If she chewed a thistle, she would die. Quite fast. One or two should be plenty. Thistle effects and thistle safety were drilled into every child from the time they were old enough to comprehend danger. She stared at the thistles.

The problem was the *way* it would happen. If she chewed it and swallowed it, the first order of business would be shitting her pants. Then she would piss in her pants. She would sit, soaked in her own mire, while snot ran out of her nose and drool flowed out of her mouth until it started to become hard to breathe, and then she would finally stop breathing. She recoiled from the image in her mind. She was not going to eat a thistle.

By this time, the weather was down to a light rainfall. The solid ceiling of gray cloud was still low over the land. Downhill, ahead of her, only gray murk was visible. Had she hallucinated that vision of dark green in the far distance? No way to know. Not in this weather. But it was light. How long had she slept? Long enough, obviously, to feel the need for a bathroom. She ought to be hungry, too, after this much time, but she was not. Still, she pulled out a strip of jerky and chewed it because that was an act Thorny expected of herself.

She started the rover and began to drive slowly forward. She went that direction in equal parts because that was the way the rover was facing, she refused to turn back, and she felt a vague curiosity about the dark green she recalled. But the primary reason for driving at all was that it helped take her mind off her bladder.

. . .

THE LIGHT WAS FAILING WHEN THORNY HEARD THE SOUND OF RUNNING WATER FROM off to her right. She had driven through the daylight hours with only a single break to relieve herself once the rain had trailed off to a drizzle. The land in this area formed itself into a sequence of ridges and valleys, each ridge lower than the one before it so that the overall trend stayed downward. The soil was thicker than it had been, even if the grass over it remained sparse, with the result that the rover's tires dug deeply into brown mud. Other than the occasional shellhound, this land was devoid of obvious animal life. Her brain had been devoid of thought in much the same way, until that rushing of water caught her attention. She wanted to see it, if for no reason beyond it being the only change that had occurred in the dull and somber landscape around her. She angled the rover a bit more to the west, to the direction the sound was loudest, and she pressed on.

Past the next rise in the ground, clumps of low trees formed a line in front of her, running from east to west. They were widely spaced at first, so the rover had no trouble passing through. This time, she was careful to avoid hitting branches. The trees appeared similar to the ones around Dead Lake, none of them more than ten feet tall. Of greater interest: the sound of water splashing off rocks was louder once she was into the tree line.

It happened all at once. She had steered the rover through a thicker screen of trees, and as she cleared those trees, the ground sloped down sharply, dropping to the bank of a broad river. Thorny hit the brakes, but not before the rover had gone far enough that the dirt under the front wheels gave way. The rover tipped. More earth crumbled and the machine slid forward, coming to rest at the water's edge.

"Shit." Thorny hopped out of the passenger compartment to survey the situation. Her boots sank to their uppers in the soft mud. The rover tires had sunk as well, with mud reaching to the wheel rims of the front tires.

An exploratory rover could handle a slope of forty degrees. The tires had been designed for a variety of terrain, deep mud included. After a quick look, Thorny was certain that the rover could handle the riverbank. She had not, however, been trained to drive the rover through this sort of muck. The rocky, uneven ground between Saint Peterstown and Dead Lake had been the greatest test of her ability with the machine.

"I guess we'll learn by doing, Rover," she said to the vehicle. "That's what my dad always says. The more interesting question"—she looked up from the mud—"is the river."

The water was flowing east and to the north. The south bank was bare and brown. The trees on her side dwindled in number and density as she looked to the east. This had to be the Happy River, far upstream of where the farms were located. If she turned east and followed the river, it would lead her to the Staircase Falls above Happy Valley. Then what? The rover would not be able to descend the cliffs at the side of those falls.

I could swim out into the river there. Let it carry me over the falls.

That would be a theatrical death, it truly would. Of course, no one would actually see her take the plunge. Still, the river would carry her body past the farms, out to White Sands Bay. They would all wonder at the mystery of how she came to be in the river; they would be sad they had let it come to that; they would grieve; and it would serve them right. Except . . . with her luck, her body would be hung up on a rock, or caught in the reeds, and be half-eaten by one of the Heaven gators that would find her to be as indigestible as the human community already had.

That was disgusting. She was not going to follow the river back to the falls.

Could she cross the river?

Thorny stared across at the southern bank. The river was wide, but not impressively so. Maybe a couple of hundred feet. Judging by the ripples in the middle, the water was flowing over barely submerged rocks. It might be shallow enough to ford in this area. A rover could not swim, but it could wade. Its electrical systems were carefully encased in waterproof sheathing. As long as the passenger compartment did not flood, it would be possible.

Thorny pulled out from the equipment section a pole that extended to five feet in length. It had been designed for a different purpose, but it would do for what she needed. Then she took out the spear that had become standard equipment in every rover. She did not extend it to its full length. It did not look like gators—or any creatures more advanced than algae—lived in this stretch of river, but caution was so ingrained as to be instinctive. Gators and sawtooth roos, another carnivore, were real dangers in Happy Valley. But on a world that had experienced an extinction event on the order of Earth's Great Dying, the humans had chosen to stay on guard rather than hunt down the predators in their territory.

Thus armed, Thorny stepped into the water, using the pole to check ahead of her for depth. The river was shallow, no more than knee deep as she reached the middle. That was when she made a thrust ahead of her with the pole and struck bottom a foot down, but her foot slipped on a rock. Her leg plunged into a hole and her boot caught under a rock. She toppled into the water with a splash and a curse. Frantically, she wrenched her leg free. Pain shot through her ankle. She floundered in the water, trying to get her feet under her. She slipped again and fell forward, hands finding the bottom, face in the water. Finally, she was able to push herself upright. Her ankle hurt but held her weight.

That would be so like me, to drown in two feet of water.

"Fuck!" She was soaked from head to foot, with water dripping from her hair, standing in the middle of a river. Dusk was coming. Thorny was not pleased with herself. She had lost the pole. She still had the spear, but only because of the retrieval cord fastened at her wrist.

She was going to finish what she had started. Using the spear to check depth, and hobbling because of her ankle, she completed the crossing and then made it back across to the rover. Inside the rover, she took off her boots, poured them out, and then examined her ankle. It was a little puffy, but there was no bruising. Call it a mild sprain, she decided. The emergency medical kit had elastic tape. She wrapped the ankle and pulled her boots back on. By that point, her teeth were chattering. She turned on the heat and laughed. That was a first, she thought, that someone had turned on a rover's heating system on Heaven.

The clouds at the western horizon were still lit by the sun, but it would be night soon. Those clouds would block most of the moonlight.

"Rover, we are doing this! Now!"

She eased the vehicle into the water and drove slowly across the river, headlights shining off the ripples, her eyes fixed on the far bank. Her assessment of the river's depth did not betray her. Like a huge, ungainly turtle, the rover made its way across to the other side, where it churned up the dirt bank.

Thorny stopped the rover at the top of the bank. She was on the south bank of the Happy River. The rover's lights shone out ahead across a broad expanse of ground that was little different from the land she had already crossed. Now what?

Beyond knowing that she was on the south bank, she had no idea where she was. The starships had taken images of the entire land surface of Heaven. Almost certainly, those images were stored in the databases in Saint Peterstown. However, images of the region this far from the town were not stored in the rover, and she could no longer connect to the network. She neither knew where she was, nor could she tell what the land in front of her might be like.

"Rover, I think this qualifies as being lost."

Those words led to another decision. She would head south and keep driving south as long as she had enough daylight to keep some charge in the battery. When the battery ran out, she would stop. She was going to be the first human to see the polar night of Heaven. That would be an accomplishment. It would be a good place to die.

She did not care about being lost. She started the rover forward.

Danijel

Danijel awoke to a typical dark late-fall morning. In fact, he could not tell it was morning until he checked the time. Exhaustion from too little sleep and too much stress over the past day had taken its toll. He shook his head and tried to remember what he was doing. The trees around him were barely discernible as deeper darkness against the dark. He turned on the headlights. Clear in the beam and lying directly ahead was a snapped-off branch. Memories knitted together.

He shifted back and forth in his seat, his mind trying to reassemble the pieces of the previous day. He was astounded by what he had done—that, and more than a little afraid of it. He reached out to pat Thorny's pack. It was all real.

He had a few hours yet before sunup, but with the headlights on and his brain somewhat refreshed by sleep, he could make out the path Thorny's rover had taken. He was going to continue. That was one decision. He would catch up to Thorny. That was a second decision. He would convince her to come back to Saint Peterstown. There was really no other choice for her, but he liked the image of saving her. How he would do that, the words he would use; those details were hazy. Her pack figured into his daydreams of her being overjoyed that he had come, and so he would not need to say very much. There was a point in this chain of mental images where his decisions converted to hopes, but he did not recognize that boundary. His plan for the day was clear.

The battery still had plenty of charge. Once the sun was up, the rover's skin would help to maintain that. Power would not be a concern, not for a long while. Danijel started the rover forward.

He had to travel slowly to make certain that he stayed on the trail. Not every swath of ground illuminated by the headlights showed rover tracks and not every tree had a broken branch. He panicked once when he could see neither tracks nor tree damage. Convinced he had lost his way, he turned the rover around, then felt ice in his stomach and against his spine when he could not make out his own tracks. His breaths came too rapidly; he fought to bring that under control while his eyes scanned the ground.

The tracks from his rover turned out to be right in front of him. In his fear of losing his way, he had been looking off to the sides and far ahead, into areas where the light from the rover was blocked by trees. He was all right, he told himself, even as the sweat dripping down his side told a different tale. What he needed to keep under control was himself.

He backtracked to a point where he had a sure sign of the passage of Thorny's rover. Indeed, her path seemed to run left of the direction he had taken. He swore to pay better attention. He swore at himself for not having been attentive enough. He redirected his rover, this time moving with greater caution.

The sun was well over the horizon by the time the trail brought him out of the trees. Ahead of him was a wide plain of grass, extending out to a line of far-off mountains. He could see rover tracks headed west.

"I hope you're not planning to go all the way to those mountains," he said as though Thorny were sitting next to him.

That was when the first raindrops hit his windshield. Within minutes, the rain was pelting down faster and harder until the view ahead was hidden in a flood of water.

"No, no, no!" He could not continue to drive in this rain. More accurately, he could drive but had no way to pick up Thorny's trail. With a sigh born of desperation, he sat back to wait for the storm to break.

The monotonous duration of falling water extended out to forever in his mind and ate up precious hours of daylight on the clock. When at last it slowed, and the clouds and mist lifted away from the ground, another blow landed against his hopes. The rain had washed out all evidence of the other rover's track.

"Now what? Now what?" Danijel gripped the steering wheel hard enough to cramp his hands. Part of his mind wanted to bang his head against that wheel even as a more rational part told him that would be theatrical, useless, and childish. He settled for clamping his jaws so tightly that they ached with strain.

He checked his main screen on the dashboard. The Saint Peterstown network was not available. His phone indicated that it had no signal. He hadn't noticed that he had driven out of communication range with the town. Would he even be able to find his own way back? That could not matter, not at the moment. He had to find Thorny.

You're supposed to be bright, he thought. *Prove it.*

Rovers were designed to operate in the wilderness. An obvious component of that function was to have ways of finding an explorer who became separated from the main party and, for whatever reason, was disoriented or unconscious. As long as the missing explorer had their phone, as long as it had some scrap of power, the rover had a built-in base station that could ping the phone. His father had shown him a backup method while having him practice on the rover's circuitry. There was an always-on chip in a phone that the rover's base station could ping, even if the phone had been turned off.

"It's not documented," his father had said, "but it works. Nobody is going to turn their phone off in the wild, but you might as well know about everything this machinery can do."

Naturally, distance and terrain imposed limits on the technique, but it was worth a try. Danijel had learned the rover system well enough not to need to consult the manual. He sent the ping.

Joy flooded his nerves at the immediate response. Thorny was out here. But where, precisely?

Normally, if a strange world was being explored, a starship would be overhead to take the role played by the GPS satellites around Earth. That would yield the exact location of the phone. No starship had orbited Heaven for twenty years. Danijel did not have a second pinging location available that would allow him to triangulate. The communication equipment on the rover did support a voice channel, but when he tried it, Thorny did not answer. Probably because her phone *was* off.

What the rover's instrumentation did leave him with was a reasonable estimate of distance and approximate direction from his location. If he was correct in the heading he picked, he would reach Thorny during the remaining daylight. If he failed to magically pick the correct direction, after he moved a distance, he could re-ping and make a crude attempt at triangulation using his current data. As long as Thorny stayed where she was. A minor additional constraint, he thought.

The next question was power. He knew how many hours of daylight he had. He could guesstimate the battery drain if he drove the rover at a constant speed and kept unnecessary components turned off. The charging via the photovoltaic skin would not completely keep up with the expenditure. If he drove in the dark, which he almost certainly would, it would exacerbate the situation. He could go a long way with the rover, but he could not go forever. Of course, neither could Thorny. The depressing part of his conclusion was that if she drove away from him at the same rate, they would both run out of power and be as far apart as they were now. He decided not to think about that.

As Danijel set out, he took multiple images of the land on all sides of the rover. He hoped those would be good enough in the absence of any true landmarks to let him bring the rover back to its current point. In the worst case, he would set the rover on an eastward heading, figuring that eventually he would pick up the signal from the communication tower in Saint Peterstown or the one on the hill near Highway 1 before it reached Happy Valley. It was not as though he were really lost. Even if it felt that way in the pit of his stomach.

After thirty minutes of driving, he put his plan to the test and pinged again. The responding signal told him that he was still able to pick up Thorny's phone, but after some work and puzzlement, he concluded that she was moving, headed south.

Why did I think this would be easy? Danijel changed course.

He continued the process of drive, ping, and course-correct. Thorny was definitely headed south. Even though the pinging made him feel that he was in close contact, it was not as though he could stand on top of the rover and wave and shout for her to stop.

The land broke into a series of small valleys and ridges that ran mostly east to west. Sometimes his ping was not returned. He tried, with varying degrees of success, to ignore the panic that ensued. He told himself that it was a quirk of the terrain blocking the signal, and he continued to drive. The next time he pinged, or the time after that, he would get a response.

More gratifying, as the daylight began to draw to an end, he spotted a set of tire tracks pressed into the wet dirt. He was offline, yes, but not so far offline that he could not see them, a double line of brown scored into a green hillside. The tracks led him to a mass of trees, but even as he was forced to depend on his headlights, the ruts were deep enough in the soft earth that he could follow them. That is, he could follow them until the rover tracks brought him to the edge of a river. Crossing that in the dark was out of the question.

DECEMBER 26, HY 21

REALITY

MY WIFE AND I ARE COMING TO TOWN TO BURY OUR SON ON THE 28TH. ALL WHO WISH TO ATTEND MAY DO SO. I AM HOPING WE FIND SOME EXPLANATION TO HELP US CLOSE THIS. The last sentence of Guillermo's message her chip projected on her field might as well have been branded on her brain. Especially the words *explanation* and *close this*. The message was a general broadcast—everyone on the Saint Peterstown network by chip or phone had received it—but to Reality, it had been directed to her alone.

She might say that high-seniors were supposed to be responsible for themselves. But not many people thought this. Gordon having come out and said it only made that knowledge more real. She knew that whatever had happened could not be her fault, but that most people would still assign the blame to her, as though the only possible way to expiate her acts of twenty years before was for the school to run perfectly. Even after all these years, she could not run away from her history.

She could only hope Dr. Song had figured out the mystery. Or that she would figure it out. Soon. The twenty-eighth meant she had only another day and a half.

·   ·   ·

WHEN REALITY WALKED INTO THE CLINIC SAYING THAT SHE NEEDED TO SEE THE DOC
but was cryptic as to why, Yuki showed her to one of the diagnostic
beds and told her to wait, as Dr. Song was busy with another patient.
Should have messaged her, Reality told herself three times while she sat
contemplating the dangling diagnostic lead that would interface with
a chip. However, she had become accustomed to her messages being
ignored—not that Dr. Song would do that—and Saint Peterstown was
small enough that it was easier, sometimes, to go see someone.

Well, it might be easier, but she did not like coming to the clinic.
The beds, the screens, the chip interface reminded her of when Dr.
Song had removed the cancers from her face and then the freckle on
her arm, part of which had turned purple and had been even more
dangerous, a melanoma. Fortunately, Dr. Song had said they caught
it early enough, so all she had to do was cut it out and give Reality
a drug. All that remained was a white scar. But Song had told her
she had to watch carefully for any others because the volcanoes had
stripped so much of the ozone from the atmosphere that a lot of UV
came through. That was bad for someone with very pale skin like
hers. Penny had made a sunscreen out of the zinc oxide in shellhound
shells—which was why, dumb as they were, shellhounds thrived—but
it was too lumpy and ugly white, so almost no one used it. It was
another reminder that another part of her—her skin—was *not good
enough* for this world. *Stop thinking like that*, she told herself. She went
about as she had before, and so far, she'd been lucky.

Sitting in the clinic, however, she could not wrench her mind from
that freckle. She traced the scar with the tip of her index finger. Who
would wield the surgi-bot to remove one when Song was too old or
gone herself? Who would do it and how, if the surgi-bot no longer
worked? That would happen eventually. Those were very uncomfortable thoughts.

Song Jing picked that moment to walk in, a welcome invitation for
Reality's thoughts to return to the purpose of the visit.

"How are you?" Song asked. "Yuki didn't say why you're here. It's
not another skin lesion, is it?"

"No!" Reality almost jumped off the bed as the question connected with her thoughts and sent sparks jumping across her nerves.

Song took a step back, her eyes wide. It took a lot to startle the doc, so Reality scrambled her words out rapidly to move the conversation away from herself. "I'm fine. I'm fine. This isn't about me. It's Fernando, or about Fernando. You saw Guillermo's post. I've been on the phone with him and Donna. Is there anything more I can tell him, anything I can say when he is here? Have you found anything?"

Song leaned back against the diagnostic bed opposite Reality and took a moment before answering. "I don't know any more than I've said. Something happened to him, and I don't know what. Not yet. Not all tests can be done in a day or two." She folded her arms across her chest. "I never thought I would say this, but this is one time I wish we had a police department. Not Cam and Jess. Although maybe you can help."

"With what? How?" Reality almost jumped at the question.

"The students get chemistry lessons, right?" Reality nodded. "There is some practical—that is, lab work. Right?"

"There is some hands-on work," Reality said. "I mean, we don't have a lot of equipment or reagents, but they need to learn that there's more to chemistry than tapping a button on a cell foundry panel to synthesize compounds."

"No need to be defensive." Song appeared relaxed, even if Reality was not. "Any of the students good at it?"

Reality was puzzled at the question but searched her memory for an answer. "Sonia Janasch, maybe. They only study it as high-seniors, so I can't tell you about younger ones."

"Sonia. Could she, or anybody else, have cooked up something kids might use as a drug? Fentanyl and methamphetamine aren't that hard to make."

"I . . . don't . . . know." It struck Reality that she should have thought of this, should have checked even before she went to see Song. "I'll go through our inventory, check the use records. I'll let you know."

"Thanks. If you find anything, I can run some more tests, although as I've said, this clinic isn't close to a forensic lab." Song stood straight as if to leave, but then had one more question. "Speaking of knowing anything, you haven't heard from Dani or Thorny, have you? Still no word?"

Reality shook her head. "Hiep will go get both of them."

Song nodded. "He is certainly the right person to do it. We can't have half the town out in the wild looking for them. We'd probably lose half of them. Now, if you'll excuse me, I need to see what Norma and Yuki are doing."

As Reality walked back to the school to begin checking the chemistry supplies and records, she could not shake the feeling that Song had left something unsaid when she spoke of a search. Had Sonia Janasch tried to cook up some recreational drugs? Reality was chipped in; she connected to the system, where she had access to any activity of the students. She checked every one of Sonia's log-ins over the past year. Sonia had searched for information on methamphetamine multiple times. Those searches had included how to synthesize it. Pages she had viewed on the synthesis had remained open for remarkably long periods of time. A number of her log-ins were after midnight, not the time an indifferent student would be in the lab. Had she actually produced some?

Reality checked the stores of reagents and the analytical instruments the students used. Then she pulled up chemistry texts that she barely remembered from her youth. Chemistry had not been one of her stronger subjects.

Sonia might have made methamphetamine. Maybe more than once. How much? It could not have been large amounts, but Reality was not sure how much a person would need to take. She shook her head and left a message for Dr. Song. She resolved to put in a new protocol on the use of the chemistry facility in the school. It had never occurred to her before to do that. After all, they were not on Earth. She told herself she was not facing another failure on her part—what could happen in a small town isolated by tens of light-years?—but the thought gnawed at her throughout the night.

DANIJEL

DANIJEL'S INSIDES COULD HAVE BEEN A MOP GOING THROUGH A WRINGER THE WAY they squeezed and twisted on themselves as he waited in frustration for the light of the new day to show itself. His attempts to ping were no longer answered. He paced up and down the edge of the Happy River hoping that he was wrong, that Thorny had not crossed, that she had driven along it either east or west and that he would come across her tracks if he looked closely enough. No such luck. Even in the dark, with nothing but the light of his phone, it was obvious that no rover had traversed the northern bank. He gave up and waited for daylight.

The gray of the late-morning dawn showed him what he did not want to see. Across the river on the southern side, deep tracks had been dug into the bare dirt of the bank. Thorny had crossed the river. The question now was: What was he going to do?

Danijel checked his phone. Even with the rover acting as a base station, he had no connection to Saint Peterstown. He could not ask for advice or for another's decision. The choice of what to do would be his alone.

He *could* cross the river. Thorny had driven across, and there was no reason his rover would not be able to do it as well. Making that crossing, however, felt like a huge step into the unknown. No one lived south of the Happy River. No one had ever gone this far from Saint Peterstown, except Thorny. The chill that caused a shake down in his bones had nothing to do with the wind, sticky-warm as it was at its coolest.

He *could* turn back. That was probably the smart thing to do. He would not risk a second rover, every rover being an irreplaceable machine the settlement could ill afford to lose. Thorny would probably come back on her own once she had gotten whatever devils bothered her out of her system. Danijel had figured the probable battery life several times. A rover could make it back from this point, even with the shortening days. If she did not come back, the town council might authorize an expedition, a properly outfitted one, because the rovers were that valuable. Having taken this rover this far on his own, his judgment would be severely criticized. If he crossed the river, the risk to the rover, never mind to himself, would be greater, as would the reprimand. However, if he went home and Thorny did not return on her own, she would die out in the wild. He would live for the rest of his life with the knowledge that he had turned away, no matter if his judgment was validated by others.

"I can't do that." He said it out loud and the wind blew his words away, so he shouted them out. "I can't do that!"

Danijel climbed back into the rover and started the motor. Carefully he drove into the water, aiming for the tire tracks on the other bank. The water was shallow. The rover had no difficulty with the crossing. When he had forded the river, he drove up the bank on the other side and saw that the rover tracks continued south. Without looking back, he followed them.

Danijel Petrovic had crossed his Rubicon.

DECEMBER 27, HY 21

JING

REALITY'S MESSAGE ABOUT SONIA'S ATTEMPTS AT KITCHEN CHEMISTRY CAME through too late for Jing to consider starting to work on it that night. It would keep until the next day. There would still be a whole day before Guillermo and Donna came up for the funeral, and that would be enough time, she hoped, to solve this particular problem.

She was at the clinic early to check the samples of blood, plasma, and urine from Fernando that they had stored. Should be adequate. Jing chipped in and pulled up her references.

Laboratory kits for detecting all manner of abused compounds existed. They were easy to use and very accurate. None of them had been included in the supplies ISC had sent. She stared at the inventories on her projection field and mumbled a few choice phrases. Had the ISC really believed that people would be so consumed with the work of building a human settlement around another star that no one would think of abusing psychoactive compounds? If so, why had they included cannabis in the plant inventory? And did they think no one would ever figure out alcoholic drinks? She shook her head. None of this rumination was solving her problem. There were other ways to figure out if a compound was in a person. Jing pulled up references on methamphetamine and its metabolites, then took her samples a short distance around Town Circle to the Lab Unit.

The main part of that building was always busy. That was where some of the cell foundries were located, churning out the different molecules, night and day, that the technological civilization of Heaven required. That was also where the embryo banks were stored, along with the artificial uteri that helped provide Heaven with Earth animals the colonists needed. Jing did not enter those parts of the building. Instead, she went through the doorway to the true laboratory area, with its ranks of benches topped with the equipment to analyze the strangeness of a new planet.

This area was quiet, devoid of people and machine activity. Twenty years into the colonization of Heaven, little new analysis was happening. It was not that everything about the planet had been discovered and understood. It was more that the humans from Earth had learned enough to survive and were too busy with the work of maintaining their settlement to spend their time on what they did not know.

It had been, in fact, years since Jing had needed to use any of the instruments. She took a moment to reorient herself. The molecular analyzer, the tool she wanted, was near the back wall. It was easy to find, set apart from the other instruments and marked off by strips of tape warning of the strong magnetic field.

Who knew the last time someone had used it? Jing powered it on and was gratified to see the screens flash, the self-check run, and the READY FOR USE image displayed. She quickly reviewed the process she needed to follow, as this was really three instruments combined. She followed her references carefully to prepare the samples, then drew up some of the resulting liquid from a test tube into a syringe and injected it into the primary port. The first part of the analyzer, a gas chromatograph, vaporized the liquid and separated the mixture into its component compounds by how long it took each compound to transit the column. Each of the compounds that came through the column was then analyzed in a mass spectrometer and a nuclear magnetic resonance spectrometer to determine their structures and identify them. If Fernando had been using meth that night, the compound and some of its metabolites would still be in his body. The instrument would pick them out.

She waited for the results to come up on the output screen. When they did, she scowled. Nothing there. At least nothing in the sample said Fernando had taken meth. Maybe she had made a mistake. She did all the work again, checking each step. Still nothing.

With an oath, she shut the instrument down and the screen blanked so that she did not need to look at it anymore. Almost a whole day gone, and she was no further than she had been the day before in solving the puzzle of Fernando. It also left the question of who was using the products of Sonia's chemistry projects. Reality ought to have better control of this, but obviously, she did not. The town needed a detective. When they'd had the trouble at the start of the colony all those years ago, Leif had been a pretty piss-poor detective, but he had tried. Now? Calling Cam and Jess was useless. Another question for the Demos? Maybe. None of that helped her right now.

MIROSLAV

IT WAS LATE BEFORE MIROSLAV CALLED IT QUITS FOR HIS WORK ON THE ROVER. HE WAS not finished, far from it, but he was not going to continue and short-change himself on sleep even more. The conversations with Hiep and Reality from two days ago still rankled. Especially what Reality had said about Danko. He shut down his instruments and put his tools away, but he did not head for his own hab. He did not have a partner currently, so there was no need to account to anyone for his comings and goings. There was a student he wanted to talk to before he went home.

During the dark term, which ran from the fall equinox on September 35 to the spring equinox on March 35, children attended residence school, which meant they lived with other students and not with their families, although most of them did not physically live in the school building. The students were divided by cohorts based on their age at the beginning of the term. The lowest juniors, ages eight and nine, did live in dormitory rooms in the school building. The rest of the juniors, those ten through twelve years old, lived four or six to a hab as assigned by the school, which meant by Reality Busby. In addition to—theoretically—ensuring greater concentration on schoolwork during that time of year, they were less likely to be needed for work in the town or on farms. It was also an opportunity to improve their socialization and social networks, since young children in the valley might rarely see another child their age, either there or from the town. This was becoming a particular concern as the Originals aged and produced fewer children each year, and it would remain a concern until the older cohorts of Heaven-born had school-age children of their own.

Senior students, in the age cohorts from thirteen to seventeen, were allowed to have a hab with only a single habmate. The pairings for the high-seniors, those in the sixteen- and seventeen-year-old cohorts, were of their own choosing, the only requirement being the same biological sex. Miroslav ran through in his mind what he knew of Kojo Owusu, Danko's habmate. It wasn't much. He had no shared personal experiences he could use to lubricate a conversation.

The hab door opened at his touch. It still surprised Miroslav after two decades how unlocked Saint Peterstown was. The only locked doors in the original town were in the school building itself and the old nuclear reactor that had been disabled and no longer provided power. Hab doors were not designed to lock. They were intended to be the interior door of an air lock, an assembly that could be fitted to the front of the hab unit so that the same living quarters could be used under inhospitable conditions. Heaven was habitable by humans, so the air locks had been left out of the construction, but manufacturing standardization meant that the front doors had no locks. Some people wanted locks, and it was possible to print them and add them to the doors, but the printers were always busy, so personal locks waited in line until the people running the printers decided to do one or two. It was not as though you could simply buy a lock and hire a locksmith to install it.

Miroslav called out a greeting as he walked into the darkened front room. He was gratified that there was no smell of cannabis in the air. The students were forbidden pot and alcohol in their rooms. Miroslav and probably every other adult knew that the kids used both, but he found it a comfort that they obeyed the rules in their habs. A foolish and meaningless comfort, he knew, but he would take what comfort he could from rules in a world they barely understood.

A light switched on in the back unit of the hab, where the personal and sleeping quarters were located. Shortly thereafter, a yawning Kojo Owusu stepped into the front room, barefoot and in pajamas. When he saw Miroslav, his eyes widened and he covered the yawn.

"Mr. Petrovic. Is something wrong?"

"Many things are wrong. Danko not being back is only one of them." Miroslav told himself that was not the friendliest way to start the conversation, but it fit the mood he was in.

Miroslav had not asked a question, but Kojo said, "No, he's not," anyway. "He could have contacted you."

"I know." Miroslav rubbed at the knuckles of one hand. "What I want to know is if you know anything about the night Fernando died and Thorny disappeared." His eyes narrowed as he scrutinized Kojo. Danko had roomed with Kojo the year before, but Miroslav did not think the two were friends. Kojo was sensitive about his need to use his mother's last name. It had become accepted to think that if a boy did that—and vice versa for a girl—they were from a storage tank embryo or did not identify as cishet. Either of those exposed a child to teasing or worse. Danko, good boy that he was, would not do that, which made him a comfortable habmate for Kojo. This went both ways. Danko was not much of a socializer, and even though Kojo ran around with Dalton's group, he left Danko alone. That suited Danko and Miroslav. "Danko was the one who found Vargas," he added. "Do you know why he went out there?"

"Dani said Regan called him and said she was worried about Thorny."

"That much I know. Do you know what Thorny was up to? Was something going on with her and Vargas, or any of his friends? I know you hang around with them. You know Danko is out looking for Thorny, don't you?"

Kojo looked uneasy. "I didn't know for sure, but I'm not surprised."

Miroslav decided to say nothing more and wait. The silence drew out a little longer before Kojo cleared his throat and started to talk again.

"Look, Mr. Petrovic, nobody knows what goes on in Thorny's head. She keeps to herself most of the time, except every now and again she suddenly wants to be part of things, as though she's been everybody's friend forever. And then you say one word wrong, you don't even know it's wrong, and she's at critical mass in a second. Runs off by herself. Then she comes back like nothing ever happened. Or her father brings her back and she still acts like nothing ever happened."

"I wasn't asking for a psych profile of Thorny Panagiotidis. I was asking if something happened the night Vargas died that would make her run and would have my son chasing after her."

"No. Nothing happened with Thorny. Not that I know anyway. And Dani . . . look, you know Dani has a . . . thing about that girl. He's had that for years. I have no idea why. I think he's a nice guy, a good habmate. Nothing like her. But somehow, he thinks she's this gorgeous, fantastic person and he'll talk about how he's going to get her to notice him and what he'll say to her when she does. I'm not saying Dani talks like this all the time, or even often," Kojo added with haste, "but he has more than once." Kojo shook his head. "I've told him to just do it and get it out of his system, but that doesn't happen. If he does catch up to her, she'll probably curse him out and tell him to get lost."

Miroslav decided he did not want a dissertation on his son's infatuation. Certainly not from another seventeen-year-old. "I'm aware of Danko's interest in this girl. That's not the point." Well, that might be the reason he was asking questions, but Miroslav was not going to discuss that either. "Do you know Vo Hiep?"

"Thorny's father," Kojo answered. "I know who he is. Everyone does."

"Yeah." Miroslav shoved his hands into his pockets, suddenly uncomfortable. He did not want to go too far into what was happening, but if there was any chance of learning more about Danko he would take it. "He spoke to me on the twenty-fifth about Thorny being gone, the day after all of this happened. The man was concerned. I have known Vo Hiep for twenty years, almost from the day I landed on this planet. You could stand this man up against a wall and tell him he was going to be executed in five minutes and I don't think he would show you any greater concern than if you told him he would have to stand in the rain. I can't count the number of times Thorny has run and Hiep had to get her and he never looked any different than he ever does.

"But I am telling you, he was concerned when he spoke to me. He wants a rover put back in service so he can search, and he has been working on it with me. That tells me he thinks something happened, something out of the usual, and something not good. And it will be about Thorny, because Hiep wouldn't give a shit about anyone on this planet except Penny and their kids. Now, are you *sure* you don't know about anything odd that went on that night?"

"I don't. I'd tell you if I did."

Miroslav spent a minute taking in Kojo's stance, his face, how he held his hands. Kojo's denials had been too quick, almost sounded practiced. He tried to tell himself that he was reading too much into all of that. "I don't know that I believe you, but I think I'll have to leave it at that for tonight. Just one thing. If something *did* happen, you'll want to be telling people before Hiep finds out on his own. And trust me, that man will find out."

KOJO

HIS HAND WAS POISED OVER THE TOUCH PLATE TO THE DOOR OF IBIANA'S HAB. KOJO hesitated. He was not sure he wanted to go through with this. No. He was quite sure he did *not* want to do this. He was too old at seventeen to be running to his mother with his problems. However, this was a problem where he needed to speak to her, needed to have her advice. To do or not to do; both directives had warred in his mind all the way up the street. Had anyone seen where he was going, it would have been enough to dissuade him, but Dani had not returned, it was pitch-dark, and none of the other students were about. No witnesses had seen him come to this hab.

With more of a convulsive jerk than a controlled movement, his hand hit the touch plate. The door slid open. Kojo stepped through the doorway to find Ibiana and Vanessa Huggins seated at a table in the front room, steaming cups of tea in front of them. Surprise lit up both of their faces.

"Kojo, is something wrong?" Ibiana asked. "Usually you call first, and this is late."

"No . . . ah . . . yes, dammit!" The conversation was off to a bad start. Kojo gnashed his teeth. "I need to talk to you."

"Okay. We're here to listen," Ibiana said. "What's the problem and how can we help?"

That was, in fact, part of the problem, part of why he had hesitated at the door. From the time he had understood about families, he did not want to play the mom-one, mom-two tag team that Ibiana and Vanessa used with their children. Kojo had nothing against a two-mom family. He knew he had a father—unlike Ibiana's other two, who had come out of the embryo bank—but the man's identity, beyond being white, had remained a mystery. That was why he had to use his mother's last name. It was a minor blessing that no one in his group of friends had made an issue of it. Vanessa's four all came from different men, but they all knew who their fathers were, and the one boy used his father's last name.

Still, the family dynamics were not the cause of his unease around Vanessa. He had never felt comfortable with her, never trusted her, which was why he thought of Ibiana alone as his mother. He had never understood why, in a world where partners came and went on what seemed like a daily basis, Ibiana had stayed committed to Vanessa for all those years. Vanessa was a curvy strawberry blonde who was the opposite of his bio-mom in almost every way. What did his mother see in that woman?

No matter. He was far too committed now to do anything but

go forward. He could hardly tell Vanessa to leave. "It's about what happened the other night. To Ferdy."

Both women sat up straight.

Kojo licked his lips. "First, I need to ask you about Vo Hiep. I know all the talk, but you knew him from before, from Earth before you left. He's a killer. For real. Is that right?"

"Hiep was one of the Sicarii," Ibiana said in a measured voice. "He was a member of the Sicarius Free Company, mercenaries who specialized in assassination. Before that, he was a soldier in the Dragon Free Company. Yes, he has killed people. What does Hiep have to do with Fernando Vargas? He was not in town the night Fernando died."

"It has to do with Thorny." Kojo wanted to stop, to take it all back, but he could not. He had to finish it. "Look, that night, Thorny was out there, was kissing Ferdy, going hard. Maybe Ferdy thought there was more . . . you know . . . She started it! She hit him and he went down."

"Wait a minute." Ibiana put her hand up. "We all heard that no one else was out there that night. No one saw what happened. That's what you said, what everyone said. Now you're telling me Thorny was with him and somebody else saw them. Was it you?"

"Yes, I was there! Our whole group was there! That's the truth! That's where we go to have a smoke and drink, and I've never hidden that from you. But . . . Thorny was there too. She's not part of our group—who would have her?—and *she* started in with Ferdy and then *she* hit him and he went down."

Ibiana locked eyes with Vanessa for an instant before she spoke again. "Fernando is . . . was a strong young man. A big young man. Are you telling me that little Thorny Panagiotidis hit him once and killed him? What did she hit him with?"

"Her hand . . . fist, I guess. That's what she hit him with, Mom!" Kojo felt himself starting to sweat. He wanted to appear cool and collected but was afraid he was starting to look anything but that. "You live in town; you never leave town. You don't know this girl. Everybody says Hiep started training her when she was five. You know how Koch has been making concrete? He made some blocks, an inch and a half thick, weighing about seventeen pounds each. Summer before this past one, Davis set up two of them in a stack on top of supports, with little spacers between the blocks. Thorny smashed her hand through both of them. One of the guys who lives in the valley got a vid of it."

"Okay, okay." Ibiana made a downward motion with both hands, as if that would lower the rising pitch in Kojo's voice. "Let's say she knocked him down. What did all of you do?"

"Nothing! I mean, we thought maybe she knocked him out. She was screaming that she was going to leave forever, and we should all die, and she would like to kill all of us. We thought somebody might hear, she was so goddamn loud. And then she ran, so we all got out of there. Figured Ferdy would come to, come back to his hab. We never thought . . . not until Dani was out there and called."

"So, nobody checked Fernando and you all left. How long between then and when Dani was out there?"

"I don't know exactly. A couple of hours, I guess." Kojo could tell how bad all of this sounded from the way his mother was looking at him. Even Vanessa looked shocked.

"A couple of hours," Ibiana repeated. "Nobody tried to call him? He didn't call any of you?"

"No. I mean, I don't know. I mean, when Watanabe came out, Ferdy's phone wasn't there." Kojo told himself that maybe Dalton was right, that it was better to say nothing than to be careful what you said, but it was already too late for that.

Ibiana shook her head. "This is a mess. Why the story that nobody was there?"

"Dalton said that was the best way." Kojo found his words coming faster and faster, as though if he didn't say them quickly he would not be able to say them at all. "Dalton said that even if Thorny came back, she wouldn't say anything because she's the one who hit him, and she's not stupid enough to say anything when nobody else is. I mean, she's a fucking mess and nobody wants anything to do with her, but she's not stupid. So, Dalton said that would be the end of it."

"Why not say what happened?" Ibiana asked. "You said she is the one who hit Fernando, and it's not like you or anyone in your group cares about her."

"Mom, there are . . . other . . . reasons." Kojo could feel the heat in his face. "Can we leave it at what happened? Just what happened."

"We can." Now Ibiana's tone went stern. "Then why did you come here now and tell me this? What do you want me to do?"

"It's because of Vo Hiep. Mr. Petrovic, Dani's father, came to talk to me. Said Hiep is worried about Thorny and may go to search for Thorny and for Dani because neither of them are back yet. What do I do if Hiep comes to me? What if someone else tells him something?"

"I'd say that's something you should have thought of first. Not just now." Ibiana stood up, then walked across the room and back, hands clasped behind her neck. "If Hiep starts asking you, I'd say tell him what happened—because if he's asking you, he'll be asking others, and someone will slip. Count on that. I wouldn't go to him first, because maybe it won't come to that, but if he's asking, yes. And between now and then, you think of a good way to tell the story. And for goddamn sure don't tell him what you think of his daughter."

Kojo was saying, "Yes, yes, I'll do that," as he was nodding his head and backing out the door.

IBIANA

WITH KOJO GONE, IBIANA BEGAN PACING BACK AND FORTH IN THE ROOM, HER hands clasped at her chest and her head bowed head in a position that suggested prayer. "This is a huge problem," she said on her second trip across the floor.

"Because of what happened, or because our son is in the middle of it?" Vanessa asked.

"Kojo was a bystander. That's all that matters about Kojo. He'll be fine long as he can keep his mouth shut; that's all that matters about Kojo." She broke her hands apart and then pounded them back together. "The problem is that we need Penny to be mayor again, and I'd asked Hiep to talk to her about doing it because I know damned well she doesn't want to do it. The one thing that you can get townies and valley-folk to agree on is that they don't like Penny, and Penny is tired of it."

What started as a giggle from Vanessa ended as a full-blown laugh. "Putting up a candidate everyone hates is not a recipe for winning an election. That's not your style, Ibi."

Ibiana answered with a scowl. "When they're scared we're all going to die, they yell for Penny because she'll figure out a way to save us whether anybody likes her ideas or not. Once their asses have been saved, they vote her out. This time, they don't realize their asses need saving, but I do and Sonal agrees with me, and we don't have time to wait. That's why I need Hiep." She let out a great sigh. "Most men have whatever brains they possess in their prick. They fight and they kill from lust, whether it's about women, money, or power."

Vanessa leaned back with a faint smile. "Tell me something new, Ibi."

"Hiep is not most men. Sicarius had a code. Hiep operates on that code. Malachi and the other free company people found that out and died."

"It was the starship pilot that killed most of them," Vanessa pointed out.

"Hiep killed the others" was Ibiana's response, "and he would have killed them all if Yang hadn't gotten some of them. Now Hiep is going to be focused on Thorny, and if he does hear about what Kojo said, he will follow his code and protect Thorny and be no help at all to us."

"Do we really have such a crisis?" Vanessa picked up her tea, took a sip, and realized it had cooled completely. She made a face and put it back down. "Jacoby Grubb isn't great, but it's not like he's the worst thing around. And Penny . . . is Penny. Hard to take."

"Jacoby wants out. And Ajit wants in, if you're thinking about what could be worse. Ajit wants to take care of Ajit. That's all he ever cared about. And we need Penny. Give me a minute or two to think." Ibiana walked around the front room and the kitchen area, scrutinizing every inch. The rooms were on the spartan side, like all habs, but they were precisely organized, each piece of furniture, every object, exactly where it should be. It was not, however, immaculate to the standard

Ibiana wanted. She swept a finger across the top of a cabinet and looked at the result with disapproval, a microcosm of all the pieces of Saint Peterstown that were failing embodied in that streak in the dust.

"Our air filtration system needs to be checked and cleaned." Ibiana brushed the dust off with her other hand. "I will need to find a way to get someone to do it, but even when it comes up on the work priority list, there is no telling if or how well the work will be done. There is no downside for poor work or no work. Food is apportioned in equal shares, same for clothing, same for whatever other needs may be, with a randomly generated priority list when there isn't enough to go around. Sometimes I feel like I've fallen into Eugen Richter's nightmare."

"Who?"

"Eugen Richter. Wrote *Pictures of Our Socialist Future* in 1868, possibly the first Marxist dystopian novel." Ibiana almost smiled. "I always find it surprising, Nessie, that I know more European history than you do."

Vanessa did smile. "That's because you, dear Ibi, were a swindler, and your cons went better if you could appear a sophisticated member of the intelligentsia. I simply had to manage my boys and girls so that the movers and shakers could move and shake in entertaining ways. That worked very well, thank you very much."

"It all worked well," Ibiana said, "until it didn't." Saying that reminded her of meeting Nessie for the first time when they were both in jail and finding common ground in how many of their family members, along with bunches of other people, wanted to see them dead. That had led to companionship and the decision that taking the starflight together was an attractive alternative to what they faced on Earth. They were not very different, in that respect, from the rest of the Originals on the *Daredevil*, with the exception of the ones from free companies. And Hiep was the only one of those left.

Thinking about Vanessa brought her mind back to the way material things were parceled out. Her partner was wearing a bright red and black top over pants of black slashed with red. The fabric was, without question, that shimmery filament that Klaus Koch had started to produce from bamboo. Vanessa always had nice clothes, ever since they had been able to make them, and they were always well-fitted to her full figure. The possibility that they had come through the usual equal share system was near zero.

No, it was zero. Vanessa always had a way, always had an angle, and those angles usually ended up with material items. Of course, Ibiana had played plenty of her own games in the past on Earth, but for her, it had been a craving for the thrill of making the scheme work almost as much as the money in a bank account. On Heaven, she had been abstinent; Nessie had not.

"We need to fix our system," Ibiana said. "I hear Penny has been able to cultivate coffee trees. Maybe she can put this place on the coffee standard, and we can use that for money."

"Is that what you expect Penny to do? Create money out of coffee?"

"It would be a new take on the tragedy of drinking through your money." This time Ibiana did smile, but it did not lead to a laugh or touch her eyes. "Money that is actually worth something is part of what we need. Right now, it's only equal shares, which the computer decides, or personal markers. That won't do it. I can send a marker to your chip, or to a phone if it's to a Heaven-born, or even write it down, but the point is it's a *personal* marker. I'll pledge you an egg out of my equal share or I'll do you some service, but what's worth an egg to one person isn't to someone else, and it's only my obligation."

"Between that and straight barter, it works okay." Vanessa made a point of plucking at the fabric of her shirt.

"What it works for is gambling and some trade, and never mind your shirt." Ibiana knew the argument would go nowhere, but they would have it anyway. "Too much of what we have is starting to wear out. Too many problems aren't being solved. If people don't see a reward for tackling tough problems, they won't do it. Slackers don't save your ass. Penny is the only one with the smarts to come up with a solution and the stubbornness to shake everyone up and keep shaking them until they agree to it." Even after all their years together, she was not sure how to explain that to her partner.

"If she does take it on, Ibi, don't be surprised if you don't like what she invents. In fact, you probably won't."

"I'll take that risk, Nessie."

"And what are you going to do if Hiep won't take the role of being the persuader?"

Ibiana straightened up. She dusted off her hands against each other again, although they did not need it. "I'll speak to her myself. Take a trip to Happy Valley if I need to. I used to be very good at talking people into things."

THE FUNERAL OF FERNANDO VARGAS WAS A SOMBER AFFAIR THAT BROUGHT NO closure. It was held at midday, after the morning arrival on horseback of Guillermo Vargas and Donna Billingsly from the highway way station. Usable wood being in short supply in the vicinity of the town, the printer facility created a coffin from plastic feedstock. The only rover in Saint Peterstown was the one Miroslav was still working on, so the coffin was placed on one of the old construction bots for transport to the cemetery.

The graveyard was east of town, out in the direction of the landing zone the spaceplanes had used and near where the fighting took place twenty years before. The bot with the coffin could not move much faster than the walking pace of a human, so those who were going to attend—essentially the entire population of Saint Peterstown over the age of eight excepting Gordon and Poppy, who stayed back to mind the young children—trooped along with the bot. On the way, they passed the old WELCOME TO ST. PETERSTOWN billboard sign the Originals from the *Daredevil* had put together from packing materials. The paint had been bleached by the sun and had now faded to the point that in another few years it might no longer be legible. That might not matter, because one of the stanchions supporting the sign had cracked, dropping one end of the sign to the ground. From the way the sign now rattled in the day's light breeze, the next storm might knock it flat. From the stares and mutters as the people walked past it, the symbolism was not lost on the walkers.

The burial ground was a lonely place under the silent, empty sky. No church building mounted a watch for the souls of the departed. No fence encircled it, and there was no sign to announce its presence. It was differentiated from the surrounding plain only by the markers that stuck up from the dirt. White plastic, with names and dates etched in black ink, they told a story of their own. Grouped together and away from the other three were the graves of five free company men and women, along with one of the Pioneer Youth. They had tried to subjugate the settlement and had been killed in the fighting.

Reality was the only one who walked over to those markers. She spared only a brief glance for the one of Malachi Oates, the man who had seen himself as dictator. The grave she stood over for a while was that of Bjorn Gudmundsson who, like her, had been a cohort leader in the Pioneer Youth.

There but for the grace of God, she thought. Too many memories she could not forget, even if the others would allow her to do so. The message she had received this morning before the procession out to the graveyard ran through her mind: "Hey, Busby, lose any more kids today?" That had come from one of the townies who did not usually bring up the past with her. It showed what everyone really thought, even those who were polite on the surface. Reality shook her head and rejoined the crowd, now arrayed around the open grave dug by bots in the early-morning hours.

Saint Peterstown did not have any religious functionaries. Its people did not profess any religion beyond the occasional reference to God in heaven, which had become a joke on a world named Heaven. A burial, however, pried their thoughts away from their immediate concerns and pleasures. It forced them to confront the brutal fact that they now had one less human on a world that barely tolerated them, that they had one less person between them and the awful finality of extinction. One less for sure, and it also made them think of two more who were missing.

They bowed their heads while Jacoby Grubb pulled up a suitable prayer from the database and read it off his projection field. Then they prayed, silently or in murmurs, to a God they did not really believe in that no one else would die before a ripe old age, that no one else would die without leaving at least two to replace them. During those prayers, the bots filled in the grave.

After that brief service, many stopped by Guillermo and Donna to say a word of sympathy. Guillermo was a big, bluff man with a full beard and a robust mustache. He wore a short-sleeved cotton shirt with cotton pants dyed blue to match Donna's dress, also of cotton. The clothing befitted the family that supplied the largest amount of cotton to the settlement; it was also an announcement of sorts that they paid attention to having their own share of what they produced. He kept one hand on Donna's shoulder and maintained a stoic pose through the condolences, but when he spotted Jing, he broke away from the group clustered around the two of them.

"Dr. Song, can we speak for a minute?" His voice was loud amid the subdued tones others were using.

"Of course, Guillermo." Jing stepped close to him. "I'm sorry for Fernando, for you and your family."

"Thank you. But tell me. Do you still not know what happened? Why he . . . died? Fernando was young; he was strong. People like him do not simply . . . stop."

"No, they do not." It was clear from Jing's body language that she wanted a better answer to that question, or at the very least an explanation, but she had nothing but the uncomfortable truth. "Unfortunately, the only answer I can give you is that I do not know why. There are some bruises from how he landed on the ground, but nothing that would be serious, and nothing to suggest why he fell. Everything I have checked has come back negative.

"Plenty of the flora on Heaven is poisonous to us, but I have tested for the toxins we know, and I do not find any. It was definitely not thistle. It still could have been an allergic reaction to something, even though my testing so far is negative. I will say, at the risk of sounding distasteful, that the brain is not ready for examination yet. That may tell us something. For now, I am sorry to say, it remains a mystery."

"That is not very helpful, Doctor." Guillermo could not keep the frustration out of his voice even if his words remained mild.

"No, I understand that it is not. I do understand your frustration and your anger. You have a right to both." Jing brought her hands together in front of her. "I do have other samples remaining at the clinic. As we test more plants and creatures over time, if we find a new toxin, I will check those samples. I do have to say, though"—and her face turned down to the ground—"that the native biodiversity on these plains is very low. I can't say that we will find something new."

Guillermo straightened himself, which, at six feet tall, put him nearly a foot above Jing. "I should thank you for your efforts. I did not mean to be rude."

·   ·   ·

From where she was standing, Reality could hear the conversation between Dr. Song and Guillermo. She watched the doctor shake Guillermo's hand and step away. Vanessa Huggins was nearby as well, shifting her weight from one foot to the other as though debating whether to approach Guillermo. Reality decided that if she waited for Huggins to make up her mind, she would lose her own nerve. This would be an unpleasant business, but she had to do it. She stepped in close to Guillermo.

"I am so sorry. Fernando was a wonderful young man." Reality was not sure that Fernando was all that wonderful, but she reminded herself of her mother's instruction never to speak ill of the dead.

The conversation, the entire situation, was surreal. She remembered meeting Guillermo at the first gathering of the Pioneer Youth volunteers for the *Dauntless*, both of them twenty-three and thinking only of the positives their futures would bring. She remembered him taking the seat next to her on the Miles Richmond Space Elevator when they went up to the starship. She had thought then that he was interested. It had not worked out that way.

Guillermo's eyes went cold as they focused on her. "I doubt you are sorry enough," he said. "I hold you responsible for this."

For all she had worried over exactly this point, the verbal assault caught Reality unprepared. Had she and Guillermo ever been two kids themselves in a youth group? She fumbled for words. "We don't know what happened. I don't see . . . how you can say that."

Guillermo folded his arms across his chest, a position that emphasized how large his arms and hands were. "I can say that because you do not know what happened. Just as you said. You do not supervise these children closely enough. You do not really know what they do. You do not maintain discipline well enough. If my son is dead because of something somebody did, I will find them and hang them from the roof supports of the Community Dome. You would not do that. You are not good enough at what you do. Are those enough reasons for what I said?"

Each statement was a stab into Reality. It was a wonder, she thought, that they did not leave her bleeding. *You are not good enough.* The same accusation she leveled at herself time and again. It pulled the breath out of her chest. It was all she could do to whisper, "I am sorry." A gust of wind blew her words away.

It was a prayer answered when Vanessa Huggins chose that moment to step between them. "I heard you speaking to Dr. Song before," she said to Guillermo. "There is something I think you should hear."

Reality gave a sigh of relief as Vanessa looped one arm around Guillermo's and drew him away.

Miroslav

Miroslav watched the scene between Guillermo and Reality play out. He was close enough to hear the words that were spoken—that is, he was close enough to hear Guillermo. It was enough to bring a smirk to his lips. When Huggins captured Guillermo's attention, he turned away.

Whatever came next was not of interest to him. With that turn, he found Hiep standing close. Hiep's eyes were on him.

"She does not deserve this," Hiep said.

Miroslav rapidly brought his face to a neutral expression. It was impossible to tell if Hiep was commenting only on what Guillermo had said or whether it included Miroslav's satisfaction. Miroslav had no intention of placing himself on the opposite side of any position Hiep took. Hiep's voice might have a soft, almost disinterested tone, but Miroslav knew better than to ascribe any meaning to that.

"I'm surprised to hear you defending Reality." That was about as far as Miroslav would go in questioning anything Hiep said, but he was, in fact, surprised.

"I do not think any of us do our jobs so well that we cannot be criticized, and it is hard to control, at all times, the actions of any person without the apparatus of a security state. I was coming over to see you, however. I have already extended my sympathies to Vargas."

And I will bet Guillermo had no sharp rejoinder for Hiep. Miroslav fought to dismiss that thought. There was no reason Guillermo would have criticized Hiep. "I assume you want to ask about the status of the rover."

"Yes. Can it be ready tomorrow?"

Miroslav considered that, having seen Hiep work with him on the machine over the past days, Hiep probably had the answer already in his mind and was only being polite. "It will be operable tomorrow morning, on the assumption that I can get away from this and finish the work I have to do that is my actual job." Miroslav struggled to keep any acid out of his voice. Thorny might have created this problem, but Danko had definitely contributed to it, and he wanted Danko back. "You have to understand, though, that when I say operable, that means you can drive the vehicle over rough terrain as you normally would, and the battery will recharge through the photovoltaic system and hold a charge about as long as you would expect. Not like new, of course, but no worse than the others we still have. What it does not have, as you have seen, are most of the standard supplies. The inflatable boat was sent to the valley to replace one that was damaged. We pulled out the usual weapons and emergency supplies when we decommissioned it."

"I will supply my own weapons and food. I do not need a boat."

"Okay. But you need to know about communications. I pulled out most of the base station assembly in order to repair one of the other rovers. You have seen what I've been able to do with this one. The jury-rigged system will let you connect to the network as long as you can pick up Saint Peterstown, but you are not going to be able to use the voice channels from the rover independently."

"I agree with your assessment," Hiep said. "I am not criticizing your work. I could not do better."

Yes, Hiep could be very polite when he wanted to be. "Sometimes I think we would do better with old-fashioned radios, but we don't have them."

"The people who made the plans for what we have are not here. They thought, I am sure, no further than that our phones interface with our chips and network, so why would we want any different communication devices?" Hiep's lips twisted up in a hint of a smile. "You are correct that radios would have advantages here, but it is not worth wishing for what we cannot have."

Miroslav worried that the slight reproach he heard in Hiep's last sentence was more meaningful than the smile. "I've talked to Jorge, who is still in the valley, and he says they can free up one of the other rovers to come here in two more days. It might be safer waiting for that." Those were not words Miroslav wanted to say, not with Danko away and out of touch. But he wanted Hiep to bring Danko back, and the odds of that would be better with a fully equipped rover as opposed to one that lacked the rover base station and could not reach out to a phone.

"No" was Hiep's answer. "I have already misjudged the situation and that error may be serious. I will not let any more time pass than is necessary. Let's say that at eight a.m. I will pick up the rover."

"You are driving out tomorrow to search for Thorny and Dani?" The question came from Reality. Miroslav had been so focused on Hiep that he had not realized she had stayed nearby. It was not surprising that she had seen the two of them together and, given that their children were involved, was butting into the conversation. Not after her mess with Guillermo.

After Hiep confirmed his plan, Reality said, "I'm going with you."

Hiep's eyebrows went up, probably the closest to an expression of surprise Miroslav had ever seen on the man's face. "That is not a good idea. I am skilled in tracking and skilled in surviving under adverse conditions in unfamiliar territory. You are neither."

"I've survived on this damn planet as long as you have!" The heat in Reality's voice was obvious. "That's for damn sure adverse conditions."

"Not the same thing," Hiep said. "I would prefer to work alone."

"Your preference doesn't count. Thorny and Dani are my responsibility. Tiffany, Gordon, and Poppy are capable of covering the school in my absence. I realize that Gordon and Poppy are only a couple of years older than the high-seniors, but the generation gap is what it is and they need to learn to take over. I cannot shirk my responsibilities."

"Ah." Silence followed, as if Hiep was considering her statements in light of his earlier words. "You make a valid point. Please consider tonight that I do not know how far they have gone and that this will involve risk to us. If you still wish to come, bring weapons, food, and spare clothing. Meet me at the rover park at eight a.m."

"There is nothing to consider. I will be there."

Miroslav was glad that Reality's final words were enough to have both of them take their leaves and go their separate ways. He would be happier going back to town and doing double work than spending any more of his day with the two of them together.

THORNY

THORNY AWOKE IN DARKNESS TO MATCH HER MOOD. THROUGH THE WINDSHIELD OF the rover, she could tell the sky was still clouded over, for no stars were shining. The only light came from two bright splotches where the clouds could not completely hide two of the moons.

Suddenly the image was disorienting. Her mind spun, searching for an anchor. Where was she? It took the feel of the seat under her and the steering wheel when she pushed against it to ground her. Yes, she was in the rover; in the rover and in the middle of nowhere. She had driven a long way since she had crossed the Happy River. The rover could tell her how many miles she had covered. It could tell her, based on her south-by-southwest course, exactly how far south she had come. She stopped her finger before it tapped the screen. It did not matter. Not really. She was nowhere.

Nowhere. The word burned in her mind. Nowhere and nobody.

She leaned back in her seat while her mind ran through the miserable compilation of days that constituted her life. She felt hollow. Her stomach had become a huge pit, and all the worthless pieces that Thorny comprised were falling into it. Big problems weighed on her: What had happened that night with Ferdy. That she had no friends. Little problems bothered her almost as much. That her hair fell straight like her father's except when it was wet, when it would curl—thank you, Mom—just enough to be a problem keeping it in place without being curly enough to be pretty. She had used scissors to cut her own bangs but did not manage to make them even, and now they had grown out enough to fall partway over her eyes so that she had to pull them to the sides anyway. Too many problems. Too much weight. It would be a relief never to wake up again.

She opened the console between the front seats. By feel, she drew out the bowie knife that was sheathed there. She let the blade rest against the skin of her left wrist. She needed only to work up her courage. But not yet.

She had said that she would go south to total darkness, to be the first to reach polar night on Heaven. She did want to do that. It would be an accomplishment, one they could not take away from her or belittle.

She did not have that far to go. Between the waning of the year toward the solstice and the distance she had already driven, the sun was above the horizon for only a few hours each day. The daylight had already diminished to the point that it was not nearly compensating for the amount of electricity the rover was using. The battery was draining. She ought to be able to calculate how long she would be able to drive, but that felt like too much of a bother. When the battery ran out, that would be as far as she could go. Total darkness or a dead battery. Both were good metaphors for how she would end.

No use wasting time getting where I'm going. She switched on the rover. Caught in the glare of the headlights, a huge monster opened its jaws wide.

Thorny jerked upright in her seat, her heart hammering and her breath coming in short gasps. Focus! The creature was not the size of a three-story building. That maw, full of teeth, could not swallow a rover whole. It was squat, in fact, less than half the height of the front end of the rover as it stood on legs reminiscent of a dog's. Its body was ten feet long, covered in knobby plates out to its tail. The head was pure evil, leathery skin tapering to a needle-tipped beak, with two horns projecting from above blinking rows that could be eyes. The gaping mouth showed off two rows of razor-edged teeth before it snapped shut.

Thorny brought her breathing under control. This thing had to be a variant of the river gators they had in Happy Valley. The rover was not near a river. Was this a gator that hunted on land, a land gator? She had seen plenty of shellhounds on the way; the gator probably feasted on them. What had brought it to the rover? More importantly, could that beak tear through the rover's sheathing? In her fear, Thorny realized that she did not welcome being torn apart by the land gator.

The beak opened wide again, this time displaying four writhing, snakelike tongues that thrust into the air. The gator belched out a sound like a foghorn. Unthinking reflex made Thorny stamp down on the accelerator. The rover lurched forward, its front end banging against the gator's beak.

Thorny hit the brake the instant she realized what she had done, but the gator scuttled backward a few feet and it gave out another roar. Its tail wagged side to side. *Try that again,* Thorny thought. She pushed down hard on the accelerator.

Bang! The rover slammed into the gator with enough force to dent the vehicle's sheathing. The gator backed up again, one horn snapped off halfway down its length. The tail lashed the ground on either side. Then, with a sudden jerk, the gator turned and vanished into the darkness in search of easier prey.

"Oh my God, Rover, oh my God!" Thorny hunched forward in the driver's seat, as if doing that would let her see farther into the dark. There was no sign of the gator. She needed to check the rover for damage, but she was not leaving the cab. Not then. Not there. The readouts on the dash said the rover was operational.

"Okay, Rover, okay. We've got places to go and things to do. Let's go do them."

·   ·   ·

THORNY DROVE STEADILY THROUGH THE DAY. HER COURSE REMAINED SOUTH BY southwest, but that was less by intent than because that direction was the path of least resistance across the terrain. The sun came up, a glow low over the horizon behind still-solid clouds. Her path sloped down at a modest but constant grade.

To her left, to the east, the ground rose sharply into foothills and cliffs. Trees dotted those slopes, different in shape from the ones she knew from home. These rose fifteen to twenty feet in the air, taller than any trees she had seen before except in images of Earth. Turning to the east would have been difficult at best. She did not consider it.

To the west, the ground seemed to fall away as if there was a valley there that she could not see. Whitish stone, possibly limestone, even farther to the west caught the light in patches as the sun sank back to the horizon. Limestone made another Mom-lecture—number-what-ever—pop into her head. Running through limestone took the acid out of water and helped heal the land from the effects of the acid rain. Maybe that was why she had seen dark green in this direction before. Maybe she would find out. The indicator for the rover's battery sank along with the sun. She continued to drive.

Overhead, the clouds began to break after sunset, allowing the moonlight to give her some idea of her surroundings beyond what the rover's headlight revealed. The slopes to the east crowded closer, forcing her more to the west to avoid climbing into them and being caught among the trees there. The audio pickups of the rover transmitted the sound of running water again, although neither her eyes nor the rover's screens showed evidence of a river.

Quite rapidly, the grade she was on steepened. The rover tipped a little to its right as the land sloped not only down but to the west. The gradient was within the capability of both the rover and its driver, so she continued down because the only alternative was to go back. There! Off to the right was water. She was sure of it. The white crests of rapids slapped against rocks. Beyond, farther to the west, the light of the moons through breaks in the clouds shone off white rock and spoke of cliffs hemming in the water there.

As the rover finished its descent, the ground leveled off and the land she drove across was now little above the water level in the river. Her headlights picked out a rising cliff in front of her. She was forced to take the rover still closer to the river.

The riverbank, the space available for the rover to drive, narrowed. Rock wall to her left, running river to her right. That rock wall curved in front of the direction she was headed, but Thorny thought it ended in a sharp line near the river. Perhaps she could curve along with the wall, along the bank of the river, and at the end of the rock wall find an opening to the south. She gritted her teeth and wished for better visibility.

When she reached the point that she thought was the end of the rock wall, however, she realized that she had reached the entrance to a narrow canyon. The space between the canyon wall and the rushing water might have made a footpath. The rover could not drive along it, not without putting two wheels in the river. That was an invitation to having the rover flip over sideways into the water. Thorny shone a light across the river. The bank on the other side might be wider—the light did not show it clearly—but that did not matter. As she played her light on the whitecaps and the turbulence of the river, she knew there was no way the rover would be able to cross this one. The battery charge was dangerously low, down near the safety cutoff. Going back to search for another route was not going to work. This was the end of the line.

Despair rose up from her stomach to engulf her. She would die here, in this meaningless place. For all that she had thought of death, she had expected to make it to the polar night, the first person on Heaven to reach that far, so that when they found her, they would be impressed with what she had done and sad that they had driven her away. Now she would not even have that. Never was she allowed to have what she wanted.

The idea of being denied was enough to anger her, and the anger catalyzed her thinking. Anger was her friend. Her first impulse was to grab the rover's emergency pack and start hiking into the canyon, go as far as she could. That would not be very far, however. It would lead to an end as ignominious as staying in the rover.

But wait! The thought hammered through her brain: *Rovers are equipped with inflatable boats.*

She scrambled around to access the storage compartment at the back of the vehicle, all fears about what might be lurking in the dark forgotten. Was the boat in the rover, or had it been transferred to one of the others or pulled out for some other use in the valley?

It was still there in its storage compartment below the floorboards. When compressed and folded, the boat was the size of a large backpack, with snap-together paddles clipped to the side. A small electric motor could be hung from the pack and carried along with it.

Going downstream, she would not need that motor, but it was good to see that its battery pack was fully charged. *You never know what you're going to find*, she told herself. The pack was bulky for someone her size to carry on their back, but she was not going to carry it very far. Simply putting it down behind the rover put it near the edge of the dark water flowing past.

"Okay," she said in the direction of the river, "Mom got to name the Happy River. I'm naming you. You are the Lost River." She nodded with satisfaction and turned to the boat.

The boat inflated without difficulty. It was big enough for four, which meant she had plenty of room for supplies. Spear, knife, bow, and arrows went in along with a supply of poison to refresh what was currently on the blades and arrowheads. The emergency pack was next, with her remaining supply of food, vitamins, and methionine. It was not a lot of food, but she had not been very hungry so far. It would last her several days; she was sure of that. Beyond that, she could eat shellhound—assuming they lived this far south, which seemed likely—and she could test plants for edibility. The limiting factor would be the vitamins and methionine that did not exist in Heaven's biota. She was not going to count the number of pills. Whatever was there was what she had.

She dithered over the tool pack. It was bulky and awkward, and some of the tools—the ones for working on the rover—would be useless. In the end, though, she threw it in the boat. She did not want to waste time sorting out what could be left at the rover, and the boat, with only one occupant, was big enough.

When the packing was done, she climbed back into the rover and deleted the log. There was no need for anyone to listen to her conversation with the rover. Let them wonder at her thoughts. Then it was time to leave.

"I guess this is goodbye," she said to the rover. "You've been a good friend and a good listener. I don't know where I'm going, but I won't be back." She gave the rover a friendly pat on a fender and turned to the boat.

With all the gear she had tossed into it, the boat was heavy. She had to crouch low, knees almost to the ground, and shove. The boat lurched forward across the last stretch of dirt and into the water, where the current tugged it downstream. She slipped, fell forward. Her chin struck the sidewall of the boat, driving teeth into her tongue. She cursed and spat blood, all while she grabbed onto the safety cord along the sidewall to keep the river from taking the boat away from her. She stepped into the water to keep up with the boat. One foot slipped and went off an underwater ledge. She went down with a splash into cold water but kept her grip on the cord. The boat dragged her out into the river, but she was able to swing a leg over the sidewall. She tumbled into the bottom of the boat, soaked and with chattering teeth for the second time on her journey. It had been a damn good decision, she told herself, not to try to drive the rover half into the river.

Thorny pulled a handheld LED searchlight from the tool pack and played it across the canyon walls as the boat was swept downriver. It was a long hallway with walls of stone. The canyon widened not far from where she had embarked, with a broad gravel bank on her left. She could beach the boat there, but what would be the point? She put the light down in the bottom of the boat and let the current take her while she focused on squeezing water out of her clothes. Intent on that, she paid no attention when the canyon walls fell away on each side. What she did notice as she finished wringing the last drops out of the bottoms of her pants was that the light was growing. That was odd. It could not possibly be sunrise. She brought her head up to peer over the inflated prow of the boat and saw a broad river winding into dimly visible lowlands ahead. There was enough light to show that the land on both sides of the river was covered in trees, lower bushes, ferns, and reeds, all of unfamiliar types. White strands, they could not be netting—they had to be webs—hung across the low growth and from the lower branches. And those trees! Some of them went up thirty or even fifty feet. The trees and the growing light made her look up to the sky.

"Oh God!"

The clouds had cleared while she traversed the canyon and worked at her clothes. Above her now, a drapery of green and red luminescence hung across the heavens in lofty folds. Stars twinkled in the black sky and through the luminous sheets. Rivers of brilliant color flowed across the sky from horizon to horizon. Thorny sat back in the boat. She turned her face up in awe while God raised his hand to paint a vivid artwork on the heavens above her.

PART II

It was the best of times, it was the worst of times, it was the age of wisdom, it was the age of foolishness, it was the epoch of belief, it was the epoch of incredulity . . .

Charles Dickens, *A Tale of Two Cities*

DECEMBER 29, HY 21

HIEP

I T WAS A GOOD BET THAT THE ROVER WOULD BE READY WELL BEFORE EIGHT O'CLOCK. Miroslav was not going to leave anything to the last minute and risk having to confront Hiep with the job not done as promised. So it was that when Hiep arrived at five in the morning, three hours ahead of the set time, the rover was waiting for him, plugged in at one of the charger stations. It had already been plugged in long enough to have a full charge. Miroslav was nowhere to be seen.

He checked the instruments on the dash and the computer screen. The rover was functional, with the notable exception of the communication equipment. Hiep smiled, just a little smile to himself. His backpack went into the rear storage area. The sound it made when it hit the flooring of the compartment belied the ease with which he swung it.

He was ready to leave. In fact, he would have preferred to leave at that instant, without any further delay on a mission that had already waited far too long. However, Reality had been told 8:00 a.m. He did not want her along, saw no value she could bring, but he had made the agreement, so he would wait. Not a minute past the set hour, but until that time he would wait. He leaned back against the rover and let his mind replay the book he had been reading the previous evening.

At ten minutes to eight, Reality's footsteps sounded across the packed earth of the rover park before she stepped into the light of the LEDs mounted over the charging station. Tendrils of mist curled in the actinic glare of the light which also cast her facial scars into harsh prominence. She was garbed in stained and heavily worn baggy cargo pants with a shirt in the same shade of tan. A red kerchief was knotted around her neck, with the knot on the left side. Hiep watched her approach, his eyes more on the clothes than the person.

"I thought all of the Pioneer Youth uniforms had gone into the recycler years ago," he said.

"Not mine." She stopped right in front of Hiep. "The last time I wore it was the day I went to speak to Penny after that Demos meeting, when I asked her if I could set up a day care center in the school building to take care of the kids people were going to start having. After she agreed, I took it off and put it away. Why I didn't throw it away is a good question, but I didn't, and it seems appropriate for today."

Hiep inclined his head a fraction of an inch in return. "Whatever reason makes sense to you is fine with me." His clothing was the same T-shirt and cargo pants he had worn the day he came up from the valley. What had Reality staring as he straightened up from the rover was the M8 automatic rifle slung over his shoulder.

"Are you expecting to go to war?" she asked.

"It's better to be prepared for things that you do not expect. My spear and arrows are already in the storage with my pack." He opened the driver's side door of the rover and placed the rifle where it would be easy for the driver to take it up. "The facts that neither of them have returned and both rovers appear to be out of contact with our network tell me they have gone a long way. Our knowledge of this world is restricted to a very small area. I have no idea what may exist beyond its boundary."

Reality's lips twisted into a wry grin. "Here be dragons, in other words."

"Excuse me?" Hiep pulled himself back out of the passenger compartment to face her.

"In ancient times, before we had mapped all of Earth, European mapmakers would write that in the spaces beyond the borders of the lands they knew."

"That makes sense," Hiep said. "You brought your own weapons, I would assume?"

"Of course."

"And food and vitamins and other supplies?"

"Standard wilderness pack," Reality said. She opened the storage area to stow her gear and stopped for a moment to look at Hiep's pack. "I would guess you have twice as much."

Hiep put his hands on his hips. "Most of the bulk is equipment that may be useful. Listen. Shellhounds are everywhere we have been on this planet, so we will probably find them. We can eat them if we go through our own food, and some plants are edible. If necessary, the test kit will tell us if an unknown plant has one of the toxins we need to be careful about. That takes care of calories. No food from this planet will supply any of the vitamins we need, nor the methionine, but pills do not add much weight."

Reality eyed the bulky pack. "Equipment for all sorts of contingencies, I guess. You are prepared to be out for a long time."

"I will return with my daughter or with her body." Hiep's voice was very soft. "If you would like to reconsider going with me, this is the time to do it."

REALITY

THEY WERE WELL ON THE WAY TO DEAD LAKE BEFORE ANOTHER WORD WAS SPOKEN, Hiep silent because he did not indulge in unnecessary conversation and Reality lost in her own thoughts. It was the land near Dead Lake, with its thickening vegetation, that pulled Reality away from the useless spirals her mind was pursuing and to the realization that she had joined Hiep out of need but without a plan. She did not know his plan either, but Hiep was the sort of person who always had one.

"How are we going to do this?"

"The search, you mean?"

"Yes."

"I have the path that Dani's rover took stored in this machine's memory," Hiep said with neither hesitation nor inflection. "Dani drove to the exact latitude and longitude that mark the position Thorny's rover dropped from the network. From that location, we will follow the route Dani's rover took. It went into the trees past Dead Lake, and I would like to traverse that ground during the daylight hours because signs of a rover passage will be more difficult to spot among the trees. My expectation is that there will be evidence of two rovers. The two tracks may diverge if Dani lost her. He is not adept at this, and there has been rain since they went. If there is no sign of a separate track, I will follow to the point Dani's rover dropped from the network. That should be in open land. Given the thin ground cover and the nature of the dirt, I expect to be able to follow their path from there."

"You're sure Thorny kept going? That Dani is not chasing a will-o'-the-wisp because he is misreading the signs? I'm told Thorny's rover dropped off abruptly. That suggests malfunction. She could still be by Dead Lake."

"Thorny probably disabled the network connection." Hiep's voice betrayed no emotion.

"She disabled the network link?" Reality's voice went up an octave. "I didn't think it was possible to do that!"

"Any electronic system can be hacked or disabled. It is only a matter of knowing how to do it. That is one of the reasons I am convinced I misjudged the situation and that there is a serious problem with Thorny."

Reality shifted in her seat to face Hiep. "How would she learn this? I doubt there is a how-to vid in the database."

"I taught Thorny a great deal of my tradecraft."

"What!" That word was nearly a scream, but at Hiep's glance, Reality went silent and shrank back against the door. Hiep could be frightening with only a sideways glance. "You trained your daughter to be one of the Sicarii?" she said more calmly.

"No!" The heat in that one syllable was more than Reality had ever heard from Hiep. "I would not do that." His voice was calm again, the emotion a momentary lapse. "In any case, Sicarius existed on Earth. It has no role or presence here."

"Then why would you . . ."

"Teach her my craft?" A ghost of a smile played around Hiep's lips. "Thorny is a difficult child. She lives up to her name. Perhaps we should have chosen a different one." He paused for a moment while Reality resettled in her seat. "My tradecraft, certain portions excepted, naturally, is very useful here. The purposes are different, but being able to bypass, penetrate, and manipulate our electronic systems is a valuable skill, especially as those systems begin to malfunction and fail with age. With the nature of my work and some of the regions on Earth Sicarii were employed, these also included wilderness skills. I taught Thorny not to make her one of the Sicarii, but to have—" His voice softened even further and then the words stopped.

"To have a relationship with her." Reality finished the sentence.

"That is a fair statement." Hiep chose his words with care. "I thought it worked. She learns fast. Learns everything. Like her mother in that. So, if the rover suddenly dropped its connection to the network, she has done it."

Reality considered the implications for a moment. They were far more ominous than Hiep's voice suggested. "You're thinking that this time she is running away and does not want to be found. That's why you think you misjudged the situation and that it's serious. But you said there was more than one reason."

"Yes. Her pack was missing."

"Her pack?" That made no sense to Reality. "She took a rover. I would think she would take her pack."

"Not her main pack, although that was actually left in her hab. Her small accessory pack. She always leaves that in her storage area at the school. But it was not there. It was not at her hab, either. I checked."

Reality had no doubt that Hiep had been through both the school and the hab without anyone knowing what he had done. "What makes this pack special?"

"It is an arrangement we have. A pact, if you will. Her flute is in the pack. If she has gone off, I take her pack with me. I will play the flute. Nothing else in the vicinity of Dead Lake can sound like a flute. She knows it is me. It's a signal, and she will come back."

"You play the flute?" Reality had thought she could no longer be surprised by any of the people in the colony, but that was apparently not true.

"It was a challenge," Hiep said. "She wasn't older than eight, just started at residence school. She found the flute in a storage area at the school. She brought it home at the end of the term, at the spring equinox, and taught herself from vids. Then she challenged me, said that if she had to learn my skills, I would have to learn the flute. So, I did, although Penny does not appreciate my playing." Hiep smiled at the memory, but it was a wistful smile. "It has become a return call, I suppose. Thorny always leaves the pack for me. When she hears the flute out there, she comes to meet me. But this time, she has taken the pack and the flute."

"I'm sorry." Reality had never put feeling sorry and Hiep into the same thought, but she did on this one occasion. "You should have called me about that. I would have checked right away and let you know."

"No," Hiep said. "This was our signal. I had no reason to suspect it would be different this time. This is not something you need to be sorry for."

"Yeah." Reality's eyes were on the sky, now showing a grayish light through the clouds. "There's plenty of other stuff I need to be sorry for."

Hiep did not comment further.

HIEP

REACHING DEAD LAKE IN THE ROVER TOOK ALMOST AS LONG AS WALKING THERE. Dead Creek, the primary outlet from the lake, often overflowed its banks in the heavy rains that drenched the Saint Peterstown area. The ground they had to cover was still soggy with standing water in numerous places. The rover churned through the mud well enough, but it was impossible to do it fast. Even at slow speeds, muddy water splashed up onto the rover, which led to stops to wipe its photovoltaic skin clean, and that added even more time to the trip. When they did reach the point where the transmissions from Thorny's rover had stopped, no tracks from either rover were visible on ground pockmarked with puddles.

Hiep grunted and checked the screen in the dashboard that displayed a map with the superimposed trails of both rovers. He tapped on his phone. A red dot joined the screen, showing their location. "As long as our phones have signal from the town, we should be able to duplicate the route they took."

"The only information we have beyond this point is what was in the system from Dani's rover," Reality said. "You are assuming he was able to follow Thorny before the rain hit this area. Correct?"

"That's why I want to follow his path as closely as I can," Hiep said. "Yes, he will be following Thorny, but, as I said before, he is not expert in tracking. We need to be alert to any sign of another rover's track moving off in a different direction. And unless I can see evidence of *two* rovers, we will be limited to the daylight hours. My chip was enhanced by Sicarius, so I have better night vision on my field than even the rover display, but it is still not as good as a combat visor from the armies of the Powers back on Earth and not nearly as good as daylight."

"Got it." Reality sat back. "That also explains why you're not going to take the shortest route to the last point on the map where we had signal from Dani's rover. He might be off track."

Hiep nodded.

"Okay. If it will help, I'll do my best to check to the sides."

The drive through the trees went smoothly and at a reasonable pace as the higher ground was drier. Only occasional depressions in the ground gave evidence of a rover—much less two rovers—but the track of Danijel's passage did coincide with recently snapped-off tree limbs. There were no signs that a rover had taken a separate path.

It was after they cleared the trees past Dead Lake and came out onto the featureless plain that it became difficult. They found a single set of rover tracks pressed into the earth.

"Could we have missed one of them turning in a different direction?" Reality asked.

"Always possible" was Hiep's answer. He pulled up some information on his field, then scrutinized the map on the rover's screen. "From the information we have, I think it is likely Thorny reached this area before the rain hit, but Dani came through after the rain. That would explain why we see one good set of tracks. Whatever track Thorny left was washed out, while when Dani came through, the ground was quite soft."

"But then how could Dani have followed her? As you said, he does not have expertise in this. How can we be sure he hasn't missed her?"

"We can't be sure." Hiep rubbed absently at his chin for a few seconds. "However, look at this track. It goes straight as far as we can see. Dani's rover came here, so these are his tracks, and he must have been certain he was following her. His track does not wander. Also, consider that we could make a zigzag search pattern across this plain to see if we pick up another track. That will take time. Too much time. The best of bad choices is to follow the track we have."

Guillermo

The sickly sweet odor of cannabis smoke wrinkled Guillermo Vargas's nose as he stepped inside the hab on the Avenue of Asia. Guillermo had no objection to a bit of buzz, even a lot of buzz after a hard day at the farm, but he preferred it from the alcohol they served up in Happy Valley, whether distilled or in beer. Cannabis grew primarily in the hydroponics facility—there were only a few small patches in the valley—and for all the valley produce that was hauled up to Saint Peterstown to create equal shares for the townies, he never saw cannabis being brought down to the valley. He supposed he could make the trip to town and claim a share, but the smell of burnt cannabis that lingered in his nose was not to his taste.

The men in the front room of the hab were not to his taste either. Ajit Mistry met him as he entered, coming across the floor to express sorrow once again at Guillermo's loss. His precisely trimmed mustache sloped down from his nose to the end of his lips and made all the contours of his face appear to slant down along with it. Guillermo accepted the sympathies with proper grace, the words of neither man being more than formalities. Once that was done, his eyes flicked across the other three.

Oscar Gradison lounged on the room's couch. He was one of the oldest Originals, in his late fifties now. Age had turned his thick eyebrows gray and scooped out hollows for the eyes underneath them. He had lost all the hair on the top of his head, so, in apparent compensation, he had grown the rest of it long and pulled it into a ponytail with an elastic band. Herschel Northrup leaned against the counter that served to divide the front room from the kitchen and eating area. A joint smoldered between the thumb and index finger of his left hand. He wore a sunny smile that Guillermo was willing to bet was insincere. Everett Jones was the last, seated in a chair with his sandals against the edge of a desk. His skinny legs stuck out of his shorts and ended in feet that needed dirt cleaned off them, with nails that had not seen a clipper in too long.

All four of them were Originals who had come out on the *Daredevil*, and Guillermo associated that with "criminals" in his mind. Pioneer Youth Originals, particularly those who lived in the valley, did not associate with townie criminals. Other than Jones, who worked in IT, Guillermo would have been hard-pressed to think of any useful work they did for the colony.

The enemy of my enemy is my friend. His father's favorite saying ran through Guillermo's mind. He had had little use for his parents—nor they for him, mutual sentiments that had motivated many of the Pioneer Youth who had come out on the *Dauntless*—but that phrase had stuck with him. It had proved true on multiple occasions.

"Vanessa Huggins told me that you know how my son died. That you can help me to have justice done. Tell me." Guillermo folded his arms across his chest and focused on Mistry.

"Direct and to the point," Ajit said. "I like that. We can avoid unnecessary conversation."

"Let us avoid it, then." Guillermo's voice was harsh. If these men knew something, he wanted to hear it. Immediately.

"The Panagiotidis girl did it," Ajit said. "She killed him."

"What?" Guillermo's arms dropped to his sides. His hands wanted to choke something; they came up but closed only on thin air. "That *girl*? My *son*? Tell me how this is possible."

"She hit him," Ajit said. "A lucky punch, or an unlucky one, as it may be. He went down and she kicked his head in. Or stomped on his head. We're not certain what, but those details don't matter. I know it's hard to hear, but that is what happened. A witness came forward. Privately."

Guillermo looked from one man to another. This was not possible. Penny's wild child. That girl was bad news, crazy but . . . how was it possible? Wait. "I spoke with Dr. Song. She said she couldn't tell why Ferdy died. A kick in the head, you say. A doctor could tell that."

"Yes, indeed, Guillermo," said Gradison from the couch. "A doctor *could* tell that. However, this doctor rode in from the valley with Vo Hiep. The two of them had plenty of time to fix the story she would tell. And you don't think either of the two practitioners we've got here is going to contradict her. Do you?"

"No. But—"

"But nothing." Mistry cut off the objection, his voice forceful now. "We've been told she started off by kissing him. Took him unawares. You know a punch in the right place can take a man down. It doesn't matter how big a man is. She took his phone. If you ask, you'll find that no one knows where it is. And you know what her father is. And there is a witness."

"More than one, in fact," Gradison added.

Guillermo fell silent. Too many disgusting images warred for preeminence in his mind.

"And you see," Mistry picked up the thread, "that it is only now, with Fernando buried and the story secure, that Hiep is going out to bring her back. He has covered it well, or so he thinks. But he does not know what we know."

The criminals of the *Daredevil* were all despicable. Guillermo had known that from the day he landed on this world. Through his mounting fury, however, he held on to the thought that even people of foul character could know the truth. They could be useful.

"You said there was a witness, more than one witness. Who were the cowards who watched and did nothing? Who?"

Mistry stroked the tips of his mustache, then smoothed down the front of his shirt the way he might brush off bits of food or an unwanted question. "I think those names need to be confidential. I am sure you understand that."

Of course I understand, Guillermo thought. *I also understand that what I have is a story. He knows I need more than a story.* His eyes narrowed as he thought about that. Nothing for nothing, not with people such as these.

Guillermo fought to keep his voice even. "You have already told me your tale. A story, if you will. I do not believe you have done that out of the goodness of your heart or from an interest in justice. You know more, confidential as it may be. Today. You want something. I want proof that what you say is true, and I want action when it is proven. What proof, and what else will you offer me, and what is the price you want for that offer?"

"Direct, as I said. To the point, as I said. I like this." Mistry made show of making sure his shirt was tucked in all around to display his neatness in contrast to the others. "It is simple. Jacoby Grubb is going to step down as mayor. He cannot handle the pressures of the job."

Mistry's voice dripped scorn. "Ibiana plans to have Penny run again, and it is essential that she is not elected. I will also be proposed. You are well respected among the valley-folk and among the Pioneer Youth Originals. I want you to bring enough votes from the valley to put me in and keep Penny out. I will safeguard our equal shares and also propose a change to our rules that will allow the mayor to set priorities for printer and cell foundry manufacturing without either town council approval or a vote of the Demos. I need support for that vote as well.

"In return, I will see to it that a charge of murder against Thorny Panagiotidis is proved to your satisfaction and receives a successful vote in the Demos, and that the Demos leaves the decision on punishment to you. Votes of the Demos are binding, as you know. As a side benefit, a bonus to you, if you will, the names of the witnesses will be disclosed in front of the Demos, and they will testify. As I have said, there were multiple witnesses and their testimony will corroborate each other. That is part of your proof."

Guillermo pushed his fingers into the beard at his chin, then kneaded his temples. Yes, he wanted justice for Fernando—even call it revenge, he wanted it—and he knew it. Mistry knew it, too; knew that he needed the right person to be the subject of his vengeance. The asking price was not trivial, however.

"You are asking me to have my friends in the valley vote against their own interests. What makes you think I can get them to support a townie, never mind give you that kind of control over production even before it is divided for equal shares?"

"You can explain to them that the valley needs Saint Peterstown and that equal shares are vital to us," Mistry said. "It is in both of our interests to keep the valley productive. On the other hand, Penny would gut Saint Peterstown, ruin us, and turn this into a ghost town. I am sure that you can explain this so your friends will understand it. In return, we will see that you obtain justice for your boy."

Yes, Mistry had found what Guillermo wanted and he was holding it out for Guillermo to take. Guillermo could feel the burning in his gut. He wanted it more than a farmer needed the cool of a hab at the end of a scorching summer day. That aching desire did not blind him to the risk of a double-cross. He did not trust Mistry. He did not trust townies, and he did not trust *Daredevil* Originals. Yet . . . could they give him what he needed? Was it worth the risk that what Mistry presented at the Demos would be proof?

"You will bring the charge in front of the Demos before Jacoby steps down," Guillermo said. "The trial, the proof, and the vote must take place before we elect the new mayor. I must have that."

"You shall have it."

Mistry's response was so smooth, so immediate, that Guillermo worried he had missed a trick. "What if she does not come back? What if Vo Hiep cannot find her?"

"We will still make the charge," Mistry assured him. "With the defendant gone for good, I don't imagine there will be much of a defense. You will still see the proof. You will still have your verdict, and if you cannot punish the guilty directly, the Demos can vote a punishment against the family. The Demos does not have restrictions on what it can vote on and decide. I can deliver votes if you can."

"The family," Guillermo repeated. The word brought up a problem, a threat, in his mind. "What are you going to do about Vo?"

"You may leave Vo Hiep to us," Mistry said. "Now, if we have a deal, would you like to smoke on it?"

Guillermo waved off the offer and managed to make it through the door with only one stumble. He would have revenge. That was what it was and what he wanted. As for what Mistry wanted, he would test how it played with one or two people in the valley. Jordie Longfellow, a Heaven-born, did work for him and Donna. He was a believer in equal shares, although otherwise decent enough. He would start with Jordie and a few like him when he returned to the valley. Right now, however, he needed a drink to rinse his mouth and clear the taste of the bargain he had made.

AJIT

"Do you trust him?" Gradison asked after Vargas had left. His frown pulled his eyebrows together so they touched.

"Of course not," Ajit said. He regarded the joints Vargas had refused and lit one for himself. "You can't take the word of a valley-boy. However, when the tool you need falls into your hand, you use it." He drew in the smoke, held it, then blew it out.

It had been Vanessa Huggins who had put the tool in his hand, but he did not want to go into that with the others. She had been clear about what she would want afterward, and he would make the payoff when he was mayor. Solving most leadership issues came down to transactions. In fact, life was basically transactional. He took another satisfied drag on his joint and enjoyed the way Gradison, Northrup, and Jones looked at him.

He knew Vargas had the fault of being an essentially honest man, would need proof of the story, would not be content to take vengeance without knowing he had the right person. Once the story had set the hook, Vargas had almost reeled himself in. He would not even try to explain that to the others.

"If Vargas is to do his part, he will be talking to his friends in advance. We will know if he does not do that. The day laborers in the valley who do not have their own farms, they will be easily moved, and they will talk about what they hear. Even the *aristocrats* down there will talk. For all that she lives in the valley, people have not forgotten why Penny was voted out the last time. Ending equal shares, moving people to the far south. It's all craziness, and she does herself no favors when she starts to talk. She can't shut up. Vargas will get it started because we have what he wants. And then later, he will not want the deal he has made to be known. We do not need to trust him."

"But what about Hiep?" Gradison's frown etched deeper lines into his face. "You said we would deal with him. Was that just to shut Vargas up? What will we do? That man is dangerous."

"Hiep can hardly go to war against the entire Demos. As dangerous as he is, he will not do anything that would endanger Penny. That is his mortal weakness. We simply need to keep Vargas from going too far with whatever ideas for punishment he comes up with. That is how we will keep control of Hiep at the Demos. Quite simple, actually."

The other three all nodded and delivered platitudes about how cleverly Ajit had figured out the process. That was what they did all the time. That was what most of the townies, especially from the

Daredevil, did. Which was why Ajit told himself that this time was his time to win. He had been careful to stay in the background in the early days, especially when Malachi had been alive. After Malachi, he had continued in the background, for why would he want to be mayor when the hard choices had to be made and the difficult work done? But now the colony was stable. The valley could support the town. All that was needed to lead in comfort was to maintain the primacy of the town and keep it repaired. It was ironic, he supposed, that as a young man he had chased celebrity and fortune only to realize that true happiness came with respect, comfort, and stability. That was what was worth having, and he had set it up all so well and so carefully. He only wished that he truly felt the same assurance he had given the others about keeping Hiep under control. That man was dangerous.

·   ·   ·

It was late that night, by the clock and not only by the darkness, that his phone buzzed. Ajit was out in the front room of his hab watching a vid because his wife had gone to bed with expectations and he preferred to wait until she fell asleep before he went in. Since the children were in residence school, the hab was quiet, the way he liked it. He looked to his right at his projection field. The notification opened to show the caller's identification. Everett Jones. That was unusual enough to make him answer it.

"What's happening?" Ajit saw no point wasting time with a salutation.

"I was thinking about the way it ended with Vargas," Jones said. "When he was scared about Hiep and you said we would handle it."

Ajit noticed that the weight of handling Hiep had been put on him. He chose not to remark on it. "So you remember the conversation. Why bring it up now?"

"I thought of a way we can handle it even better at the Demos. In fact, it will help with the votes at the Demos even if Vargas doesn't do much. Are you interested?"

"Depending on the price, I am interested in many things. What are we talking about?"

"I want to be secretary on the town council," Jones said. "You're not going to want Sonal Davis to stay on. Once you're elected, you can see that they put me in as secretary."

Ajit considered Jones's request. Among other administrative tasks, the role of the secretary included setting the council's agenda. The position would give Jones an excellent position to receive bribes and favors of various sorts. Ajit was fairly sure he knew the type. Ajit also considered that he would be able to intervene to block some of Jones's maneuvers if necessary. That would increase his own popularity at Jones's expense and could bring favors of its own. "I think that would be very workable, Everett," he said, "assuming that this idea of yours is a good one."

"It is, it is. You remember the guns the *Dauntless* brought?"

That was a silly question, Ajit thought. Whatever the reason the ISC had sent eight M8 assault rifles with the *Dauntless*—a sudden fear of alien predators overrunning the colony being likely, though ludicrous in view of the actual ecology of Heaven—Malachi Oates and his free company followers had almost been able to use them to become rulers of the settlement. All the Originals remembered being under those guns. "What's your point?"

"Hiep locked them up in the control room of the old nuke when the fighting was over. Two sets of locks, and Hiep has rigged them for a code his chip generates. Alarmed for sure, but I can suppress that, and Hiep is away into the wild. What if we could get in and take them? If we had the guns at the Demos meeting, we wouldn't have to do anything with them. I mean, we wouldn't have to actually shoot anybody. People would see them and draw their own conclusions when they had to vote. And if we had them and Hiep didn't, well, for sure he's not going to do anything at the Demos. What do you think?"

The prospect was enticing. Ajit always liked to have insurance. He remembered how it felt when the guns had been in the hands of the free company people. If they were in his hands, his and a few followers—just a few who he knew would take his lead—those same feelings would run through the Demos. Guns sway votes. He knew that. As for Hiep, that man was dangerous with or without a gun. However, Jones was right for a different reason. Hiep would not risk Penny or his family. "Are you sure you can do this?"

"Give me a little time. I'll call you. Do we have a deal?"

THORNY

THORNY SAT IMMOBILE IN THE BOAT AS IT WAS SWEPT DOWNSTREAM, HER HANDS FLAT against its bottom on either side of her butt. Her phone told her that the past hours had pulled her into a new day while the river swept her into a new land, but she spent little thought on that. Her face stayed as it had been when the aurora first caught her eye, her head tilted up to keep the heavens in full view with no regard for the ache that developed in her neck. The shimmering folds of light transfixed her, triggered an ache inside her. It was a long while before she even closed her mouth.

A curve in the river and a channel in its bed took her close to one bank, and shadows cut across the lights. That interrupted her gaze, and she focused on the shadows. They were the trunks and branches of trees that grew near the waterline in that area, now skeleton bare with the advent of dark winter. Trees! These were tall trees, the way she had seen trees in books and vids from Earth. Her initial glimpse of them when she came out of the canyon had been correct. They soared thirty feet and more into the air. Thorny had never seen a live tree that tall. She recalled another of her mother's endless talks, this one about how the combination of heat, high carbon dioxide, and poor soil dwarfed all the trees in the vicinity of the town and valley. None grew over ten feet. But these did! She had enough light from the sky to confirm that white threads billowed from the lower branches and across the low bushes and ferns. Webs? Maybe. The light was too low to grasp any detail.

The river broadened, flowing toward a wide bend up ahead. Behind that bend a hill rose, black against the lights in the sky. As she closed in, she could see that trees grew all around its base and on the lower slopes, but the crown stuck up bare. When she was seven, Thorny had drawn in crayon a picture of a treed hill past a river bend. On top of that hill, she had drawn a little house and, in the awkward printing of a seven-year-old, had titled the picture, MY HOUSE. Mom had taped it up on the wall of the hab unit's front room and it had stayed there for two years until her bratty brother Leif ripped it down. She remembered pummeling him for that, and that *she* was the one who was punished, but what all of that did was ensure the picture remained etched in her mind. And here were the trees, and the hill, and the river. Right in front of her.

"This is *my* hill." The words were little more than a mouthed breath. "My house is going to be on this hill."

Spurred into motion, she grabbed one of the paddles. With furious strokes, she dug furrows in the water and pulled the boat to the side. A bump and a grinding sound announced that the boat had beached on a dark, stony shore. She leaped out of the boat, her boots skidding on small pebbles and rocks that were scattered across the dirt. With both hands, she got a tight grip on the rope that ran along the sidewall of the boat. She dug her heels into the dirt and pulled, teeth clenched tight, straining from her hips and back to drag the heavily laden boat high enough on the bank that there was no risk the river would take it back and wash it away.

Once off the beach, she found the ground at the base of the hill and partway up the slope to be covered in fallen leaves. This had to be the accumulation of years, each fall's worth layered on top of the previous, down to a spongy layer that merged into the earth below it. She had to pick a path upward because everywhere she looked, white webbing—and they were webs, she saw when she turned her phone light on them—coated all the lower growth and draped from low-hanging branches. The webs ranged from strands as thick as a sewing thread, woven in big, boxy sheets that could have been hung as a net for a ball game, to gossamer filaments, glistening but barely visible in her light, woven among leaves and even in the spaces of the largest webs. A touch of a fingertip told her they were all sticky. Webs meant spiders, from her books about Earth—or something like them—and she thought she saw movement as her light swept across the webs. She would check more closely later. What she wanted most at that moment was a way to the top of the hill.

The trees themselves were odd, with wide, round trunks—too wide, seemingly, for their height—that tapered rapidly very near the top. They were anchored by a broad spread of shallow, lumpy roots that she tripped over more than once as she hustled past them. All around the trees were low bushes with long branches that drooped under the webs. Those branches still had leaves; they hung off in tight rolls. She unrolled one leaf out of curiosity. It could have been a fern, the same as the plants that sprouted even lower among the bushes.

At long last, she gained the open summit of her hill, breathing hard. Hands on hips, she turned around, found a view of the river she had come down, then looked again at the lights in the sky.

"This is mine." For as long as she lasted, even if that was not long, this was hers.

It took several trips back to the boat to pull out the packs and weapons and lug them, all at a dead run, up the hill. She was gasping for breath after the last run but had no intention of taking even a momentary break. The tool pack from the rover should have a vibro-saw. It did. She regarded it with satisfaction. Downed branches and trees littered the woodland around her hill and provided a ready source of wood. By this time, dawn was breaking, orange to yellow at the northeast horizon replacing the rainbow spectacle of the night sky.

Her father had taught her how to build an A-shape hut for fast shelter in the wild. In the valley, they had used bundles of bamboo tied together to simulate logs. Here she had plenty of real logs already on the ground. The wood of the big trees was soft; the vibro-saw cut it easily. She had no nails, but she could cut notches in the wood to jam pieces together. There were also vines to tie one to another. Even better, she was able to wad up webs into a sticky rope that also helped fill gaps. The shelter, really two slanting roofs held together at a single rafter, was finished rapidly. She plastered fallen leaves from the lower, partially decayed layers and twigs into the gaps with gobs of sticky web. This would hardly be waterproof against a heavy rain, but it was the best she could do at the moment. It would suffice. By the time she was done filling up every hole she could find, her hands were mitts of glue from the webs, with leaves stuck to her halfway up her arms. She had to take time to scrape her hands and arms clean because she was sticking to everything she touched.

She had resented her father for insisting on building those structures at the farm—and even more resented the way he had made a race out of it, because she hated to lose and could not do it as fast as he could—but that work now served her well. A plastic sheet out of the rover pack served as her back wall. With that up, she was able to stand back and admire her place. Home sweet home.

The only problem was the bare dirt floor. She did not relish sleeping on that. As a compromise between the dirt she had and the bed she wanted, she gathered up armloads of fallen leaves and spread them across the floor of her hut. It would be better if she could build a wooden bed to go underneath, but for now, she would hope it would not rain.

Her work took her through the small number of daylight hours. She still had a little time to explore before the light died again in the northwest. Those webs were home to spiders, or something like them. They ranged from creatures with bodies as big as her palm, with three legs fore and three aft, which built the big webs, to tiny ones with twenty legs in a circle around a body she could barely see, which built webs of glittering fairy dust fastened inside the big ones. There was every size and arrangement of legs in between. Bugs and wormlike things crawled up from the dirt to eat leaves and climbed into the bark of the trees and got stuck in the webs. Flimsy-looking fliers, some barely large enough to see, also landed in the webs. The spiders had a feast laid out for them.

She captured a few spiders, macerated them, and pushed the pulp into tubes. The reagents from her toxin test kit—an invention of her mother's, hence its nickname of Pennycounter, and part of every rover's emergency pack—went in next. After a ten-minute wait, all the tubes stayed blue. No toxins. If she was willing to take the risk of allergy or an unknown toxin her kit could not detect, she could probably even eat them for protein, although they would not supply methionine any more than any other food on Heaven did. She looked at her hands, turned them over and back again. No redness, no swelling. *Should have thought of testing before you started grabbing all those webs*, she admonished herself, *but for once, you were lucky.*

As the dusk deepened, Thorny decided to celebrate by catching and cooking a shellhound for dinner. She did not need to go far to find one; they were as numerous in the southern polar forest as they were in the valley. They were also every bit as dumb and sluggish, with plenty of evidence around that they supported a variety of small to midsized carnivores, a point she told herself not to forget. Along the way, she saw two types of plants in the flatland below her hill that looked different from any she had seen before. On impulse, she uprooted one of each and brought them back to her hilltop. She pulped them and put samples into her test kit. One of the tubes turned red, indicating the presence of a known toxin. The other was blue. That plant might be edible. Thorny shook her head. She did not require vegetables with her shellhound steak.

It took more doing than she expected to start the campfire. Butchering the shellhound into steaks for cooking was messier than she believed possible. Her father should have included those tasks in his teaching.

Can't do anything right on my own was the refrain that ran through her head.

In the end, though, that was not enough to dampen her enthusiasm. She sat by her fire with chunks of shellhound meat roasting on spits and watched the stars twinkle between branches while the overhead light show began. One moon—Gabriel, the biggest—hung low in the sky over the northern horizon and provided some light in addition to the auroras. A huge, deep breath whooshed out of her chest and took her accumulated tension with it. Her muscles ached from the day's work. She was hopelessly lost, forever alone, and undoubtedly doomed, but for the first time in a long, long time, she was relaxed. Doom could wait. *There's probably a message in that*, she told herself.

"Eep!"

The high-pitched sound, a squeak really, came from behind her. Few sounds broke the evening silence on Heaven. No birds flew in the air; most insects, even winged ones, did not buzz. She turned as the sound was repeated.

A few feet behind her, the face of a tiny fox was mounted on a tubular body that stuck up from the piled leaves. Thorny pulled out her phone and thumbed the light on. The face and body were covered in small feathers, with bands of color ranging from light pink to deep red. At the light, the back ends of a pair of linear openings, one on each side of the head, squeezed shut, as though they were sensitive parts of eyes.

"Eep!" A V-shaped mouth opened, revealing upper and lower teeth.

To leap from a sitting position to standing is difficult at best, but Thorny would have jumped out of her skin if she could. "Holy shit! Holy shit! What are you?"

The body of the creature did not move. Its face did turn, however, to where one of her arms was outstretched wide to her side, her hand holding a skewer with an uncooked piece of meat.

Thorny brought herself under control. "Hungry, are you? I can understand that." She pulled the meat to the very tip of the stick and held it out.

The creature slithered forward through the leaves like a feathered snake. The mouth opened wide and the head struck with a sudden move. A small bulge worked its way down behind the head.

"Eep!"

"Still hungry?" There was plenty of raw shellhound left. Thorny hacked off a small piece. Before she could put it on the tip of the skewer, the creature struck again, this time taking it neatly from her fingers.

The creature had not bitten her, nor did it make any move to go after Thorny's hand, which still hung out in the air not far from its head. The two episodes had also given Thorny a good look at the teeth.

"Omnivore, aren't you?" Thorny asked. "You like meat when you can get it, but humans don't smell right or look right, is that it? I suppose that makes sense."

Slowly, Thorny extended her hand to the creature. *You are being stupid. This is going to cost you a fingertip or maybe a whole finger.* She extended her hand a little bit farther.

With a slither in the leaves, the creature's lower body formed a coil and pushed its head up higher. A pair of small, birdlike feet reached out from the body and grasped one of Thorny's fingers. It pulled itself forward, then wound upward along her arm. Another pair of little feet grabbed her fingers to assist in pulling itself up. Slowly, it wound its way upward, assisted by more pairs of feet, six in all, until it had formed a coil from her wrist to her right biceps, where the head projected forward, peering back into the darkness. Its feathers were soft and smooth against her skin. The body below them was a rope of muscle, cool to the touch.

Thorny sat back down by her fire. The creature adjusted its coil as her arm bent. It showed no disposition to leave. She fed it another piece of shellhound, then cooked a strip for herself. The creature showed no interest in the cooked meat.

"Thorny makes a friend," she said. "Another first in the history of the universe. My mom gave me an Icelandic name, so we'll go Norse for you too. Your name is Fenris." She took a bob of Fenris's head for agreement.

When she was done eating, she smothered the fire and yawned. It occurred to her that she had not slept at all the previous night. She wanted to sleep in the home she had built, but Fenris's appearance made her wonder if other, less benign, creatures might come calling. Heaven-life was more plentiful in this southern forest than anywhere around Saint Peterstown or the valley. The rover pack had a set of campsite wards. She set the disks on the hilltop encircling her home, as she now thought of it. Those would create an electric fence that would give any intruder a discouraging jolt. If she was careful to turn them on only when she went to sleep and shut them off as soon as she woke, their charge should last several nights. The pack did have a small photovoltaic panel that could charge a phone or camp lights. With the limited daylight at this latitude and time of year, it might prolong the time the wards could be used, but it would not keep them charged indefinitely. She decided she would worry about that when the power failed. She did not need to worry about "indefinitely."

Thorny pulled the thin, silvered thermal blanket from its pouch in the rover's pack. In the hothouse that was Heaven, it had never been used, but away from the campfire, the breeze this far south felt cool. Blanket in hand, she retreated to her house, yawning all the way there. She lay down in the leaves as though they made a fine mattress and converted the blanket to a cocoon. Fenris did not like being covered up that way. It slid off her arm and burrowed into the leaves at the opening to her shelter, where it formed a coil, head up and facing out.

Maybe I've got a feathered-snake Norse deity for a guard. With that thought, she fell asleep.

DANIJEL

DANIJEL DROVE OVER THE INCREASING DOWNSLOPE WITH A GRIM DETERMINATION that came to replace all other reasons for what he was doing. In the course of this pursuit, his view of his worth as a person, his very identity, had become fused with the image of catching up to Thorny, of rescuing Thorny.

That latter image was a worthwhile one. Thorny must need rescuing. Her run into nowhere had long since passed any standard of reasonableness. She was fleeing. Why that was the case, Danijel did not know. His imagination supplied all sorts of conjectures. It had to be connected with Fernando's death. He convinced himself, at least for fifteen minutes at a time, that Fernando had done something to Thorny, said something, made her fear something that had sent her into headlong flight.

The "what" was the piece he could not supply. Thorny had run off plenty of times since she had first come to residence school, had stayed away more than a night or two often enough. Everyone made fun of her for it. Well, he had not—not to her face, not ever. But she had never done anything like this. No one else at the school had ever been dead before, either, but in Danijel's circular train of thought, Fernando's death was less significant than Thorny's run.

He had scope for his mental meandering because Thorny's trail was now easy to follow. The ground cover grass was even thinner south of the Happy River. The rover's tires tore up the surface and left deep indentations from their tread. The clouds broke up as he drove, which let in moonlight and starlight. Southern lights in a variety of colors—occasionally visible from the valley and town—also flickered low on the horizon. While this did throw some illumination over the trail, it was no substitute for the sun. The night-vision sensors of the rover that fed the forward image to the screen compensated fairly well and provided a reasonable view of the land in front of him. If that were not enough and he was willing to burn the electricity, he could turn on the brilliant night-piercing headlights. As he went along and the open land constricted between the hills and cliffs on one side and a drop-off on the other, the likelihood of losing the track diminished further. Where the tracks did become indistinct across a harder stretch of ground, an occasional ping was returned to confirm his direction.

What did concern him was the remaining charge in the battery. The long drives in the dark drained the battery and the brief sunlit time restored less and less charge. Sooner or later, the battery would reach its cutoff and the rover would be out of power. Danijel told himself that Thorny's rover was subject to the same limitations. He should be able to continue as long as she did.

How either of them would return if this chase ended with two rovers having fully discharged batteries was another question. It was one that Danijel shied away from whenever he happened to glance at the battery gauge. First, he had to reach Thorny.

To help him avoid dwelling on the question of returning, he focused instead on what he would do when he found her. What would he say? If he had been able to summon up the fortitude to talk to her before, this current situation would never have arisen. So he told himself. He would have to say something when he found her. It would have to be memorable. What?

He thought of her eyes. Those eyes were full of mischief—not only the eyes but the way they narrowed with crinkly lines around them from time to time. Those eyes had captivated him from the day he realized he was attracted to her on a level far beyond two children playing together at school. A girl would not like being told her eyes were mischievous. He discarded that idea.

He thought about the way she spoke, which was limited to school because that was the only time he was able to hear her speak. Her voice was strong, clarion clear; it made him feel his heart beat in his chest. She was so smart. He was the top student in the school based on exams, but he knew that the only reason she did not beat him out was that she did not care about the exams. In group classes, she always knew every answer; she would destroy the line of argument anyone else could make. A girl would not like being told she was a know-it-all with a lacerating tongue. He discarded that idea.

Concentrate on how beautiful she is. She wore loose shirts and baggy pants, so he was not actually certain about her figure, but he had seen her wear short pants a few times and her arms were always bare. She was slim, her muscles sharply defined. Her waist was slender. Her hips tilted in a bewitching way when she walked. He constructed in his mind an image, eyes and voice and body with a face that would light up if she would only smile.

Danijel began to build in his mind the words he would use. This was not a conversation; it was beyond a mere speech. It was a paean to her brilliance and beauty and the feeling she awoke in him. He rehearsed it in his mind. He rehearsed it out loud as he drove, having first made certain that the rover's audio log was shut off.

What would she do in response? She would run into his arms. She would say how grateful she was, that if she had only known how he felt, she would never have run away. She would kiss him, a heartfelt, passionate kiss. He was not certain what would happen next, but he knew it would be perfect.

·   ·   ·

THE SUN ROSE AT LAST. CLIFFS WALLED HIM IN ON THE LEFT AND STOOD ACROSS HIS path ahead. The melody of running water came from his right. The ground turned stony, with only scattered clumps of grass. Pings were not returned, had not been for some time. The power level on the battery gauge was dangerously low, but with the sun in the sky, he would not be forced to stop. Yet.

But had he lost her? Did he miss a turn she had taken, either because the ground ceased to be favorable for tracks or because of his stupid, useless ruminations? He could not have lost her. There was nowhere else for her to go.

It was one thing to tell himself that she could not have gone anywhere else; it was another entirely to fight down the despair he felt rising inside. If all he had done was to get himself hopelessly lost, he would cry. He was, in fact, almost ready to cry when a flash of light ahead made floaters dance in his eyes. Light off a mirror? A signal? With renewed energy inside, he pushed down on the accelerator.

Soon enough, he realized that he was seeing reflection off the rear window of a rover. The other rover was directly ahead. He had managed to track it successfully through the wilderness and through the dark. Thorny was here! His heart leapt.

Thorny did not come running up the slope to greet him, however. There was no sign of her outside the rover. Asleep? His mind was quick to supply other, more doleful, ideas.

He braked the rover to a stop close behind the other one. No sign of an occupant at all. He was out the driver's door and sprinted to the other rover. It was, in fact, empty. It did switch on when he hit the Power button. He checked the audio log. Deleted. Foreboding swept through him.

No. This was not possible. Where was Thorny? The place was a dead end—rock ahead and to his left, a river to the right. He backed out of the passenger cabin. That was when he looked down for the first time. Boot prints marked the ground around the rover. She had been here. At the rear of her rover, almost concealed because he had pulled so close, was a track, as though something wide and heavy had been dragged across the ground. He clambered into her rover to check the contents. Emergency pack was gone. Tool pack was gone. Weapons were gone. She could not have carried all of that. His mind whirled.

That was when he spotted the open compartment in the rear storage area. The boat! He went back outside and looked at the ground, where something had been pulled. Thorny had put the boat in the river.

Why would she do that? He had no idea. He could have told himself she was crazy, but instead, he thought, *If she can do it, so can I.* His rover would have a boat pack as well. The consequences of doing this did not enter his mind.

Danijel moved in a frenzy to prepare. It was already daylight. The remaining time of good visibility was ticking away while he was on this riverbank. Once launched into the waterway, he would be dependent on his ability to spot wherever Thorny had gone ashore. The possibility of pinging her phone was gone the moment he left the rover. Once darkness fell—dusk would actually be the limiting time since it would be too easy to miss a beached boat with only a handheld light from the tool pack—he would be forced to beach his boat and wait out the night. If she stayed on the river at night, the distance between them would increase. Let more than a day or two pass, and he would never catch up.

He had the boat on the ground and inflated even as the worry about finding where Thorny went ashore percolated through his mind. He practically threw his supply pack from the rover into the boat. Then he grabbed his weapons, ran to the boat, and hesitated. Thorny had taken the tool pack from her rover. He might need some of its contents as well. That meant another trip to and from the rover. He dithered.

Dammit! He told himself, *In the time I'm wasting thinking, I could have done it!*

He turned back to the rover. And froze.

Out of the cliffside shadows, past the first rover, a gator had crept forward. This was not a huge specimen, being no more than twelve feet from tip of its tail to its murderous eagle beak, but it had enough power in its squat body under the armor plate of thick leathery skin to rend a human into bloody fragments.

Danijel gauged the distance to the door of his rover. The doglike rear legs of the gator would launch it forward in a lunge of frightening speed. He would never make it.

Danijel licked his lips. His bow was unstrung. In the same way he had no chance of reaching safety in the interior of the rover, his odds of stringing the bow to draw and shoot an arrow were close to zero. That left the spear.

He had one advantage. A gator was stupid. The head was fundamentally a mount for the jaws, teeth, and beak. It did not have a true brain. Small, distributed clusters of neural tissue served to control and coordinate limbs, mouth, eyes, and the rest of the body. Its mode of attack was stereotyped and lacked all subtlety. It would creep forward slowly, then, once in range, drive off those rear legs in a straight-ahead attack.

Danijel, like every Heavener child, had been drilled in how to defend himself since he could hold a spear. He dropped everything but the spear. He grounded the butt end of it into the dirt ahead of his feet and tipped the spearpoint down to aim it forward at a low angle. With a click and a snap, the spear shot out to its full length. The gator crept toward him.

He positioned his hands on the shaft to anchor it against the ground, willing his hands to be steady, to keep the point directly at the gator. The concept was for the gator's leap to impale it on the spear, the point taking it either in the mouth or in the softer skin beneath the jaw. He hoped his head was far enough back from the tip so the beak would not reach it.

Theory and practice. Always a difference. That was what went through his mind.

The gator lunged.

An open maw lined with rows of needle teeth filled his vision. He could not help squeezing his eyes shut at the last instant. A shock made his hands shake as the gator hit the spear. The spear was ripped from his grasp.

Danijel forced his eyes open. The gator lay on its side, its beak close enough for him to reach out and touch it. The spear point had been driven through the upper palate and out the top of its snout. In that instant, every part of the gator had convulsed in spasm and then gone flaccid as the poison on the spear shut down every sodium channel in its nerve and vascular tissues.

"Oh God." Danijel's entire body was shaking. He thought he might collapse as well. Then his mind processed the fact that the gator was dead and he was unhurt. More remarkable, his pants were dry.

Danijel looked at his hands, shook his head. Then he wrenched the spear out of the gator. The impact had bent the shaft a little, but with a quick twist, it retracted to its shorter length. It would still be serviceable. He would refresh the poison on its tip from the supply in the rover tool pack.

Danijel finished loading his boat. Then he pushed it out into the water and pulled himself in. When he looked back, the rovers were already out of view.

Nothing on Heaven can stop me now.

·   ·   ·

THE CURRENT SWEPT DANIJEL'S BOAT THROUGH THE CANYON AND OUT INTO THE broader river beyond. He pulled himself to the front of the boat and clung to the safety cord that ran across the inflated wall, his head pivoting from side to side, searching for any sign of Thorny's boat on either bank or in the water ahead. He kept one of the paddles next to him in case he should need to beach his boat or push away from rocks, but while the light held, he found no reason to use it.

He stayed on the river as long as he dared, but when the light began to fade, he dared not take the chance of continuing. The risk was too great, he judged, that the current would take him past a boat pulled out of the water without him realizing it. With a lump in his throat and his stomach a bottomless pit, he used the paddle to bring the boat to shore, then pulled it up onto the bank.

The kit from the rover held campsite wards. He hefted one in his hand while he debated with himself whether to set them up. The more he used them, the sooner they would be discharged, and then he would not have them at all. He set them out anyway. He was by the water, and the memory of the gator was still fresh in his mind. A tap on the button atop the main disk sent a rod from each one extending up seven feet in the air. A thin streak of green glowed along each rod to show its location. It was the visible green, even more than the knowledge of the electrical field between the rods, that made him feel secure. He fell asleep in the boat, watching the green that fenced out the wild world.

DECEMBER 30, HY 21

GORDON

ORDON DURHAM-POLE SLIPPED INTO REALITY'S OFFICE, HIS LUNCH, A meager sandwich, in one hand. He took a chair facing Reality's desk and sat down to wait for the others. With Reality now gone, there was no reason not to use her office for a meeting. In fact, there was every reason to use it, to avoid snooping students in residence, but it still felt like trespassing. He hated that feeling. He was the proctor for the senior cohorts. That was his job, his real job. He had a right to use this office.

Tiffany Williams arrived not long after. She walked past Gordon's chair and took the seat behind Reality's desk. Gordon resented that almost as much as he disliked the sensation of being somewhere he was not allowed to be. There was no arguing with her right to the desk, however. Tiffany was a chipper, like Reality, with some training from Earth in early childhood education. She ran the day care and set the home instruction schedules for students younger than eight, those too young to be in residence. It was her status as a chipper with training from Earth, though, that made her Reality's Assistant Head of School and gave her the right to Reality's desk.

Gordon took in her dark hair, eyes, and face with the frown lines that never curved upward while he appeared to focus on his sandwich.

Tiffany wore a recycled-textile shirt like his except the sleeves were chopped off at the shoulders and underarm, the way chippers who complained of the heat and humidity, even in winter, often wore them. As she leaned forward, elbows on desk, to bite into her own meal, that T-shirt gave Gordon a view of breasts that needed the support of a bra. That was not a sight he appreciated. She was a townie, like him, which should have made them allies, but she was a chipper. Sometimes, Gordon thought, having that chip created a gulf as big as the one between town and valley. It did not make them smarter, even if they acted as though it did. It only meant they were older and retained all sorts of useless thinking from Earth.

Before Gordon could go any further down that well-worn track in his mind, Poppy Merriwether slid past the door with a "Sorry I'm late."

Her recycled blouse was dyed pink, a hue that did not successfully overcome the underlying sprinkle of random colors from the recycler. Could she have picked a worse-looking shirt, Gordon wondered. Maybe she was trying to emphasize the point she had made the other day about never having a new cotton shirt. Gordon did not doubt Poppy's claim. He had known her since she was eight, so he knew her as well as a townie could know a valley-girl. If she had new clothes, she would have worn them.

Ugly sort-of-pink recycled shirt or not, he did wish she had cut the sleeves off the way Tiffany had, because a view of her chest would be worth having. They had slept together a couple of times when they were in the second-to-seniormost cohort. It hadn't been anything special for either of them, so they had moved on to others, but it had left him with an appreciation of her body. Possibly it had been the political split of valley and town that had made it not special. Possibly it had been him. He snapped his head up straight and felt a flush in his cheeks at where those thoughts were going. He told himself neither of the other two could possibly divine what had been in his mind, yet he excoriated himself for thinking that way. He was nineteen, an adult, a proctor, with no time to be dwelling on youthful lust. Townie-boy and valley-girl—Heaveners or not—were not on the same side. Poppy had said that too.

Poppy had a brown stick jammed into one side of her mouth, actually several very thin stems twisted together. She made a point of working it around her mouth with her tongue and lips when she caught him looking over. Aspergrass. That was a native plant that grew in the valley, and the valley-boys and -girls made a great affectation of chewing on it, as though that made them more Heavener than the townies. One of those sticks had been nearly omnipresent with Poppy since the start of this term.

When he kept staring at it, she asked, "Want to try one?"

"No, thanks. It makes your piss stink."

Poppy bit the stick almost in half and chewed noisily. "That's from the asparagine it's loaded with, as you should know, and it's good for you. Like asparagus from Earth."

Gordon grimaced. "I'll still pass."

"What was this about, anyway?" Tiffany asked. "Not aspergrass, I'm sure."

"Yes." The abrupt word from Gordon pulled their attention to him even as he hoped it did not betray his drifting thoughts. *Get to business*, he told himself. "Dalton and that little group of his are doing something out back of the hydroponics. It's time we put a stop to it."

"Reality told them they are confined to their habs after nine," Tiffany said.

"Which is going to have the same effect as everything else Busby says," Gordon retorted. "They don't listen to her. Nobody over the age of ten does."

"What do you think they're doing?" Poppy asked. "Beyond smoking, drinking, having sex, and being outside the town—barely—where they're not supposed to be. Or do you think something they're doing is why Fernando died? Because if you think that, you should be thinking about Thorny and why she ran away."

The chair behind Reality's desk made a loud squeak as Tiffany pushed it back. "That girl would get pissed off and run off if the computer hung when she was doing a design. Thorny running doesn't mean a goddamn thing unless you're thinking that *she* did something."

"Okay, okay." Gordon felt color rise in his face and the heat rise in his voice. He fought to keep himself under control. "This is not about Fernando and it is not about Thorny, and I know all about Thorny because I have to supervise that cohort. This is about discipline." He paused, hoping the word would sink in. "Our cohort"—he waved in Poppy's direction to include her—"and the one behind us that graduated last year, we knew we were going to be the first adults to grow up on Heaven and how important the jobs we were going to take were. We do our work. These *kids* in this cohort seem to think Heaven owes them an easy life. Well, it won't work that way. They're only the third cohort of Heavener adults. They need discipline to help keep Saint Peterstown going."

"Good speech," Poppy said, "but it's the valley that keeps the town going."

"Excuse me." Now Gordon did not care if his irritation showed. Had Poppy always been this partisan? "Without what the town produces, your little valley would be in a world of hurt."

"Oh, please!" Tiffany put her fingertips against her temples. "I didn't come in here to listen to more townie-valley bullshit."

Gordon scrambled mentally to return to his plan. "Right. Right. This isn't about that. What I want to do is catch them out there. Give them a good scare and tell them that if there is a next time, they'll get moved into the school building. Give them a week in the dorm rooms in school. Which have locking doors. We need to stop this benign neglect shit Busby has been doing. We are responsible for them and what they do. So maybe some of it is about Fernando and Thorny."

He could see he had their attention. Both of them were leaning forward in their seats.

"How do you know they're going to be out there?" Tiffany asked.

"Busby's gone," Gordon said. "It's a guarantee they're going to test us."

"That makes sense." Poppy leaned back and stretched her legs. "But do you really think this will change anything?"

"Would you want to be stuck in the school building with the day care and the lowest juniors?" Poppy shook her head. "They'll be the laughingstock of every senior cohort—your junior cohorts, too. It will tell them we mean what we say."

Whether that would truly make a change in Dalton and the ones who hung around him, Gordon could not say. What he did believe was that the town needed to know it had Heaveners who meant what they said. Who understood their responsibilities. Who could be relied upon for leadership in the future. If it took having Dalton and his cronies cooped up in the school dorm rooms for the entire winter to prove to the townies—Heavener and chipper alike—that Gordon Durham-Pole understood responsibility and was a leader for the future, it would be worth it.

Poppy and Tiffany took in the concept in silence. Poppy certainly understood what it would mean to give up the privileges of a hab, to go back to being treated as a young child. Her face assumed a calculating mien, her eyes focused on the distance beyond the office walls.

"Okay," Poppy said at last. "Say we do this. How are we going to make it work? Even without Fernando, there are seven of them to only three of us. They'll be high or drunk or both. What happens if it turns into a fight? What do we do then? Charge them in front of the Demos? I don't want to get hurt. Or did you get your hands on one of those guns Vo Hiep locked away?"

Gordon allowed himself a small chuckle. He did not think bravery was among Poppy's character traits. That was why Busby had her with the preteen juniors, one of the few decisions Busby had gotten right.

"Nobody can get those guns," Gordon said, "and even if I could, that would be a stupid thing to do." He watched the flush rise on Poppy's dark skin. "If we're agreed on this, I'm going to call Cam and Jess, and I'll show you how we handle it."

"What do you expect the two of them to do?" Tiffany's frown almost brought her eyebrows together. "They've been useless since the day they landed."

"All tools have uses," Gordon said. "You just have to use them correctly." He could see from the way Poppy and Tiffany were looking at him that he had them. Manipulating people, he was coming to realize, could be enjoyable. "This is what we're going to do."

· · ·

THE THREE OF THEM WERE BACK IN REALITY'S OFFICE THAT NIGHT. THEY SAT READING— or pretending to read—on their phones. Dinner was long over; darkness had blanketed Saint Peterstown for even longer. The lights were out in the corridors of the school and in the rooms occupied by the lowest juniors.

It was close to midnight when a light began to flash on the screen at Reality's desk. It was the indicator for one of the motion detectors in the infant and toddler area of the school. There were no children there at this hour, however. Gordon had taken one of the motion detectors and planted it out behind the hydroponics facility. Connected to the network, it still performed its function in its new location.

Gordon grinned. "They're out there."

"Unless it's a dumb shellhound eating grass," Tiffany said.

"Not there. Not at night." Gordon stood up. "If it is, you can laugh at me. Let's go."

Gordon led the way from the school building to the stable by the Community Dome. Cam and Jess were waiting for them with five saddled horses.

"Are you sure this is going to be okay?" Cam asked.

"Absolutely," Gordon said. "All you need to do is yell when I do. You don't even need to yell words. Just be loud. Now, are the lights working?"

"Yes." Jess held out a small tray. Resting on it were five elastic headbands, each with a battery-powered, ultrabright LED mounted on it. "Do you want to check them?"

Gordon flicked the switch on each one in turn. In the dimly lit entrance to the stables, the light that flashed out was blinding. "They'll do," Gordon said. "Leave them off until we get there."

With that, the five of them saddled up. They rode out of the stable and down the Avenue of the Americas. Saint Peterstown was quiet; it could have been deserted. The intermittent streetlights gave enough illumination to see, but they could just as easily have been the dying lights of an abandoned town where the power was running down.

When they reached the junction with the Perimeter Road and the entrance to the hydroponic facility, they heard a shriek and giggles coming from behind the structure. The odor of burning cannabis floated over to them.

"Told you," Gordon said. He kicked his horse into a gallop. The other horses ran after his.

They rounded the curve of the building at a full gallop, switched on their headlamps, and began screaming like banshees. *The first cavalry charge on Heaven*, Gordon thought with pride. Caught in the glare of the LEDs and faced with five horses pounding at them, seven people froze.

"Hands on your heads!" Gordon shouted. "Sit down where you are! You are all in detention. If you don't walk back to the school with us, it will go even worse. I promise you that!"

Six of the seven did exactly that. All appeared somewhat intoxicated; two were raving, apparently at hallucinations. None of them offered any resistance when Gordon dismounted and used ties to bind their hands. But one boy bolted for the darkness at the back of the facility, tossing an object to the side as he went. Poppy, still on horseback, easily ran him down. The boy flung his hands in the air, but Poppy was already swinging out of the saddle to grab him. One foot caught in a stirrup as she latched on to his shoulders and the two of them went down in a heap. Poppy rose from the ground. He did not. "Not so damned tough, are you, Ethan?" she panted. "Gimme a damned hand."

Poppy tied that hand to a stirrup then backtracked, using her headlamp and phone light to find what had been thrown away. It was a stoppered flask with a small amount of clear liquid in it. She pulled the stopper, sniffed, and wrinkled her nose at a smell of saccharine mixed with hot sauce. She stuffed it into a thigh pocket of her cargo pants and remounted.

MIROSLAV

THE MESSAGE, ARRIVING AT ALMOST THE SAME TIME AS HE PLANNED TO SIT DOWN FOR lunch, announced a problem that needed his immediate attention in the printer facility. It was worded more like a peremptory command than a request. He took in the identity of the sender and decided that lunch would need to wait. If he sat down and started eating, he could count on receiving a barrage of messages at diminishing intervals. He could ignore the notifications as they popped up in his field, but he would need to go there eventually, and the greater the number of messages he ignored, the greater the aggravation when he finally went.

The argument—and it did sound more like an argument than a discussion—was in full swing when Miroslav opened the door to Chloe DiMasi's office in the printer manufacturing building.

Chloe was in charge of both the printer facilities and the cell foundries, not because she had a background in print technology or cell and molecular biology, but because the *Daredevil* crew, who had constructed Saint Peterstown, had trained her to run the machinery. She had been doing it ever since.

Her real background, as Miroslav had learned eight or nine years ago when Chloe started to talk about it, was a series of scams that had bankrupted a swath of towns across Wyoming, Montana, and Idaho. The lurid details that came out at her trial of how she had used the money was such that her life expectancy would be quite limited both in prison and if she ever got out of it. Even her relatives to the second degree feared for their lives. It had all made the prospect of colonizing a distant planet and being wiped from the databases attractive.

She was a middle-aged white woman with narrow, squinty eyes above puffy cheeks, possessed of a well-known choleric disposition. She might have been suspected of sneaking drinks from her hometown church's supply of wine, but not of gamboling through Las Vegas strip joints and drug dens on the townspeople's dollars.

"About time you got here," Chloe snapped at Miroslav's entry.

Knowing the way her temper worked—and who did not?—he

ignored both the tone and the gibe. "You said I needed to look at something, which is why you couldn't do it on a call. But does it involve the clinic? I heard something about cyclosporine as the door opened, and I'm guessing that's a med."

His questions were sparked as much by what he had heard as by the other occupant of the office, Song Jing, who perched on a chair across from Chloe's desk. Dr. Song, he thought, looked mostly the same as she had when she came down from the starship *Dauntless* on what was supposed to have been a brief surface mission. *Time is kind to some. Well, she does look older and a bit tired, but we're all older and tired*, he told himself.

"I didn't realize you two had to work on something," Song said. Her posture said that even if she had, she would not have hesitated to intrude, and with the deference she was given, she could have intruded as she wished. "You did hear about cyclosporine. It is a medicine, and we need more output from the foundries because of this eye reaction we are seeing in young children, thanks to this greenhouse of a planet we live on."

"And I was saying, and I will keep saying," Chloe said, "that every tank we've got is running at capacity and I can't swap out a cell line unless the Demos votes to change prioritization. Penny insisted—damn near threatened the whole Demos with a spanking, which only makes you wonder why all the rest of her kids aren't as screwed up as Thorny—that we keep stockpiling vitamins and methionine in case there is some disaster like a flood or tornado, or God knows what, that'll destroy our supply of Earth food from the valley."

She paused for a breath but not long enough to be interrupted. "Well, that's fine, but that ties up those tanks. The one for the methionine isn't that efficient because even though we have a cell line that can be tweaked to produce reasonable amounts, it's not as though it's optimized for that. We had to do all the work to set up the cell line here. I can't just decide that we need your cyclo whatever instead of something else."

"Okay, okay." Song had her hands up in surrender. "I'll plan to propose this to the Demos. And I will talk to Penny. I understand where her concern comes from. That flooding we had in the valley nine years ago had us on tight rations, and we have more to feed today. We could have worse."

"It can always be imagined to be worse. We may have more people, but we have lots more farms down there today. Penny is a one-woman catastrophe imagination machine." Chloe's grumble lacked heat, an indication that she had been mollified. Somewhat.

Dr. Song stood up. "Before I go, how is your son, Dalton, doing? I know he was friends with Fernando. I was going to ask earlier, but our discussion became quite involved rather quickly. If he needs help dealing with this, let me know and I will make time for him."

Chloe slouched back in her chair and folded her hands over her stomach. Her eyes narrowed until they were almost closed. The doctor's expression of interest in her son was clearly not the way to end matters on a friendly note.

"I don't know what goes on in that boy's head anymore. Nothing, is my guess. Anyway, he doesn't talk about what he's doing or thinking, so I don't know. Neither does his father. I'll tell you, if he had been my first and I could have seen how he would be, there never would have been another, replacement-plus be damned."

"I'm sorry to hear that," Song said. "It's a difficult age anyway, and I think it's harder on our oldest cohorts of children because of the demands they know they'll face. The lack of any newly adult role models because of the generation gap doesn't help. Does he know what he wants to do after residence school?"

Chloe slapped both arms down against the arms of her chair. Then, with a grunt, she used her hands to help shove herself upright. "No idea. Doubt he does either. I've shown him all the workings here, tried to train him for it. It's not that hard, for God's sake. You see the readouts, that tells you the commands to enter or the buttons to tap, and there's a manual if it's not in your head. Granted, he'd have to do a little extra tapping to pull the manual up on his phone since he's got no chip, but how hard is that?

"But no interest from him. He'll probably take shifts harvesting in hydroponics, and I'll hope he harvests what we need to eat and not only what he can smoke." She turned her squint on Miroslav. "Your oldest will be an engineer like you, right? And you trusted him to bring back the rover and that girl."

"Yes." Miroslav was proud of Danijel's aptitude and school record, but he did not want the conversation to go in the direction of "that girl," which was where he knew Chloe wanted to take it. In particular, he did not want to dwell on the fact that Danko was not back yet, with or without the girl. "Can you show me what the problem is here? I've got everything from building maintenance to IT stuff I need to take care of, and there's a big difference between what I know and what a fully trained engineer would."

"Come on then and stop wasting time." Chloe moved out from behind her desk with a speed that belied her build, brushed past Miroslav, and was out the door of her office, headed to the part of the building devoted to the printers.

Miroslav rolled his eyes at the ceiling and followed her. He noticed that Dr. Song tagged along as well.

The printer area was pervaded by what sounded like the steady hum of a million bees as the machinery laid down piece after piece of feedstock to form everything from an axle for a horse cart in the valley to a coffee pot for a Saint Peterstown hab. Chloe wended her way past partitions, machines, and the occasional worker to reach the back wall of the building. She stopped at a plastic tank anchored to a wall. Piping with release valves ran from the tank, one of them to an opaque cylinder from which more pipes and tanks emanated, some of which led to yet another cylinder. Signs on the wall proclaimed MAINTAIN SEALED ENVIRONMENT and, by the distal tanks and pipes, AVOID VAPOR. Screens alive with data adorned the wall around the main tank.

"It's one of your dedicated cell foundries that's the issue." Miroslav knew he was stating the obvious, but he was not going to let Chloe speak first.

The cell foundries were biological manufacturing plants. Inside the tank lived suspensions of immortalized cells in which specific genes had been inserted. When fed sugar for energy and the proper substrates, the cells produced enzymes that churned out a wide variety of useful materials, everything from vitamin B_{12} to the organic material for the photovoltaic cells. Each foundry tank had one type of gene-edited cell and produced one product. Tanks in the main foundry area could have their cells taken out and stored, replaced by a different cell line to make a different product. This one, in the printer area, was integral to the manufacturing process and could not be changed.

"It produces the monomer for our altrubber," Chloe said. "The polymerization is catalyzed by gadolinium, and then the polymer is converted to feedstock for the printers. We use a lot of it because we need new altrubber as we expand and because, well, when you recycle an old, worn tire, you don't get nearly as much material as was in it when it was new. Every gasket, every damn tire we print, whether it goes on a rover or a horse-drawn cart, comes out of this process." Starting from the tank itself, Chloe tapped each piece of the apparatus, rattling off a list of what went on where until the feedstock reached the storage bin.

"And your problem? At least, the problem you need me for?" Miroslav asked.

"Something is wrong with the lines, or the tank. Or both. We're losing yield. Shit, it's basically not producing anything right now," Chloe said. "Not like the problems with some of the other foundries. It was intermittent when I first saw it, which makes me think it's mechanical or structural, and that's not something I'm going to figure out. Worse than that, we had contamination in the foundry tank itself. Had to take that offline, dump the tank, and start up a reserve cell line, but I don't want to put that in until we've got this figured out. We're also losing gadolinium, and that makes no sense because it's a catalyst; it's not used up. We're losing some, though, and that's a problem because while there has to be gadolinium somewhere on this goddamn planet, we've got no damned idea where. If this system crashes hard, we've got no altrubber except what we recycle, and that won't be a good thing. So, can you figure it out and fix it?"

Miroslav sighed. It was too much to hope that he would see a puddle on the floor resulting from liquid dripping out of a leak in a tube. He chipped in to the Saint Peterstown network to access the database and bring up the manual for this system. He was not surprised to discover that it ran to 432 pages. He was able to identify each section of the system in front of him and flag the appropriate section in the manual.

While he was doing that, he did his best to tune out the commentary from Chloe. She started in again on her son Dalton, how she had tried her best to show him how all of the systems worked, and that it was not that the kid lacked a brain in his head but that he simply didn't care, and she had shown him how this system worked, in particular, because she wanted him to understand how important this was, and that his generation would have to take over this work soon, and all he had mustered up was a mumble about, "Yeah, the shit goes in here and comes out there," and even she had paid more attention when she went to school, and it was for sure his father's fault.

"If you want to send him over to the clinic, I can speak to him," Dr. Song said. "Or he can talk to one of the practitioners, if he would prefer that."

"You'll get better results talking to a shellhound," Chloe said. "Good-looking, I'll give him that. Somehow he's popular. Fucking useless."

"I'm going to need to spend some time with the manual and then come back here," Miroslav said. "I can't do this on the fly. And it will be better if I can come back when I can work alone."

Miroslav regarded the equipment with a sour taste in his mouth. A leak here, a loss of irreplaceable catalyst there. What would happen next, and how would they manage to fix it? With the exception of the two former starfolk at their jobs and Penny at farming, none of the colonists were truly expert at the jobs they performed. How had they ever thought they could keep this place functioning? It was a joke. And the joke was on them.

HIEP

Sleep for both Hiep and Reality was fitful given their desire to resume the chase. They were, in fact, awake with plenty of time to fret before it was light enough to follow the track of what they had concluded was Danijel's rover. It was not long before they were rewarded by a second set of rover tracks headed in the same direction. Reality let out a sigh of relief. They followed the dual tracks, making note in due time of where they lost the signal from the town.

It was the band of trees and then the river that slowed them again and then brought them to a halt.

"Happy River," Hiep said. "Far above Staircase Falls, which in turn is above our valley farms."

"They can't have crossed this," Reality said.

"They did. Both of them." Hiep pointed across the river and a little downstream from their position to where two sets of rover tracks were dug deep into the side of the riverbank. "It makes no sense that they would have joined up and gone farther south together. So Thorny crossed first and Dani must have continued after her, even past this point. I would never have known he felt that strongly about her. He never spoke to either me or Penny. And Thorny never mentioned him. We know Miroslav and Dani's mother, of course, but neither of them ever said anything." Hiep rested his chin on one palm and stared at the tracks. They told him what the two had done but not *why*.

"There was some talk around the school, some things you pick up from other kids." Reality's face flushed enough that it was obvious around her scars. "I've heard Dani had a crush on her . . . from a distance . . . quite a distance . . . for a few years. I can't imagine having a crush, nothing but that, and being willing to dash, quite literally, into the middle of nowhere."

"I can." Hiep's thoughts turned to Penny with those words. There were times and situations, special ones, where feelings trumped even logic and discipline. This was no time, however, to indulge in reminiscing. "If they were able to cross here, so should we, even in this salvaged, reassembled, and partly reconditioned rover. Let's hope that Miroslav was careful about shielding the electrical components."

The rover did successfully ford the Happy River and they continued down the long slope to the south that followed, with the other unnamed river on their right. Since no additional rain had fallen since Thorny and Danijel had passed this way, their pursuit picked up speed. Visible tracks existed in many places, and there was no other reasonable direction to take.

DANIJEL

HE WOKE IN THE DARK AFTER A RESTLESS SLEEP. TRIPLE MOONLIGHT, ALONG WITH THE southern lights, reflected off the water only a few yards away, but he feared he could still miss a boat or a person on the banks from mid-river. At the same time, he was unable to go back to sleep. It was the worst of both worlds.

After a few hours of sitting with nothing to do other than review every mistake he had made and startle at every sound that came from the brush farther up the bank, he saw twilight begin to glisten in the sky. The northeastern sky glowed with bands of red and orange above the dark land. The sun finally deigned to poke above the horizon. Danijel quickly shut down the wards and put them back into the kit.

In a few minutes, he was back on the water. Once there, however, nothing changed. To either side, a low, stony bank glided past as the current took the boat along. Farther away from the water grew reeds, grasses, and fernlike plants all draped with odd white webs. Even farther back grew ranks of trees—taller trees than he'd ever seen except in books, their branches bare of leaves. No movement anywhere. He was forced to contemplate how long he would continue. How far could he go before he would be unable to return? Had he already passed that point? He shivered.

A bend in the river lay ahead of him. Behind it, a low hill rose. A lonely hill, he thought. He was so in the grip of his thoughts and so focused on how alone that hill appeared that he almost failed to notice the boat pulled up on the shore in the bend.

"My God! You idiot!" He was screaming at himself as he fumbled with the little motor and flailed away with the paddle to avoid being carried downstream past the hill. It was only with his lungs on fire and muscles burning that he was able to bring his boat to shore in almost the same spot.

By the time he had dragged the boat up far enough to be safe and alongside Thorny's, his breath was coming in gasps. Whether that was from the exertion or anticipation, he could not tell. He started toward the hill, remembered Thorny's small pack, ran back to the boat for it, then pivoted again to sprint up the hill, small stones flying out from under his boots as he went.

"Thorny!" he yelled into the stillness that was the landscape on Heaven. "Thorny! Where are you?"

He was almost to the top when he heard the beat of footsteps from the other side. He halted, chest heaving, legs trembling. Thorny came over the crest at a run and skidded to a halt several feet in front of him. The stupefaction writ on her face in open mouth and wide eyes gave Danijel the chance to speak, but he could not organize his brain and his breathing to do it.

It was Thorny who spoke first.

"Dani Petrovic. What the fuck are you doing here?"

All his fine speeches, all his carefully rehearsed words, fled from his mind. She was right there in front of him, speaking to him. *Say something,* he commanded himself. "I . . . I . . . I came for you. I came to get you . . . to help you . . . save you . . . help you get back. I brought your pack." He hoisted the pack with one hand.

"What? Why? Oh my God, the pack." Thorny planted her fists on her hips and stared down at him from the higher ground. "Why the fuck would you do any of that?"

Danijel desperately searched his mind for all the phrases he had prepared, the scenarios he had planned. He managed to force out the words that said what he felt. "Because you're brilliant. You're beautiful. You're everything to me."

"Brilliant? Beautiful?" Disbelief ruled Thorny's expression. "You need corrective lenses! And antipsychotic meds!"

The sting of those words finally broke the lock on Danijel's thinking. "Hey, listen," he said. "When a guy goes to the end of the world for a girl, the least she can do is say thank you."

"Okay. Thank you." The tension in Thorny's stance left in a sudden rush. Shoulders slumped; hands came off her hips. "You still need corrective lenses and antipsychotics." Her tone was much softer this time.

"What happened, Thorny? Why did you run away? I mean, why did you come all the way here?"

"I don't want to talk about it."

The note of finality in her voice was enough to warn Danijel away from the subject. He searched for a different topic. "What is that?" He pointed to the creature coiled around Thorny's left arm.

"What? Oh, I call him Fenris. Well, him, her, it—who knows?" She reached over to tap Fenris on the nose with the index finger of her free hand. Fenris stretched its neck forward and flicked a tongue out to lick her fingers. "I'm calling it a snakeipede, a Snakeipedus thorniensis to be specific. I disturbed its burrow maybe. I fed it some shellhound meat and it eats these leaves and other things too. I think it actually has a central processor unit, not like the distributed neural controllers in the other animals, and it's an endotherm—cold-blooded, that is—which is why it likes to coil around my arm because this weather is chilly for Heaven, and these feathers are interesting." She paused to stroke them and hold a couple up for display. "My mom says feathers appeared on Earth early in the Triassic, so that could fit with where this planet seems to be evolutionarily, although I don't see any signs of early wings, but that's not really necessary since feathers could evolve for heat conservation—"

She cut off abruptly. "Oh my God! I'm sounding exactly like my mother when she gets going on a tangent." Her voice dissolved in a series of giggles. "Oh my God," she said again when she could speak past the giggles, "I haven't laughed at myself or anything for so long. I really do thank you for that. Come on up."

She turned and led the rest of the way to the top.

"Welcome to Fort Thorny." A wave of her hand took in the clearing at the hilltop and the small shelter she had erected.

Danijel picked up—or thought he did—a stiffening again in Thorny's posture and a strain in her voice. Did she expect him to scoff at the crude structure, dismiss it as something a child might build in a yard? He was not going to do that. His eye took in the geometry, proportion, and balance.

"You did this? How long did it take?"

"I did it in a day. During daylight." There was no missing the defensiveness of her tone. "And, yeah, by myself. Fenris isn't much help with this sort of thing."

"It's impressive. Really, really impressive."

"You think so? For real? You're not just saying that?"

"Why would I say it if I didn't mean it?" Danijel felt surprise at her obvious surprise. "How did you learn how to do it?"

"My father taught me. He made me practice with bamboo bundles, and I hated him for every minute of doing it because what's the point of learning to do anything like this? Until all of a sudden you need one, of course." She gave a short laugh at the irony.

"It's really well done." Danijel looked at the trees all around, then back at her. "You know, with all the wood around here—real wood, not like what we have around town or in the valley—I'll bet if the two of us work together, we could build a real log cabin. Like in the Earth histories." Enthusiasm rose in his voice as he went along.

"You think *you* could help?" Abruptly, her voice rang with challenge. "I've seen you at school. I handle a vibro-saw better than you. I can do the cuts better than you."

"You think that?" The words jumped out of his mouth of their own volition. "I'm training in engineering. I will be an engineer."

"On a computer," she said. "I can build it for real better than you."

"Excuse me," Danijel fired back. "I can judge the angles, the supports, and the stress better than you. I can build it better than you."

Why did I say that? ran through his mind immediately afterward. *I've pissed her off. All of this, and I've pissed her off.* It was a moment before he dared to look at her face.

Mischief flickered in her eyes.

"Tell you what," Thorny said. "We'll each build half and see whose side falls down first." She laughed. "We can start on it tomorrow. For now, come on, go grab your bow and arrows—which you better have brought, because who knows?—and I'll show you around my empire. Well, maybe it's more like a small duchy, but it's all mine."

Danijel was back from the boat, near breathless and as close to instantaneously as possible, to see Thorny, quiver on her back, brandish her bow and skip off to the other side of the hill. Danijel scrambled to stay behind her. Leaves flew away from her feet as she picked an opening in the web-covered bushes beneath the trees. Halfway down, she peeked over her shoulder, pushed a branch heavily draped in web to the side, stepped past, and let the branch go.

The branch whipped back over the top of Danijel's head, catching him in web from head to toe. He gave a strangled yell and spun to go back, but accomplished nothing beyond twisting even more web around himself. He pulled at the strands, lost his footing on the path, and fell into the piles of leaves that covered the ground. He sat up, enmeshed in web, with leaves stuck to the sticky web filaments all over him. Tiny and not-so-tiny spidery creatures ran across him.

His first reaction was to curse, to scream at her. But before he opened his mouth, he saw her come to stand over him. He looked at her. The mischief was gone, replaced by worry on her face, tension in her shoulders. *She's afraid I'm angry. She's afraid she made a mistake. This was supposed to be a joke.*

"Well," he said. "You have snared me in your web!"

With those words, he saw her nervousness dissolve. Mischief and giggles returned. "You're quite the mess, aren't you? There's a stream at the base, just a little farther. Let's get you cleaned up."

Thorny held out a hand. When Danijel took it, lightning coursed up from his hand to his heart. He no longer cared how he looked. That lasted until a six-legged spider the size of his hand crawled into sight on his arm. He froze, afraid to move.

In that instant, Fenris's head shot out from Thorny's arm. Its jaws chomped down on the spider. The head retracted to her arm, its face almost comical with three hairy spider legs protruding from its mouth. Then it gulped, and the legs and all the other content in its mouth disappeared into a bulge in its body.

"Holy shit!" Danijel had to laugh. The situation was too ridiculous to do anything else. He did not let go of her hand all the way down to a little brook of clear water that splashed over rocks.

They sat there on a pair of large rocks and Thorny helped him peel leaves and web from his clothes and exposed skin. The touch of her fingers against his cheeks made him wish he had more web to pull off. *I should lean over and kiss her*, he thought. She was close enough, practically next to him, but he was not sure that was what she wanted. He could not do it.

"Are spiders going to take over this world?" he asked as a way to distract himself from what he was feeling. "These webs cover every-thing here."

The first answer was a giggle accompanied by the touch of her hand on his shoulder. The touch was soft, barely any pressure at all, but it was enough to make lightning strike again. "I think it makes sense, in a way," she finally said. "If you look, there are little insects and worms everywhere. They eat the leaves on the ground and on the branches. I think some of them eat into the stems and even the trees too. It's a smorgasbord for all these spiders. At the same time, Heaven doesn't have birds or anything like birds yet—or maybe they died out in the extinction—to eat the spiders. Fenris eats them, so some of the other animals must also, but that's not enough to keep the spider population down. So this is what happens." She plucked another clump of web off his neck.

"I wonder if this area, this whole polar forest, really, is left over, a survivor hanging on from what was here before the volcanoes and the extinctions, or whether this is a new ecology evolving. We'll know, I guess, in another hundred thousand years or so."

Danijel laughed. "I'm not sure *we* are the ones who are going to know."

Thorny laughed too. "True enough. Either way will work for us. Come on, I want to show you more."

Thorny popped to her feet and headed off alongside the brook. Danijel followed, wondering if he had missed an opportunity that would never come again.

.   .   .

THEY WANDERED IN THE WOODS WHILE THE DAYLIGHT LASTED, PAST PONDS AND SOME soggy bogs. The ground was predominantly low-lying, broken up by stretches of open water and small hills placed seemingly at random. Here and there, small white flowers poked up from the stems of trefoil leaves, both along the shores and seemingly floating on the water. The thistle was the only other plant with flowers, and the ones with the white flowers did not grow in the valley or on the plains around Saint Peterstown. Thick drifts of dried leaves carpeted the ground and made a layer across the surface of the ponds.

Bushes three to five feet high dotted the landscape, some with large spade-shaped leaves, others with their leaves tightly rolled, all draped in webs. Reeds and thistle grew thick around any water. Trees were widely spaced, all of them apparently the same type. Their branches were bare, the lower ones being wider, with webs hanging from them, and the trunks rapidly tapering to the top at thirty to forty feet, rather like a squat Christmas tree. Fallen trees littered the ground in all directions, creating an obstacle course on land and a network of bridges across water.

Shellhounds were omnipresent as usual, chomping through the leaves on the bushes, munching on dry leaves on the ground, and burrowing their heads into piles of leaves to eat God knows what underneath. Occasionally, calf-high creatures with long tails, oversized rear legs, and far too many teeth for their small jaws to close completely ran through the landscape on missions of their own. One of them was busy pulling strips of flesh off a newly dead shellhound. They paid no attention to the two humans. Thorny and Danijel did see one twin to Fenris hanging from a branch, swallowing a spider.

Thorny played tour guide through all of it, chattering about the animals, the plants, and the land—how far south she thought the forest might extend. Danijel did not think he had heard her talk this much in the entire nine years they had attended residence school.

"Shellhounds are just like at home," Thorny said. "Mom says they're one of the few species that came through the extinction, whether that's because they concentrate zinc oxide in their shell and it protected them when the volcanoes stripped out the ozone layer, or through just dumb luck; they filled all these empty ecological niches. I find it hard to believe an animal that dumb could be the future of the planet, but that's nature at work."

Danijel had to laugh. "My father always says it's remarkable that humans became the dominant species on Earth, given that our greatest talent is killing each other off."

"And on it goes." Thorny squeezed his hand. "God does play dice with the universe." She let go of his hand and squatted down to pick up a foot-long leaf in the shape of a blade. She walked over to put her hand on one of the tree trunks and held the leaf out to Danijel. "I've named this type of tree a glosso because if Mom saw them, she would say the trees in the polar forest are like a tree called Glossopteris was on Earth. They were everywhere on the planet until the great extinction at the end of the Permian, which was like what happened here. Then they were gone."

She rapped her knuckles against the trunk. "These must photo-synthesize like crazy during the summer to get through the dark time. The wood is soft, pretty light, and cuts easy." She looked up. "Maybe these are survivors. Large animals and plants don't do well with the high carbon dioxide and heat we have. The CO_2 is the same every-where, obviously, but it's not so hot here, so maybe. I don't know. My mom might."

"Sounds like she taught you a lot."

"Yeah, except she's like a textbook that won't shut off and chooses sections with a random number generator. My father, he listens to every damn word she says. She could read the dictionary off the screen and he would listen.

"Yong pretends to be perfect and lets it all flow past her. The twins are boys. They don't care. And Xeno—that's short for Xenophon, in case you don't know—and Thuy are too young. I'm the one who suffers." Thorny let out a sigh. "Fuck it. You know, I always thought both my parents were assholes for finding something to teach me damn near every minute of every goddamn day and demanding I learn it, but maybe I'm just a little shit who didn't appreciate any of it. Maybe I'm the reason I'm such a fucking mess." She put her forehead against the tree and leaned on it.

"Why are you so goddamn hard on yourself? And please turn around and stop staring at the tree."

Thorny turned around but kept her eyes down. "Maybe no one ever went to the end of the world for me before. Come on, we should go back. I've got a good sense of direction, but this would be a bitch in the dark."

.   .   .

THE SHADOWS OF THE NAKED TREES HAD GROWN LONG AND THE GROUND UNDER THE lower brush and webs was hidden in gloom by the time they neared the base of the hill opposite to the river. As much as Danijel had enjoyed Thorny's company and her chatter about what they were seeing, he had his head down, putting one foot in front of the other, looking forward to the opportunity to sit and rest. It took him unawares when she thrust out an arm across his chest to stop him.

"What's wrong?" he asked.

"There. Look there."

She was pointing at a rent in the network of webbing. The ferns that grew there had been trampled.

"Something went through there. Something fairly big, at least as big as us, and it went through very recently. If there is something lurking around my hill, I want to know what it is. Come on." With one hand held out behind her to wave him forward, Thorny followed the trail that had been cleared of webbing.

Danijel followed and took some quick steps to come even with her. Webs dangled and waved in all directions, but the lower growth was not dense enough to impede them. Broken ferns made a clear path to follow, and the webs had been ripped along it as well. The track went around a particularly wide-boled glosso. They stepped around it and froze. They had found the maker of the path.

Only a few yards farther on, partly screened by ferns, a carnivore was stripping flesh from the body of a dead shellhound. It rose up as they came around the tree to stand six and a half to seven feet tall on the two massively oversized rear legs. These had led the Originals to call them roos, after the kangaroo of Earth. The body was covered in green scales, all coated in a sort of fuzz, and a crest of red feathers grew from the top of its head. Dark blood coated the claws of its forelimbs and its jaws. It fixed its eyes on them and blew out a hissing whistle that made bloody giblets drip off razor-sharp teeth.

"Oh shit," Danijel said.

"It can reach us easy with a leap." Thorny's voice was a low hiss of its own. "Listen, those things can't think; no real brain. I'm going for the ferns and bush to the left. You go exactly opposite, to the right. It will hold in place for a sec, give us a chance to shoot at the sides. Go now!"

Thorny did just that, spun to the left, made a three-step dash and a diving roll into ferns, bush, and webs. Danijel was an instant behind in his turn to the right. It was a delay of no more than a fraction of a second, but it was enough for him to see that the roo had already chosen which target it would attack. Its head turned promptly to track Thorny. It crouched back on those rear legs. Muscles rippled under the scales.

"No!" Danijel shouted. "Hey, stupid roo!"

The head swung back to him. Lips peeled back and away to show the full length of the needle-tipped teeth. Its legs shifted position. Its hiss sounded again.

Its repositioning gave Danijel just enough time to pull an arrow from his quiver, give thanks they had been carrying the bows strung, nock the arrow, and shoot.

And miss.

The arrow glanced off the side of the roo's head. All it did was cause a shake of that head, which flung more droplets of blood around. It crouched back on those hind legs.

Danijel pulled another arrow from the quiver. Could not nock it. Some sticky web strands from his earlier encounter with the webbing stuck to this arrow. He fumbled with his grip. Dropped the arrow.

Jaws gaped in front of him.

An arrow suddenly sprouted from the roo's flank. It let out a high-pitched bellow, swung neck and forelimb claws around to try to reach the shaft in its side. Another arrow struck right next to the first one.

The roo faced to Danijel's left. Leg muscles bunched to propel it in a leap. But all it did was topple forward, its snout digging a small trench into the soft dirt.

Thorny stepped out of the greenery on the left, web strands trailing from her hair and across her shoulders. Her face was the face of an angel—an angel of death.

"You are amazing!" Danijel screamed. "Just fucking amazing!"

"You're pretty fuckin' brave yourself." Thorny walked over to where Danijel was standing. She put one hand lightly on his shoulder, then quickly withdrew it.

"Your shooting was amazing," Danijel said. "You saved me. I missed."

"You don't have Vo Hiep for a father. And it was your shouting that saved me." Thorny turned to stare at the dead roo. "Maybe we should skip the mutual congratulations and admit we're both fucking lucky."

"Yeah."

They approached the roo cautiously even though it was obviously dead. Thorny went to pull her arrows out of its side. "I've only seen one in the valley," she said. "This one is bigger."

"What's the fuzzy stuff?"

Thorny brushed her hand along the roo's side. "Protofeathers, maybe. And look at that crest. This one is different. Different species, maybe. You can see"—she indicated the partially eaten shellhound—"it rips and pulls the meat off. Its bite isn't that strong. Those jaws wouldn't be able to crack your bones."

"That's a great comfort." Danijel laughed because he was sure she expected him to laugh, but it sounded forced, even to him.

Thorny let out a long breath. "I'm glad we got rid of the one whose territory includes my hill."

"Territory?" Danijel was puzzled. "I didn't think they were smart enough to have a territory."

"It must take a certain amount of land to support one of these. And this one seemed to have some kind of central processor. Like Fenris." She stroked the head of the snakeipede, who had stayed coiled around her arm throughout the encounter.

"So, new species," Danijel said. "Do you want to name it?"

"No. Not now. I want to get back to my hill."

·   ·   ·

Later that evening, after the cookfire was extinguished, Danijel and Thorny sat at the opening to the shelter and watched the skies over Heaven unfurl their display of color.

"I have to tell you something," Thorny said.

Her words were quiet, not much above a whisper. It was the kind of quiet that made a sense of foreboding rise in Danijel. He waited for her to speak again.

"I came all the way out here so I could die. I intended to die out here."

"Thorny, no! You can't mean that!"

"Do you want truth, or only the same lies everyone expects when they ask how you're doing?"

Danijel flinched at the intensity in the question. "I'm sorry. The truth. Always the truth."

Thorny nodded. With the bow of her head, her hair slid forward to shroud her face. "That's what I wanted. To die. That was it. To make an end of a life I hated living." The anxiety was gone from her voice. These were statements of fact, nothing more. "But I've been thinking," she went on. "Starving to death takes a long time and it's pretty ugly. I could eat a thistle, of course, and that would be quick, but I'm told it's a real nasty way to die.

"I could take a knife and slit my wrists or my throat, but that would hurt and I'd have to watch the blood pour out. I could hang myself from one of these trees, but with my luck, the noose would give or the branch would break. What I'm trying to say is that maybe this is all telling me I should keep living."

Danijel reached out to put his hands on her shoulders and turned her to him. He brushed the hair away from her face. "Thorny, don't joke about this. Please. I just found you. I don't want to lose you."

"Now, I'm sorry," she said. "I shouldn't joke about it. What I mean is that the sky is beautiful and someone came for me, and no matter what else is wrong, living is worth it."

Danijel saw longing in her face, felt the same longing in his chest. The light hold on her shoulders turned into an embrace, the embrace into a kiss, equal parts long, powerful, and clumsy. After they separated with a mutual gasp, Thorny slid next to him, her head on his shoulder, hand in hand.

She loosened the hand clasp after a few minutes and stroked his palm with the tip of her forefinger.

"Dani, can I ask you a question?"

"Sure. Anything."

"Why do we still have our clothes on?"

DECEMBER 31, HY 21

JING

THE MEDICAL CENTER BUILDING IN SAINT PETERSTOWN THAT WAS NOW SONG Jing's clinic had not been constructed with discrete exam rooms. Instead, it had diagnostic beds that could be curtained off to provide a little privacy. This design may have been to make the most efficient use of the interior space —or more likely, to reduce the number of walls requiring bot self-assembly. Whatever the reason, the only truly private places were the physician's overnight room and the doctor's office.

The type of visit Jing was having with Athena Markopoulos, the type of visit she always had with Athena, required privacy. That meant Jing used the office, where she could have a desk between the chairs the two of them occupied, the on-call room having only one chair in addition to the bed and barely enough room to stand up from either the chair or the bed.

The office was still too small. It had a good-sized monitor on the desk next to a nice, printed pic of Jorge and another of Jing and Jorge with their children when they were little. Beyond that, the walls were bare and the floor concrete. It felt now like those walls were pressing inward to squeeze them together. Talking to Athena made the office frankly claustrophobic, although, Jing reflected, Athena's conversation could make a grand ballroom claustrophobic.

"I told you when I came in, Jud left me." Athena had said that immediately upon her arrival and already three times since. "He's moved in with an Original from *Daredevil* and she's eight years older than I am. And she's not even attractive." Athena's words were flat and heavy. Sad as they were, they carried no heat, nor was there any animation in her face. "I don't know what I'm going to do. I don't. I don't. Tell me what to do to feel better."

Jing wished the bare walls of her office would offer some inspiration, but none was forthcoming. She had no magic words to offer. Jud had been Athena's third partner in as many years, and like the previous two, he had lasted only months. Jing's eyes fell on the pics on her desk. They served only to remind her of her own good fortune and offered no therapeutic approach to this problem.

"Are you taking your meds?" she asked.

"Yes, yes, of course. Every day. Just like you told me." Athena's eyes fixed on a spot in the middle of the desktop. "They don't work. Can you give me something else?"

"You've already been on the others I can give you."

"They didn't work either."

On Earth, Jing would have been able to prescribe from a vast pharmacopoeia of treatments for depression, drugs with varying mechanisms of action, drugs with tweaks in the molecular scaffolding so that one might work better for a particular individual than others. Here on Heaven, however, she was limited. The cell foundries produced the medications; each drug needed a distinct cell line. It was impossible to have the same variety as they had on Earth. The ISC program had selected the drugs that would be available to the colony and sent the necessary cell lines in the *Daredevil*. That was the limit, until the day the settlement developed the wherewithal to synthesize their own drugs from scratch. And, Jing told herself, there were some depressions that no drug therapy could lift.

"Can you tell me something you enjoy doing?" Jing asked. "Maybe we should try to focus on what gives you some pleasure."

"Oh, I enjoy lots of things." Athena's voice lacked any trace of emotion. "But I can't do any of them here. I like having my hair done, with color streaks sometimes. I'd like to have my nails done. A manicure and a pedicure. I know just the shade I want. But no one ever opened a salon here, although I thought someone would. And I'd like a new pair of shoes. Nice shoes. Not another redone pair of boots."

Athena stood up and walked to the side of the desk to be sure Jing could see the ones on her feet. Those had been remanufactured often enough that the uppers had no shape at all. "But even if I could get them, I wouldn't wear them on dirt roads. And new clothes would be nice. I mean real clothes, with some shape to them." With a thumb and forefinger, she pulled a loose fold of her sleeveless cotton top out into a tent and tucked her chin down to view the fabric.

Jing watched the display of fashion, or lack thereof. Athena had taken scissors to her above-the-knee shorts—one of the five standard types of pants the textile recycler could spit out—and cut the legs off a bare fraction of an inch below the crotch. The length of bare leg from the bottom of her buttocks to where the boots covered her ankles might have looked flirty on a woman in her early twenties, but Athena was closing on mid-forties and no longer so lithe. Jing asked her to go back to her chair.

As Athena seated herself, she added, "And I'd like to go skiing. I'd just like to see snow."

"Athena, wait." Jing tried to keep her own tone gentle as she held up her hands to break into Athena's recitation of wants she could not have. "I suppose if enough people wanted their hair and nails done, we could get hair coloring and polish into the production queue and you could do them, or someone could make a business of it. Why don't you ask around?" Jing sneaked a look at her own hands and thought there was some merit to the idea.

"Why would anyone bother when all they get in the end is their same equal share? No one is going to do all that extra work for nothing. And even if somebody would, they'll never give priority for production," Athena said. "Or they'll say we're not set up to make it. I'd like to go out for sushi too."

Her last sentence hung in the air. Jing tried not to sigh. "Athena, there are a lot of things we had on Earth that we can't have here. We all knew that when we decided to make the trip. I think it would be more helpful if we talk about what you like here and what you enjoy here. That will help you feel better."

"There's nothing here I like or enjoy. Every time I go out of my hab, all I see is a dirty, shabby, little town. With the number of people who've moved to the valley, it sometimes feels like a ghost town, and it's too hot and it's too humid, and it's always the same people."

A knock on the door was a welcome interruption for Jing, who was running out of soothing words. Yuki stuck her head in the opening.

"I'm sorry, Jing, I know you're having a session and your phone shows DO NOT DISTURB, but I need you in the clinic."

"Athena, it looks like we'll have to cut this short." Jing wondered for a scant second or two if she was going to regret welcoming this interruption, since it was probably a crisis of some sort. "I'm going to add one of the meds we tried before to the one you're taking now. Yuki will get a supply for you." She wasn't sure if there was a good basis for the combination, and the AI might well scold her later on, but nothing else was working. It was worth a try. The depression in some of the remorsers was the worst she could remember seeing. She tapped the prescription into her phone and sent it to Yuki.

"Why don't you show me what's going on," she said to Yuki, "and then get Athena her meds."

.   .   .

JING COULD BE FORGIVEN IF HER MIND CONJURED UP ALL SORTS OF CATASTROPHES, because those were the types of events that summarily pulled a doctor out of a therapy session. She did not, however, find a bloody mess waiting for her in the clinic. What she found was Poppy Merriwether sitting on one of the diagnostic beds, kicking her long legs in the air and humming a tune. One hand held a small flask. Why was Poppy here? She had a level head and was not given to malingering or hypochondriasis.

Even without the answer to her question, Jing let herself relax a bit. Poppy's family had moved to the valley to set up a farm a dozen years ago. Jing, naturally, knew her well. She had delivered Poppy, as she had every one of the Heaveners, and had seen her for well-care and sick visits both.

Jing shook her head to clear the memories. "What's up, Poppy? What brings you in today?"

Poppy looked around quickly, as though her mind, too, had been somewhere else. She held up the flask. "We broke up a party last night out behind the hydroponics. Dalton Watson and that little crew that hangs around with him, being where they shouldn't be and doing what they shouldn't do.

"Thing is, it wasn't just drunk or stoned. Two of them were seeing things. They said the panels of the hydroponics were melting and flowing down to the ground, and dragons or a gator were talking to them. Ultra-strange, you know. We put all of them in dorm rooms in the school building and locked it up. This morning they were fine, didn't remember any of it, but I wanted to talk to you about it, even though Gordon didn't think we should bother since it went away."

"They were having visual and auditory hallucinations."

"Yeah. I guess that's what it was." Poppy held out the flask. "One of the boys—Ethan Cappelletti, who is Dalton's habmate—tried to throw this away when we caught them. Smells odd, but then I thought I probably shouldn't be playing with it. Can you tell if there is something in here that could make people hallucinate?"

Jing took the proffered flask. A small amount of clear liquid sloshed around the bottom. "Did you ask Ethan what it is?"

"He said he didn't know what I was talking about. Same with the others."

That figured, Jing thought. "Okay," she said. "We can find out what's in here with or without cooperation."

·   ·   ·

Jing took the flask with her and walked out of the medical center, turning left at the intersection of the Avenue of Africa and Town Circle to reach the Lab Unit. This was her second visit to the molecular analyzer in a few days, probably as many visits as she had made in all the years since the *Dauntless* left. If nothing else, she told herself, her failed attempt to find evidence of meth in Fernando had refreshed her on the use of the instrument. This time would be simpler. She had a compound. She was asking only one question: What was it?

Once the machine had powered on and shown the ready message, Jing drew a small sample of the liquid in the flask into a syringe and shot it into the instrument's port.

She pulled up a chair and sat down to wait while the machine did its work. Soon enough, results began to flash up on the screen. When the instrument was finished with its work, she scrolled through the results. The readings brought a frown to her face that deepened as she reached the bottom. She went back to the top and scrolled through the output again. A second look improved neither the results nor her frown.

The flask contained one specific organic monomer, along with dimers and various sized polymers of that monomer. It did not match any known biological molecule in the database, nor did the structure match any in the toxicology database. The computer failed to extrapolate any biological activity from the structure the molecular analyzer had determined. A message at the bottom of the results said that a small fraction of the material could not be analyzed through the gas chromatograph. And that was it.

Jing stood up, arms folded across her chest, and glared at the instrument. There was only one person to call when the results made no sense. Penny.

JORGE

"Penny, where are you? We have to go!" Jorge shouted as he ran back into the fields beyond the farmhouse, his field of vision constrained by the tall stands of bamboo in one direction and the fruit trees in another.

Ultimately, her location was given away by the sounds of dogs yipping and children laughing. Penny stood on a narrow dirt path, a small stanchion besieged by three dogs with their forepaws up by her belly looking for a treat and seven-year-old Xeno along with six-year-old Thuy tugging at her arms. Penny was finding the whole situation comical enough to be laughing herself and not managing any movement back toward the farmhouse where Jorge had left the rover.

"I'm sorry, Jorge," she said when she caught sight of him. "I said I would be waiting for you, but I had to check on that stupid goat. You know, we always figured goats would be terrific animals for the settlement because they give milk and they eat anything, but the problem is that they do eat anything, and if we can't keep them away from the damned thistle and some of those reeds close to the river, we lose the goats, and they don't take well to conditioning, so I wanted to check the paddock before I left and I was intercepted on my way back."

Jorge gave Penny a chance to run out of breath before he tried to speak. "It looks like they don't want you to go."

"They never do." A smile erased some of the fatigue from Penny's face. "You know, before we came here, if I had told anyone I was going to have kids, they would have offered condolences. To the kids." Her smile broadened as the children released her arms to hug her, one on each side. "I mean, I still have no idea what I'm doing, but they do seem to grow up anyway. Like farming, I suppose, as long as you pay attention to what you're doing. Except for Thorny." The smile faded. "Some plants are hard to cultivate. No matter how much you worry."

"Hiep will get her," Jorge said. "He always does. It will be okay. That's why you're making the trip to town now, isn't it?"

"I need to see Ibiana and some others ahead of the Demos meeting. Not simply on a call, but in person, and getting them out of town is almost impossible. I swear, it gets worse every year. Which is part of it. And, yes, I want to see Thorny as soon as she is back."

"There you two are!" Yong came running down the path and gathered up the two children. "I thought they were doing lessons, but they sneaked out. You two, finish what you started!" She shooed the children off in the direction of the farmhouse. "Seriously, Mom, Austin and I have this under control. He'll be here with me until two days before the Demos meeting, when he'll ride up. I'll call in and keep watch here. We're Heaveners. We know how to live here. I would think that by now, you could relax a bit."

"I am relaxed."

Yong's smile showed she didn't believe a word Penny said. She gave her mother a hug, then walked up the path after the younger ones.

Penny directed a tiny smile to the ground, where her dogs now sat patiently on their haunches, still hoping for a treat. Then she linked arms with Jorge and they walked toward the road, leaving the disappointed dogs behind.

"I *am* relaxed. About the kids," she insisted. "Yong can't remember, of course, but I was totally paranoid about her as a baby. I think I was on the phone with Jing twice a day every day, and I don't know what I would have done without her. So, when Thorny came along, I thought I knew what I was doing. We all see how that turned out. But then I had the twins and I was too busy to think about it. And with these two, I'm fine. For me, anyway." She blew out a snort. "The big difference between my kids and my farm plants and animals is that the kids grow up and give you their opinion of everything you do. My plants and animals don't do that. Except the damned goat!"

·   ·   ·

THE ROVER WAS PARKED ON VALLEY ROAD IN FRONT OF THE HOUSE. IT WAS NOT only the rover. Attached to the rear of the rover via a trailer hitch was a wagon that was an odd amalgamation of old and new. The hitch itself, the two axles, the flooring, and some of the side panels were printed plastic, while the tires were made of printed altrubber. Valley-grown bamboo made up the other side panels, the wagon's interior benches where people sat, both the framework for the roof and the roofing itself, and stacked crates filled with farm produce. Each of the crates had a handwritten note card identifying the nature and quantity of its contents, which had been entered into the computer to be figured in the calculation of equal shares. The faces of a half dozen people seated in the cart watched Penny as she walked up with Jorge.

"The front passenger seat in the rover is reserved for you," Jorge said. "Since you're an ex-mayor and expecting, I'm giving you the privilege."

Penny blushed as he held the door open. "This isn't necessary. Tell me all of you didn't take a vote on it."

"No vote. My executive decision since it's my job to drive this rover trip." Jorge walked around the front and settled into the driver's seat. "If I let you sit on the cart benches, your whole trip will be listening to a litany of complaints about how what little the town gives the valley doesn't come close to the value of the food the valley sends up."

"That's part of the discussion I need to have with Ibiana if she really wants to put me up for mayor again. The bit about money." Penny smiled. "I'm pretty good with that argument, and most of the valley people agree with me."

Jorge started the rover. Although the electric motors were silent, the vehicle shuddered and a rattle came from the rear. "Yeah. I don't think anyone on the planet can outtalk you." He laughed. "However, even if you would talk them into submission in ten minutes, Jing will never let me hear the end of it if I put an 'elderly' pregnant woman on the outside benches."

Burdened by the heavily laden wagon, the rover groaned forward, digging a new set of ruts into the road. "I don't think we'll be able to go any faster than one of the ponies," Jorge said. "This will be a slow trip. Midafternoon arrival, I'm afraid; not that much time before sunset."

"Then I'm doubly sorry I held you up," Penny said. "I'm sure you want to see Jing."

"Always. Why do you think I let myself be dragooned into being a bus driver? Unlike riding the ponies, however, I can keep driving until we get there. Full charge in the battery. And Jing is pretty much booked solid with those patients the practitioners can't handle. She's also still dealing with a bunch of questions about what happened to Fernando. The family is far from satisfied, and talk spreads." He rubbed at the old tattoo on his cheek. "Actually, no one is satisfied and everyone is talking. It's as bad as when people would post all sorts of shit online on the Community on Earth. Cam and Jess are going around doing what they call interviewing people, and that only makes it worse."

"Has Jing learned anything new?"

"I don't think so. I think she's leaning toward calling it an allergic reaction to something, but that may be because she doesn't know what else to call it." A note of trouble crept into Jorge's voice. "Some of the talk . . . There's a rumor going around—it's all through the school and the town—that Fernando had some kind of fight with Thorny. I don't know how true that is. Some people are saying that's why she ran away."

Penny shifted in her seat to face him as the rover started up the incline of Heaven Highway 1. "I've heard it. Some of it, at least. Even if nobody will say anything to me directly, the kids at school message Yong. I'm sure she filters it, but I still get it. Whenever Thorny feels overwhelmed or angry, she runs off for a while. That's nothing new. Granted, it's never been for this long, but, still, that's how Thorny copes. But a fight? What kind of a fight? With weapons?" Penny's voice went low. "I can't believe that. Jing examined his body. What did she say? Were there wounds?"

Jorge shook his head. "Not that she told me. And she would. She said nothing looks like trauma from a fight. But there are plenty of people up in Saint Peterstown who don't do anything more productive than talk. And valley-folk do a lot of talking, too, if you want the truth. Guillermo and Donna, well, you can understand how they feel, but they're not helping the situation."

"I guess I'll see what people say when I'm standing in front of them and they can't just chip in or tap it into their damned phone. The one advantage of this place over the damned Community is that it's impossible to be anonymous."

IBIANA

THE COMMUNITY DOME WAS VACANT WHEN IBIANA AND PENNY STROLLED IN LATE that afternoon, their arms linked. Its silence was broken only by the wind whistling through the open lattice of girders and struts that held up the circular roof and the loud snaps of the banner proclaiming REPLACEMENT-PLUS! that hung below the roof. They stopped at the open space between the dais where the town council would sit and the semicircular ranks of seats for the Demos of Heaven.

"Thank you for coming to see me," Ibiana said. "I have always found it . . . difficult to travel to the valley. I understand you are expecting again, although it's not showing yet."

"A little soon for that," Penny said, "although, skinny as I am, you'd think I would show from the day of conception. I never do until late, though. It's no problem for me to come up. Jing wants an ultrasound, and I rode with Jorge in a rover, not on horseback."

"Even so." Ibiana gazed at the flapping banner. "This makes seven for you. Your Pioneers average, what, four or four and a half per couple. We Originals from the *Daredevil,* we manage replacement-plus, but it's more like an average of three."

"But you are also older than we are," Penny said. "About a decade on average. That matters when it comes to having kids."

"True. But too many of us from the *Daredevil* assumed we could pop the kids out of the artificial wombs in the Lab Unit, same as the farm animals, then ship them straight to day care. No muss, no fuss, no work. Oh sure, we all said we'd have one of our own, but after that, lab babies all that way. We never figured we'd have to populate the planet the old-fashioned way."

"There are issues growing humans in the lab," Penny said, almost as if she were teaching a class. "Bonding problems and socialization issues. We knew about that going in and we still tried with a couple in our oldest cohort, and that's what we saw. So, as long as we can birth enough children, replacement-plus"—she pointed up to the banner—"we're not doing it in the lab anymore. We don't know why this happens, but it seems to be a primate issue. They did a study on Earth in multiple monkey species looking at behaviors after completely ex utero fertilization and gestation—"

Ibiana held up one hand, then put the other one in front of Penny's mouth. "Please, Penny. No tangents today. Please. We need to talk about the Demos and the mayor."

"Sorry," Penny said without sounding sorry at all. "But why here?" She spread her arms wide, taking in the empty seats and unoccupied council table. "I could have brought coffee to your hab and we could have had a cup or two. There's a certain symbolism in being in the center of the Demos with the Demos absent . . ." She brought her eyes back to Ibiana with a smile. "But you weren't trying to set a mood, and I'll skip the symbolism tangent."

Briefly, Ibiana was disconcerted. Conversations with Penny could have that effect. It was too easy to end up nowhere near the course you thought you had charted. "Not the hab. Too many arguments with Nessie recently. We've always had fights over the years; what couple doesn't? But of late there's an edge to it. I'd rather she not know about this conversation. At the Demos meeting, Jacoby is going to step down. I want to put you up, and I need to be sure you'll agree."

"Hiep told me that much. And he told me you wanted him to talk me into it. He won't do anything like that. Convince me." Penny folded her arms across her chest.

"We have problems. Hah. Like that's a secret." Ibiana led Penny up the steps to the dais, where they looked over the empty ranks of seats. "A lot of it goes back to the attitudes about lab babies. Work, or the avoidance of it, and all the fights around that, plus the personalities, plus the factions." She sighed. "The remorsers want their equal shares, but they don't want to do anything. What they want is to go home, but with a few exceptions, even they realize how stupid it is to say it. The *Daredevil* Originals"—she smiled—"we were all crooks to begin with. Plenty want more than an equal share and scream about what anybody else gets. The valley-boys and valley-girls call townies parasites, and townies call the valley-folk pretend aristocrats. Both sides are ready to man the barricades, one at each end of Highway 1.

"The Demos voted for Jacoby because he's a bland guy who won't rock anybody's boat. Electing him and keeping him in was a way for everyone to pretend it's all normal. I don't know what Jacoby thought was involved when he was put up, beyond liking the idea of being called mayor, but he can't take it anymore. He's going to resign when the Demos meets. That's supposed to be a secret, but I don't think anything stays secret in a small town like this. Ajit wants it and we don't want that. Ajit won't have anything prepared if I put you up with no warning." She saw, in her mind, the seats in front of them crowded as they would be for the meeting, people trying to talk over one another or shout one another down, children running helter-skelter through all of it. How would all of them react?

"Right." Penny tapped the toe of one boot against the plastic sheeting that formed the platform on which the council table rested. A hollow boom followed. "It's an impossible job to do right, so we need to have as mayor the one person everyone can agree on hating."

Ibiana was starting to laugh when she realized Penny was not laughing. Not even smiling. "Dammit, Penny, that's not the reason. We need you in this job because stuff is wearing out, machinery is breaking down, there are no replacements, and the head-butting among the factions is getting serious. You're the one person we can count on to keep a clear head and come up with ideas. People will admit that, even while they're not liking you."

"That's a hell of a pitch, Ibi. Make the job more impossible." Penny's crossed arms turned into a self-hug. She realized what she was doing and quickly dropped her arms to her sides. "You want me to do this; I have a price."

"Which is?" The two words were slow and hesitant.

"First, we need to make changes in shares and priorities. That top you're wearing, it's cotton, right? Light, breathable, great for this damned climate none of us can get used to. Your pants. They're from viscose fibers, also really light, breathable, and stretchy."

"You're right," Ibiana said, "but I don't see your point."

"It's that the cotton comes from valley farms. Vargas is the largest producer, and there are a few others. The viscose fibers come from bamboo, also from the valley, maybe from my farm. We don't grow enough of either, yet, and the viscose needs chemical treatment, which depends on the machinery Klaus put together. We don't make enough for everybody to have what they want, but with equal shares and our priority rules a remorser who does no work, gets the same as someone busting their ass running a farm and making goods on the side."

Penny walked out to the edge of the dais, staring at the seats. "I'm as responsible for this as anyone, because when we got started and there was a real risk we'd all starve, I said I'd grow the food and show others how to farm and we would split it all evenly. Everyone got the same. Equal shares. That became the way we did everything." She stuffed her hands into the pockets of her pants and balled them into fists where they were out of sight. "That has to change. Productivity and hard work have to be rewarded. If people feel they're killing themselves and the benefit goes to others who do nothing, they'll quit doing it."

Ibiana stepped up to be even with Penny and tried to decipher her face, but she could read nothing there. Penny had become skilled at hiding her thoughts over the years. This was no longer the girl of yesteryear, eager to do whatever was needed and asking only for people to let her do it.

"What are you saying? You want to make this place capitalist?"

"I didn't say that, and you can thank me for not giving you the lecture I could." Penny's eyes roved across the vacant seats. What was she seeing in her mind? "We'll take care of everyone at a basic level, but those who do valuable work, and more of it, need to see the benefits. I want support on that from the town. I know I'll get it from the valley. I'll have Sonal work with Jorge to set up a system. A money system. We used to have that on Earth."

"Sonal might be a problem for some people. Because of Klaus."

"That's exactly my point." Penny's words began to rush out in a flood. "Klaus has set up the facilities to make us concrete; he makes most of our brick and all of the new glass in the valley. He figured out how to make the fiber for your pants. And for this, people will object to Sonal, his partner, working on a money system?"

"I'll do what I can," Ibiana said. "It's not going to be easy, but maybe people are getting scared enough."

"I'm not done. We need exploration. I said it before, and the Demos voted me out. Now we have to do it. No choice. What happens when bots and machinery, *recycling machinery*, break down for good? We don't have enough people to do everything by hand. We have to be able to build new machines. We don't have metal deposits—no iron, no aluminum, not in the valley, not up here. We don't have enough wood. Those dwarf trees are next to useless."

Penny turned to face Ibiana. Her eyes were hard, her whole face set in stone. Ibiana had never seen her like this. She felt a twinge of fear that Penny had never triggered before. "I'm going to tell you what reality is." Coldness crusted the words with ice. "We cannot keep a technological civilization going if all we have is the town and the valley. And with the limitations of this world, the town and the valley can't survive without high technology. That's the rock and the hard place we're between.

"The only place we can go is south. There is enough land that should be habitable for us to put settlements there, and we have to do it while we still have working tech. I've been thinking that maybe I could get support from the Demos for Hiep and me, maybe take our whole family and go ourselves. You want me as mayor again then it won't be me going, but someone needs to start exploring. You get me support from the town and the *Daredevil* Originals for all of this, and I'll do your impossible job."

"I don't know that I can promise." Ibiana kept her words soft and measured. She wanted to believe that Penny could not refuse because Penny would never let the town flounder, but this was an older, harder Penny. Ibiana did not want to take the risk. "It will be hard to hold majorities together."

"You used to be a mighty fine swindler on Earth, from what I've heard," Penny said.

"Yeah. Until I screwed up and got caught."

Penny's beatific smile could not hide all the harshness that had been there. "Well, we all have to learn from our mistakes, don't we?"

PENNY

THE CONVERSATION WITH IBIANA WAS OVER, AS FAR AS PENNY WAS CONCERNED. She told Ibiana that she would like to stay in the dome and think by herself for a little while. Ibiana took the hint and left her. She did not like to unsettle Ibiana, an old ally, but she had learned that people were more likely to do what she wanted them to do if they feared the consequences of not doing it. It was a little like raising kids, and not at all something that came naturally.

Quiet filled the Community Dome. From where she stood at the council table, Penny looked out at the ranked seats. She had been through so many meetings of the Demos, had led so many of them. Some had gone well, others not. A few, like her last one as mayor, had been debacles. She tried to picture the one that was coming, saw in her mind the empty seats before her as filled with the people of Heaven. Pondered the nature of the Demos.

The Demos was by design the heart and soul of Saint Peterstown and, by extension, of the entire human settlement on Heaven. The ISC had given the colony—or imposed upon it, depending on one's perspective—a constitution specifying government by direct democracy, an updated version of the old Athenian model. The people of the colony—the Demos—would meet and vote on every question of importance. It could be a charge of theft; it could be a decision on changing out a product from the cell foundries; it could be who would be mayor. The intent had been for the Demos to vote on everything. And as much as they voted, they argued. They argued on a personal level, as townies against valley-folk, and as people who felt they should receive in accordance with their work against those who felt all should have an equal share and no more. Now Originals argued with their Heaven-born children. Having Demos meetings by phone and vid link on the network did cut down on the arguing a little and, if nothing else, prevented the escalation to fisticuffs. The most vituperative arguments were saved, or so it seemed, for the in-person Demos meeting at the winter solstice, when everyone who could come in person did so and brought their children for what sometimes resembled a circus. The arguments were the only part of Saint Peterstown that had not diminished with age.

A small, elected town council, composed of a mayor, a vice-mayor, and a secretary, was charged with executing the decisions of the Demos and handling administrative tasks. Quite early in the town's history, the council became responsible for decisions in minor matters since no one wanted to meet and vote on *everything*.

The actual meeting of the Demos was another feature that had evolved over time. All the original settlers had chips, naturally, so voting was an easy process, with the voters chipped in to the town network. That meant the meetings could easily have been remote, with discussion moderated over a voice and vid channel. But that had not been the intention. The people were supposed to gather in person, again following the model from ancient Earth, to promote the sense of community. They would be able to see and hear—and, in the constant hot weather, smell—each other with their own senses. Close proximity meant they could reach out and touch each other, and some touches, from time to time, were not gentle. The Community Dome had been built with seating for one thousand. It had space where more seating could be added, because the settlement was expected to grow out radially into the surrounding open land.

No plan survives contact with reality. The land around Saint Peterstown could support the primitive ferns the settlers called grass, along with thistles, shellhounds, and little else. Human expansion went to the valley, forty-two miles away, which made repeated journeys for multiple meetings problematic. The broiling air discouraged outdoor meetings, especially in the summer. Within the first year of the colony, most questions were decided by network notification and vote. Meetings were conducted on the network whenever possible. The people, by vote of the Demos, restricted in-person meetings to a single meeting a year. It had become tradition that the meeting started just as the sun rose above the horizon on the winter solstice and had to end before it disappeared back below the horizon in the evening of New Year's Day.

Would she be mayor again at the sunset of the coming New Year's Day? What path would the colony take if she were not? What was forming, along with the knot in her stomach, was the conviction that she needed to be mayor, needed again to find a way to push the Demos like a balky, intractable two-year-old to do what had to be done. She wrapped her arms around her chest, contemplating that job. She was tired and she had another baby on the way.

That was when her phone buzzed. Jing needed her.

·   ·   ·

"So what do you have here?" Penny asked. The darkness that came with late afternoon had already descended by the time she was able to meet with Jing.

The problem in front of her now was more to her taste than the politics of the Demos. She and Jing were in the Lab Unit in front of the molecular analyzer, with Jing scrolling through the readout describing the material in the flask. "I don't know. You can take it as a general rule that when a teenage boy is someplace he is not supposed to be and attempts to get rid of something when he is caught, he has either stolen or abused whatever it is he tried to get rid of. That was how it worked on Earth. No reason teenagers should be any different here. But this stuff doesn't make sense. It doesn't fit the structure of any known abused agent. The molecular scaffold isn't close enough to any of them to suggest what kind of effect it would have that someone would abuse. It has a safety data sheet, but all that says is not to get it on your skin or to inhale it because the toxicity is not known."

"What about the material that the analyzer rejected?" Penny asked.

Jing shrugged. "I'm a doc. I trained in rural medicine, so I had to know how to use all the instruments a medical lab would have, but at the end of it, I'm a doctor, not a chemist."

"I'm not a chemist either." Penny tightened her lips momentarily and stared at the screen. "Technically, I suppose I'm not anything except a half-trained mostly do-it-yourself farmer, but I did play with almost every instrument in here back when I was analyzing the soil and the local biota to figure out what we could grow. And," in a voice gone sharp, "I did all of that by myself."

"I know that."

"Sorry." Penny patted the older woman on an upper arm. "This brings up memories of being mocked for knowing the stuff we needed to know and doing what we needed to do. After all these years, I still get defensive."

"No need to apologize," Jing said. "I saw enough when I first came down from the *Dauntless*. Tell me what you want to try, and we'll do it."

A few hours and several instruments later, Penny was staring at the readout from a boxy instrument at the end of one of the benches. "There's gadolinium in this sample," she said. "And that's strange. It's in the lanthanide series, a rare earth metal. I never found it in any of the dirt or biological samples I analyzed. I would remember. I mean, it's probably on the planet somewhere; we just haven't come across it yet. So, unless this was a strange and lucky find out on the plains here, it came from something we brought."

Jing snapped her fingers. "I was in the printer unit the other day, trying to talk to Chloe DiMasi about shifting one of the foundries to cyclosporine. She was more interested in bitching to Petrovic about how one of the lines was losing yield and she wanted him to fix it. She mentioned gadolinium. It was the production system for altrubber."

Penny was already headed back to the bench with the molecular analyzer. The words "I want to play with the output a bit" trailed after her.

It did not take long before Penny stepped back from the instrument's panel and turned to Jing. "That's what it is." No trace of doubt showed on her face. "This comes from the reaction chamber for the polymerization that yields our end product of alternative rubber. The reaction hasn't gone to completion; it's been stopped—there's even monomer still present. But that's what it is, a mix of precursors to our altrubber."

"Which explains why I found nothing in any of the medical or toxicology databases. Ask the wrong question, get the wrong answer. That's my fault. Now I wonder if it could trigger an anaphylactic reaction."

"Don't be so hard on yourself. It's like what Sherlock Holmes said about what you have left after you eliminate all the impossible answers." Penny rubbed her lower back where standing over the instruments had raised an ache. "Someone invaded that system to pull out this material. Maybe didn't know proper technique, was sloppy, or just didn't care. Doesn't matter which; they damaged the system. For the sake of a hallucinogenic high, they could leave us with no way to make new altrubber.

"What are we going to do if we get to the point where we can't make new tires? Good luck building wooden wheels. Bad for us. Probably bad for the kids who used it too. But why? I can say that after having had six kids, their ingenuity in finding trouble still surprises me."

That brought a laugh from Jing. "We should ask the one Poppy caught."

Jing

A couple of phone calls resulted in Ethan Cappelletti being brought to the clinic by Gordon Durham-Pole, who comported himself like a gendarme escorting a prisoner. Ethan slouched along, hands deep in the pockets of his cargo pants, as he worked to keep arm's length from Gordon. An abrasion across his chin spoke to the fall he'd taken when Poppy tackled him from the pony.

Jing took in the body language of the two and came to a quick decision. "Thank you for coming over, Gordon, but we're going to have a private discussion. There's no point in you staying here."

"I should know about things that concern the school and the senior cohorts," Gordon said.

"If there's something you should know, we'll tell you. That's a promise." Penny's voice was stern, a sharp contrast to the way her hands clutched her arms across her chest.

Gordon looked from Penny to Jing, found no support. "If that's the way you want it, of course."

As Gordon walked out the clinic door, Ethan turned and thrust a middle finger out at his retreating figure. "I never thought I'd be sorry to see Busby gone, but that asshole thinks he has been made king of the seniors."

"That can be a separate discussion," Jing said. "Come on in back."

The three of them squeezed into the tiny office Jing had used for her therapy session with Athena. She sat behind the desk, with Penny standing at one side of it. Ethan did not sit.

"We want to know what you were doing with the liquid in that flask you had," Jing said. "We also want to know how you got it."

"There was nothing in it." Ethan made a show of being angry. "It was an empty flask I picked up. Don't remember where. I was going to put my joints out in it. Not that I ever got to smoke one."

"Come on," Jing said. "We've analyzed what was in it, so we actually know the chemical, which means we also know it wasn't empty. And I don't believe you just picked it up at random. It's important that you tell us what you were doing with it."

"We weren't doing anything except going to smoke and drink, and that's not such a big deal. Who really cares if we're out there at night? It's not like anybody has seen anything bigger than a shellhound at the Perimeter Road."

Jing looked closely at the boy and saw tense, hunched shoulders, eyes down, brown hair falling across his forehead, hands jammed into his pockets so deep they might burst through. "You've done this before, whatever it is that you're doing. This is why you make a point of being out there." An idea came to her. "Is this what happened to Fernando that night? He drank it or inhaled it and maybe took too much? Or did he have a really bad allergic reaction to it?"

Ethan's eyes came up, narrowed. He jutted out his chin. "None of that happened." He licked his lips rapidly, came to a decision. "Yeah, we were out there that night. Fucking Kojo told his mama, so even if you don't know yet, we were. But there was nothing to do with anything in a flask. Fernando's mouth wasn't anywhere except on top of Thorny's." He made a sharp turn toward Penny, as if suddenly realizing who she was.

Then he doubled down on it. "Yeah, that's what she was doing with him. And then she hit him and that's what happened to Fernando. Stole his phone then and ran. Your kid." By the end, he was almost spitting the words at Penny. "You should be askin' about that, about what your kid did, not worrying about a stupid flask."

Penny went rigid. Her knuckles went white. Her jaw barely moved, but somehow, words came out under control. "We'll ask Thorny about that when she comes back. We'll see what she has to say. In the meantime, though, you should tell Dr. Song what you were doing with what was in the flask. We know what that stuff is. The compound blocks the production of androstenedione and of testosterone, and it channels steroid production to estrogen."

She rattled off the names of a few enzymes for good measure. "That means if you're using it, you'll end up with testicular atrophy and erectile dysfunction as well. In words you'll understand, it means your balls will shrivel up and you'll have a permanent limp dick. You may also grow a nice set of tits. It's a small town. I don't know how confidential anything stays. Not very, I suspect. I do have a habit of talking. Your gender identity is male, isn't it? Now, if you want help, you talk. Now and fast."

Fright flashed across Ethan's face and his jaw dropped open. Penny's face was cold while Jing's wore a smile. All at once, Ethan cracked.

"I don't know what the stuff is. I don't. Dalton gets it. He said there's no issue with it. It just makes you high so you see things and hear things. It's wild, a great ride. Just heat it up a bit and breathe it in. That's why we go out there. That way, no worries if the air cleaners don't get it out of the habs, and if someone is raving for a while, at least they don't go running into the street around other habs. Dalton said there's no problem, and anyway, Fernando didn't use it. Not then. And what can you do to help me?"

"I'll think of something," Jing said.

"Maybe," Penny added.

Jing smiled again. "You should get back to your hab. Unless you want me to call Gordon to come get you."

After Ethan had fled from the clinic, Jing slumped, her muscles going slack, almost as though she would flow across the desk like an amoeba. She turned to Penny, who had managed to put her hands down but was still standing in place, rigid.

"I'm sorry about what he said about Thorny. I'm as sure as I can be that Fernando did not die from a blow to the head. I've said that. I'll stand by it. Give me the rest of today, maybe early tomorrow, and let me see if this compound could have done it."

"Thank you," Penny said. "And for the rest . . . some kids grow up the hard way. I should know."

"Too true. But where did you pull all that hormone information that you used to get him to talk? What database? I didn't find anything when I looked for allergic reactions after we spoke earlier, and I'm chipped in now and searching, and still nothing."

"I made it all up." Penny smiled a thin smile. "Everybody knows Penny goes off on tangents, but everybody also knows that Penny's tangents are true. It's a good reputation to have. This isn't the first lie I've told. He deserved it."

DANIJEL

THE LITTLE SHELTER WAS EMPTY WHEN DANIJEL WOKE. HE DRESSED QUICKLY AND WENT outside. Thorny was seated cross-legged on the ground a few yards away, looking upriver at the starry sky.

She did not offer her face for a kiss when Danijel came up, so he sat down next to her and put an arm around her shoulders while hoping that was the correct move to make. Thorny shifted her position to eliminate the space between them and molded herself against his side.

"What are you doing?" Danijel asked.

"Trying to find the star that Earth circles," she said. "I can't remember the patterns, though. I'm not sure I'm looking in the right place."

Danijel peered up at the heavens. "I memorized the star patterns back when I was eight or nine, at least the ones around Earth's star. It's so faint from where we are, though, you can barely see it without a telescope." She was still focused on the sky, so he settled for giving her a gentle kiss on the top of her head and was rewarded by her arm going around him to give him a hug. "I don't think it's in the sky tonight. Not this season at this latitude. Any particular reason?"

"I had a dream about home, and when I woke up I was thinking how Mom will sometimes say home when she's referring to Earth. Dad doesn't do that, though. Not at all."

"It's funny, I suppose." Danijel gave her a hug as he spoke. "We learn all about Earth in school, human history on Earth, but the chippers all act like you're not supposed to talk about what it would be like being on Earth, or even think about Earth, and they cut themselves off when they start talking about what it was like, so, naturally, I memorized where to find it in the sky."

"Yeah, most of the chippers are like that. I mean, to Heaveners like us, Earth doesn't mean anything, but I guess it does to the chippers. The remorsers, shit, they hardly talk about anything else."

"I wouldn't want to be them."

They were quiet for a while after that, enjoying the gentle pressure and touch of being next to each other. Memories tumbled through Danijel's mind.

"Speaking of home," he said at last, "and speaking of dreaming of home, we need to think about getting back."

"No," Thorny said. "I don't want to go back. I *can't* go back."

"Thorny." Danijel reached over, his fingers light against her cheek. She did not turn her face. "Thorny, we don't really have a choice. Sure, we can eat shellhound and we can find some plants we can eat, but once we've finished the Earth food and supplement pills in our packs, that's the end for the vitamins and the methionine we need. You know what happens then. First symptoms in about three weeks from no thiamine."

"I'm not sure it's possible to go back," Thorny said. "You may have bought yourself a one-way ticket."

"If it's a ticket to you, I'm okay with it." He tightened the hug.

"You're silly. But I like that." Thorny moved, though, to create a little space. "I'm serious, Dani. It may not be possible."

"I'll bet it is. The battery in my rover wasn't fully discharged. It'll recover enough in the sunlight we have that we can limp along. I'll bet we can make it."

"No." Thorny shook her head. "You can try it if you want to. It's okay. I won't be angry."

"I'm not leaving here without you!" Desperation edged into Danijel's voice. The conversation that had been cut off the previous day resurfaced in his mind. "Thorny, tell me what happened that night. Tell me what's wrong."

"I don't want to tell you." A tear rolled down her cheek and onto his fingers. She began to talk anyway. She told him about Fernando kissing her and about what he was trying to do, and where his hands went, and how he was touching her. "I stomped on his foot. Drove the edge of my boot down his shin and jammed it into his instep. That loosened his grip, let me shove him away, but he didn't stay off. He lunged at me, so I threw a punch, hard as I could, everything I had, and then I ran. I didn't stop running until I got here." When the words ended, sobbing began.

"Thorny . . . Ferdy's dead. Don't you know that?"

"What!" She turned a tear-streaked face to him. "When?"

"That night. I found him by the hydroponics."

"How is that possible? I mean, I punched him once. I didn't even hit him in the head. Oh my God, they're all going to say I did it."

"Nobody thinks that, Thorny. Nobody knows what happened. Nobody was out there, and nobody saw anything."

"That's not true!" She whipped her head around once, twice, three times, lashing his face with the ends of her hair. "They were all out there. Dalton's group. They were . . . they were there."

"They said they weren't there. All of them said that."

"They're lying." The words were flat, brooked no argument.

"Why would they lie, Thorny? That doesn't make sense."

"You mean, why would they lie when it would be so easy to blame me?" She pulled away and turned to sit facing him. "Dalton's got some stuff, don't know what it is or where he gets it. Heat it, inhale it, you get a real psychedelic high. That's his secret, their secret. I guess whatever it is, there'll be real trouble if people like Busby find out."

"You've done this?"

"No. I wanted to. That's how . . . never mind. Maybe it's not safe. Maybe that's what happened to Ferdy."

Danijel reached out, took both her hands in his. "Look, this makes it even more important to go back, and I promise you, no one is going to think what you did . . . is why he's dead. And I told you, I'm not leaving here without you."

"You don't fucking give up, do you?" She pulled her hands away and wiped the tears from her cheeks. Then she grinned—a little strained, but a grin. "I'll make you a deal. Remember yesterday we talked about a log cabin?"

"Yes."

"Build a log cabin with me out of these glosso logs. Then I'll go back with you. Do we have a deal?"

Dani gave her a hard look, thought about it for no more than a second or two, and smiled. They shook on it and pledged to start with the first light.

·　　·　　·

The slopes of the hill and the surrounding land held plenty of the glossos with trunks or boughs of appropriate diameter, either standing or fallen. The vibro-saw cut through the wood easily enough, both to fell a tree and to chop a trunk into suitable lengths, but their first problem surfaced immediately: no bots. All the logs they would need in order to build the cabin had to be hand-carried to their construction site at the top of the hill. A bit of experimentation told them that between the two of them, they could manage six-foot logs. After they brought up several, Danijel took a break from hauling and dug lines in the dirt with the heel of his boots.

"I think six by five will be about as big as we can go," Danijel said. "If we can manage rafters, we can get some overhang with the roof and use spiderwebs and leaves, like you did on the shelter, for caulking."

"That's enough room to stretch out. You're five nine at most and I'm shorter." Thorny eyed the dirt in the middle of the lines Danijel had drawn. "If we split some lengthwise and put the flat side up, we can have a floor to put the leaves and blankets on. It won't be perfect when it rains, but it won't be mud."

"Good idea." Danijel allowed himself a smile despite his already aching muscles. "The only problem with the size is that you won't have room for a dishwasher and kitchen table."

"Hey! That's your area of responsibility!" She swatted him across the back of a shoulder with an open palm. Her own smile broadened to make dimples in her cheeks. "Come on! I can cut joins better than you can!"

"No, you can't!" It would be worth dying, Danijel decided, to see those dimples again.

With the brief number of daylight hours, the walls had barely reached chest high on Danijel when the light dimmed. The tool packs had some battery-powered lights that allowed them to keep going with the logs they had already brought to the hilltop. When they finally called a halt, both of them were breathing heavily. Every muscle—arms, legs, and back—was sore. Still, the cabin was taking shape. The opening for a doorway was there, although neither one could think of how to hang a door without nails or hinges, and, after much debate, the bottom half of a cutout for a window was in place, although no amount of playful argument had resolved what would go *in* the window. Fenris indicated its approval of the structure by wriggling in and coiling in a corner.

"I don't think we can go much higher than six feet on the walls," Danijel said. "We're not going to be able to position logs if the walls are higher than that."

"That's all right. Tell your glands that you're done with your growth spurt."

"Easy for you to say, shrimp!" They both laughed.

"We should have some dried food from our packs tonight," Danijel said. "The shellhounds are dumb, but I'm too tired to go through the woods to catch one. Maybe you've got something special in that mystery pack of yours that I brought."

"No food, I'm afraid. A change of clothes and my flute. That's all." Her face turned solemn.

"Flute?"

With that, she told him the story of how Hiep would take the pack with him the times he went out to get her and would play the flute as a way of telling her to come in. "I don't understand why he does it," she said. "And I can't imagine what he thought when the pack wasn't there. Nothing good, I'm sure."

"I think it's nice," Danijel said. "Like a secret connection between you two."

"Yeah. A weird connection from a weird father to a weird daughter."

"I like your sort of weird."

"You're weirder." She poked his shoulder with a forefinger. "I'm not very good, but would you like to hear me play?"

"Hell yes! What do you like best?"

"There was a flutist in one of the late twentieth-century rock bands I like, but my favorite piece is 'Brian Boru's March.' That seems right for where we are."

DECEMBER 32, HY 21

PENNY

"I AM, ACTUALLY, MORE INTERESTED IN WHY FERNANDO DIED THAN IN MY ULTRA-sound." Penny thought the effort she was expending to keep her hands in her lap and appear nonchalant was working. At least her hands were in her lap and were not fidgeting with each other. "If the stories running around this excuse for a town get any wilder, they'll have Thorny hitting him with Thor's hammer. The Demos is always a cross between an improv show and a cage fight. If this becomes the main attraction, I don't want to guess what will happen—and I'm speaking from experience. What do you think now? Could it be the altrubber chemicals? Is there any way to put this away?"

"I don't know. I just don't know." Jing took a moment to try to coax loose strands of hair back into her bun before she gave up and gazed at Penny across the desk of her small office. "I've rechecked everything. Some minor inflammation in his bronchi I saw earlier when I was looking for signs of anaphylaxis. I can't say it was due to those chemicals, and even if it was, that couldn't have killed him. At the same time, I can't disprove it, because anaphylactic shock can hit so damned fast.

"Some of those kids had hallucinations. The brain has to be fixed properly, and it won't be ready to make slides for another week, so I can't know if there are abnormalities from those chemicals there.

Could it have caused seizures? Maybe. Could that be fatal? Don't know. Yes, sudden death can occur in epilepsy, but I can't tell if that was what happened here. I do know he did not aspirate and asphyxiate." She sighed. "Inhaling reactive chemicals isn't a good idea. Never understood why kids did it on Earth. It makes no more sense here." She stood up and brushed at the front of her white coat.

Penny shook her head. "I know you're doing your best, but I need better." She could not keep her hands still. They grabbed her elbows. No matter what she did, she could not banish the nervous habits from her youth. "Ibiana is going to put me up for mayor again. I know Ibi. She'll do it whether I agree or not and dare me to turn her down in front of that circus."

"I'm sorry I don't have anything better on Fernando. Believe me, Guillermo is on the phone or popping notifications on my field every day, and he is not as polite as you." Jing made a gesture for Penny to stand up. "However, I have you here so we can do your ultrasound, which you need no matter what you say. If you don't mind, I'll do it with Yuki and have her shadow watch so she can learn."

Penny decided she could not argue with Jing if the doc was going to switch the conversation back to medicine. Jing was as stubborn about medicine as Penny was about everything else. No, Penny did not mind if Yuki and her shadow were present. People needed all the opportunities they could have to learn their jobs.

When they stepped out of Jing's office, however, what the two of them found was Yuki and the shadow coming toward them at a brisk pace. Yuki's face was grim but not panicked, which Penny took as a good sign. The shadow was a townie-girl named Jewel whom Jing had selected as a possible future practitioner. This was her first year as a high-senior, a year younger even than Thorny. Her job was to shadow Yuki and begin to learn what a practitioner did. She looked so young that her way-too-large and no-longer-so-white coat seemed to be a costume for a child. Could she possibly learn enough, fast enough, to be able to function in the role before Jing was too old? *Dear God, was I ever that young,* Penny wondered, *and when did I get old?*

"I'm glad we caught you before you went off to something else," Yuki said to Jing. "We've got a couple of the boys out front who've been in a fight. I think I've got it taken care of, but I'd like a quick check from you."

So much for the ultrasound, Penny thought.

Jing followed Yuki and her shadow to the front of the clinic. Penny trailed behind, because Penny was always curious about everything and no one told her not to come along.

Dalton and Ethan sat on adjacent diagnostic beds, both looking rather the worse for wear. The left side of Dalton's face was swollen and bruised, with a half-inch laceration under the eye. His lower lip was split and swollen. In one hand he held a cold pack that rested on his thigh. Ethan had a bloody wad of gauze stuffed up his right nostril. He winced as he inhaled. Gordon Durham-Pole stood with his arms folded, facing the two of them. He did not look pleased.

"Hab-mates," Yuki said. "An argument yesterday that carried over into a fight this morning. Soft tissue contusions, basically. Except I think Ethan has a cracked rib. I've got it taped up. I'd like you to check the image."

Yuki crossed to a screen and tapped in commands. An X-ray image of a chest appeared. She placed fingers on either side of one of the lower ribs and spread them to enlarge the view."

"Yeah. One broken rib," Jing said. "I'd say you took a good shot, punch or kick," she said to Ethan. "You threw it?" She looked at Dalton.

"We had a discussion," Dalton said.

"It might need more discussion," Ethan said.

"Any further discussion and you'll lose your hab privileges," Gordon snapped. "You'll live in a school dorm room like a first year low-junior. Got it?"

They glared at each other but both nodded.

"Either of you want to talk further about what happened?" Jing received two definitive head shakes. "Fine. Then we'll leave it at that. The cold pack works better if you hold it against the swelling," she told Dalton. "You need to limit physical activity for the next two weeks," she said to Ethan. "After that, it will still probably hurt, but it's up to you how much you want to put up with. I would stay out of the gym until the pain is gone. Both of you can attend to your lessons. And avoid further discussions."

The two of them stood up from the diagnostic beds, gingerly in Ethan's case. From there, they shuffled to the exit from the clinic. Gordon did not leave.

"You said something to Ethan yesterday." Gordon's words took in both Jing and Penny. He ignored Yuki and Jewel. "Something about what was in that flask."

"That was between him and us," Penny said.

"Goddammit! I am the proctor for the seniors. I am responsible for them. It does not matter if Busby's around or it's Tiffany taking her place. I am responsible for them, and if there's something that's going to touch off a fight, I'd like to know in advance. I'm the one who will be explaining this—or trying to explain it—to their families."

"They're old enough to know better. You're not accountable for what they did," Jing said.

"Yes, I am." Gordon realized he had raised his voice to the doctor and clenched his teeth for an instant. "I know you chippers don't see me or my cohort as any different from the school kids, but this is my job, and I am accountable for what happens."

He spun around to leave, but Penny said, "Wait."

At the word, Gordon turned back, stared at her. If he could spout flames like a dragon, Penny thought, he would.

"You say you feel responsible for what happened between the two of them. Is that right?" Penny asked. "Even though it was nothing that you did or could even have known about?"

"That's what I said. It goes with having the job, even if you don't believe I'm old enough to understand responsibility."

"Oh, I do," Penny said. "I was twenty-two—that's only three years older than you are now—when I left Earth, my family, everything I knew, to come here. I didn't really know what I was doing, but I was here, and at twenty-two, I was mayor and it was all on me to keep this place from starving. So, no, I don't think you're too young for responsibility."

Gordon's eyes narrowed. "What are you saying?"

"I'm saying we need people from the Heaven-born cohorts who will take responsibility. We need to see what happens at this meeting of the Demos, but I may need to talk to people who can do that."

"I've already told you that I can." With those words, Gordon stalked off to return to his work.

Penny turned to Jing. A smile played around her lips. "I need to make a few calls, Jing. I'm sorry, but I need to put off subjecting myself to your ultrasound for another time."

·   ·   ·

"GORDON DURHAM-POLE? OF COURSE I KNOW HIM. HE'S IN MY COHORT AND there are only sixty-eight of us. It's not like we were spread across the planet." Yong's voice came through the hands-free speaker of Penny's phone. "Why the sudden interest, Mom?"

Penny lounged back on the bed in the hab she and Hiep used when they were in Saint Peterstown. This was a question she wanted to ask Hiep, even though Hiep would not have known the individual nearly so well as Yong, because Penny trusted Hiep's judgments of people. For all Penny had learned—been forced to learn—over the years, she did not trust her ability to read people. And she missed Hiep. She told herself she had no time to indulge in those emotions.

"What kind of person is he?" Penny asked. "What is he like?"

"Very sure of himself" was the immediate answer. "Opinionated too. I can't give you a lot of detail. It's not like we were friends. Actually, I'm not sure he had friends. He's a townie, a real us-versus-them kind of townie."

"You said he is sure of himself. Can he back it up?"

"From what I saw, yeah." A short silence followed. "What's going on up there? I can hear the gears of my mother's brain grinding together from down here in the valley."

"I'm not sure yet." Penny rubbed a hand across her belly, thought of the new life beginning to take shape there, wondered if the baby would be like Yong or like Thorny. Children were hard to figure out. *People* were hard to figure out. "Do you think he can be trusted?"

Yong laughed. "Those gears are definitely grinding. He put a lot of stock in doing whatever he said he would do. But don't forget, it's been a year and a half since I've had anything to do with him. I've hardly seen him since school. He's a pure townie."

"Fair enough," Penny said. She had to think of the way Hiep would react. Would he search for a counterbalance if he was not sure of a person? "Do you know a valley-girl or valley-boy who is up in town, preferably also from your cohort? I need someone you think is reliable, someone I could talk to. And no known friend of ours," she hastened to add.

"No problem with that. Poppy Merriwether. She also works at the residence school. She's solid."

"I know the parents," Penny said. "If not the girl."

Before Penny cut the connection, Yong added a hasty, "Hey, Mom, don't drop off yet. One bit of buzz you ought to know. I was talking to Jordan Longfellow yesterday. He's kind of an equal shares person, but he'll help us with transporting our building materials in return for me helping him pick a farm site. Not a personal marker or anything, just a trade, but that's not the point," she said quickly. "He was doing some work for Vargas and Billingsly. Said that Guillermo was going on and on about Thorny and what he says Thorny did.

"Jordan thinks Vargas is planning something at the Demos. I'm going to see if Jordie will watch the farm, Xeno, and Thuy so I can come up. I know Thorny can take care of herself, but the Demos is a different kind of creature. And Thorny may be a different species, but she's *our* different species, if you know what I mean."

"I do," Penny said. "Thank you for the warning. I'll figure it out for the Demos. You know your father and I will take care of her."

·   ·   ·

"Aspergrass stick?"

"Sure." Penny accepted the proffered stiff, twisted stick of brown-green reeds. It snapped off in her mouth as she bit down. A faint almond taste permeated her mouth as she munched. They did not have almonds on Heaven yet. Penny suspected they never would.

"Does your family send these up from the valley for you?" Penny tried to make herself as comfortable as she could in the plastic chair of the Dining Hall, where Poppy had arranged to meet. The tables around them were deserted. Even the people picking up food shares were few in number.

Poppy smiled as she chewed on her own stick. "Yeah," she said between bites. "Mom thinks I need a taste of home during the residence period when, as she puts it, I'm in exile up here in the town."

"What does she fry them in? I'm trying to place the taste."

"Oh, that'll be different with each batch. She'll fry 'em in whatever she's got left over." Poppy chuckled. "She says that keeps it interesting, but like I said, it depends on what she's got."

"How's the farm going?"

"Pretty well." Poppy looked at the stick instead of taking her next bite. "It's a lot of damn hard work, though, and I'm sure they wish their oldest was working with them instead of herding residence school juniors.

"When they're not in residence, Micah is old enough to be a big help and the younger ones can do some, but still . . . They're really grateful for what you showed them when they started the farm, about the soil and which plants and, like, keeping the aspergrass in a separate field so we've got a real nice growth we can share. It's been years. They still talk about it."

"That's the funny thing about aspergrass; all of the Heaven plants, really," Penny said. She had never known quite what to do with a compliment and preferred to talk about the plants. "Earth plants grow fine anywhere as long as we pay attention to soil quality, acidity, and minerals. We can establish a hybrid biome and they do fine. Heaven plants seem to need their own biome. Except the damn thistle." Penny laughed. "I can usually figure out what to grow where and how. I helped with all the farms at the beginning."

"Well, thank you from me too."

Penny wished she could stop the blush in her cheeks. "You're welcome. It's not a problem. I was always better at relating to plants than people. Plants come naturally. People are sort of a learned process."

Poppy started to laugh but cut it off when she saw that Penny's face stayed serious. "I'm sorry if I said something wrong. What was it you wanted to talk about?"

"Work. In a way, work." Penny fought to segue her train of thought to the topic she had originally planned. Indeed, it had always been easier to deal with plants and farm animals than people, who often had their own ideas about where to take a conversation.

"It's like your parents with their farm; how hard they work. Do you think, now that they've made the farm successful, that they should be able to get more than the equal share or be able to buy more, if that's what they want to do?"

Poppy's back stiffened, brought her upright in her chair. Then she smiled. "You sounded like Gordon then."

"Gordon? Gordon Durham-Pole? Why?"

"That's his favorite topic," Poppy said. "If you work hard and you're successful at what you do, then you should be able to have more."

"And do you think the same way he does?"

Poppy clapped her hands together and laughed. "Me think like Gordon? Maybe on the thirty-sixth of a month. I'll grant you, on that one point we may agree, but otherwise, he's a complete townie-boy. Thinks the valley exists only to support the town; everything should be done to build up the town and keep it like new. You know the line: The town was designed to last two hundred years before we would need anyplace else.

"He'll say it even though you can see systems are starting to wear out and we can't recycle all the tech stuff, never mind make new. And then, when he gets going on equal shares or different shares, he'll tell you valley-boys and -girls hold back some of what they make so it's not equal shares anyway."

"Well, what about these sticks?" Penny held up the nub of the one she had been eating while she wondered which side Poppy was on. "Heaven biota aren't registered in the computer system, so they're not figured in when equal shares are calculated. Your folks can do whatever they want with the aspergrass. Trade it for what they want. Right?"

"True." Poppy grew a rueful smile. "I'm sure, if you're working at the viscose plant for Klaus, you're probably more likely to have a new shirt or pants than if you're a townie, even if you're a townie who works hard. But"—she held up a forefinger—"if you're a townie, you're more likely to have bot help with your job even though we really need the bots on the farms because of all the physical work. If we bring it up, the townies will tell you most bots aren't designed for agriculture and they can't reprogram them and we don't have the materials to build new ones."

"So, equal shares really aren't equal," Penny said. "Some people are just better than others at hiding what is unequal."

"Yeah." Poppy slid down a bit in her seat. "Everyone has their own way of gaming the system. Which sucks, to be honest."

"Do you think we should find a different way? Not necessarily equal, but open and honest?"

"If you can come up with one, I'll sign on to it. I've even told Gordon something like that. But, I'll tell you, even among Heaveners who work hard, the townie-boys and -girls and the valley-girls and -boys will each think the other is hiding an advantage somewhere. Put a bridge across that canyon and you're an engineer of miracles."

HIEP

THE TRAIL ENDED FOR THEM, AS IT HAD FOR THE OTHERS, WHERE THE CLIFFS CAME down to the riverbed and blocked the way forward. Ahead of them, nestled in the cul-de-sac, they could see two rovers in the golden light of the afternoon.

"Thorny! Dani!" Reality was out the passenger side door as soon as Hiep stopped the rover. Her voice echoed back from the cliffs, but that was the only answer she received. She raced to each rover in turn, yanking open doors and peering inside. They were empty, naturally.

Hiep stopped and kneeled down in the dirt to examine the picked-over carcass of a gator. Only after he was satisfied with what he saw did he stand up, brush the dirt from his cargo pants, and join Reality by the rover nearest the cliff. He reached in, hit the power switch, and was rewarded by the rover's systems turning on.

"Had the battery been fully discharged, it would not recover on its own; therefore, it did not reach that point. The driver chose to shut down the system and abandon the vehicle." He studied the instrument panel and computer screen. "There are not too many hours of daylight, and this area is shaded for much of that time," he said, "but sitting here with no drain on the systems, it will recharge. Slowly." He tapped a set of commands into the computer. "Interesting."

"What?"

"A series of entries were made in the log system from the day the rover left Saint Peterstown until, I assume, the day it reached this point. They were deleted. By time stamp, deletion was a few minutes prior to system shutdown."

"Any way to retrieve them?"

"No. Not here. That much is certain."

"Delete your entries and vanish into thin air. Where the hell did they go?" Hands on her hips, Reality yelled the two names at silent forested hills and lonely cliffs. The landscape mocked her with echoes. "This is almost enough to make you believe in alien abduction, never mind that we're already seventy-six light-years from Earth."

"One of them killed a gator back by the other rover," Hiep said. "It has to be one of them. No signs to indicate another large predator. Also, nothing to indicate that either one of them was hurt. I want to check the rovers and see what was taken."

While Hiep climbed into the storage area of first one rover and then the other, Reality walked back to stand over the dead gator.

"Shit," she said when she finally mustered up a word. "Goddamn shit. The thing is right by the rovers; whatever happened was at close range. I can't imagine using a bow and arrow this close. It must have been with the poisoned spear. No sign of an arrow. Holy shit!"

"The boats are gone from each rover," Hiep said. "Rover kits and tool packs too. I would assume their own packs as well. Come, look here." He was standing by scored dirt, pulled-up ground cover, and trampled ferns in the short space between the rovers and the water's edge. He pointed at the river that splashed and rippled on its way to the canyon. "Each of them launched from here."

"We don't have a boat."

Hiep said nothing, merely turned and followed the short path down to the river. Reality followed. The water flung foam over rocks, the current increasing as the riverbed was constricted in the approach to the canyon ahead.

Hiep gazed into the canyon. "See, there is a ledge, or a shelf perhaps, at the base of the cliff between the rock wall and the water at the canyon's entrance. As long as it continues, it should be possible to hike through the canyon. With a little additional luck, I should be able to reach wherever they beached their boats. Once they are on foot, I will find them."

"I'm going with you," Reality said.

"You do not need to do that." Hiep did not consider himself compassionate, except with a few certain people, but he felt it at that moment. He did not allow it to show on his face. "The rover we have been driving has some charge remaining in the battery. If you husband it, allow the battery time to recharge in better sunlight, you should be able to make it back to Saint Peterstown. I know that you do not drive rovers," he said in anticipation of her concern, "at least not outside the town, but if you proceed slowly and cautiously, the rover has systems that should make it possible for you to retrace our route."

Reality shook her head. "I said I would continue."

"Please consider the implications of proceeding on foot this far into the wild. I have said I will not return without my daughter. The likelihood of you returning, especially if you need to do so on your own, is quite low." Again, he allowed no emotion to surface. When she did not respond, he added, "I have already told you that you do not need to go."

"I do need to go." Heat rose in Reality's voice. "I need to far more than you can ever know."

"Very well." Hiep shrugged. "Let's ready our packs. If our rover has campsite wards, we will want to take them. They have been taken from the other two."

Heavily laden with packs that bulged with whatever supplies and tools could be stuffed into them; spears, bows, and arrows lashed to the packs; and Hiep's M8 slung over his shoulder, they made their way down the embankment to the mouth of the canyon. The rocky shelf was wide enough to stand single file with both feet side by side and the sides of their packs just brushing against the cliff face.

To their right was only the dark rush of water, the sound of its churning filling the canyon with a dull roar. The water splashed across the narrow path that they had to traverse, and once they were into the canyon, the rock ledge sloped to the right, toward the water.

"Shit!" Reality cursed as her boots slipped down the rock, her right boot finding purchase only at the very edge. "What happens if we fall in?"

"Shed the pack as quick as you can," Hiep said. "Then try to float feetfirst downstream until you're out of the canyon and can swim to shore. Or drown."

Reality had to laugh. "You make it sound like such a simple choice."

"It is."

The ledge did remain passable. With the last of the light, they were able to reach the exit from the narrow portion of the canyon, the place where the river broadened again with an open bank to their left. They dropped their packs farther up the bank, away from any likely flooding. The only semblance of a camp that they made was to set out the campsite wards. Even the display of lights in the sky above made no impression. They were both asleep as soon as they lay down.

PART III

All happy families are alike; each unhappy family is unhappy in its own way.

Leo Tolstoy, *Anna Karenina*

DECEMBER 33, HY 21

AJIT

FOUR SWEATY MEN WALKED ACROSS THE OPEN PLAIN IN THE PREDAWN DARKNESS. Two of them carried a long box by its plastic handles. Their destination was close now, an isolated hab distinguished only as a blacker black against the stars visible at the horizon. The black spear of a comm mast stuck up from the building.

"Ridiculous to have to walk this far in this heat," Oscar complained from where he held the front end of the box.

"Be glad it's not summer," Ajit snapped. "And there's no rover available in Saint Peterstown right now. In case you hadn't noticed. The one Olivares drove up was taken back to the valley so that more people can come up for the Demos."

"There should be one here," Oscar said. "Ought to be a rule that there's always a rover available here in case we have to go out of the town."

"Which is why I need to be mayor, so that the town can have its priority restored. All of you remember that, and you make sure your damned townie friends know it by heart. And, in the meantime, you can talk about the crazy girl who ran off with one of the few rovers we had. And while you're at it, talk to Petrovic about his stupid son, who took another one and went after her and isn't back. And all of that is why Hiep is gone, which is why we can do this in the first place, so shut up."

"Yeah, okay," Oscar said, "but it's too damn far."

"What did you think they were going to do?" Jones chimed in. He liked making Oscar look foolish, which was not hard to do. "Bury the nuke under the Community Dome? Safer out here."

"Well, it was then," said Northrup. "Just an old, dead reactor now."

"Fine." Ajit's patience with the griping he had been hearing since he had roused them to do this was nearing its limit. He remembered another Western saying his father had adopted, that it was a poor workman who blamed his tools. That was true, but he deserved better tools. "This radioisotope decay generator should have been good for a couple of centuries, two and a half maybe, but it was sabotaged, and we all know how that happened, so it's kaput. It used to be a functioning nuke, so it's out here, and the place locks up, which is why Hiep stashed the guns here after they killed Satan and Satan's Five." He paused to blot droplets of sweat from his forehead with a cloth that should have been made of a better material and to clear a stone that had wedged itself into his sandal. "Now, are you sure you can get into this place, Everett? Hiep is a Sicarii, you know."

"Yes. You've only asked me that question twenty times already, and I've told you yes each time." Jones came to a halt in front of the building, the outline of the door and its touch plate faintly visible. He set down the small pack he had been carrying, arched his back with a moan, and then bent over to open the pack.

"How are you going to do this?" Ajit asked.

"Simple, actually." Jones spoke as he pulled tools and a small plastic bag from the pack. "I know Hiep made this into a security lock. It's rigged for eye plus chip code. Look into the detector to have your retina read, the computer generates a ten-digit code that your chip has to match. Code changes every ten seconds. I know it's there because I can see it in the system, but I can't change it. I'm sure there are people who could, because every computer system can be hacked, but I can't do it."

"Then what's the good of all of this, and what good are you?"

Naturally, Oscar would take a shot at Jones any chance he had. "You just said you can't get past his lock."

"I can't pick it electronically, is what I said. However, as good as Hiep may be with electronic locks, the door is the door. He can't do anything about that."

Jones aimed a small hand tool at the physical door lock. The target glowed red, then puffed out a bit of vapor. He picked up the plastic bag, inserted a wide-bore needle attached to a syringe, and pulled back on the plunger. Then he put the needle into the hole he had made. With gentle pressure on the plunger, he extruded the contents of the syringe into the channel that had been cut into the lock.

"Not all theft is done with electronics," he said as he worked. "These materials are astonishingly easy to come by. Even here, if you go through leftover construction supplies. It's only a matter of knowing how to use them." He finished by sticking a pin into a small blob of material at the end of the filled channel.

"You would know, I suppose," said Ajit.

"I do indeed," Jones replied.

Jones stepped back and the others did as well. He made a series of taps on his phone. A flash and a bang came from the door. It slid open.

"The hatch down to the underground control room also has a lock," Jones said. "I'm assuming Hiep upgraded that lock as well, so we'll repeat this process. No problem, like I said."

"The problem is going to be that it's obvious someone broke in here," Oscar said. "Hiep is going to know, and he is a Sicarii."

"Trust me, Hiep has alarms on the code generator for the lock. If I even try to pick that, he's going to know—and a whole lot faster than him finding this." Jones wore a broad smile. "The notification in the system for the door opening, however, is part of the system build. There are limits to what he can do with it. I checked and I can—and did—suppress it."

"Enough with your pansy-ass shit, Oscar," Ajit said. "What's he going to do when we have the guns? Are you in, or are you just going to suck your thumb and take whatever damn crumbs Penny lets the town have?"

.   .   .

THE INTERIOR OF THE HAB WAS STERILE AND EMPTY, WITH NOT EVEN A CHAIR TO SIT ON. The whole purpose of the building was to shield the entrance to the control room of the old nuke from the elements.

Jones pulled open the trapdoor and went down the stairs to deal with the control room door in the same way he had the exterior door. When his shouted "Done!" came to the three waiting upstairs, Ajit signaled to Northrup.

"Go down there and help him bring up the guns and the ammo. Oscar, get all of it into that box so we can get it back to my hab."

Five minutes later, Jones's voice called out. "Hey, Ajit, I thought you said there were eight guns down here."

"There are," said Ajit.

"No. There are only seven."

"Look again. More carefully."

"Dammit, you come down here and look yourself!" Jones came to the bottom of the stairs and looked up at Ajit. "There's barely enough space to stand in front of the control screens and consoles. No storage areas, no closet, no hidey-hole. The seven of them are just stacked against the wall. Are you sure about the number? It's been twenty years."

"I am sure!" Ajit made certain Jones could hear the heat in his voice. "Malachi and the other free company people each had one. That's six. Then there was all that competition with the Pioneer Youth leaders over who would get the last two, and Busby and Gudmundsson had them. That makes eight."

"Well, there are only seven here now," Jones said. "Vo Hiep must have kept one out. Or he took one with him."

"Look," Ajit said, "if he took one, he took one. The Demos meeting is in two days. If he's not back, what difference does it make? If he is back, we'll figure it out. What we can't do is stand around here all day like a debating society. Get the guns and the ammo and let's get out of here."

JORGE

THE BLINKING NOTIFICATION AT THE PERIPHERY OF HIS FIELD CAUGHT JORGE'S ATTENtion the instant he opened his eyes and cleared away the tattered memory of what had been a pleasant dream. Back on Earth, it had been common to see notifications on waking. Someone, somewhere, was always sending something. His mind had trained itself to pay no attention until he was ready. But twenty years on Heaven, where such notifications were rare, had resensitized him. He sat up abruptly—immediately regretting disturbing Jing, who had been snug against his shoulder—and looked at the blinker to open it.

"What's wrong?" Jing's question was distorted by a yawn.

"Alarm." Jorge took it in as he spoke. "The doors to the old reactor room." He chipped in and brought up the main panel for Saint Peterstown. Saw nothing. "The alarm on the main panel has been suppressed. Jones is the only one who could do that, but he wouldn't know about this."

"I don't understand," Jing said.

"After the fight twenty years ago, Hiep took all the rifles and stored them in the old reactor control room, because other than the residence school, it's the only place in Saint Peterstown with doors that lock. He set a separate alarm, separate from the one that goes to the main system panels, to send him a notification if the doors were opened. He also set it to send to me as a backup. He didn't trust Jones or anyone else who might get the alarm from the main panel."

"That man doesn't trust anyone. Except Penny. You never told me about this."

"He asked me not to say anything." Jorge pushed his hair around with one hand, but it was too short to smooth back and too long to stay in place. "I'm a starship pilot, or was, who was a computer jockey for fun in my spare time. That's how I took an IT job here, and Hiep trusted me on this, probably because I was a starman. Well, he trusts me more than Jones, which isn't saying much." Through his chip, Jorge located the light panel for the hab and turned on the bedroom lights.

"Hiep always messaged me ahead of time if he was going in there, like if he needed to clean the rifles or get one to kill a roo. He messaged me the other day before he took the rover to go after those kids." Jorge sighed. He noted the time stamp on the alarm. "This happened a few hours ago. Middle of the night. I better go put eyes on the place and see what the situation is."

"You do that," Jing said. "I'll be in the clinic. I've been bugging Penny to have her ultrasound done, and we might as well do it early. That will give me more time to argue with Chloe and others about medication supplies. It's not as though I'm going to miraculously solve the mystery of Fernando Vargas with any amount of spare time." Jing swung her legs over the side of the bed, leaving Jorge in the sheets.

·   ·   ·

ONCE JORGE REACHED THE HAB SHELTERING THE OLD REACTOR CONTROL ROOM, THE blown-out locks at the exterior and interior doors were obvious. The rifles were gone. One magazine that must have been dropped lay on the floor. It took only seconds to determine that he could not reach Hiep, so Jorge left a private and encrypted message. When Hiep reconnected to the network, he would learn about the rifles.

That done, the foremost thought in Jorge's mind was that he needed to tell Jing what had happened. He wanted her safe, wanted her to return to the valley, but he knew she would never agree. She would call that running away, and she would be stubborn. *We share our lives and all our risks.* That had been their wedding vow after they told the starship pilot, Yang, that they were staying behind. He had to admit to himself that there would be few, if any, safe places on Heaven if something bad were to happen again. He looked around the empty control room one more time, but the rifles did not suddenly materialize in front of him. Trouble was coming. He wished he knew when and from what quarter. He wished that Hiep would return soon.

·   ·   ·

"Hey! We've got a problem!" Jorge dashed into the clinic, making a sprint to the last of the diagnostic beds, where Jing and Penny turned in surprise. That pulled him out of his self-absorption with the matter of the missing rifles. It dawned on him that perhaps he should not be where he was. "Am I barging in on something I shouldn't be? I checked the hab, but you were gone by the time I got back, and I figured you would be in the clinic and I didn't want to do this over the system. Yuki said you'd be back here . . ."

"A doctor-patient discussion," Jing said. She moved away from the bed and smoothed down wrinkles on her white coat that popped up again the moment her hand had passed.

"It's all right." Penny swung her legs over the side of the diagnostic bed, then let herself drop to stand on the floor. "It's not my first kid, and based on my own observations, they're much more complicated after they come out than before. In fact, most mammalian physiology, which includes us, follows certain basic patterns. So, we don't have a veterinarian, which was a clear mistake by the ISC, but this summer when one of the horses was having trouble delivering, I was able to work from a vid and deliver the foal, which, when you think about it, can be more difficult than with a human because you can't tell the horse to push—"

"Penny, please." Jing patted Penny's hand. "Yes, it's far from your first, but you're in your forties and I know you're nervous. Everything is okay." She turned to Jorge, who now felt more embarrassed than at any time since his first date and was certain his face had achieved the color of an engine ready to melt down. "This is about the alarm that woke you," Jing said. "Do we have a crisis?" She gave him a flash of a smile and a quick peck on a cheek as a way of de-emphasizing the last word.

The word "crisis" exploded in Jorge's head. Embarrassment vanished. "The guns are gone."

That flat statement wiped any amusement from the faces of the two women. Jing found her words first. "The guns? They're gone? The old M8s that came from the *Dauntless*?"

"Yes."

"That's not possible," Penny said. "Hiep has them locked in the old reactor control room. That's double locks, and I know how you like to say that anything electronic can be hacked, but the way Hiep rigged them, nobody here would have the skill."

"I got an alarm this morning that the door opened. That's what Jing meant. Not hacked," Jorge said. "Or you could call it a different kind of hack. Explosives. The doors were blown open. Crude but effective."

"And all of them are gone?" Jing asked. "That's what, eight automatic rifles?" She kept her face impassive but could not keep fear out of her voice.

"I'm sure Hiep took one with him," Penny said. "And Reality went with him, so maybe another. Malachi's people taught her how to use one, but that was twenty years ago. I know she hasn't touched one since. Actually, I doubt Hiep would have taken one for her."

"It doesn't matter," Jorge said. "Whether it's six guns or seven, that is effectively the entire firepower on the planet unless you want to count bows and arrows, which I don't. True, the printers have the capability to print firearms, if not as sophisticated as an M8, but the ammunition is a different story. I argued with Leif before the ship left, and with Hiep after, that we might be better off destroying them." Jorge threw his hands up in the air. "The argument then was protection from gators or sawtooth roos, so we left them there. After we came up with the sodium channel poisons, we never got back to it."

"No point moaning over past decisions," Jing said. "The questions now are who took them and why? Who could use explosives that way?"

"It's not someone following a vid," Jorge said. "The odds of doing it right the first time are pretty low, I would think."

"It can't be any of the Pioneer Youth," Penny said. "That's my old group. None of us had that kind of training."

"And except for Hiep, the free company people are all dead." Jorge's eyebrows pulled together, accentuating the widow's peak of his hair. "The criminals who came on the *Daredevil* are another matter. Their backgrounds were wiped. That was an incentive for them to come. All that information was erased from the databases, which gave their families relief from all the crap they were getting on the Community." He ran a hand through his hair. Short as he now wore it, it still felt limp from the humidity outside and he wished it would stay in place. "Jones has to be involved somehow." Jorge explained the alarm settings. "Whether somebody bribed him or he is actively involved with the weapons, I can't tell you. Maybe the more important question is why is this happening?"

Jing snapped her fingers in the air between Penny and Jorge. "It has to be about the Demos. Ever since people were able to stop worrying we would starve the next week, we keep splitting into more and more factions. We've got Originals and Heaven-born. *Daredevil* and *Dauntless* within the Originals. Then there's townies and valley-folk. Remorsers and workers. Equal shares and work-for-reward.

"You would think that with only one small community on this entire planet, we would just be humans, but I guess we don't function like that. Well, it's not stable. Any idiot can see that. Someone is going to stage a coup at the Demos meeting."

"That won't work," Penny said. "What we can grow out of the hydroponics can't support the town. Not with so much of it devoted to the sugar cane for the cell foundries and the cannabis they can't quit smoking. All the valley has to do is cut off the food shipments."

"No," Jorge said. "Embargoes don't work if the other side has all the weapons."

"The other side does not have all the weapons." Penny mimed an archer aiming at Jorge.

"Spears, bows, and arrows against assault rifles? You can't be serious." Jorge slumped back against one of the diagnostic beds in a way that suggested it might need to be used for him.

Penny clutched her arms across her chest the way she often did when stressed. Her voice stayed even, however. "I'm not being ridiculous. This isn't like when we were dealing with Malachi and his killers. Whoever is working with Jones, and I can guess one for sure, doesn't know anything about fighting. If we daub the thistle poison on the arrowheads instead of the sodium channel agent, any hit would be lethal, and everybody in the valley can use a bow and arrow because of the predator risk, which is why Hiep trained all of us, and Yong is almost as accurate as Thorny."

Jorge's stomach clenched into a knot at the talk of weapons. He was too young, hadn't been born, when fighting in the Troubles—the decade of warfare that had threatened to pitch Earth into apocalypse—ended in 2062, and he was only a toddler when the Treaties of 2065 brought the dawn of the New Golden Age, the durable time of peace and prosperity on Earth.

Yet on the *Dauntless*, he had known Leif Grettison, the exoplanetary scout, and Yang Yong, the pilot. They were much older, having made a previous starflight, and had fought—against each other—in the Troubles. They had spoken of what the fighting and the fear had been like.

On Heaven, he had come to know Hiep, a member of the free companies, men and women who carried on the fighting as proxies of the Powers in parts of Earth where the New Golden Age was not so golden. From those associations and the sliver of fighting he had witnessed when the settlement was established, Jorge was afraid of what could happen when men and women had weaponry in their hands. What would come of this mess? He fell silent, lost in thoughts he did not want to have.

"I don't want a war, though," Penny said. "Winning a war here is just another way to lose. We can't be killing ourselves off."

"Then what do we do?" Jorge was acutely aware that he was not standing up as a staunch defender the way men did in storybooks. He was certain he could face emergencies in space and had done so before he had been selected as the junior pilot for the starship *Dauntless*, but starship pilots did not need to be fighters, and he knew he was not one. His upbringing in the New Golden Age had taught him that fighting—not to mention war—was wrong. "I wouldn't know where to look for these weapons, and it's not as though we could search every hab in town in the time we have, not without people knowing what we were doing."

Jing tugged at a sleeve of each of them at the same time. "Let's back up to what's important. The Demos meeting is the target. It has to be, given the timing. You have everyone who matters there—damn near every competent adult on the planet except for a few caretakers in the valley. So the first thing to do is postpone the Demos meeting and keep people dispersed."

"Good thought, Jing." Penny extricated her sleeve from Jing's grasp, which also released the death grip her hands had on each of her arms. "I'll talk to Ibi and Sonal. Grubb won't like it, because he wants it done and over with, but I'll come up with a reason for them. Sonal is the secretary. The system will accept the change if she makes it, and then everyone gets the notification. Nobody will question it when it comes from the computer system like that." Penny found a loose flap of shirt and tucked it into her waistband. "There's no reason the meeting has to be on December thirty-fifth. The solstice was just a convenient date when we set this up. Sort of symbolic. We'll push it off a couple of days. With any luck, Hiep will be back by then. He'll know how to handle it."

"No, push it back more," Jing said. "Maybe cancel it."

"Can't cancel it," Penny said. "People won't accept that, and Jacoby will probably resign right away, which will force the issue. But, yes, if we push it back more, say at least a week, maybe two, people will stay in the valley or go back to the valley. That puts pressure on whoever took the guns because people will be spread out. It gives them time to make a mistake. It gives Hiep more time too."

"If Hiep's not back in a week—" Jing cut off abruptly.

"Hiep will be here." Penny's eyes glistened but there was no trace of doubt in her voice. "I'll have Ibi and Sonal push it out. We'll try for two weeks, whatever they can get Jacoby to live with. We can't have him resign suddenly."

"I've already put a notification about the theft into the system for Hiep," Jorge said. "I've rigged it so that Jones can't read it. When Hiep gets back in range of the signal, he'll know. Which brings us back to Jones. He has to be involved."

"By itself, that may not tell us much." Jing now released Jorge's arm as well and began ticking off points on the fingers of one hand. "He has had three partners in our time on this planet, no marriages.

Currently single. From what I know, and I hear a lot of this kind of thing, none of his exes are talking to him. He has four bio-kids. Don't think any of them has much of a relationship with him either."

Jorge ran an index finger around his cheek's tattoo. "When I'm in town, he and I are both in and out of the computer center. I know he has contacts with others from the *Daredevil*. Both in the system and in person. After we finish here, I'll check his message and phone contact frequencies. That will tell us who his primary contacts are. In all the time we've been working together on the IT here, I don't think he has ever mentioned any friends."

"Are any of those bio-kids in seniors?" Penny asked.

"Oldest son," Jing answered. "Low-seniors. But I told you, I don't think his kids have much if anything to do with him."

"You never know." Penny grew back her smile. "It may make it worth having another conversation or two with Gordon Durham-Pole."

DECEMBER 34, HY 21

AJIT

THE HAB WAS FAR OUT ON THE AVENUE OF ASIA, CLOSE TO THE INTERSECTION WITH the Perimeter Road. It was an unoccupied hab, officially not initialized if anyone looked at the registration information in the Saint Peterstown system. Jones had turned the hab's power on while maintaining its status in the system as uninitialized. He had rigged a few unoccupied habs that way, which made for good places to have meetings that snoops, acquaintances, partners, or wives could not pry into.

Jones was useful that way, Ajit thought as he watched Jones enter along with Northrup. Northrup might be good in a different way. That man said little, even now, about his past on Earth, only that he had been in pharmaceuticals. From the man's build and his occasional comments about physical retribution to certain people, Ajit was quite sure that the pharmaceuticals were the kind obtained in the street and that, despite the ISC's limitation on colonists to ones with nonviolent criminal histories, Northrup was no stranger to physical violence. Well, when the ISC had needed a few more to fill out the crew, they had taken those free company people. They had about as violent a set of backgrounds as could be found, so who knew what the truth was about Hershel Northrup. Anyway, a person like that could be useful—all the more so in the situation that was developing.

That left Oscar Gradison, who slunk in ten minutes late with his long gray hair half out of its ponytail and clothes that looked like he had slept in them and then rolled out of bed onto a dirty floor before coming over. Gradison was an odd fourth to depend on in his inner circle, but Oscar did have one trait Ajit valued. He was an obedient dog who was still several kicks short of the point where he would snap. Ajit could tell him to do virtually anything.

When Oscar was in the front room with them and his eyes had focused—or appeared to focus—Ajit said, "You've all seen that fucking notification. Right?"

"About the Demos meeting, you mean?" Northrup asked.

"What other notification would make me call a meeting here?" Ajit snapped out the question sharply enough that the three others flinched. Part of him would have liked to mellow out with a joint, but another part of him was glad for the irritation that showed in his voice. Ajit had kept the notification open on his projection field. He glanced over to his right and read it one more time. DUE TO UNFORESEEN COMPLICATIONS, THE DEMOS MEETING WILL BE POSTPONED UNTIL JANUARY 9. WE WILL FILL YOU IN ON THE ISSUES THEN.

"The council has postponed the annual in-person meeting until the ninth. There is only one possible reason. They are waiting to be sure Hiep is back for that meeting."

"Or they know about the guns," Northrup said.

"Not possible. Nothing has been triggered. I would know." Jones's defiance was undermined by the shakiness in his voice.

The problem with IT people, Ajit thought, was that they often forgot that people sometimes went and looked at objects, not only at computer screens. In this case, though, he agreed with Jones. No one would ever walk out to the old reactor building without a reason.

"If someone knew about the guns, this place would be going crazy right now," Ajit said. "So they don't. They're playing for time to have Hiep here."

"He went after his daughter, not on a starshot," Jones said. "It would be nice if he was not here, but we said—you said—we'd figure it out if he was."

"And that is what we need to do." Ajit wished he could breathe fire like a dragon. "Remember, he has a rifle."

"Does it matter?" asked Oscar. "We have seven guns. Do we need more people to carry one?"

"Yes, it damn well matters!" Ajit was shouting even though they were all together in a confined space. "The whole idea was that we would show up at the Demos meeting with the guns. That would be enough to convince people which way to vote—enough people, anyway. And we're going to charge Thorny with murder. That's the deal with Vargas. Hiep wouldn't be able to do anything about the vote, not for mayor and not about his kid. But now you're talking about one of the Sicarii loose with a gun, and they are waiting for him to get here, which means they expect him to use that rifle to make things come out the way *they* want. How dead do you want to be?" He bit at a thumbnail and spat out the piece.

"Then we need more people carrying guns," Jones said. "For once, Oscar has an idea. Confront Hiep with seven armed men, and he won't try anything. I can think of one for sure we can add."

"In addition to that, we could grab Penny," Gradison said. "Her or one of their kids. Hiep won't do anything if one of them is hostage."

"Now you're back to stupid." Ajit let the contempt show in his voice. "Stupider than usual, in fact. Touch Penny or any one of their kids, you sign our death warrants. Hiep will kill all of us. It would only be a question of when, unless he happens to die first."

"Maybe we should just forget this." Northrup's voice was soft. Maybe, Ajit thought, he was no stranger to physical violence, but he was not a killer.

"Are you crazy?" The fear in Jones's voice was obvious. "There's no way to put this back like nothing ever happened, and whatever else Hiep is going to do, he will figure out who stole the guns. He'll figure me for sure, and he won't care about proof."

"Don't go in your pants," Ajit said. He needed to take back control. "We need to change our plan."

"Are we going to just let the Demos meeting happen?" Oscar asked.

"Don't bother bringing the guns? Figure Vargas will deliver enough votes and afterward it won't matter if Hiep finds out about this? Penny won't have him threaten to shoot people unless they vote for her. That's not her style."

"Hiep is not going to sit there while we have his daughter convicted of murder," Jones said. "That's what Penny is counting on, and that's why the council delayed. It was her idea, I'll bet. But if we don't deliver on that conviction, Vargas will blow up the vote on mayor. Count on it."

"Wait." That was Northrup. "You saw it. Hiep did just sit there back when Malachi put Penny on trial. And that was as much a show trial as anything I've ever seen."

Ajit remembered. He remembered very well. It was not as simple as Northrup said. "Yes, he sat there, but that was before he switched sides and helped the starfolk kill Malachi and the others. You have to figure that he planned all of that in advance, him and Penny being what they are. We can't take a chance on what he will do, what Penny will have him do." Saying this was bringing out agitation in his voice. He knew the others could hear it.

He paced back and forth in front of them, skirting the standard hab furniture that had never been used. He needed a new plan, and he needed one fast. This crew of his was not helpful when it came to planning. That was part of what made them useful, but he needed a better plan before they fell apart.

"We can't give up," Jones said. "I already told you Hiep is going to figure out who pulled the guns out, and I will tell you that I'm not going down by myself."

I would never think that you would, Everett. Ajit tried to force himself to concentrate. The fear these fools were putting out was interfering with his focus. "I never said we were giving up!" He took a deep breath, cleared his throat, and closed the notification on his field. He had the answer. It was the right one and the obvious one now that he thought of it. He had actually said it, in a way, a few minutes before. "Here's what we're going to do. When Hiep comes back, he'll bring the other rovers with him. Right?" Three yeses answered him.

"Fine. The rover Petrovic recommissioned that Hiep took, that one doesn't have a working base station for the phones, but the other two do. The moment one of them comes in range, it's going to connect to the network. Right, Everett?"

"Correct," Jones said.

"Good." Ajit bit off another piece of thumbnail. "We know the direction those two kids went. Hiep will follow their route, so he'll come back by Dead Lake. Jones, you set an alarm in the system so we know when he's in range. When he has signal, you send him a message. We'll work on the words. The message will bring him to the rover repair shop at the Perimeter Road. We'll have plenty of time to get there ahead of him and set an ambush. At that point, I don't care how it looks or what anybody sees. They see guns, they'll stay out of the way. Hiep will never expect it, never know what hit him. If we can find a way to only take out Hiep, that's fine, but it's not essential. We don't wait for him to get out of the rover. He'll have his gun, so it's not like we can stand in front of him and shoot. When his rover pulls in, we shoot. Nobody will care if Busby gets hit. Same for Thorny. Vargas will thank us. And Petrovic talks, but he never stands up for himself. Then it's done. You can count the Demos votes right then."

"Fuck!" shouted Jones. "I've never fired a gun, much less at someone. We need more people."

Northrup put a hand on Jones's shoulder. "This can be done, Everett. Ajit is right. I've been keeping track of the talk. Guillermo is so fucking furious about Thorny. He's not only saying she did it; he's screaming that Hiep showed her how. I'd say you could shoot both of them in front of the whole Demos and Guillermo would make a motion that you did a good thing. Donna would second it."

"Thank you, Herschel. And don't worry about your aim. Those are automatic rifles," Ajit said. "Point it at him, pull the trigger, and hold it down. It'll spray bullets like a hose sprays water. You can't miss."

"We're going to ambush one of the Sicarii?" Oscar's voice rose into a squeak.

"He's a Sicarii, not a goddamn superman," Ajit growled. "He's not going to see this coming." *You can't make an omelet without breaking the eggs,* he thought. His father did not eat eggs, but he had been fond of that saying.

DECEMBER 35, HY 21

GORDON

F MESSAGES THROUGH PHONES AND CHIPS COULD BUZZ, THE WHOLE TOWN WAS buzzing over the postponement of the Demos meeting. The winter solstice meeting had never been delayed since it had been established in HY 2 of the colony. Not even the floods nine years ago, which brought panic over the food supply, had been enough to change the date of that meeting. What had happened? Was Dr. Song preparing some dreadful disclosure about Fernando's death? Did Thorny's disappearance have anything to do with that death? Was it about Hiep?

Gordon walked slowly along the Avenue of Australia out toward the Perimeter Road. He went slowly because most of his mind was on the *why* of the meeting he was about to have, not the physical reality of it. Jones had started the whole business around sunup with a message asking if Gordon were available for an important meeting. His positive response—what else could he really say?—set off a string of messages to establish the time and place. Nothing in them had spoken of a purpose, and his direct questions to that point had been ignored. It was only natural to tie this to the postponement of the Demos meeting, but try as he might, he could not divine why there was an association.

He stopped where he was and kicked a loose stone. The puffball white clouds mixed with gray that took up most of the sky offered no inspiration. The idea flashed through his mind that maybe it had nothing to do with the Demos, that this was about sex. The secretiveness, almost furtiveness, of the messages was consistent with that.

He discarded the idea, however. Jones's ex-partners spent plenty of time discussing the man's habits and failings. In a place the size of Saint Peterstown, those had become well known to everyone. A preference for men was not among them. Gordon grinned up at the sky. He was sure his preference for women was equally well known. But if not sex, that brought him back to the Demos, and that made no sense either.

Equally puzzling was the location Jones had given him: on the Avenue of Australia nearly out to the Perimeter Road. Gordon knew the numbers by heart. Counting chippers and Heaveners who had graduated from residence school, the town population occupied only ninety-two of five hundred habs. Even including the habs used by the residence school students, the majority were vacant. The preference of most people—and a requirement for the students, as Gordon knew well—was to take habs at close as possible to the town center. After all, other than exterior color, one hab was the same as another. Consequently, none of the habs in the area he had walked to were in use.

His smile turned to a grimace. The town would be filling up the way it had been intended if people had not kept moving to the valley. He knew perfectly well that the town needed the valley for food, but it was wrong to neglect the town, the one center of technological civilization on the planet. Keeping the town vital was important. He made sure his seniors knew that when they started to think about finishing school. It was a mission for Gordon.

He chastised himself for letting his mind drift away from his purpose. That was a waste of his time. Standing in the middle of an empty street would not tell him what the meeting would be about. *Once you get there, it will be obvious*, he told himself, and kept walking.

·　　·　　·

Jones was waiting for him in the open door of the next to last hab before the Perimeter Road. That was odd. In fact, Gordon thought Jones looked nervous. From the blood on Jones's fingertips, he had been biting or picking at them while he waited for Gordon.

"Come in, come in," Jones said. "I don't want to have any of this conversation outside."

"There's nobody else in sight, but okay." Gordon quashed the uneasiness in his stomach and pushed past Jones to find whoever else was inside as quickly as possible.

No one was inside. From a quick glance, this was a hab that had never even been initialized. No personal items could be seen. He spun back around to face Jones as the door closed behind the two of them.

"What is going on?" Gordon demanded.

"I'm going to tell you." The lights in the ceiling reflected off a sheen of sweat that coated Jones's face. "You believe in the importance of Saint Peterstown. We know that."

We. The word reverberated in Gordon's head. That had to include Ajit Mistry. "Of course," he said, because it seemed Jones was expecting an affirmation.

"Of course," Jones repeated. "The question, though, is whether you will defend the town. Will you really put the town first? Will you stand up for the town and for people's equal shares?"

The words "equal shares" set off an alarm in Gordon's head. He hoped he blocked any of that from showing on his face. "I'm for the town," Gordon said. "I will do whatever the town needs." He avoided mentioning equal shares and did not think Jones noticed its absence.

"Good, good. Gordie, I told Ajit you were the one we could count on out of all the boys who've come out of the school."

The use of the diminutive and calling him a boy were additional reminders that these people still looked at him as a child. He kept the feelings to himself. If they needed him, that was a start on the road he wanted to take. "Count on me for what?"

"Let me show you something."

Jones led the way to the sleeping quarters section of the hab. Gordon followed and stopped dead two steps in. Jones was standing next to the closet, and the closet door had an add-on lock attached to it.

"Why is there a locked closet in a hab that has never been occupied?" Gordon asked.

"Because of what is in it." Jones stared at the eye scanner.

The lock released and Jones pulled the door open. The only object in the closet, resting in a rear corner, was an M8 rifle.

"One of Satan's guns." The words came out of Gordon in a rushed breath. He was immediately angry with himself for using the words to describe it the way it was in the stories the colonists told their children when they were young.

A harsh laugh told Gordon that Jones had picked up on that point. "*Dauntless* brought them," Jones said, "and it was Malachi Oates who took them. That man might well have been the devil, but the truth is that a gun is just a tool. It doesn't kill. The person using it does."

Gordon struggled to get past his anger at how he had allowed himself to look like a child. That gave Jones a reason to confirm the way he thought of the Heaveners. "What's the point, and how did you get it?"

"You don't need to know how," Jones told him. "What matters is that Vo Hiep has one with him. That, and the Demos meeting was postponed to make sure he will be present at it. We know what is coming. Valley-folk and Hiep with that gun, they want to make the townies their servants. They'll take away our equal shares. We can't let them do that. We need to stand up and stop them. We want you to join us."

Gordon was having trouble believing what he was hearing, except that the reason for postponing the meeting could be correct. The valley-folk were waiting for Hiep to return. "Stop them how? With guns?" He fought to keep his voice level, as though these were routine questions.

"Vo Hiep has a gun. He will use it, unless we . . . ah . . . stop him, which may mean . . . ah . . . kill him first. But nobody else gets hurt. When the Demos sees we are serious and we have the guns, they will vote to preserve the town and our equal shares. Do you want to be one of the leaders? You've said you do. Now is the time to stand up and be counted."

Gordon felt his throat close for an instant. The idea of taking a gun and killing someone was a shock, a thought he had never had before. He could see sweat standing out on Jones's face. He said, "I don't know anything about using one of those."

"It's simple," Jones said. "These were designed so that illiterate peasants on Earth could use them. There are plenty of vids in the computer system."

"And you want me to take this gun for when Hiep comes back?"

"Not like that. I'll set this lock to open for your eyes. I'm monitoring the network. When Hiep comes in range, he'll connect and I'll know. I will let you know, and you'll pick up the gun and join us. Are you ready to be a leader?"

HIEP

THEY WOKE IN A BLEAK CAMP ALONG THE RIVER THE MORNING AFTER A FULL DAY'S march, during which they saw no sign that anyone had been on the riverbank. They started the day with no more than a minimal meal, a dose of vitamins and methionine, and a quick drink from their canteens before they hoisted their packs and resumed hiking down the river. They could hunt shellhound away from the river for calories and they might spot vegetation they knew to be edible, but the time spent on that would only prolong their journey. At the same time, they were reluctant to use up the food they had brought since that set an immutable limit to their expedition.

This hike began as little more than a repetition of the one before. The silence of the wilderness on Heaven was only occasionally broken by a buzz or roar from back in the trees, nothing like the wild places on Earth where Hiep had fought. No birds flew to enliven the air with their calls. The occasional rustling among the ferns up the bank and in the trees had an ominous portent, enough for Hiep to walk with his rifle at the ready, eyes scanning the vegetation inland. But no creature emerged to be seen. The webs increased in size and density as they went south. Hiep eyed those with interest, but he was unwilling to waste time in examining them. With darkness starting to fall yet again, they headed for a hill that stuck up beyond a bend in the river. That was when a sound rang out through the air, rising and falling, a lilting and compelling march.

"My God, is that a flute?" The moment the words were out of her mouth, Reality saw Hiep turn and walk a few paces away from her.

It would not be fitting for anyone to see a member of Sicarius cry.

Danijel

The notes from Thorny's flute soared into the dark sky, up to where a thin veil of shimmering green was beginning to form. Danijel thought the lights pulsed in time with the music. Thorny played each evening, and he would sit and listen to her play all night if she would. They sat close enough that he could feel her warmth against him although not so close as to interfere with her playing.

Every muscle in his body ached: legs, shoulders, and back. He could not tell which was the worst. It was true for Thorny, too, he knew. Nevertheless, they had finished their cabin. He turned his head enough that he could see the log structure illuminated by the flickering campfire. It did not give them more than five feet of headroom at the sides, but that was because they had laid down some shorter logs, centered at the front and back. Those allowed them to position crossbeams, which supported a slanted roof. They had cut logs down to flat-surfaced planks for the roofing, as much to reduce the weight they had to hoist as anything else, and with a combination of notches and vine ties, it held together. Oh, it would need some work before it was truly waterproof. They would need to figure out how to get up on the roof and seal the gaps with web and leaf, a task that Danijel's mind worried over, as the more he thought about it, the more difficult it became. He told himself they would figure it out. He was prouder of that cabin than of his solution to any engineering problem posed by the school computer. The kiss Thorny had given him when the last piece was in place . . . he felt he was up in the sky with the lights.

He wished they could stay here, just the two of them. He knew it was impossible, but he could wish. For this one more late afternoon and evening, he would enjoy that daydream.

That was when an "Eep!" came from Fenris where it circled Thorny's arm. The music from the flute stopped. Danijel's eyes searched the darkness beyond the campsite wards, but the fire spoiled his night vision. Thorny rose in one fluid motion without needing her hands to push off from the ground. She gripped her flute like a weapon.

Danijel was on his feet an instant later, ignoring the protests of muscles that had stiffened while he sat. Their weapons were at the cabin. Poor planning, although the wards, marked by the glowing green along the rods, should be proof against local intruders. The sawtooth roos people saw occasionally in the valley could jump high enough, sometimes, to clear the wards, but since they had killed that roo the day Danijel arrived, they had not seen another one. No animal that had come to the hilltop had come close to clearing the defenses on their hill. Yet. What might live in the polar forest that they had not yet seen?

A rustle and crunch of leaves came from the side of the gentler slope of the hill. A form moved across the ferns and trees, then stepped into the clearing and the light. It was Vo Hiep.

"Dad?" Thorny's question turned into a squeak in the space of the single syllable. "How? From where? How did you find me?"

"I heard the flute," Hiep said. "From Saint Peterstown, I heard the flute. And I am here. Instantly."

"Of course." Thorny said that as though Hiep's statement were the most natural course of events.

Danijel managed enough of a coherent thought to dig into his pants pocket for the controller and switch off the wards. As the warning lights on the poles blinked out and the rods retracted, Hiep walked up to the fire.

"Did you build this?" Hiep's eyes had moved to the cabin.

"Together" was Danijel's one-word response. His mind moved

immediately to what Hiep would also assume they had been doing together, and no further words came.

"Good." Hiep's voice was soft. "I am glad, Thorny, that you have such a good friend."

"Oh, Dad!" With that, Thorny was in convulsive motion. She rushed to Hiep and the two of them locked in a tight embrace. That lasted only seconds before they released each other with a glance at Danijel suggesting they were embarrassed at their mutual display.

That was when Thorny spotted Reality, who had come up the hill behind Hiep and was also standing in the light of the campfire, her Pioneer Youth uniform now heavily stained and bedraggled.

"What are *you* doing here?" Thorny managed to pack a lot of disbelief into that short question.

"I . . . ah . . . well . . . Two students from my school were . . . ah . . . missing."

"Of course." Again, Thorny said the words as though the most natural action for the Head of School to take was to journey hundreds of miles through trackless wilderness to find two students.

"Why don't you sit by the fire with us?" Danijel asked. "I can offer you shellhound any way from pretty raw to completely burned. And some plants we've found that seem to be okay and are a little juicy." That would be a normal response to guests who stopped by unexpectedly, he told himself, although nothing about the situation was remotely close to normal.

The four of them did sit down by the fire and shared some meat on skewers. Thorny and Danijel, in alternating fashion, told a carefully abbreviated and edited tale of how and why they had come to be there. Danijel was certain, at many points, that explanations would be demanded, but none were. What they said was simply accepted. In return, Hiep told the story of how Reality had joined him and how they had found their way to the little cabin on a hill. Hiep did ask many questions about the building of the cabin, and with a technical subject and a job well done to celebrate, the conversation flowed more smoothly.

At least, it was smooth until the topic of the roo came up. Hiep had many more questions this time, about everything from what they were expecting when they picked up the trail to what was in their minds and why they acted as they did during the frantic seconds of the fight. Danijel thought the questions were reasonable, and Hiep did say that he thought they had shown themselves to be very capable, but he noticed that Thorny's answers became shorter the more they talked, and she seemed stiffer.

When Hiep was finished with the roo, he asked about the gator back by the rovers. Danijel found he was a little embarrassed to recount what he had done and realized that he had not even told Thorny. Compared to finding Thorny, it was not that important in his mind.

"I just did what I had to do," Danijel said at the end of the story of the gator. "There wasn't much choice."

"There are always choices," Hiep said. "We are all known by the choices we make."

"Well, I'm just glad I didn't go in my pants." Danijel forced a chuckle. Self-deprecation felt more comfortable. Thorny squeezed next to him when he did that and put her arm around his waist.

A small smile crossed Hiep's face. Danijel was certain that was what he saw. The heat in his face was not from the fire. He searched for a topic that was not himself, one that had nothing to do with him or Thorny facing danger. He was sure she was uncomfortable with Hiep's questions even though he did not know why. "I still don't understand why you came with Mr. Vo," he said to Reality. "I mean, he came for Thorny. I understand that. But me . . . my father hates you, you know. He really hates you."

Reality found a loose stick and threw it in the fire. Then she poked at the dirt with another one. "He has reason to."

Danijel did not know what sort of response he had expected to hear, but those words were definitely not it. "I don't understand."

"Shit." Reality's focus was where the stick dug into the dirt. "In the early days here, Miroslav, your father, was whipped. A punishment he did not deserve. He blames me for that. I did not do the whipping, but

I was part of it, part of what happened. He has a right to feel the way he does." She paused. "He never told you about this?"

"No." Danijel found himself temporarily at a loss for words. "I know something happened from things I remember him saying to my mother when they were partners, but nothing specific. Neither he nor my mother ever talked about anything like that, at least not where I or any of the other kids in our family could hear it. Now that you say this, though, it makes me realize that he never takes off his shirt, no matter how hot it is."

"It's true, though." Reality's head was still down. She was speaking to the ground.

"Right," Thorny said. "Satan and his Six, not Five. That's the story. You were the sixth. The only one who is still alive."

"Yeah." Reality dropped the stick and sat with her elbows on her knees, fingers buried in her hair at the sides of her head. "I should be dead too. Do you know that? Do you know," she said to Thorny, "that it was your mother who saved my life?"

"No." Thorny's voice dropped to a whisper.

"She did. Your father was going to shoot me, but your mother saved me."

"Dad?" Thorny turned to Hiep.

"It's true," Hiep said. "Penny said not to shoot. That's why I did not."

"If you had fired, you would have killed me," Reality said. "Correct?"

"Also true," Hiep said. "I would not have missed."

"Why?" Thorny's whisper was down to the point where it was barely audible.

Reality still did not look up, but her voice strengthened. "Malachi, the one people like to call Satan now, he was going to kill your mother. He was going to have us do it. It would have been horrible. In spite of that, your mother saved my life when she could have let me die.

"Afterward, when she was first mayor, she said I could set up day care for the children who would be born, what has turned into the school since then. I have tried to pay her back . . . tried to do it by paying it forward . . . every day of my life." She picked up the stick again and stabbed it into the ground. It snapped off in her hand. She held the broken piece up in front of her face, focused on the place where it had split. "For all of that, I'm not good enough at what I do. Any of it. And that's why I'm here, to go back and answer your first question." She tossed the part of the stick she was holding into the fire, where it was rapidly consumed.

Danijel had never heard Reality say a word or act in any way to suggest that she was less than top-notch at what she did. There had never been a hint that she felt that way. That slid off his mind, like a droplet off his waterproof, because it was too strange to credit. The rest of that brief conversation did grip his mind, however.

"My God," he said. "I know people talk about the bad times, but it's never specific; it's always like one of the chippers—the Originals—will wink and another will nod, and they know what they mean even though they don't say anything. It's been twenty years. No Heaveners were even born then."

"Wait." Hiep broke in, his voice was hard, but he did not move from where he sat cross-legged, hands on his knees. "Before we talk about guilt or about horrors, we should remember that the Demos elected Malachi Oates as the mayor. The Demos voted for him. He was chosen to be our leader, and we followed his orders. All of us."

"Until you didn't," Reality said. She did not look at Hiep, kept her eyes on the fire. "You had the courage I lacked."

"Malachi crossed the line into evil." A judge passing sentence could not have sounded more final than Hiep. A loud snap from the fire punctuated his words. "Some orders are not to be obeyed. That is an old principle. What I am saying, though, is that the Demos voted for him. The Demos is responsible for the choice they made and the consequences. All of them. They cannot force the burden to be carried by only a few, most of whom are conveniently dead. They cannot leave it with you. At least your generation, Thorny and Dani, does not share in the burden. I hope you will not make similar mistakes. It is all too easy to do."

With that pronouncement, a general silence descended on the foursome. Each of them was lost in their own thoughts. Looking over at Hiep and Reality, Danijel suspected—no, he was sure—they were reliving memories of those days and of things that had happened long before, back on Earth. Danijel lacked those memories, but that did not stop his mind from dwelling on what he had heard people say and what the meanings might be beneath the sanitized phrases. He thought Thorny was in the same place he was.

After a while, Thorny simply began to talk. It did break a quiet that had become oppressive. She spoke of what she and Danijel had seen in the area around their hill, the types of plants and animals, how it differed from both Saint Peterstown and the valley, and how life this far south was more abundant and varied. She showed off Fenris as an example. The tension around the fire dissipated.

Finally, Hiep said, "You can show us the area tomorrow when it is light. For now, I think we should get some sleep. Your cabin is not large enough for four, so Reality and I will sleep by the fire."

Both Thorny and Danijel blushed at his unspoken implication.

JANUARY 1, HY 22

DANIJEL

HIEP WANTED TO RETURN NORTH AS SOON AS POSSIBLE, BUT HE WAS WILLING to allow an additional day's grace for Thorny and Danijel to lead them farther into the land past the hill, to see more of the trees, the open land, the ponds, the webs swaying in the wind, and the lights in the night sky. Hiep wanted to report to Penny—and he actually used that term—on the nature of the land around Thorny's hill. It was not convenient to Saint Peterstown and the valley, but it was not all the way to the South Pole either. It would be important to let Penny know if it was suitable for settlement. Danijel suspected Thorny's grimace was for the idea of other people coming into her territory.

Thorny did take over and led the group in a wide-ranging and circuitous path through the surrounding land. Danijel suspected it was designed to take up as much of the day as possible, but he did not say anything, and neither Hiep nor Reality made comments about that.

Hiep proved to be a student of the land. He examined each area closely, especially the low-lying land by the ponds, where he dug into the dirt with his fingers to check how moist it was and took multiple pics on his phone. When Danijel asked him what interested him so much, he said, "I am working from memories of where I grew up, but I think it would be possible to grow rice here. I will show these to Penny, and we will talk."

Danijel thought he saw Thorny wince as Hiep spoke. He could not be sure of that, but what he was certain of was that Thorny turned the route to the south, taking them even farther away from the hill. In addition to the interest Hiep took in the lay of the land, he also spent time examining the webs. It was not the spiders but their webs that caught his eye. Hiep brushed a finger across the strands of the largest ones and rubbed the sticky liquid that came off between his fingers. He poked at the small ones and watched them rebound. He hardly noticed when Fenris made a snack of one of the large spiders.

"You have the test equipment, from what you said," Hiep remarked from a squatting position in front of a multicomponent web. "Have you analyzed these at all?"

"We could eat the spiders. If we had to." Thorny showed no sign of enthusiasm for the idea. "Plenty of protein, but no help on vitamins or methionine."

"I didn't mean the spiders." Hiep was still intent on the web in front of him. "I was asking about analyzing the webs."

"We haven't," Danijel said. "What would we be looking for?"

"I remember being taught on Earth that spiderwebs are good for helping wounds heal cleanly," Hiep said. "They were said to have a lot of a vitamin that is important for blood clotting. Vitamin K. Also that they have compounds that kill bacteria. I will grant that it would be very unlikely to find vitamin K here, although perhaps it has something to do with the general structure of webs that we do not understand, but if these webs have compounds that kill the bacteria of this planet, it would be very significant. Our antibiotics are useless against infections from Heaven bacteria. Antibacterials that are effective here would be a major find."

"That sounds like a speech Mom would give," Thorny said.

"No." Hiep shook his head gently and with a smile. "Penny is not fond of spiders or webs. In any case, this is military lore, not what you can pick up at a pharmacy. I was taught it because in the field, in action, when you have no other supplies, we could try spiderwebs on wounds."

They went on with their exploration with no further discussion of spiders or webs, but Thorny had obviously not put it out of her mind. When they returned to the hilltop, she announced that they would be having a local specialty for dinner. She dashed back down the hill using her phone for light and returned with a collection of large spiders. She speared them, four to a stick.

"Spider roast tonight," she said as she started the campfire.

They sat around that campfire, each with a skewer of flamed and roasted spiders. Thorny crunched her way through hers without hesitation and with no room for words while she was eating. Danijel regarded the blackened mass, somewhat like a child's drawing of four stars done in charcoal. There was no way he would refuse it, not with Thorny sitting next to him. He pulled off a leg and bit into it. It snapped and crunched in his mouth, and he was thankful that it had little taste. He was able to finish the ones on his skewer.

Hiep sat cross-legged by the fire and ate his more deliberately than Thorny did. He finished all of them and licked his fingers. On the other hand, Reality's eyes went wide and seemed ready to fall out of her head. She could not bring the skewer closer than a foot from her mouth. After a prolonged staring contest between her and the roast spiders, she put the skewer down and covered her mouth with one hand.

"Thank you for an excellent meal," Hiep said. He let his hands rest on top of his knees. "I am glad to see you can improvise well in the field." He spared a brief look for Reality and shook his head slightly. "Now that we have eaten, we need to plan for our return to Saint Peterstown. We should leave tomorrow with the first light."

Thorny's face fell at Hiep's last words. Danijel saw it because he was looking at her. He did not think the others noticed.

AJIT

THE NEW YEAR'S CELEBRATION FOR HY 22 WAS A MUTED AFFAIR COMPARED TO THE usual event. The population of Heaven did not celebrate New Year's at the stroke of midnight the way the Originals had done on Earth.

Instead, the celebration began at sundown on January 1, the official end of the solstice Demos meeting. The Demos would migrate from the dome to the Dining Hall, which even with the growth in population was still large enough to accommodate everyone. The food engineers would cook up whatever food had not been used during the meeting as well as food that had been withheld from the equal shares accounting and squirreled away for this purpose. Extra shares of beer and cannabis were distributed. That might not generate a "forgive and forget" attitude to the arguments and fights of the meeting just past, but it did allow people to paper them over and mostly enjoy themselves.

This year was different. The Demos meeting had not happened. Most of the valley-folk had either returned to the valley before the solstice or not come up at all. The hall echoed with its emptiness. The extra food, drink, and cannabis had not been broken out, because it was being held back for the meeting to come. There had been neither fights to make up for, nor gossip to share, nor new rumors to spread about the mess that decisions just made would trigger. All in all, it was a glum affair.

Ajit was contemplating without enthusiasm the skewer of roasted vegetables he had picked up when a hand the size of a ham descended on his shoulder from behind. He turned to come face-to-face with Herschel Northrup, and it was Northrup without his usual geniality, whether that was affected or not.

"Hoped I would find you here," Northrup said. He pointed to the skewer. "Is that all you're having? I'm pretty sure you eat meat."

Ajit did not like being touched by other men. He looked at Northrup's hand before he spoke and was glad to see it removed. "I do eat meat. What is here is awful. But this isn't about meat. From the way you look, something is wrong."

"We may have a problem. You know we have people in town, some at the residence school, some Originals, who like something with a little more kick than alcohol or pot."

"So what else is new?" Ajit shrugged. "We could start with Oscar."

Northrup moved closer than Ajit liked. "My point is that talk and messages are circulating, things that I see. It seems that Dalton Watkins, one of the high-seniors, cooked up some psychedelic out of material he pulled out of a cell foundry line. That's his mother's area. What's important is that the doc is starting to think that is what killed Fernando Vargas."

Ajit found a table to put the vegetable skewer down. "How do you know that? The bit about the doc, I mean."

Now Northrup did grin. It was not borne of good humor. "Our little Practitioner Yuki doesn't get a lot of attention. I make sure to supply some, and she appreciates it. That's how I know. You see the problem?"

Ajit did, and he did not like what he saw. "If this kid's, Dalton's, happy juice killed Fernando, then Thorny is clear and we lose our hold on Guillermo. I don't want to give up on the valley votes."

Northrup gave an emphatic nod. "What do you want to do?"

Ajit needed only a moment's consideration. "I'm going to talk to his mother, Chloe, make sure she understands that people would blame her, that she needs us to have this go on Thorny. Maybe she can come up with something that says the stuff is harmless, but I won't bet on it.

"What I want you to do is get word to Dalton and his friends, Fernando's friends, anyone who hung around with Fernando. Make sure they understand that they need to say Fernando never touched this stuff, or at least that he never touched it that night. And stay close to Yuki in case there is anything else we need to know."

"I can do that," Northrup said. "And we can have a different conversation about food and meat another time."

JANUARY 2, HY 22

AJIT

"**J**ONES? JONES, WHERE THE FUCK ARE YOU?" THE WORDS ECHOED HOLLOWLY off the ceiling and walls. Mistry's eyes scanned the interior of the deserted Lab Unit.

"I'm here." The voice came from an unlit office with an open door. An instant later, Everett Jones walked out of it. "Let's take a little walk, shall we? We can talk outside."

Mistry stood still, a baffled expression on his face as Jones walked past him and out the door to Town Circle. Then he turned around and hustled to catch up to the other man.

"What kind of bullshit game is this?" Ajit asked when he was close enough to grab Jones by the arm. "You leave me a message about this big, beautiful thing you've done, and then you won't answer my calls or my messages except for 'I'm at the Lab Unit.' What the fuck?"

"We can take a stroll around the Community Dome and talk," Jones said. "Or go out to the Perimeter Road. It's a nice day for a walk, and that's better than standing in one place."

Past where Jones stood in the middle of Town Circle, Ajit could see the banner proclaiming HAPPY NEW YEAR HY 22! fastened to the latticework below the overhang of the roof. A crew had put the banner up yesterday for New Year's Day, one of four such banners at the cardinal points around the dome. Naturally, a group of bots had put them up. The crew had not climbed up the lattice with the banners. They had stayed on the ground, tapping control panels while cursing about the heat. He wondered whose idea it had been and if the banners would be taken down before HY 23.

Ajit wiped one hand across his forehead, where the heat of the winter sun was already raising sweat. Heaven reminded him of visiting his relatives in Mumbai during his life on Earth. In his opinion, the nicest of Heaven's days was as bad as the worst of Mumbai's. He had hated Mumbai. "Why? Why are we doing this?"

"I don't trust Olivares." Jones converted the conversation to a walking one by the simple expedient of breaking away from Mistry and heading around Town Circle. "That man is good with the computer systems, including phone and messaging. Exactly how good I don't know, but he was a starship pilot and he has been working on our systems for twenty years now. I don't want to take a chance that he's snooping."

"Olivares?" The pitch in Ajit's voice rose with the question. "That doesn't make sense. I'll agree, he's part valley-guy, okay, and he was off *Dauntless*, yes, but the computer systems are what he does, which are here, and he's an Original. He's got to believe in equal shares and the town. He's got to be on our side."

"The only side Jorge Olivares is on is the doc's. And for all the ups and downs over the years, she is a bit closer to Penny than I like. Nothing is secret in a town like this. Women talk, you know, and I talk to women."

They went a quarter of the way around the dome to where another of the banners was above them while Mistry digested Jones's words. "Fine," he said at last. "You'd rather bathe in sweat than talk on the network. Fine. What did you do that you think is so great?"

Jones turned hesitant. Ajit could see it. He had seen it often in men and women who had raised the stakes but, at the last minute, were afraid to show their cards.

"I've got us another man," Jones said at last. "I've got someone else to stand with us when we need to fight."

"No," Ajit said. "I thought I was clear that we were not going to do that."

A muscle jumped at the side of Jones's jaw as he clenched his teeth. Then he relaxed enough to continue. "That was a discussion, not a final decision. And, anyway, I've done it. It's all set."

Ajit peered at the man, who was now sweating profusely, and not from the heat. *You weren't going to tell me at all*, he thought. *Just have him appear when the moment comes and I can't even argue. Dumbass.* "If you've done it, you've done it. Don't expect me to congratulate you, though, and be damn glad you let me know before Hiep shows up." Ajit told himself to try to make the best of a bad situation. "Who is it?"

Jones kicked up a cloud of dirt with his sandals. "Young Gordie."

"Gordon?" Ajit was glad no one else was in sight because he could not keep his voice down. "Why did you tell Durham-Pole about the guns? Why did you let him in on what we're doing?"

"Because we need reinforcements." Jones was defensive. It showed in his eyes, in his shoulders. "We have the guns but we don't have enough men. Not for what we've decided we have to do. And who we've got . . . the only way Oscar is going to be a stand-up guy is if the part of him standing up can get a blow job. We can't be sure how many rovers will come back, and if there's more than one, we won't know which one Hiep is in. We didn't think about that when we planned this, and I'm not happy about it. If we focus on the wrong rover and Hiep gets loose, that's not a good situation. We have to be able to take them all at once."

To Ajit, the bare dirt of Town Circle looked as hot as asphalt in Mumbai. "And what makes you think we can trust Durham-Pole? He's nothing but a kid. He's certainly not one of us."

"Yeah, he's nothing but a kid." Jones scowled. He seemed intent on walking in the blistering heat, and this was the goddamn winter. "But that's part of my point." His approach shifted to that of a salesman trying to close a deal. "It's easy to know the buttons to push. This kid wants so badly to be a big man. For everybody to see him as a big man. It's so obvious it's pathetic. He leaped at the idea of having the gun, of using the gun. I could see it on his face, how he was seeing the way people would look at him if he was one of us. It was the same, you remember, back at the beginning, when Malachi gave guns to Reality and that other Pioneer kid. You remember how they went for it."

"That is not a time I like to remember," Ajit said slowly. "I don't think other Originals will want to remember either. And what I also remember is that Hiep and that Leif Grettison killed the other Pioneer and Reality dropped her weapon, screaming, 'Don't shoot!'"

"That's not the point." Jones scowled. "Hiep doesn't have that starship pilot throwing dive-bombs, and he doesn't have Grettison either. It's just him. For all that people go, 'Ooh, he was one of the Sicarii,' he's one person, and he's not a superagent out of a vid. If we are going to do this—and we are—we need enough shooters to be sure. Durham-Pole will want to be a hero. I could see it in his eyes. What's even better is that if Hiep does put a bullet in one of us, Durham-Pole trying to be a hero makes it more likely the bullet goes into him than me. I prefer it that way."

"All right. I get your point." When the cards were down, the hand was over. No point moaning about who held what. "I want to get back to air-conditioning."

"Sure. But listen. Before you go running off, I think we should have one more person in addition to Gordon. That's the reason I wanted to tell you now. Gordie's good, and I've made sure of that, spoken to him a few times now, but Hiep's not back yet, so we still have time to add another. I want to talk to Herschel. I think he has the nose for the right kind of people."

At those words, Ajit's eyes shrank down to narrow slits. His mind threw off the heat and turned to the true nature of the problem. Jones did not look impressive standing there with Town Circle dirt across his sandals and toes, but Ajit had not forgotten that Jones wanted to be secretary of the council. Was Jones really afraid of Olivares, or had this been a play to pull Ajit outside, where he would not think critically and might make a hasty decision? Joseph Stalin had made his start by being general-secretary and leveraging that position to take over the Soviet Union. Ajit did not trust the combination of Everett Jones and Herschel Northrup.

"No. No more. We are not bringing in anyone else. Understand? I'll buy Durham-Pole, but nobody else. We can't have this leak." Ajit thought the last point was adequate reason to keep the group small. It was a point that could not be argued with. *Nice try, Jones. I'm still sharper than you, heat or no heat.*

Danijel

Leaving the little cabin on the hill was bittersweet, with far more of the bitter part than Danijel had expected since it was not a choice at all. It took only a cursory glance into their packs to see how little he and Thorny had left of their Earth foods, vitamins, and methionine. Hiep and Reality would share theirs, of course, but spread over four people, that would not buy too much more time. Once those were gone, the inevitable deterioration of an Earth physiology in the environment of Heaven would begin.

Hiep had not been willing to wait until they reached that biological endpoint. After the spider dinner, he had been polite but adamant that they cram their packs as full as they could be and prepare to depart the next day.

Danijel paused on the trail down the hill for a final look back. That cabin might not be much, but it was theirs. He and Thorny had built it; a part of both of them was in it. Somehow, someway, he told himself, there would be a way for them to return. They had built something out of themselves too. He felt a twinge of loss when he thought about that relationship as well. Since the arrival of Hiep and Reality, Thorny had been a little reserved, a little irritable. More so than usual. He blamed Reality for that, but there was nothing to be done about it. He would love Thorny even when she was irritable, he knew that, but he did prefer it when she was not.

"We should take one of the boats," Hiep was saying when Danijel came, last of the four, to the riverbank.

Thorny's eyes flashed. "The little motor the boat has might go upstream here, but it won't manage against the current farther up, never mind the canyon."

Danijel noticed, not for the first time, that any position Hiep took, Thorny would find a way to take an opposing view.

"Using the motor when we can will conserve our strength. With all four of us rowing in addition, I think we can make it through the canyon," Hiep said.

"Well, if we can take only one boat, that means we have to leave behind a lot of stuff," Thorny responded. "With four of us in one boat, there won't be that much room for anything else."

"If we hike out, we will be leaving all of that and more," Hiep said.

"Then we should take both boats," Thorny said.

"Two people rowing plus the motor will not make it through the canyon."

"Then the river will just push us back down and then we can do it the other way." Thorny was not giving up the argument.

Hiep shook his head. "The way the water is in that canyon, it will be safer with four rowers in the boat. We can also mount both motors on the one boat."

"Well . . . fine!"

Thorny dropped her pack on the bank, gave it a kick, then boosted it up and tumbled it over the sidewall and into the bottom of the boat. Danijel put a hand on her shoulder. She shrugged it off, did not even look at him.

Danijel sighed. This might be a difficult trip.

•   •   •

IT WAS EASY AT FIRST FOR THEM TO WORK THEIR WAY UPSTREAM AGAINST THE LANGUID current in the river near where the hill rose. The motor alone was almost sufficient. The current quickened as they went north and the river began to narrow, however. That increased the effort required and slowed their progress. It was clear they would take the full day to reach the outlet of the canyon. They would not make their first attempt at navigating the canyon after a day on the river and in the dark, so there would be yet another day added to the journey.

JANUARY 3, HY 22

DANIJEL

REALITY SAT UP AND STARED AT THE BLACKENED REMAINS OF LAST NIGHT'S SMALL campfire. She kneaded first the muscles of her lower back and then each of her upper arms. "I think it is just as well we've got four people rowing. If we ever come down here again, we should arrange stronger motors."

"We could do this with two in a boat and one motor," Thorny said. "You're just old." She was already up and had pulled her small pack close to her so she could check something inside.

Danijel moved so that he sat next to Thorny, legs touching. "Whether we could or not doesn't matter anymore," he said quietly. "Maybe better to just let it be."

"You don't need to be taking my father's side in this!" She scooted her butt across the ground to open a six-inch gap between them.

Danijel looked across the fire to where Hiep was examining the boat. He saw a minute turn of Hiep's head from side to side. "The best use of our time is in preparation," Hiep said. "Right now that means a decent meal, even with our short supplies. Today will be a strenuous day."

It proved to be every bit as strenuous as Hiep's words suggested. The river had a malign intent of its own to thwart their desire to go north. The current worked against them to fling them back toward the river bend and hill they had left the day before. The motors by themselves were insufficient. It was only with Danijel calling out a count to coordinate their strokes, and with each of them digging deep into the water with every bite of their oars, that they were able to fight their way upstream. To their dismayed eyes, each stroke appeared to bring them no more than a few inches forward despite the effort it took.

Halfway up the canyon, Thorny yelled out, "Okay! I was wrong! I don't think we can make it even with four!"

"We have to!" Reality shouted back. "We won't have enough strength for another try."

In fact, that exchange caused them to lose focus and the river sensed an opportunity. It pushed them back south as the rowing lost coordination.

"Danijel! Call the strokes! Loudly!" Hiep's voice projected over the rush of the water. "Keep over to the edge. The current is stronger in the middle."

"Pull!" Danijel shouted. "Pull!" With each cry, he put his back, his shoulders, every muscle he had, into the row. With agonizing slowness, the boat crept forward against the current.

Danijel lost all track of time in the canyon. The sky overhead was grayed out with cloud. He had no sense of the sun's position. He was aware only of the increasing ache in his arms and his back. The sides of the canyon in its narrow upper segment offered no place to pull the boat ashore for a rest. If they did not make it through, the river would sweep them back downstream and all their effort would have been for naught.

"Pull!" Danijel shouted with a voice as hoarse as the ache in his muscles. "Pull!"

Ahead he could see where the canyon walls fell away on the sides. The exit was in sight.

"Pull!" He tried to use the shout to mask the aches and weariness from his awareness.

They could not fail so close to the end. All four screamed with every thrust into the water. Danijel could taste blood from where he had bitten his lip or tongue. It did not matter. Nothing mattered expect one more effort and then another after that.

The boat shot past the mouth of the canyon. The water calmed; the pull on the boat to send it back downstream eased. Ahead was the sloping riverbank that still bore signs of where they had put the boats in the water. They jumped into the shallows to pull the boat ashore, frantic to complete the task before their energy drained away completely. Then, with the boat far enough up the bank to be secure, they stumbled a few feet farther and collapsed on the dirt, heedless of their surroundings.

Thorny dropped next to Danijel with a moan. He put his arms around her and hugged her tight. She fell asleep in his arms.

AJIT

ANY GAIETY INSPIRED BY THE NEW YEAR'S CELEBRATION, EVEN AT A SUPERFICIAL LEVEL, was gone after two days. Saint Peterstown was back to being the same boring place where nothing new ever happened and no one new ever stopped by. Well, it wasn't entirely true that nothing new ever happened. Two weeks had passed since Thorny and Dani had disappeared from the town, followed by Hiep and Reality in search of them. Nobody ever disappeared for that length of time, and the town and the valley together were nothing more than a speck on a vast inhospitable planet, so speculation about their fate, almost all of it downbeat, filled the messages and conversations in both valley and town.

It was not so much the individuals involved that generated concern for them. Reality Busby's name was often mentioned in association with the words "good riddance," and similar sentiments were put forth about Thorny. No one other than his family felt comfortable around Vo Hiep, so even if the words were never said—in case he did come back and heard about them—the same feeling was there. Dani Petrovic was, everyone acknowledged, a nice boy, but he had always kept to himself so that people hardly noticed he was gone. That is, people other than Miroslav hardly noticed, and Miroslav had with-drawn into himself and was not talking to anyone.

If people were not worried about the specific individuals who were missing, the number that were missing did cause concern. This was four more people on top of Fernando, whom they had buried only a week and a half ago. In a settlement where the census was always at the forefront of everyone's mind, this was a big deal. The town and valley could not sustain big losses. They all knew that, even the ones who were happy to say they were glad to be rid of a particular individual. When they spoke of the number of losses, just as many people fixated on the three missing rovers. It was easier to replace people than rovers.

All of which did weigh on Ajit's mind as he counted the days, but he was worried more about the days until the Demos meeting finally happened. It would be so much easier if the meeting came and Hiep did not. He could stop worrying about Jones talking to someone else or Durham-Pole talking to anyone, and they could be done with Jones's increasing paranoia over Olivares plucking some interaction out of the system and learning the guns had been taken, although he tried to tell himself that anyone learning about the guns would mean nothing because *he*, Ajit Mistry, controlled the guns. That is, it would mean nothing unless Hiep returned.

Jones's obsession with secrecy had even infected Northrup, which was why Ajit was shivering as he stood next to Northrup, waiting to hear what the man wanted to say. Ajit hated the heat outside, but that did not mean he wanted to meet in one of the walk-in refrigeration and freezer units of the Dining Hall, private though it might be. Northrup showed no sign of discomfort, but that man had substantially greater insulation under his skin than Ajit did. Subhas Chandra Bose had not hidden in a damn freezer to lay his plans against the Raj, Ajit thought with rising irritation.

"You see what I've got here?" Northrup tapped the clear plastic door of one of the freezer units.

"Food. Obviously." Ajit hoped his teeth would not chatter. "What's your point?"

"That it's not simply food. We have some chicken parts here; some ham down there." Northrup rapped the plastic in front of the respective shelves. "In the summer, we can have some nice honeydew melons. Not frozen, of course. The point is, the farms enter what they ship for equal shares, but there is always the opportunity for a little to disappear—shrinkage, if you will—and we adjust the inventory in the system so that it matches. We know the valley-crats do the same with what they pack up to ship. That doesn't match what they actually harvest. Someone wants a little extra, a personal marker can do a lot."

"So, you're skimming off some of the food. I'm not surprised." Ajit was not surprised. What he wanted to know was the reason for the conversation. There was always a reason.

Northrup grew a very wide grin, an announcement that he was about to make his pitch. "When you're mayor, you could organize the collection, the food inventory, and have storage here. Right now, I can manage a piece here and a bit there. Organize this right—I'll tell you who we can put in which post—and I'm sure we can pull ten percent off the top, and that's after paying off those people. We can split it. It would be, shall we say, mutually profitable."

And there's the reason, Ajit thought. And it would be profitable, especially if, with Jones as secretary, he could have Northrup looking over Jones's shoulder. There was potential here, potential to have Jones and Northrup wary of each other and wanting to keep alliance with him.

"I need to be mayor" was what Ajit said. "That and we need Hiep out of the way. You follow my meaning?"

"Of course." Northrup's grin almost reached his ears on either side. "I've talked to Dalton and to each of his little groupies. Fernando never touched that stuff. They'll all swear to it."

"Do you know if he did—I mean, for real?"

"Who knows and who cares?" Northrup said. "I wouldn't trust anything those kids say, but they will say what we need them to say when it matters. That's what counts."

That was true, Ajit thought. That was all that mattered. "Anything more from your friend Yuki?'

"Nah." Northrup shook his head. "The doc doesn't know anything more than she did two weeks ago." He laughed, and his breath came out as smoke, which made Ajit even more aware of the temperature in the unit.

"Can we get out of here?" Ajit asked.

JANUARY 4, HY 22

JING

JING REGARDED FERNANDO'S BRAIN WITH DISTASTE. IT WAS FIXED AND READY TO be sectioned, its tissues ready to yield up their secrets to Jing's tests and microscope slides. And yet . . . Jing was unhappy with the work in front of her because she did not know what she was doing. She had plenty of reference works, naturally. The library that was part of the computer system had no shortage of those. However, it was one thing to read about the work and another to do it. She had never done this before, and she had no one to show her how to do it, no one to teach her. Being the highest authority on the planet in the field of medicine was wearying at times. It would be worse in the future. How much of her skill would she be able to pass along? How many generations would it take before the Heaven-born were forced to reinvent medicine? She could not escape these recurring emotions and worries.

She felt a shiver run from her head through her torso. *Focus, Jing!* She rechecked the reagents she had set out. She had, maybe, a quarter of the ones mentioned in her references. The ISC had not included them; the cell foundries could not produce them, and creating them out of what was available on this barren plain was beyond even a fever dream. It would not be that long, not so many uses before the same could be said for all the marker tests that needed to be conducted.

How long would it be before they could manufacture new monoclonal antibodies or sequences of nucleic acids? A long, long time, she thought. The shiver repeated itself, a warning that the only respite from her wandering thoughts would be in work.

She was working alone in the laboratory section of the clinic. This was a job that could be done by one as easily as, if not more easily than, two. For all that she anguished over not being able to teach everything she knew to the others, Yuki had become too invested in the rumors that ran about the town about some sort of fight between Fernando and Thorny.

Yuki was convinced now that some kind of trauma had caused Fernando's death, and when people were convinced of what they would see, they tended to see it. That was a bad trait for a diagnostician, so Jing had assigned Yuki to seeing walk-ins. Norma had declined anything to do with the autopsy, and Michael was in the valley. So, let's get it done, Jing!

•   •   •

Hours later, Jing pushed her chair away from her desk, shut off her microscope, and stared up at the ceiling. All that work had failed to give her an answer. The problem was, she thought as she let the ceiling lights make multicolored sparkles in her vision, that she did not know if she had missed something because she did not have the reagent she needed or because she had made an error or because there was nothing there to find. The only solace she could take from the frustration of the day was that she had not had to listen to Athena, who had not been able to wait a full week for a visit. That had been Yuki's problem.

Danijel

Danijel was dreaming. It was a dream about Thorny. They were lying together on the sandy beach of an island that his mind must have pulled from a vid or a book because Heaven had no beaches shaded by coconut palms. They were close. She was nibbling at his ear.

Suddenly he sat bolt upright as a bite stabbed through his ear. That part was no dream! It was dark out, alleviated only by the beginning of a glow at the northeast horizon. Thorny was curled next to him, still sound asleep.

He fumbled with one hand for his phone to trigger the light while his other hand went to his throbbing ear. In the beam from his phone, he saw blood smeared across his hand. He swung the light out and around him. Caught in its glare, a small creature froze. It wasn't more than eight inches long from snout to whip-thin tail, its leathery body held just off the ground by six birdlike legs and feet. It opened its jaws, revealing rows of tiny, needle teeth.

"Thought I was breakfast, did you?" Danijel said. "I hope you die of food poisoning."

With a groan, Thorny sat up at his words. Danijel pointed at the creature still motionless in his light and explained what had happened.

"Give me the light so I can look at your ear." Thorny plucked the phone away from him before he could hand it over. The tiny carnivore took the opportunity to scoot back into the darkness. "Looks like that thing took a little chunk out of your auricle. I guess that means you've been officially wounded on this expedition." She giggled. "I could kiss it to make it better, but some antiseptic and a bandage is probably the way to go."

Danijel did not think the situation warranted humor, but he was happy enough to have Thorny back to her normal self that he swallowed the first words that formed in his mind. Instead, he leaned over and kissed her lips lightly. Then he stood up and extended a hand for her to pull herself up.

"I guess lying around here is an invitation to be snacked on," Danijel said.

Within a minute, he had both Hiep and Reality awake. Hiep brushed dirt from his clothing, then walked off in the direction of where they had left the rovers, giving no indication that the night on the ground or the previous day's exertion had left any mark on him. Reality, by contrast, had trouble standing up straight, and her first tentative steps in a circle around where she had slept showed a pronounced limp.

"I am not that old," Reality said. "I am simply not that old."

"Maybe if you keep repeating that, you won't feel that way," Thorny told her.

"Sounds like a line someone like Torquemada would use." When Thorny made no response, Reality said, "Yeah, no reason for you to get that. Let me see what Hiep is up to." She limped off, also in the direction of the rovers, her gait improving with each step.

.   .   .

"THE ROVERS ARE FUNCTIONAL," HIEP SAID FROM WHERE HE STOOD BY THE DRIVER'S side door of the middle one. "The problem is the charge level of the batteries, which is not a surprise to any of us." He folded his arms across his chest and continued in a soft voice that did not suggest anything was wrong. "All of these were largely discharged when they reached this point. Not completely discharged, and not to the point where the safety cutoff would have been triggered. Again, we all know this." Hiep could have been giving a talk on the principles of battery technology at the residence school.

"There has been minimal further drain since they were shut down, and the photovoltaic skin has been recharging during the daylight hours; however, those hours are very limited at this time of year and this location is quite shaded, especially with the sun so low on the horizon, again due to the date and latitude." The echo off the cliff wall that loomed behind him emphasized his point.

"What are you saying?" Reality leaned against the rover, frustration leaking out of every word. "They are not completely discharged and the rover powers on. We'll pick up more charge in the sunlight. We can move them. Even if it's stop and start, we can move them."

"Yes." Danijel broke in. "That's true, but the point Vo is making is that they will discharge faster than they will charge, even if we only drive in the daylight, and if we keep the base station on to pick up the network when we can get signal, and if we want to use the computer for mapping and making sure we're going back the way we came, it will accentuate the drain. It's not like when we started out. We had fully charged batteries, and even without being able to fully recharge, we had plenty of charge to burn. Now we're starting from very low levels. We're going to spend a lot more time stopped than going."

"Are you saying we're going to run out of Earth food and our pills before we get back?" Thorny asked. "We can keep going for quite a while without them and longer if we space out the doses. It's not like you drop dead instantly if you miss a vitamin dose."

"True." Hiep's lips curved in a tiny smile when he looked at Thorny, but she was looking at Danijel. "We will make it, assuming there is no mechanical problem we cannot fix. Dani has done the same calculations I have. Correct?" Danijel nodded. "It would be better, however, to recharge the battery of one rover to a higher level before we start. The margin of safety will be greater, as the return will take fewer days. The charging ports on the rovers have circuitry that allows them to manage a charge transfer, one to another. Dani, you know how to monitor this also. Again, am I correct?"

"Yes, I can do it," Danijel said.

"If we are all in one vehicle and there is a mechanical breakdown we can't fix, it's a much bigger problem," Reality said.

"No free lunch," Thorny said. "I'm not arguing this time."

"Then it is settled," Hiep said. "Before we start on the rovers, Dani, I want to look at that ear."

The bandage Thorny had applied was liberally stained with blood when Hiep removed it. He flexed the ear and looked at the raw flesh. "There are a couple of punctures that have closed over. I can't tell if they were adequately cleaned, and there is no good way to open them up to do it now. Could this result in an infection from something in the mouth of that creature? Possibly."

Thorny's grimace was plenty of evidence that she took his

assessment as criticism of her technique. She stalked away toward the cliffs. When Reality moved to join her, she put a hand out behind her as a stop sign and did not turn around. Hiep took no notice of the byplay.

"I am going to take some of the spiderweb samples and use that as a dressing," Hiep said. "It may be unnecessary; the wound may heal cleanly anyway, but it is worth doing."

Danijel did not think his agreement was being solicited, but he agreed anyway. It took Hiep only a few minutes to dress the wound to his satisfaction.

After that, they started working on the rovers, or Hiep and Danijel did. The physical work was simple enough. Each rover carried a spare charging cable that could be used to connect to the charging station at Saint Peterstown. Those cables could not connect directly to another rover, however. Instead, a small, blocky device connected to both and handled the current conversion and current flow, and monitored the process, sending outputs to the computer on each rover. Hiep sat in one vehicle of the pair they were working on and checked the progress on that computer, while Danijel did the same on the other.

Danijel was scrunched over on little more than half the driver's seat because, with the issue of his ear now in the past, Thorny wanted to watch. Instead of taking the front passenger seat, she took the outer part of the driver's seat and peered over Danijel's shoulder at the screen. She was, in fact, draped across his back, her chin resting on her hands, which cupped his shoulder.

He did not notice her weight. She was light as a feather on his back but a very warm feather. He was very aware that her cheek was next to his undamaged ear. He could feel her breath across his cheek. He knew that if he turned his head, his lips and her lips would connect. It was difficult to focus on what he had to do.

"What are you watching for?" Thorny asked. "Doesn't the computer manage this?"

"Mostly," Danijel said. "But this isn't a standard process. Do you remember the lessons on old internal combustion engines, how we were supposed to learn them because in the future, when these batteries are dead, we can make engines that run on alcohol? Well, we can if we can find metals we can use; but never mind that."

Thorny's nod was a warm and distracting rub against his cheek. Danijel fought to focus on engines. "Well, if these were two rovers with IC engines, we could just siphon the fuel from one tank to the other. Transferring electrical charge is different. Same concept, but the process is way different. On top of that, we are bypassing the computer safety shutoffs, the vehicles are old, and the systems have been modified. There are things we don't want."

"Like what?"

All of her was now very close and very against his side. He was acutely aware of the fact that her father was one rover away and Reality had nothing to do except stand around and watch.

"We don't want"—Danijel managed to say while thinking more of what he did want, which had nothing to do with the computer or the batteries—"the battery we're drawing from to go completely dead. Normally, the computer has a safety shutoff, but that's turned off for this. If it discharges completely, that leads to chemical changes in the battery and will make it a harder job when we come back here to retrieve the other rovers. May damage the battery permanently. We also don't want the temperature to go too high or rise too fast. That could start a fire, and that would be really bad."

A soft giggle came from beside his cheek. "Yeah. It's amazing how sparks lead to flames, isn't it?"

What was amazing, Danijel thought, was that he was able to keep his mind on what he was doing. Mostly.

·   ·   ·

THE CHARGE TRANSFER PROCESS TOOK MOST OF THE DAYLIGHT HOURS. THE ROVERS they were drawing charge from were not designed to rapidly charge another rover battery, and having the converter in series between the rovers slowed the process even more. By the end of the transfer, the sun was at the horizon and long shadows covered the cul-de-sac where the rovers stood.

"We should get started anyway," Hiep said. "We can retrace our route well enough even in the dark, and more time here is a waste."

"What's a waste is driving in the dark and burning off the charge we just put in without the photovoltaics to compensate." Thorny had not been with Hiep when he made his comment, but she appeared next to him as if by teleportation to argue the point.

"The voltage is adequate, and the sun will come up tomorrow," Hiep replied. "As it is, the Demos met days ago and we have no idea what transpired. The sooner I am back, the better it will be."

"That's not an answer!" Thorny spun on her heel and stomped off toward the treed slope. She walked into the lower bushes before she stopped, her face to the hillside and her upper body barely visible in the failing light.

Danijel grabbed a spear and went after her. He did not want to think about what might be in the dark woods. He had been lucky once with a gator. He would hate to bet on being lucky twice, but he was not going to leave Thorny. She kept her back to him when he reached her. He put his free hand on her shoulder, but she shrugged it off.

"I really wish we weren't going back," Thorny said with her face aimed at the darkness under the trees. "I wish my father and Busby hadn't come, had never found us. We could have stayed in the cabin."

"We couldn't do that." Danijel tried again for her shoulder. She allowed the touch but would not turn around. "Even if they hadn't come, we would have needed to try to get back the way we're doing it. We were getting close to the end on our supplies, whether it's Earth food or supplements."

"I was saying how I *feel*." Thorny's words were bitter. "You know the word from all the schoolwork on relationships, don't you? You're supposed to *validate* my feelings, not give me a lecture on how Earth life is incompatible with this environment. Maybe I wish you hadn't shown up, either."

With that, Thorny bolted past him back to the rovers. Danijel did not follow immediately. He stared into the gathering dark, trying to think of what he could have said that was so wrong. Perhaps a part of him would have liked to confront another gator or a roo as being an easier task, but the woods were quiet.

When he did walk back to the rovers, he saw Thorny face-to-face with Hiep. They were not speaking loudly but did not appear to be in agreement. As he came up, he heard the tail end of what Thorny was saying.

" . . . your plans always fail."

"Which is why," Hiep said to her, "understanding and planning what you do is important. That way you can adapt when the plan fails."

Danijel did not want either of them to think he was eavesdropping, so he kicked a pebble across the ground. Both of them looked around. When she saw him, Thorny pressed her lips together and walked off toward the river. Hiep offered him only a faint smile. Danijel turned away and spotted Reality by herself, loading the supplies into the one rover they had charged. He deflated the boat and helped her pack that into the cargo bay as well. When the packing was finished, Thorny rejoined them at the rover.

They maneuvered their chosen rover out of the cul-de-sac created by the rock walls and river and headed upslope. After several hours, Hiep decided by himself that it was time to break for the night. The rods of the campsite wards were blinking, their batteries almost out of power. With Danijel's experience with his ear in mind, they chose to sleep in the rover. It was an awkward and quiet night.

JANUARY 5, HY 22

GORDON

ORDON SAT IN REALITY'S OFFICE IN A DAZE, HIS LUNCH UNTOUCHED IN front of him. He had been that way for a while. He was not so much occupying her office as he was hiding in it. *Face it, you're in a funk. A total funk.* He had not slept since that conversation with Jones on the thirty-fifth. Well, more correctly, he had hardly slept, which was almost the same thing when it came to exhaustion, but still, he knew the difference between that and a funk. What was he going to do?

He could not quite believe what had happened in those few minutes with Jones. Yet it had not been a dream; he was not delirious with a fever. This was real. Jones checking in with him at the New Year's celebration—not that it had been much of a celebration—and again the day after only confirmed how real it was. Jones had not said a word for the last two days, but Gordon could not shake the idea that he was being watched. He could readily imagine what people in surveillance states on Earth felt like, places that had cameras everywhere. There were no cameras on Heaven, but he still felt that every move of his was being scrutinized.

What was he going to do? The high-seniors needed to be checked on and kept to their work, now more than ever. The low-seniors were an even bigger problem, with no one doing anything except speculating about Thorny and Dani. Thorny's twin brothers were perhaps the biggest problem. He could not move to control any of that. His work felt trivial. He felt like he was pinned in the chair by an immense load that had landed on his back.

There was no question he saw himself as a leader-in-waiting, only in need of his opportunity. Was this offer from Jones real? Even if it was not, could he find a way to make it so despite whatever plans Mistry had? He knew Mistry and the others underestimated him. That could be their fatal mistake. With that weapon in his hands and determination to steel his mind, what might he be able to do? The prize of being a leader—the true leader—might be there for the taking. But what was the price? How often had other men and women justified doing evil to accomplish what they saw as worthwhile? Did the ends ever justify the means? What if others saw the ends as corrupt? What if corrupt means corrupted even worthwhile ends? How would people see him? What would Poppy think?

The stories from his childhood kept bubbling up in his mind. Satan and his Six. He was sitting in Reality Busby's office. Was this the temptation Busby had yielded to? The barrenness of the office struck him for the first time. No personal items, no pictures, not even of her children. She had borne three, he knew that, knew the oldest was in low-seniors, that all of them lived with other families, and that none of them used her name despite being from the embryo bank. If he had thought about it before at all, he assumed it was because she was no good at raising children, an ironic counterpart to not being good at running the school. Was it possible that it had been a decision to spare them growing up with her guilt by association? He would never, ever put himself in the same position as Unreality Busby.

What was Mistry's real purpose; what was behind Jones's talk? Did Hiep really have a gun? If so, was he really planning to use it at the Demos, or was it only because he had gone off into the wild looking for his kid? Were Mistry and Jones playing him for a fool? If indeed he was a fool, what were Mistry's ends that he would help accomplish?

It was not about whatever might befall Vo Hiep, a man he knew as little as it was possible to know someone in such a small community, a man he had learned mostly was one to fear. Anyway, Vo Hiep might never return. It was about what might happen to Saint Peterstown and everything he told himself that he believed.

It dawned on him as he sat there battered by worries that would not quit, a sudden insight borne out of fatigue and inability to move past the questions that plagued him again and again, that he knew the answer. Had known it all along.

He knew what he needed to do. He knew whom he needed to see. But how?

Gordon pulled out his phone. Hesitated. Jones's words came back to him. Jones was monitoring the network to see when Hiep returned, to detect him when he was still well away from the town. Was Jones now also monitoring him? Not merely those vague feelings he had, but under surveillance for real? If he made a call or sent a message, would Jones know? Could Jones read the message or listen to the call? He wished he knew more of the systems he had grown up using and took for granted. They might as well be magic. Would any of the Heaveners know? Dani, maybe—or maybe he would with more years of study and practice—but that did not help now because Dani was out somewhere with Thorny and, presumably, Hiep. He decided he dared not use the phone. He also dared not go physically himself. It would be far too easy for someone to be watching him.

There was, however, one person he could talk to without anyone seeing anything amiss. Poppy.

He found her in the gym, working with the low-juniors. She had them doing stretching exercises. Warm-up? Cooldown? Maybe it was yoga. He didn't care.

"Poppy, I need to speak with you."

"I'm a little involved right now. These kids won't go through their routines properly if I'm not on top of them." Her attention went back to her class. "Feet shoulder width. Knuckles to the floor."

"Have them do vids for a period."

"Is the building on fire?"

"What? No."

"Then our conversation can wait," Poppy said with an air of finality. "Now, palms flat on the floor," she said to the class, demonstrating. With her eyes up at Gordon from that position, she added, "Why don't you find something important to do?"

Gordon stood there, arms folded, and watched Poppy spend another solid five minutes on more exercises without deigning to acknowledge his continued presence. Then she did send the kids off to work on vids to the accompaniment of cheers from the low-juniors.

"All right," Poppy said as she walked over to Gordon. "What's the crisis that's brewing in your fevered imagination?"

"A real one," Gordon said. "And not here. Come to Busby's office."

That caught Poppy's attention, and she matched his quick pace out of the gym. When they were in Reality's office, he shut the door behind her but did not bother taking a seat. In harsh, clipped phrases, he recounted his meeting with Everett Jones.

Poppy's eyes went as wide as her face would allow, and her mouth dropped open. "If you weren't Gordon Durham-Pole, I'd be sure this was a joke. But you don't have a sense of humor."

"It's no joke." Gordon's face was grim. "Not with a real gun in that closet. They're planning to shoot Vo Hiep and then force the Demos to vote the way they want. Like a coup out of the histories."

Poppy was shaking her head, either from disbelief or an attempt to shake those concepts out of it. "Why are you coming to me with this?"

"I need your help."

"Why *me*?" Poppy shook her head yet again. "We don't agree on *anything*. I'd think you would be on their side, happy to put the town on top of the valley—or have you changed your mind about that?"

"Yes, I do think the town should come first, and no, I haven't changed my mind on that." Impatience shot through Gordon's words. "It's not about that. They're going to use the guns. I bet that bothers you as much as it does me. And there is one thing we do agree on. You believe that people who work hard and produce should have priority over those who don't. Jones kept talking about equal shares. That's what this comes down to. A bunch of those damn, lazy chippers—and some Heaveners, too—looking for us to do the work so they don't have to. I know you don't think that's right."

Poppy put her hands on her hips, over the edges of her untucked shirt. "Okay. You're right about the guns, and we talked about the other bit. So, yeah. What do you think I can do about any of this, though?"

"I want you to go find someone. Old Lady Penny, maybe. She's married to Vo Hiep; she'll listen. Or Dr. Song and Olivares. They're both in town, and they were starship crew. They'll get it. Find one of them. Tell them what I told you."

"I don't see why you don't call them or message them yourself. Or go and find them yourself. Why do you need me?"

"Dammit. Didn't you hear what I said? Jones is monitoring the network for Hiep. He said he'll know once Hiep is in range of our signal. I'm sure that after we spoke he started watching my phone. If I make a call or send a message, he'll know, and he'll read it or hear it too."

Poppy looked doubtful. "Can he really do that?"

"I don't know!" Gordon stared down at the floor, his fists clenched. "I don't know enough about how these systems really work. I don't think any Heaveners do. I can name a few who probably have the brains to do it—you can, too—but none of us have had the time yet to learn enough. And right there is part of the problem.

"Who is going to work that hard on top of everything we have to do here? Who is going to do that if they can't have any more than the same equal share as a lazy ass whose job is harvesting cannabis and who spends their time smoking it? Anybody who would do that is probably too crazy to be safe having around. I'm not walking around Saint Peterstown looking for these people. Someone will see me, and it will get back to Jones."

"Okay. Let's not get dramatic." Poppy brought her hands up as if to restrain a physical charge.

"I'm not being dramatic." Gordon punched the top of Reality's desk, then had to bring hurt knuckles up to his mouth.

Poppy bit her lower lip. "You've made your point. I'm working with you. On this. Don't let it go to your head."

·   ·   ·

When Poppy returned from carrying the message, she had nothing to tell Gordon beyond that she had spoken with Dr. Song. "She said she would talk to some people and they would see what to do. Neither Fulton nor Watanabe were around. Doc said your secret is safe with her."

"That's it? Nothing else?"

"Nope." Poppy patted him on the shoulder. "She's the doctor. She's pretty damn good at not giving away information she doesn't want you to know."

With that, Poppy was off to see what her juniors were doing and make sure it was what they were supposed to be doing and checking that the lowest juniors were getting ready for bed—all unlikely events, in her estimation. Gordon was left to stew.

Darkness had long since fallen, with Gordon sitting in Reality's office again, when his phone buzzed. It was Penny. He had to read the message twice because the first time through it made no sense.

"I've heard from Dr. Song Jing that she got a report from Poppy that some of the seniors have been allowing juniors, and my sons Leif and Huan, to access vids that should be off-limits to them. I would like to talk to you about it early tomorrow morning and have Jorge work out a way to block this from happening again. Don't do anything about this until we speak."

Gordon fired off a reply that said he would be at the school building an hour before the students started their day. Then he had to endure another night of lying awake, thinking of all the awful ways this could play out. It did not matter how he tossed in the sheets or tried to bunch up his pillow to cushion his head. His mind would not shut down.

Danijel

After they broke camp, which meant little more than relieving themselves and pulling some food from their packs, Hiep piloted the vehicle while Thorny made it clear that she did not intend to sit in front with her father. Danijel thought he would sit in back with her, then thought that Hiep might not appreciate driving with the two of them in the back seats, then decided that Thorny's frosty mien meant he was better off in front anyway. Reality was oblivious to his frantic internal decisions and did not seem to care where she sat, so she had the rear with Thorny.

The drive was mostly silent and without stops. Hiep was intent only on the vehicle and the surroundings. He drove as fast as the terrain would allow, as if in a race with the sun as it arced across the low section of the northern sky permitted to it at this time of year. Reality tried to start a conversation about Penny's contention that the south polar land was good for settlement. Hiep started to agree, only to have Thorny cut him off with, "If you thought it was so great, you should have let me stay there."

Her words were not dangled as bait to start an argument. Instead, they were uttered in a way to shut down any conversation. In fact, they sucked the oxygen out of the rover's passenger compartment. Danijel could not bring himself to say *I know how you feel* or even *It must be awful to feel that way.* He could not actually imagine feeling that way, and he was not sure she really did.

At the same time, he could not think of anything else to say that would not sound like a rejection of her feelings. Time passed while the thoughts whirled in his head. The silence became self-reinforcing.

The night's camp and meal were quiet, conversation limited to their progress, the remaining charge in the battery, and the expectation for the next day's drive.

JANUARY 6, HY 22

GORDON

He was standing outside the door to Reality's office nearly an hour before the time he had given to Penny, clad in the same pants and shirt he had worn the day before. His head felt like a kettlebell that was too heavy for his neck to hold up. Dark circles stained the skin under his eyes.

When Penny arrived, in the company of Jorge Olivares, exactly at the time appointed, Gordon waved them into the office with what he hoped was a confident manner that betrayed neither his nerves nor how long he had been waiting.

"That message you sent was a cover, a code," Gordon said before either of them could say a word or take a seat. "That means Jones can read our messages in the system or listen to our calls."

"Maybe." Jorge pulled a chair away from the desk for Penny to sit down. Then he waved at Gordon. "Sit. Pick a chair, but sit. Stop looking like you're going to have a heart attack before anything ever happens."

Gordon thought he would take the chair behind the desk but then he thought that would be an awkward place for him in this conversation. He took a chair on the same side as Penny, while Jorge leaned his butt against the edge of the desk.

"Better," Jorge said. "So, the answer to your comment is maybe.

The system has the capabilities to do what you said, if someone knew how to hack it. Any electronic system can be hacked, and if you think otherwise, you're wrong. Those are parts of a set of rules I made up years ago in what now feels like an alternate universe, but they are true. The real question is whether Jones has the skill to do it. He was never trained as an IT professional. He is a good enough thief and accustomed to hacking systems, enough so that ISC put him in charge of the system here, but I don't know if he is that good. We think it's safer to assume that he is. Do you agree?"

Gordon answered with a sharp nod.

Jorge looked at Penny, who also nodded. "I knew the automatic rifles had been taken before we got your message, and I knew Jones was involved. Never mind how. I'm fairly good with these systems also. I left a message for Hiep that he will pick up when he gets a signal again, and I thought I'd protected it from Jones finding it. I didn't know the other stuff, though. Now, I'm going to assume Jones knows I have left the message. It's encrypted, but even if he can't break it, the fact that it's encrypted may be enough for him to guess the content. That would explain why they will try to ambush Hiep. We need to let him know what is happening."

"How are you going to do that?"

"Much the same way you alerted us." Jorge's features formed a thin smile, his lips pressed together.

It was Penny who continued. "I will call Hiep, once we pick him up on the network, and tell him to wait for a messenger to come to a specific spot by Dead Lake." Penny's smile lacked any trace of warmth.

"That will give you plenty of time to go out to the lake and meet him," Jorge finished.

Gordon glanced from one hard face to the other. They were playing with him. Something he did not understand. "How is that any good? Jones will hear what you say. They'll know someone is going out. Do you think you are going to sneak past them?"

"Jones is not going to know," Penny said. "When the children were little, Hiep would speak to them in Vietnamese, his language. His English sounds like he grew up in the American Midwest, but he learned to speak that way in Sicarius. He'd play a game with the kids, like Vietnamese was a secret language only for us. Thorny was quite good at it.

"It was our family secret, in a way. The Saint Peterstown computer system lacks translation software for spoken language. Why would it have that for a settlement where one of the criteria was all colonists had to speak English? Anyway, I had to learn a little Vietnamese, too, even if my pronunciation is atrocious."

Her tight, hard smile returned. "Vietnamese is tonal. Even if the system could translate, it probably wouldn't be able to work out its meaning, the way I butcher it. I can manage enough for a message that Hiep will understand. Not enough to tell him the situation, but enough that he will wait. At least a day. I am sure of that. So, Jones may hear that call. He won't know what it means, and I will get out of town before one of them thinks to take a hostage."

"Wait. If you're doing that, then you're not the one going out there."

"That's right," Penny said. "Dashing cross-country was never one of my skills, and my leg hasn't been right since that gator sliced it open. You need to be the messenger."

"What? How?" Gordon's stomach dropped to infinity.

"It's really simple," Jorge said. "I'll make sure the location of the rover can be found on the network. I'm not giving away a secret, because Jones will know it anyway. You can pick up the latitude and longitude from the rover's base station. You can navigate to that, I assume. I am betting that Hiep brings back one of the rovers with a functional base station."

"Wait a minute. Just wait a minute." Gordon had his head down, fists clenched in his lap, trying to make his brain think. "We've all just agreed that Jones can monitor us on the network. That means he can know where I am by my phone. I know you can locate a phone with the network, not precise—and less so out of town because we only have a few antennas—but I know it can be done. He'll know I'm out of town, which means he'll know what I'm doing and he'll know it's me."

"No. He won't." Jorge broke into a grin that split his face. "You're going to use this phone." He pulled a shiny gray pouch out of his pocket. "The material for this pouch will shield a phone from detection. When it's time to go, slip your phone into this pouch and leave it in your room. Having it turned off would be best." He tapped the pouch. "This other phone has the coordinates of where Penny will tell Hiep to wait. Don't take it out until you're ready to go. Maybe an unnecessary precaution, but I don't want it on the network until then."

Gordon took the pouch with fingers suddenly grown cold. "Even with another phone, he'll still see it's me on the network."

"No." Jorge's grin drew his face into a broad V. "I pulled this phone out of the supply we're holding in storage for the young kids. It has never been used, and it is now registered on the system to Xenophon Vo. It took a little work, and then I had to cover my tracks in the network, which is why we didn't have this meeting yesterday."

Gordon stared at Jorge. "Who?"

"My younger son and child number five," Penny said. "Xeno is seven, too young for a phone. Jones won't look for him, won't know to look for him on the network, won't associate him with you. If you need to contact Hiep, he will understand from the ident."

Gordon swallowed hard. "What happens if Hiep doesn't come back? Or he doesn't come back before the Demos. That could happen. It's only a couple of days away."

"It could happen," Penny said. Her mouth tightened, as if she had bitten into something bitter. "I'm not asking you to be a hero. If that's the way it happens, keep yourself safe. Just don't do something you'll spend the rest of your life regretting."

"Okay," Gordon said. This was the moment of decision. If he turned them down now or shirked his duty later, he would forfeit any chance at leadership. Retreating back to Jones and Mistry was not a possibility either. He had committed himself. "All right. Yes, I can do this and I'll find the rover. I'm your man," he said. "I'll do it."

"Good." Penny stood up. "One bit of advice. When you go out to Dead Lake to meet Hiep, don't carry the rifle. My Hiep has a well-earned reputation from Earth as a killer. I don't want him to make a mistake."

JORGE

"I'M GLAD THAT'S DONE. I DON'T WANT TO WAIT ANY LONGER TO GET YOU OUT OF town to the way station hab," Jorge said to Penny as they walked from the school to the hab she and Hiep used when they were in town. It might be dark, but the air was thick and wet, as Heaven's air often was, and it was not cool. Jorge ran his hand through his hair and glanced with disapproval at the wetness.

"I needed to be here for this. We can leave now if there is a rover," Penny said.

"There is one that came up today bringing people for the Demos, so we're in luck. Most people will come up the day before, which means the rovers will be back down in the valley. Being short three rovers doesn't help." At the look on her face, Jorge said, "Sorry."

"Don't be sorry for the truth," Penny said. "I'm still hoping it will turn out okay, and I think Gordon will play his part."

"I swear that boy looked like he was going to shit his pants in there."

"He's young," Penny said. "Younger even than I was when Malachi was planning to kill me. There's nothing wrong with being scared as long as you do what you need to do."

"Do you trust him?"

"'Trust' is such an interesting word," Penny said. "Most people equate trust with friendship, you know, and no, I would not consider Gordon a friend. I do think we can rely on him doing what we want and what he agreed to. Because I understand what he wants, and he has no choice."

Jorge laughed. "You've grown hard and cold in your old age, Penny."

"Maybe I didn't have a choice either."

DANIJEL

THIS DRIVE WAS ALSO LARGELY SILENT, WITH THE EXCEPTION OF COMMENTS AROUND progress or spotting landmarks and tracks from the journey down. Between the speed Hiep was managing and his and Danijel's continuing calculations on the battery life—they did not care if they arrived at Saint Peterstown with a dead battery—they covered the upslope much faster than Danijel and Thorny had come down.

Danijel thought, on multiple occasions, that he should ask Hiep if there was a way to lighten Thorny's mood, but he never did. Hiep was, after all, her *father*. It was impossible for Danijel to tell if the man was angry or accepted this as a normal Thorny-storm that would eventually blow over. Whatever his feelings, they did not show. In any case, Hiep was totally locked in on the drive. Reality, as far as Danijel could tell, was lost in her own thoughts.

They were able to recross the Happy River without difficulty and swung east on the high plains in the direction of Dead Lake before they stopped to camp.

"We will make Saint Peterstown tomorrow," Hiep announced.

JANUARY 7, HY 22

Hiep

IT WAS HIEP, IN THAT AREA OF GRASSLAND WEST OF DEAD LAKE, WITH NO FEATURES to distinguish it from any other piece of forsaken grassland, who first saw an indicator light flash on the rover's computer screen. They had picked up the signal from Saint Peterstown. Almost immediately after that, a notification flashed on his field and Hiep brought the rover to an abrupt stop.

"We have a problem." Hiep's tone was as foreboding as the words.

Ajit

"A STORM IS COMING."

The thinly coded message from Jones on Ajit Mistry's projection field spurred him into motion. The first thought in his mind as he headed for the hab he shared with his wife was *About time*. By the time he had extracted from his personal closet the M8, packed in a long bag stuffed with towels to conceal the contents, that thought had been replaced with *Why now?*

The truth was, he acknowledged to himself, already sweating as he stepped into the street, that for all the days they had spent cursing about how long Hiep was away, they were not ready for the confrontation his return would bring. They had not practiced what they had talked endlessly about doing.

How had it come to this? The whole situation had evolved, spontaneously it felt, from his original idea of using the town versus valley sentiment and the growing concern around equal shares as a way to gather votes in the Demos, a way to finally become mayor. It had also provided a route to dissuade Penny from standing for election—or alternatively, persuading her to support him. The connection of Hiep and Penny's daughter to the death of Fernando Vargas had been a heaven-sent opportunity—and even with the sweat staining his underarms, he smiled inwardly at the apt term—to split the valley votes. Hiep's absence to search for Thorny had offered him yet another advantage: the opportunity to take the weapons that would let him overawe the Demos. That was when the milk had soured. It had turned out Hiep had a rifle himself. The idea of facing an armed Vo Hiep was suicidal. From that knowledge, it had been an easy, logical step to extend the plan to shooting Hiep before the man could possibly know what was happening. That meant, by another logical extension, that they might shoot others as well. And so here he was, rifle in a bag, murder on his mind, hurrying to his destiny.

Ajit shook his head as he walked down the street. The type of business he had operated on Earth—and the sorts of individuals who were involved with such businesses—meant that an occasional person might disappear under circumstances that clearly said they had been made to disappear. Ajit had no trouble with that, conceptually. However, he had never planned such a disappearance himself, had never *caused* such a disappearance himself.

Well, he had accepted the necessity. Gradison, Jones, and Northrup had all acquiesced to his lead, which was why they were the people he kept close in his planning. But then Jones had felt compelled to add this kid, Durham-Pole. Yes, he did seem like the perfect little lickspittle, but he was not an Original. Ajit could not be as sure of him as he was of the others.

On top of that, Jones had now developed full-blown paranoia, convinced that Olivares could not only read their messages and listen to their conversations—he was watching for the chance to do so. That was why Hiep's return was announced by a silly code. That was why Ajit could not call Jones to find out how far away Hiep was or when he would reach the Perimeter Road.

Instead, they all had to meet at the rover charging and repair station on the Perimeter Road and discuss it in person. Ajit only hoped the others had the good sense to disguise what they were carrying so that no one was walking across town openly carrying an assault rifle. One more thing that should have been discussed long before this moment. How had this plan mushroomed from a simple political maneuver to win the Demos vote into such nightmarish chaos?

At least it was cool inside the repair facility. He was glad to see Jones, Gradison, and Northrup there ahead of him. Jones's recruit was not there. Small loss. More important, no one else was there either. It was early morning, still twilight. It was too early for a rover coming from the valley to arrive. The delay in the Demos meeting, which he had first greeted with a five-minute streak of cursing, was now a blessing.

The rovers that would bring people up to Saint Peterstown were down in the valley to pick up people for the meeting, which was now set for the day after tomorrow. None of the rovers were at the station. With no rovers in town, and the one that had been designated for salvage now gone with Hiep, there was no reason for Petrovic to be at the facility.

It occurred to Ajit that they should have had a plan to ensure that Petrovic stayed out of the way. It was not as though they could shoot him, too, if he showed up. Or could they? No. Petrovic was the best engineer on the planet. They couldn't afford to shoot him. Maybe they wouldn't need to worry about it. With his son gone all this time, he had withdrawn from the town except when he was called for essential work. Too depressed, people said. Ajit didn't know the truth.

What else had they not thought of that would create trouble? A bitter memory struck him that for all Bose's organizing skill and acclaim, he had not been a military success when the time had come.

Ajit thrust that away. Bose, the Raj, and all that history were nothing more than history, both long ago and very far away.

"Where is he exactly, Everett?" he said to a red-eyed Jones. "How long before he is here?" Demanding answers made Ajit feel more in control of the situation. It was a way to *take* control of a situation.

"Still well past the lake," Jones said. "This is a rover base station I picked up, not his phone or chip connecting to the network."

"The salvaged rover he got from Petrovic didn't have its base station." Ajit rubbed his chin. "So he is bringing back at least one more rover."

"Yes. Which is why I wanted more people, but you wouldn't agree to any more." Jones had to bring up the same point he had been arguing for days.

Ajit did not like the feeling that he was being set up to take responsibility in case this went wrong. "Speaking of more people, where is Durham-Pole? Adding people is useless if the people you add don't show up."

Jones flushed. "I don't know. I've sent him the code message multiple times."

"Probably went and hid somewhere," Gradison said. "Too scared to do what he bargained for. Find his phone and find him."

"His phone must be off. I'm not seeing it on the system," Jones said after a minute. "Do you want to spend the time hunting around town for him?"

"No," Ajit said. "If he's hiding now, he'll be worthless later even if we have him. Trying to work with these kids who don't have chips is damn near impossible. Forget him. Send Hiep a message. Tell him we need a rover in town urgently because we don't have one, and he should come here ASAP so we can get it up to full charge fast. Tell him to call us when he is on his way."

Scant seconds after Jones sent that message, a reply notification blinked on his projection field and he forwarded it to Ajit.

"Message received and understood," it read. "Will do. Vo Hiep."

Ajit smiled grimly. "Now we wait. While we do, come up with a story that will get rid of anyone who shows up here. Especially Petrovic."

GORDON

GORDON COULD NOT REMEMBER ANY TIME IN HIS LIFE WHEN HE HAD BEEN SO AFRAID. That included the time he was twelve and had been picked on by those two valley-boys. He had stood up to them, knowing he would be beaten, scared but doing it anyway. This was far, far worse.

His heart was pounding hard enough to force an exit through his sternum. He could feel muscles between his shoulder blades twitch as he scrambled over the rough ground along Dead Creek, as though in anticipation of a bullet striking him there. He knew Ajit's group were at the rover facility. He knew they had their guns. He had only a vague idea what the range of those weapons was. The rational part of his brain tried to tell the rest of him that it was very unlikely any of the others would be able to look out a window of the rover station and spot him against the landscape because he had deliberately left Saint Peterstown by the Avenue of Europe, to bring him out west of the station before he turned toward Dead Creek. Even if they had seen him, the chance that a man who had never before fired a rifle could hit him at the distance he had already put between them was practically nil. Unfortunately, his adrenals and his stomach were not listening.

A new worry emerged as he approached Dead Lake and the fear of getting shot receded. Would he be able to find the rover? Olivares had given him the location where Penny said the rover would park, but would it, in fact, be there? Would his navigation be correct? He was developing an acutely new appreciation for how wild and empty Heaven was beyond the confines of the town or valley.

He pulled out the phone, the one registered to Xenophon Vo, to recheck the coordinates. As he did, the shielding pouch fell out of his pocket. He saw it on the ground and cursed himself. Had he been supposed to leave his own phone in that pouch? His phone was turned off, tucked into his bedding in his hab. There was nothing he could do to change the situation now. He cursed again and told himself to keep going.

It was only when he came to the top of a low rise and he could see the rover nestled in the fold of land beyond that relief surged through him.

He ran down the lee side of that slope, waving his arms and yelling at the top of his voice, heedless of the toll the hike had taken on his body. As he closed the distance to the rover, he became very glad he had listened to Penny's admonition not to take the rifle with him. Hiep was behind the rover and had him in his sights through his entire run. Gordon made certain both his hands were up in the air as he came up to the rover.

Ajit

With nothing happening and nothing to do, the hours stretched out as though by relativity near the speed of light. Jones did put out a general notification that error messages from the electrical system at the rover station had appeared on the system. It both assured people that the errors were probably bogus and warned them away, because if those were genuine, it would be dangerous to be in the station building or around the lot with the charging stations. Jones followed that with another message that he was working on the problem. Hiep and the other three presumably with him were excluded from the message list. Petrovic did message back asking if he was needed, and Jones told him that he was not. That sequence had the desired effect because no one approached, although it was possible no one would have come anyway. It left them to sit and wait.

Ajit told his three to review the vids on the M8s. It was not correct to say the weapons had been designed for use by illiterate peasants. They had been designed for soldiers who went through US Army basic training. There was a substantial difference. Other than viewing the vids, however, there was little to actually *do*.

Ajit believed that Hiep kept the weapons clean and in good working order. There was no point, and some risk, in taking them apart and putting them back together. They could not practice shooting them. That would attract attention. All they could do was practice removing and reinserting a clip of bullets. Ajit decided that Northrup was very comfortable in his handling of the weapon. Maybe one of them did have expertise, and that would be useful.

"I have a message from Hiep," Jones said at last. "He says he has a mechanical problem. He is trying to fix it."

"Where is he?" Ajit asked.

"System puts him at Dead Lake on the way to us," Jones said.

"Crap." That was Oscar. "That's not so far. Tell him to get out and walk the rest of the way."

"Don't be more stupid than usual." Northrup was blunter than Ajit had ever heard. "We made a point of telling him we urgently needed the rover, which is why he had to come here. Send him that and you'll make him suspicious, and I don't want him suspicious."

"Then what do we do?"

Ajit thought Oscar sounded like a child who could not tolerate a long car trip. "We wait."

And they waited some more.

The sun disappeared into a thick bank of gray cloud at the horizon. The light dimmed.

"I don't like this," Northrup said. "If it's dark by the time he gets here, it would be too easy for him to drop off the rover without us seeing him. Then he's loose in the dark. I'm not going to like that."

"What can you give me on their location now?" Ajit asked Jones.

After a few minutes, chipped in and working with the system, Jones said, "The system has Vo Hiep between here and Dead Lake. Heading toward us."

"Good. And that stupid kid you thought was so good? Still hiding with his phone shut off?"

That took several more minutes. Then Jones laughed. "I just remembered that Olivares enabled a way to ping a phone that's off when we were putting the additional antennas on the system. He thought he was very clever. Durham-Pole is in Saint Peterstown. Do you want his location?"

"Probably under his damned bed," Ajit said. "Useless. We can't be chasing him around town now. We can deal with him afterward. Next time you have a bright idea, don't bother."

"It's still four on one." Jones was trying to sound confident, but his hands fluttered about as much as his voice. "That's why I wanted more people, but even without, it's four to one."

"Against a Sicarii." Northrup slapped the stock of his rifle.

"Shut up. Both of you." Ajit did not want the Vo Hiep superman argument again. "We talked about this before. We fire on the rover as it's coming in. He does not know what is going to happen. If the others get hit, too bad, but nobody will do anything."

"When do we shoot?" Jones asked. "It's going to be dark. How close will he come before he gets out?"

"As soon as we see his lights," Oscar said.

"And you're going to hit what?" Northrup was developing a brusque tone as though he had done this before. "Wait until the rover stops."

"That gives him time to get out," Jones said.

"He's not faster than a bullet." Ajit wanted to end the argument.

"I'll tell you what." Oscar was already walking toward the exit. "If you wait too long, he's going to shoot and he'll shoot at these windows. I'm going to find a nice spot outside."

"Probably back at his hab," Northrup muttered after the door closed behind Oscar Gradison. "Another one who's useless."

GORDON

GORDON'S STORY, AFTER HE FINISHED TELLING IT, WAS GREETED WITH A MIXTURE OF emotions in equal parts disbelief and angry cursing. At least, the emotion—both the disbelief and the anger—came from Reality, Danijel, and Thorny. Hiep said nothing. He merely leaned back against the rover at much the same angle as his weapon did. His eyes stayed on Gordon, steady and calm, and did not shift their focus.

"I think we should accept this story as true," Hiep said finally. "Now we should move on to what we will do."

"How can you say that?" Thorny shouted her question. "Why would they try to kill you? This story about the Demos meeting sounds crazy. It's bullshit! Gordon doesn't know shit!"

"You are not paying attention to the facts that matter." Hiep's eyes shifted to his daughter, but no other part of his posture changed. "I told you I received a message from Jorge that the M8s had been stolen as soon as we picked up the Saint Peterstown signal. I can also pick up the same alarm that Jorge received from the doors at the nuclear facility, so Jorge's message is valid. Penny sent me an audio message in Vietnamese that we should wait here for a messenger. What Gordon Durham-Pole is saying is consistent, and in this context, the message from Jones would be a means to draw me to a point of their choosing." Hiep shrugged. "Beyond that, the reason why does not matter so much. Their intent is clear. What does matter is how to stop them."

"That's simple, isn't it?" Reality had eyes only for the rifle. She sounded to Gordon as though her mind was on a memory and a different time. "We know where they are waiting. Come back to a different location."

"That does not solve the problem," Hiep said. "That still leaves four men with M8s. Having been deprived of this opportunity, they will find another one. Right now, we know where they are waiting, and they do not know that we know it. This is an advantage for us. I have sent a message that we are stopped temporarily to fix a mechanical issue. That will buy us some time."

Gordon watched Hiep as he listened to him. He took in Hiep's demeanor, followed the way Hiep presented the issue. He noted the calm assessment, the lack of emotion. *I should study this man*, he thought.

"You're thinking of attacking them." The same words came at almost the same time from Danijel and Thorny. "How?" Danijel let the final one-word question hang in the air.

"The first point is that we will move in the dark." Hiep straightened up from the rover. "When you are one against many, light is an enemy, darkness a friend. We will use their expectations against them. I will leave the rover before they can see me separate, and I will reach the rover station on foot and unseen. I will chip out and leave my phone in the rover so, even if they are clever, I will appear to be with the rover. They will not pick me up visually or electronically. One of you will drive the rover toward the repair facility as they expect. That will fix their attention on the rover. I will neutralize the threat.

"I will note the risk involved. It is possible, perhaps likely, that they will fire on the rover without bothering to identify who is in it. For that reason, one person only, the driver, will be in the rover. The rest of you will stay at a safe distance until you receive an all-clear."

"I'll drive the rover," Reality said immediately.

"Why you?" Danijel's question came right on the heels of her words.

"I've already had my children," Reality said, "and I'm not going to have any more."

In the brief pause that followed Reality's statement, Gordon found that he was surprised. He would have expected some self-serving lament that no one would miss her or everyone would be relieved. Maybe he should respect her more.

It was Hiep who asked, "Reality, did you have a self-driving license on Earth?"

"No. It wasn't necessary."

"Have you ever driven a rover here, outside of Saint Peterstown?"

Reality tried to stare Hiep down, but that was attempting the impossible. "I know how to drive a rover. It's not that hard. You were prepared to have me drive back alone from the wild."

"Different situation," Hiep said. "Nothing would have depended on your success or failure except you." His turn away from her was as dismissive as his tone.

"I'm the best rover driver on rough terrain. Except for my dad. You trained me." Thorny aimed the words and an index finger at Hiep.

"I'm perfectly good with a rover off-road," Danijel said. "You're not doing it, Thorny. I will."

"Why is that, Dani?" Thorny shot back. "Don't go fucking medieval on me that it's because I'm a girl and we need the women to have children."

"It's because you're too important to me." That shut Thorny down. She opened her mouth, but nothing came out. Danijel turned away from the group as he realized he had said that in front of the others.

"I'll drive the rover," Gordon said. "I've sided with these people in the past. It's my chance to help fix the mess I helped to make." He tried to say the words the way he thought Hiep would say them, calm and matter-of-fact. He hoped that was the way it sounded to the others.

"I agree," Hiep said. "You should drive the rover, Gordon."

"What? Dad, you can't mean that!" Thorny slammed both her palms against the hood of the rover. "You don't see him at school. He's a crazy townie-boy. As bad as any of the others. You can't trust him."

"I believe we can trust him," Hiep said. "I have heard the words he has spoken here. More important than that, I would say that Gordon Durham-Pole has made enemies of those people, people who will regard his actions as a betrayal."

Gordon nodded at the chill he felt inside. He did not want to give voice to what he knew to be true. He could not retreat from what he had done.

"When you choose allies, it is key to understand their relationships with others, both friends and enemies," Hiep said. Thorny did not appreciate the teaching point, but Gordon could not decipher what she was mouthing, because Hiep turned to him. "Now, Gordon, they should wait for you to drive up to the facility and get out of the rover so that they will have a clear shot. Do not get out of the rover when you arrive. Drop down below the level of the dashboard. The way the rovers are built, the front wall of the passenger cabin will give the greatest protection. I will be there and I will engage them."

"What if they don't wait for me to get out?" Gordon thought that was a logical question.

"They may not and, to be clear, there is risk involved." Gordon looked for a smile or some hint of humor to go with that statement but did not see any. "It is possible, especially with untrained people, that they will start firing way too early. Possibly as soon as they see your lights even if they do not have a good shot. Those rifles do not have night scopes, and while their chips will give them some night vision, it is very limited. Mine is superior.

"Therefore, the way to do this is when you drive the rover, keep the front of the vehicle aimed at the repair facility where you say they will be. If shooting starts, drop down as far as you can, the way I told you. Make sure your head is below the top of the dashboard. Do not turn the rover so that the side faces the shooting." Hiep slapped his hand against a door panel. "These printed panels will not stop an M8 bullet. If the rover is turned to the side for any reason, get out and crouch ahead of the front door here with your head down." Hiep tapped an otherwise unmarked section of the vehicle. "That will put you behind that interior wall, which will protect you. Do you understand?"

"Yes." What other answer could there be?

.   .   .

HIEP DROVE THE ROVER CLOSER TO SAINT PETERSTOWN, MAKING USE OF THE ROUGH ground along Dead Creek and taking care not to come within eyeshot of the rover station. Then he stopped the vehicle and sent a message to Jones saying that he was still having trouble with the mechanical issue and would need to stop to work on it some more. He expected it would take, he told Jones, a few additional hours.

Those hours were enough for the low afternoon sun to drop to the horizon. They continued to wait as the light dimmed. When the twilight was far advanced, Hiep got out of the rover and slung his rifle.

"There would be an advantage in waiting for the middle of the night, when they will be sleepy and less watchful," Hiep said. "However, there is also the risk that one or more of them might leave. I want to finish this business. Gordon, you need to give me two hours to be in position at the facility. It will be fully dark by then. That is when you should begin your drive."

With those words, Hiep was gone, vanishing without a sound into the gloom. At the rover, it was a nervous and mostly silent wait for the time to pass. Two hours, especially in the dark, anticipating danger and with an eye on the clock, felt like the entire night.

"All right." Gordon blew out a gust of air when precisely two hours had elapsed. "I'm going to do this."

Reality stood up from where she had been sitting with her back against one wheel of the rover. "We can still switch, you know."

"No." Gordon shook his head. "Vo Hiep agreed I'm doing it, and I am. You know damned well you can't drive a rover for shit. Just keep an eye on my seniors if . . . something happens."

They shook hands. Then Danijel shook his hand and wished him luck.

"You've always been a townie-boy asshole, and you don't know shit about teaching seniors, but I hope this goes okay and you don't get your ass shot off." Thorny was smiling as she said that.

Gordon grinned back at her. "I'd never know how you really felt if you didn't say it." He shook her hand and managed to avoid changing his expression when she tightened her grip.

Then it was time to go.

.   .   .

THE ROVER ROCKED SIDE TO SIDE ON THE UNEVEN GROUND AND BOUNCED MORE than once as Gordon drove it at five times the speed of a man on foot. Even little ridges of dirt sent the headlights pointing up into the sky. The light of the moons, obscured by clouds, did not help much with seeing the ground he was covering.

Gordon clutched the steering wheel in a death grip. He wanted this drive to be over as fast as it possibly could. He wanted to reach Saint Peterstown so that whatever was going to happen would happen. Then that, too, would be over. He forced himself to slow the vehicle. Damaging it so it could not move would be worse than what was waiting for him.

Would they really shoot at the rover without being able to see who they were shooting at? Or was that a foolish idea, one that Vo Hiep had thrown out simply to scare him? He had seen those men around Saint Peterstown his entire life. He could not recall ever seeing one of them actually be violent. They talked plenty about acting that way, but he had never seen—or heard of—any of them doing it. That did not mean they would *not* shoot. They were out in the dark with weapons they were not supposed to have. What else were they going to do? Had they—like Gordon—stepped through a doorway that could not be reentered?

Of course, what would happen if they did not shoot, if Gordon ended up driving straight to the rover station and into their midst? The ending to that might be even worse. He did not need Hiep's words to be scared. The thoughts tumbling through his own mind were doing a perfectly good job of that.

Ahead he could see the nighttime glow of Saint Peterstown. The lights were not that numerous, their intensity not that great, but in the absence of anything else to break up the empty darkness of the high plains, they stood out like a beacon. He saw the lights of the rover facility. The charging posts could be distinguished by the blinking red lights on top of them, the actual posts hidden in the darkness. The building was marked by a few exterior lights; its interior was dark. Maybe all of them had fallen asleep. Maybe Hiep would be able to disarm and capture all of them while they slept. Maybe he could drive up unattacked and unmarked, his assistance valiant in the effort but unneeded in the end.

Orange-yellow flashes sparkled across the front of the repair-station building, followed by a *crack-crack-crack* that assaulted his ears. He had never seen or heard gunfire before, but he knew that was what it was. More flashing. More crackling. He drove the rover forward, fixed in the action he was already taking.

What was he supposed to do? Do not turn sideways; the door panels will not protect you. He was headed straight forward. Wait! Head should go below the dashboard! How could he drive if his head was down? *Get your head down, you damn idiot!* He ducked down. An instant later, a series of crackles was followed by banging noises at the rover and the sound of shattering plastic where the windshield was.

"Oh God! Oh God! Oh God!" He could not say anything else, only those words over and over again.

Somehow, the rover was still moving. Was it going forward, or had it turned to expose its more vulnerable parts? He did not dare lift his head to see. He could not have forced his body to lift his head even if that had been his most fervent desire. More bangs emanated from projectiles striking the rover. Something hit the back of his seat above where he huddled. He tried to make himself as small as possible. Gordon shuddered at the impact of more bullets on the rover and knew he was going to die.

Hiep

Hiep reached the parking area of the rover station undetected, cloaked in the cover of darkness. He could hear occasional sounds from the building but could not make out any conversation. That was okay. He had not counted on hearing what these men were saying. The interior of the building was dark, so he could not see any of them either. That was okay too.

He waited.

It was not too long before he spotted lights bobbing up and down out in the otherwise black plains. That could only be the rover. Durham-Pole had kept his word, or if not, one of the others had done it. The men at the facility had not noticed it yet, or if they had, they were waiting for it to come closer. How long would they wait? Would they wait until it was all the way in so they could capture it and its occupants without killing anyone other than the one they wanted? He doubted they had that kind of discipline. He did not intend to give them that much time, in any case.

The roar of gunfire from the building, along with the muzzle flashes, demonstrated that whatever patience those men had was exhausted. The shots gave away three positions in the building, one on the outside. That matched the information Durham-Pole had provided about numbers. The fact that one was outside would make his work easier. He might not need to gain entrance to the building. He immediately changed the tactics he had planned.

Amid the next spray of gunfire, Hiep made a series of single shots of his own. The sounds of his shots were lost in the cacophony of fire from the building. In case anyone should spot a muzzle flash from his weapon, he shifted his position after each shot. Each time he fired, a light went out. When he was done, the side of the building he was on and the parking field with the charging stations were devoid of illumination.

Another burst of fire was directed outward toward the rover on the plains. Hiep noted that the man outside the building had not changed his position. That was also good. Hiep slung his M8. He checked to make certain that it was snug against him and would not betray him with an unwanted sound. From the scabbard on his belt, he drew his broad-bladed knife. He advanced on the position of the man outside. This would be silent until it did not need to be.

After the man's dying wail had faded into the night, after Hiep had finished with his task, he withdrew away from the building, deeper into a night made darker now by thickening clouds. Then he chipped in. He sent a message on the network to the men who remained in the building, whose identities Durham-Pole had given him.

"This is Vo Hiep, Sicarius. Check the cabling hang-up hook at charger post number four. You will understand."

Shadows moved across the dark parking area. Three of them together. All headed for that charging station, with no thought to have one person keep their eyes scanning the field for danger. Lights from their phones shone on the post. Hanging from the cabling hook, and immediately recognizable by its long gray ponytail, was the bloody scalp of Oscar Gradison.

Hiep sent another message. "All of you are in my sights. If you do not drop your weapons immediately, all of you will die. Sicarii are not merciful."

THE ALARM ON THE PHONE NETWORK'S EMERGENCY OVERRIDE BLASTED HIM OUT of what had been a fitful sleep anyway. He and Jones should have been the only ones with access to the mechanism that would override any privacy setting, but the flashing red alert around the periphery of his projection field highlighted a message from Hiep. Yes, it was not surprising that man could do it.

Beside him, Jing came awake fast. "What is it?" she asked.

"Hiep wants us at the rover station. ASAP."

"What happened?" Jing was pushing hair away from her face, making a futile effort to coil it into a bun.

Jorge was already stumbling out of bed and trying to grab for his pants at the same time. "Doesn't say. But this is Hiep, and with what has been going on, I'm not asking questions. Just going."

"Give me a sec for some clothes. You'll need a doc."

It was not too many seconds before the two of them were out the door of their hab in a mix of regular clothes and sleepwear. They started off at a run for the rover station on the Perimeter Road. However, within a hundred yards, the combination of Heaven's air and the fact that Jorge had not actually run anywhere in years had his chest heaving and his brain fogged. He pulled up, fearing that he was going to need Jing's expertise if he tried to continue. A glance at her told him she was in no better shape. Having the world's only physician in need of medical attention was not going to do anyone any good.

"Can't run." Jing was able to manage only the two words.

"Me neither. At some point, I think we got old."

They settled for the briskest walk they could manage.

The scene that greeted them at the rover station could have come from a newsfeed vid from the Troubles. Backlit by one of the station's remaining lights was the figure of a man holding an assault rifle. On the ground in front of him sat three figures, hands on their heads, lined up as though they were about to be executed.

"What happened?" That was the extent of the question Jorge could get out.

"They tried to kill a Sicarii." Hiep's voice was soft but toneless and all the more frightening for that. "They failed. Gradison is over there." He gestured with his rifle.

Jing hustled off in the direction Hiep indicated. A brief period of light from her phone showed her crouched over something on the ground. Then she was back.

"Gutted and scalped," she said. "These—" She pointed at the three on the ground.

"Intact." The barrel of Hiep's rifle traced a line across them. "Penny would be against killing anyone because there are still so few of us on this world, so I chose to minimize deaths. In any case, they need to be tried in front of the Demos. I do not want people to believe I killed them out of hand, as Malachi would have, and risk them being perceived as martyrs. Malachi's shadow is still with us, and that is a burden Penny does not need when she is mayor again."

Jing nodded. "The others?"

"I told Reality, Thorny, and Dani to walk in after I was done here. Gordon was driving the rover as a decoy. The four of them here were firing on the rover—and fairly wildly. Jorge, go out, pull anyone you need from town, and check on Reality, Thorny, and Danijel. Get them back into town, back to where they belong."

"We should give them some time to readjust," Jing broke in. "I can see them at the clinic and speak with them."

"No." Hiep was abrupt, not angry but cold. An old soldier whose battle was not yet over. "That is a luxury we cannot afford. Too few of us and too much work. They need to go back to the residence school and carry on. Dr. Song, please check Gordon yourself. He is the most likely to have been hit. If he is okay, send him to me. I will need some help with these. When we are done here, I will send him to the residence school as well. Wake Miroslav and have him check the rover. It is likely to be a long day."

Jorge started to set up his own emergency override alarms and messages for people. It seemed perfectly natural for Hiep to be giving the orders in this situation.

GORDON

THE CONTINUATION OF THAT DAY—IT WAS ALREADY MORNING AND TIME FOR WORK when Gordon returned to his hab—felt like he had fallen into a surrealist painting of a normal day. He had barely enough minutes to clean himself up and put on fresh clothes before Reality's announcement of a meeting hit his phone. There was no chance at all to deal with his jangling nerves and emotions, although it is possible that no amount of time would have sufficed. He walked to the school with the sensation that his mind was floating up among the clouds, his eyes looking down from above at the citizens of Saint Peterstown, and his feelings completely disconnected from all of it.

He sat through the meeting with Reality, Tiffany, and Poppy with no sense of what any of them said. The words entered his ears but bounced off his brain. He thought he answered questions directed at him, and he must have made enough sense because the questions were not repeated and none of them questioned if he was in his right mind.

Then his schedule called for him to review the progress of his two cohorts of high-seniors and three of low-seniors. First, he checked attendance and noted that no one was ill and all were physically present at the school. There were too many of them for him to meet with each individually, so he reviewed the records of their progress in the computer system. Messages went to each student of what work they needed to complete over the next week. He also reviewed the assessments of their physical training and performance. If their goals or program needed to be adjusted, he sent another message.

On this particular morning, both Danijel Petrovic and Thorny Panagiotidis were present. He met with each of them in person, as though he had not seen them since the night Fernando died, and spoke about how far behind they were in their work—the lessons that had not been completed on time, the review examinations that had been missed. He talked to them about the need for a training review after the next high-senior gym workout to see if they were still on target, although for healthy seventeen-year-olds it would take much longer away from training for any slippage in physical performance to be detected. To his surprise, both he and they—even Thorny—acted as though it were no different than if they had missed school because of an acute illness. After he saw them, he wondered if their feelings had shut down as thoroughly as his.

It was, on the surface, a very normal school day. That was enough to make it totally bizarre.

Those reviews and meetings took his entire morning. He still felt as though he were somewhere outside his body, looking at himself. To avoid other conversations, he grabbed his lunch and found a quiet corner of the deserted gym to eat it in. A bench that would normally serve in weight training exercises with barbells was pressed into service as both a seat and a place to rest the container with his food. It was as good a spot as any, he decided, to sit, blow out a deep breath, take a few bites, and try to reconnect to his feelings.

The blizzard of whispers, messages, and phone conversations among the students about Danijel and Thorny and all the shooting blew through the school out of his sight, although he would have needed to be dead and buried to be unaware of what was going on. He knew that he figured in a lot of the buzz, but he was not sure in what way. That was disturbing. Equally unsettling was the superficial banality of the school routine. It was like throwing a blanket over a gator and pretending the creature was not there.

"So that's where you're hiding!" Poppy came striding through the gym—a stride far too jaunty for the nature of the morning, in Gordon's opinion—with a bag clutched in one hand that probably held her meal and a length of aspergrass sticking out of her mouth.

Gordon looked up at her as she came over. She must want something since there was no other possible reason for her to be in the gym at that time. "Yeah. With Reality back, I can't commandeer her office, can I?"

Poppy laughed. "Can I join you for a minute?"

"Sure. Drag over that other bench." While she was doing that, he asked, "Mind if I try one of those aspergrass sticks?"

That earned him a surprised side-eye. "What is this? A deathbed conversion? Don't tell me you're planning to move to the valley." She sat down and held one out.

"Hardly." He accepted the stick and chewed on it for a minute. "It's not bad, actually."

"Told you that before. Don't think that changes anything."

"No, I don't." He straightened up on his seat. "What brings you looking for me?"

"Seriously?" Poppy finished the stick she had been chewing and pulled another one out of her bag. "People talk and message. Kids talk. Dani and Thorny talk. Well, Dani talks. You're quite the hero today, you know. What actually happened? What did you do?"

"Hero?" That one word unleashed a blaze of emotion that burned through the numbness and felt as though it would burn right through his skin. "I'm no hero!"

Words flooded out of him. He spoke of the counterplot, of his part, of driving the rover, of the insanity of the shooting. He spoke of the trance he had been in afterward, when he could not quite believe he was still alive, when Dr. Song had appeared from nowhere, checked him for wounds, asked him questions he no longer remembered, and told him to go to the rover station to see Hiep.

He told about helping Hiep secure the surviving ambushers and then helping drag Gradison's body into the repair facility, all while a form of numbness pervaded his mind and blocked any feeling.

"I was so scared, Poppy, so, so scared. I thought I was going to die. I thought I would shit my pants. I'm surprised I didn't. After the shooting stopped and I realized I was okay, I sat up and found a bullet hole in the back of the driver's seat, right below the headrest, right where my throat would have been if I were sitting up. I couldn't breathe, felt like I would never breathe again. Don't call me a hero, Poppy. I'm not."

"Maybe being a hero is nothing more than doing what you need to do even when you're scared half to death," she said. "You did good, Gordon. We're all proud of you. All of us."

"Thanks." That one word was all he could manage.

"Any idea what happens now?" Poppy asked. "What are we going to do with Ajit and the other two? What about Thorny, and what did happen to Fernando? What's going to happen at the Demos with equal shares?"

"I don't know," Gordon said. "Nobody said anything past what we were doing last night, and nobody's told me anything since. Jacoby is going to have to say something at the Demos, though." He took a deep breath, tried to think about tomorrow and then the day after and the day after that. "When it does happen, work with me. Against the equal shares. You can see what these assholes will do, but we can beat them. Reward for work. We can do it."

"And what about town and valley? That stuff is not going away."

Gordon sighed. "Neither dominates. Can we work with that and then we'll figure it out from there?"

DANIJEL

DANIJEL THOUGHT SOME IMAGES AND SOUNDS FROM THE NIGHT WOULD STAY WITH him for the rest of his life.

He remembered standing with Thorny and Reality, watching Gordon drive off. Reality had said, "I would have driven it. I really would have."

"Hey, Busby," Thorny said to that. "Remember what you said about not being good enough?"

Reality had given her the look of a dog about to absorb one more kick.

"You came out to find us," Thorny had said. "I know you would have driven the rover. You're plenty good enough. If people say you're not good enough, the problem is them, not you. Did you ever think about that?"

"Thanks." Reality had reached out and given Thorny's fingers a quick squeeze.

After that, he remembered hiking toward the Perimeter Road with Thorny and Reality when gunfire erupted from the rover station. Reality's screams to drop to the ground still rang in his ears. She had yelled out that she did not remember the range of an M8, and she was not sure how far away they were.

That stuck in his mind. He thought she was scared, had lost her nerve, and filed that conclusion along with all his other negative opinions about Reality Busby until, long after the shooting stopped, they came to the rover. Then, by moonlight and phone light, he saw the bullet holes, and he saw Gordon trying to assure himself that he was still alive. He was ashamed about what he had thought about Reality. Remembered what Thorny had said.

His father had appeared as if out of the air, hugged him tight, and told him in a shaky voice that he was glad to see him back and safe. His father then disappeared back into the night, pulled back into the darkness by voices calling out that they needed to salvage the rover Gordon had driven. Danijel had been glad, in a way, for the brevity of that encounter because it had provided no chance for the conversation to turn to the other two rovers—two rovers the settlement could not replace—that were still in a valley far to the south.

Reality had appeared again with Jorge alongside her, a vapor suddenly substantial in front of him. They told him to go to his hab and get some sleep. They probably said the same thing to Thorny, but he had lost track of Thorny in the chaos of the night. After an unproductive search for her, he did return to his hab. Kojo was wide awake—well, the whole damn town was probably awake by then—and wanted all the details of what had taken place. Danijel ignored him and fell on his bed. He thought he slept for at least a few hours.

After not nearly enough sleep, an all-student communication blared from his phone on the override circuit. That had him sitting up with a headache in an instant. Busby was holding a meeting that morning with the proctors. All students should attend to individual work until otherwise notified.

Danijel tried to organize his thoughts and silence his phone at the same time. Neither went well. His clumsy fingers were unable to shut off the repeating announcement until midway through the third time.

The only thought in his head was why any announcement was needed. They would have figured it out soon enough. All the phone had accomplished by waking him was to confirm that he had been asleep. That was the point at which he realized he had fallen asleep on his bed without taking his boots off, and his sheets would need to be cleaned.

"Shit." The one word summed up his feelings adequately. He ignored the bed linen, found clean clothes, and washed up. He decided he had grown enough beard and mustache to make a shave worthwhile. That did nothing, however, for his haggard appearance, although he did notice that his ear had healed cleanly.

At the school, no one was pursuing individual work. What they pursued was Danijel, everyone from high-seniors to low-juniors, all of them wanting answers to a slew of questions: How far had he really gone? What was the Far South like? Had they reached polar night, and what was that like? What really happened at the rover station? Were people really firing guns? Had he been shot at? Had he seen Vo Hiep kill Gradison? Had he been scared? Did Thorny confess to killing Fernando? Did he have sex with Thorny? How many times did he have sex with Thorny? What was it like to have sex with Thorny?

The last four questions seemed the most important to his questioners, and to his surprise, the last three—or variations on them—were asked as often by girls as by boys.

Danijel was not accustomed to answering questions from other students except academic ones. That was true whether the others were townies like him or valley-boys and -girls. He was not accustomed to being lionized. It all felt awkward. What he wanted to do was find Thorny, to be with Thorny—preferably alone.

He thought he had a glimpse of her in the school building, surrounded by the same type of crowd that engulfed him. An instant later, she was nowhere to be seen. Fled, probably. She did not answer her phone. She did not return a message. Where would she go?

He messaged Regan.

"I'll meet you at our hab" was Regan's return message. "Not going to talk in the middle of chaos and juniors. Busby and Durham-Pole will never notice we're gone."

·　　·　　·

THE FRONT ROOM OF THE HAB REGAN SHARED WITH THORNY DID NOT LOOK VERY different from the one he and Kojo lived in. The furnishings were all standard for Saint Peterstown habs, with few personal touches. All the student habs were like that. He had never noticed the monotony before. Having built and lived in—if only for a few days—his own log cabin had changed his perspective. He had done that with Thorny. He wanted to see Thorny.

"Is Thorny here?" Danijel asked. "Did she come back here?"

"Not likely." Regan held up a plastic cup with a small amount of clear liquid in it. "Would you like some? It's alcoholic."

"No. No, thanks. I'm looking for Thorny. I need to see Thorny."

"No, you don't." Regan put the cup down on a table, crossed her arms over her chest, and ran her eyes up and down his figure. "You're a fool, you know. Nobody else is going to tell you that, so I guess I will."

"What the fuck is that supposed to mean?" Danijel was tired; he was irritated. He might be fully awake, but his headache persisted. He was in no mood for whatever game Regan wanted to play.

"You're a fool. That's what I mean." Regan pointed a finger at his face, almost poking him with it. "You go chasing around after Thorny like you think you mean something to her. Let me tell you. You don't."

"What? What are you saying?"

"That night it all happened? When I called you. Remember?" Danijel nodded. "She was out there because she wanted Fernando. It wasn't about that magic juice of Dalton's that he had for his friends. It was about Fernando. Believe me, she talked about him. Wore out my goddamn ear.

"She made me a bet she'd do him in front of the others. That's why she went out there that night. She was after Fernando and she was going to have fun. I called you because I started thinking there were too many ways for it to go wrong, and obviously I was right about that, even if it wasn't in a way I had been thinking."

"That's not . . . possible." Danijel was sorry he had come to her hab, but he could not make his feet take him away.

"Sure it is. And trust me, Fernando wasn't the first. Well, that was the first time she killed someone, but let me tell you, she's done some . . . things before. I've been stuck with her as a habmate since we entered high-seniors. I've heard all about them."

Regan let out a nasty laugh. "It was never about you. That's why you're a fool. She couldn't care less about you. Unless, maybe, the only guy on the planet was you."

Danijel was having trouble coping with what he was hearing. "Why are you telling me all of this? Why are you telling me now?"

Regan dropped her hands to her sides, then went to sit in a chair. "Maybe I'm tired of all the games, all the bullshit. I saw what was going on over at school. All of them, especially the juniors, acting like she's some sort of hero. You answering all those questions like she was the greatest person on the planet. Let me tell you, those people who know the truth are going to be laughing themselves hysterical later. About time you woke up."

"No." Danijel could not find any more words. He did not want to believe what Regan was saying. He wanted to call her a liar. In the back of his mind, though, lurked the thought that maybe Thorny did not really care about him, that his image of her and of them together had been built mostly in his mind. He had to know the truth. He had to hear it from Thorny.

. . .

Danijel was out in the street before he began thinking again. He could not remember saying goodbye, could not remember if he had been polite. It probably did not matter.

The one driving force in his mind was to find Thorny. If before seeing Regan he'd felt a need to see Thorny, to talk to her, to touch her, now it was imperative that she tell him everything Regan had said was untrue. He needed to hear that. The urgency of that need competed with the pounding of the headache behind his eyes.

The problem: Where could she have gone? She would not go back to the school. Could she have gone to Dr. Song, the way some people went to the clinic to talk through a problem? That was unlikely. Thorny was not the sort who talked about their problems.

Could she have run away again? That made more sense, but the idea of setting out for Dead Lake—assuming she stopped there—gave him pause. The rover they had brought back would not now be left for the taking, and it might not even make it to Dead Lake without more repairs. That was useless thinking. Hiep had taken it.

There was one rover, the one he had heard Penny returned in, but he would not be allowed to take it. Even if he walked out to Dead Lake, how would he find her? Had she taken her little pack with the flute back to the school? If so, the pack would be locked. Even if he could get into it, he doubted he could create a recognizable tune with the flute. Another stupid idea.

She had to be in Saint Peterstown. It was not a very big place, but in the midst of his dilemma, the five hundred habs that made up the town seemed like a city of many thousands. Then a memory surfaced. When thinking about the rovers, he had remembered the one that brought Penny back. That meant Thorny's mother was in town. She would have an activated hab, and he could pick that up from the network. Several strings of taps on his phone gave him the answer.

When he reached the hab, he did not announce himself through the speaker. He put his hand on the palm shape next to the door and it opened like any hab door would. It was only after he was through the entryway into an unoccupied front room that he realized what he was doing.

Since hab doors in Saint Peterstown did not lock, it was possible to walk into any hab, but for that very reason people considered it impolite to enter without announcing themselves or sending a notification. A chipper who was chipped in would be picked up by the door, and their chip could be set to send a notification without having to think about it. Danijel was a Heavener and did not have a chip.

"Hello!" he called out from the entryway as a belated substitute for what he should have done.

"Dani?" Thorny's voice floated out from the connector to the living quarters unit of the hab. A moment later, she stepped into the front unit, hair wild and half across her face, hands balled into fists. "What are you doing here?"

"I had to see you. You left the school." *That was a stupid thing to say,* he thought as soon as he said it.

"Yeah. Amazing observation you made." Her voice was flat. "All of them like leeching worms. All about Fernando. 'Fernando this. Fernando that. We heard what you did to Fernando.'" Suddenly her whole body tensed, and words exploded out. "Fuck all of them! I'm never going back there. I wish I'd never come back here. It's your goddamn fault I came back here, goddamn you! Fuck you!"

"Wait, Thorny. We didn't have a choice about coming back here."

"There's always a choice. You didn't need to be there. You shouldn't have been there."

"Actually, no." Danijel could feel the anger radiating off Thorny. How could he make her see it differently? "There wasn't a real choice, and I did need to be there. You don't know what you're saying."

"Damn you and fuck you too! I know exactly what I'm saying! Don't you dare say otherwise."

Thoughts tumbled over one another in Danijel's mind as he tried to think before he spoke. He had his hands up in front of him as though he were trying to stop an out-of-control rover with its accelerator jammed at max. "I don't want to fight about what's past," he said in what he hoped was a reasonable tone. "What's done is done. We're here."

Thorny's whole body seemed to clench up as tight as her fists. A shake ran from her torso to her head. Her breaths came hard but no words came with them, which gave Danijel space to speak.

"I need to ask you so I know. I heard at school . . . someone said . . . you went out that night . . . were out there because you wanted Fernando . . . wanted to—"

"What?" That was more a shriek than a shout. "I told you what happened that night! I told you all about it!"

"I know. That's why . . . I had to ask . . . and they said you and others . . . and I didn't want to believe, so I had to ask—

"You goddamn son of a bitch! My mother has nicer pigs! So what if there were others! Do you want a count? So what if it was every other guy in seniors except *you* and some of the girls too! Who the fuck do you think you are? What do you think I am? A prize you win for completing a quest? Go fuck yourself!"

"Thorny, I—"

"Get the fuck out of here!"

THORNY

DANI'S EXIT, HALF TRIPPING OVER HIS OWN FEET AS HE SCUTTLED BACKWARD THROUGH the door, did nothing to quench the rage consuming her. Her eyes fastened on a lightweight desk chair pushed under the work desk. She grabbed it, picked it up, and hurled it at the door that was closing behind Dani. It bounced away, its printed plastic unbroken. The door might have sustained a small scuff.

She needed something safe to hit. She needed the heavy bag. She needed to punch and kick it so hard that the casing would split and the sand run out onto the floor. However, the bag was at school. She would need to go back there to use it. They would not leave her alone if she did. She could guess the words they would throw at her. What ran out onto the floor would not be sand from the bag.

She wanted to run. She did not care if she had no supplies. She wanted to run all the way back to that hill by the bend in the river, with the white webs on the trees and bushes and the little cabin they'd built. Some deep recess of her mind sent out the thought that she could not do that. It was not possible. It was stupid. The word *stupid* was enough, barely enough, to check her flight, to freeze her in the hab with nothing but her fury boiling in her mind.

There was nothing for her to do. Nowhere to go. No one to vent her feelings on. She walked into the bathroom because it had a mirror so she could stare at herself. Saw hair that fell every which way, tearstained cheeks, some blood where she had bit a lip without realizing it.

"You are disgusting." The mirror did not answer.

She had not needed to say those words to Dani. Not about Fernando. Not about others. He had deserved them, but she had not needed to say them. Those were not the only words she wanted to have back, even though he had deserved them. For all he had said that deserved those words, it would have been better to have found different ones for him.

"You were the one who went to the end of the world for me," she whispered. The mirror whispered the words along with her.

She pulled out her phone. She had to make a call.

Then she burst into tears.

PENNY

"What the hell am I going to do?" Jacoby Grubb walked back and forth in front of the row of diagnostic beds in the clinic, waving his arms as he went, as though his hands might grasp the words he needed and pull them out of the air. His audience, perched on the beds or on chairs they'd dragged over, was Penny, Jorge, Jing, Ibiana, and Sonal. "What the hell am I going to do now?"

Whatever answer he might have been looking for was cut off by Yuki quickstepping into the diagnostic area. Jing did not wait for Yuki to bring up her issues.

"No." The severity of the word and Jing's face brought Yuki to a stop. Yuki's mouth opened partway, then closed without a sound. "Unless it's an emergency, anybody who comes in now, either you and Norma handle it or they have to come back later. I'm tied up in a conference."

"I can see that," Yuki said as she took in the occupants of the room. "I'll take care of it." She backed out and left them with Jacoby's question.

In fairness to Jacoby, Penny thought, it had been a crisis-filled night, morning, and now midday. The ambush—attempted assassination—and its violent conclusion at the rover station had pulled all of them out into the night, whether from their beds or, in her case, from the Highway 1 way station where she had gone to be safely away from Ajit. She could tell from their strained faces and voices that even those of them who'd suspected violence was in the offing were shocked by what had actually taken place. There had been no time to recover from that shock. She was still trying to process their stories herself.

Jing had spoken of going with Jorge to meet Hiep at the rover station, where they found Gradison dead and Hiep holding Mistry, Jones, and Northrup at gunpoint. Jing had then gone out to where two of the rover's headlights pierced the dark. Gordon Durham-Pole had still been shaking when she arrived at the rover, though he was unharmed physically. The rover itself was peppered with bullet holes, but the shielding beneath and in front of the passenger cabin had protected him.

She had sent him to help Hiep secure Mistry, Jones, and Northrup. After some discussion and work, the three were locked up in the stables at the Community Dome—to the extent that quickly printed old-fashioned handcuffs that cuffed a wrist to a strut of the dome's lattice framework could be considered locked up. Cam and Jess were rousted from their beds to keep an eye on the prisoners, although it was unlikely that any of them would attempt to flee if they did get loose or would find someone in Saint Peterstown to support them if they did.

While that was being done, Jorge had called Reality, Thorny, and Danijel. Jorge said he had told them to go to the school and just start their days as usual. He now thought that had not been the best idea. Jing was in emphatic agreement, but it was done and over.

The rover had been the crisis, on top of all of that. Three rovers had gone out from the town into the wild. Only this one had come back, and it was pockmarked with bullet holes. In the middle of tracking down Reality and the kids, Jorge called Miroslav and pulled him into the night to check out the rover. In the process, Jorge had managed to remember to tell him his son was okay.

It was fortunate that Miroslav, alternately confused, surprised, and stunned by the turn of events, assumed that Jorge's primary purpose had been to inform him about Danijel's safe return and that the rover was secondary. No one disabused him of that notion.

The rover proved to still be operational. Its battery, electric motors, and steering system had all survived without damage. One tire had been punctured—the puncture-proof rating of the rover tires not taking M8 bullets into account—but that was repaired in the field. The damage, as Hiep put it, was "cosmetic," given that no one had been sitting upright in the passenger compartment.

With the tire reinflated, they had used the rover to haul Oscar's body out to the graveyard, where, as a group, they buried him without ceremony. The only argument was over whether to bury him with Malachi and his five because of the violence involved. In the end, they chose to dig a shallow grave away from all the others. It seemed suitable, and it may have been determined by the fact that the ground in that spot was easier to excavate, a bot not having been brought along.

Then they all scurried around the town to gather up the remaining M8s. By the time they were finished with that, people were awake and buzzing with all manner of wild rumors. The sight of Hiep, rifle at his side, driving around in a bullet-riddled rover did nothing to calm people down. Once all the rifles and ammunition were accounted for, Hiep drove out of town on Highway 1 to the valley. He still did not want to destroy the rifles—Saint Peterstown remained a tiny human settlement on a wild planet—but he intended to hide them so there would not be a repetition. No one was disposed to argue with Hiep.

So Penny was willing to concede that Jacoby had reason to be perplexed. He stopped his pacing at last and stood, arms akimbo. A level of truculence crept into his voice as he repeated, "What am I supposed to do now?"

"We have to postpone the Demos meeting again," Ibiana said. "That might be simplest. Hell, we certainly can't have it tomorrow. Push it off for a while until we can figure out what to do with those three. That would be better than allowing a free-for-all at the Demos. Just as important, it will give us time to sort out where the political mess stands before the Demos has a say in that. The way this place is structured as a direct democracy, the Demos can vote for, well, anything, and it's too crazy now to take a chance on what might happen with everybody in the dome. Why don't we say February first? We've already postponed it once; we're already past the solstice."

"I can't do that!" Jacoby started out belligerent but ended up in a wail. "With all the crap between the equals and work-for-reward and then between the townies and valley-boys and -girls, shit, if I do that, someone is likely to take a shot at me. It's not impossible to print a pistol, you know."

"Printing a handgun is pretty easy, actually," Jorge said. "Ammunition is a lot trickier. I don't think anyone here is going to manage that. Your carcass will stay intact. I do agree, though, that waiting until February is too long. We have to do something with Mistry, Jones, and Northrup. That has to be soon, and it will require the Demos to meet. We can't do this one by a remote vote. If we try, it will cause even more trouble than an actual meeting. Why don't we say the day after Hiep comes back to town?"

"I can't say that either!" Jacoby now looked like he was ready to cry. "If I say that, people are going to think Hiep will show up at the Demos with a rifle. They're going to blame me! I think I should resign today."

"If you resign, the Demos has to meet right away," Jorge said. "Do that and I will fold, spindle, and mutilate you with my own hands." He smiled as though the comment was a way to lift the dour mood, but it fell flat. "Okay. I read somewhere that the government used to print that on really old cards that were read electronically. I guess it's not that funny. But you can't resign today. You really can't. The Demos meeting would be chaos."

"Make it on the tenth," Penny said. "It's soon enough that people who have already come up or were planning to come up from the valley will stay, and it gives people still in the valley time to come in person. It will give Hiep enough time also. He won't bring a rifle. You have my word."

"I'm not worried about counting days. The real question is, if we nominate you for mayor, will you stand for election?" Ibiana asked Penny. "Whenever we hold the Demos meeting, Jacoby is going to resign." Her words received an emphatic nod from Jacoby. "Ajit has been trying to position himself as a logical townie successor, but that's out the window now. I don't see a viable alternative to you."

"Which is a polite way of saying that I don't have a choice," Penny said. "I'll be seen as a valley-girl by the Originals who are townies, you know. That wasn't such an issue before, but it is now. It will split the Originals."

"You'll have to move to abolish the equals," Sonal said. "You have to do that, or you'll lose the valley support you need to win."

"And I'm not going to shut up about the need to explore to the south." Penny managed to put a tight smile on a tired face. The only part of her with any bounce was the frizzy hair that had escaped her ponytail. "I won't shut up. Everybody knows that. They know I'll say what I think."

"Which will split the town and valley into even more factions than Jacoby mentioned." Jorge's laugh came out as more of a snort. "Maybe we should let the Demos fight it out as a tag team match in the dome. If we go to a money standard instead of equal shares, we could sell tickets."

"That's not funny, sweetheart," Jing said.

"True." Jorge rubbed at his eyes. Then he planted his elbows on one of the diagnostic beds and cradled his head in his hands. "I'm tired. We're all tired. We know about the factions. I'm more worried about the situation with your daughter, Penny. Vargas has stirred up enough trouble in the valley. You know the rumor mill up here. That's the wild card in all of this if someone tries to play it."

"There's still no alternative to Penny," Sonal said. "No matter what really happened that night."

"That's another way of saying we'd better spend our time making calls." Ibiana yawned. "We need to know where we stand before we walk into that meeting. It's going to be a busy couple of days."

AJIT

As an abode, even a temporary one, the stables were a noisome place. The stalls were divided by low walls of bamboo that rattled with the stomping and bumping of the horses and also, for good measure, with the gusts of wind, which shook the sheathing that made up the roof. The delicate odor of horseshit permeated the area but seemed particularly strong in the stall next to the one Ajit, Everett, and Hershel were confined in. The horses added neighing and snorting to the cacophony, making it clear that they found the presence of the trio as unwelcome as the three men did themselves.

"Lovely mess you've got us into." Jones gave a couple of experimental yanks on the handcuff that held him to one of the struts of the dome's latticework. It was clear that the lattice was not going to come apart, nor was the cuff. His wrist might come off first. "I told you we needed more men."

"From what I heard before they stuck us in here, what we didn't need was the one you came up with," Ajit snapped.

"Can we lay off the 'who fucked up more' routine, at least for now?" Northrup's voice was a low rumble. "What I'm interested in is what happens to us now. They'll drag us in front of the Demos sooner or later. What then?"

"Don't know." Jones pulled at his manacle again. "Nothing happened to Busby, and that mess was a lot worse, but they'd already killed all the others, so who cared about her? Maybe they'll just shoot

Ajit as the ringleader, and you and I are okay." The laugh that followed was neither sincere nor indicative of humor.

Ajit badly wanted a joint at that moment. He needed its smoke and its chemical to cover both the smell of the horseshit from the adjacent stall and the bullshit coming from the two of them. Wishing for the impossible was not going to make it happen, and anyway, he needed to think. Hiep could have shot all of them at the rover station, but he had not. There must have been a reason that held him back, some reason beyond Penny's known aversion to violence. Hiep was, after all, one of the Sicarii. Ajit had no doubt, though, that Jones would gladly feed him to the mob at the Demos meeting, if that bought Jones freedom from responsibility. He needed to think. Life was, as he had always known, a series of transactions. He thought of favors he could call in, of threats he could use, of people who needed him to succeed.

"Cam!" Ajit yelled. "Cam! I need to talk to you!" He kicked at the bamboo divider, which set off the horses and added to the din.

It took a while, but the yelling and the noise eventually brought Cam by himself. That did not surprise Ajit. Cam, but not Jess, had appeared sorry to be locking Ajit up. Cam had come to almost every one of Ajit's meetings. Cam was the one he wanted to talk to.

"I don't suppose you can let me loose from this?" Ajit asked when Cam came over.

"No." Cam shook his head, seeming genuinely sorry about it. "I don't want to risk what would happen if Hiep found out."

"Okay. I don't want you to get in trouble. But if I can't get out of here, can you take a message to a couple of people? I need to talk to them, first one and then the other one after that. They'll need to come here."

After the man had agreed and then left on his errand, Ajit felt more in control. It had been a long time since a card player could literally have an ace up his sleeve, but the concept was still valid. He had the germ of an idea. He only needed to organize his own thoughts. Once he had this properly worked out, it would not matter what Northrup and Jones thought. Apparently impossible reversals of political fortunes had happened before.

JANUARY 9, HY 22

Thorny

T HE TABLE IN THE KITCHEN AREA OF THE HAB WAS SMALL, ALTHOUGH WITH FIVE occupied chairs around it, it took up most of the available space. In a way, it was the map of a battlefield being scrutinized by a general staff. Perhaps it *was* the battlefield, Thorny thought.

Mom and Dad sat on the long side to her right, trying to look as though this were a normal early dinner—not that this family ever had family dinners at the hab in town. The twins, Leif and Huan, had positioned themselves at the corners of the short end opposite her. They would have had more room on the remaining long side, but this way, they would have a better view. They were on their best behavior, and would stay that way, because any attention they attracted would detract from the entertainment they had come to see. At least Yong was not present. That was a dose of perfection Thorny was glad to do without.

The food on their plates was hot, Penny having bounced around the kitchen like a caroming billiard ball to have it prepared at almost the exact moment Hiep arrived to complete their number. For all that it was hot, little aroma hung over the table.

The chicken had been microwaved to rival the altrubber of rover tires. A portion of limp greens occupied the part of the plates opposite the chicken. Thorny was not sure what it was. The portions, thankfully, were not large. Mom might have the best farm on the planet, but she was scrupulous about staying within their shares. She had invented equal shares, after all.

At some point in time, Mom had baked bread that she brought out for this meal. It sat on the plates, flat and brittle. Mom had probably had her mind on five—or ten—other things while she was baking, since Mom always had her mind going in that many or more directions at once. She had either not given the bread time to rise, like the Jewish people in the *Cultures of Earth* text Thorny had studied, or had forgotten the yeast entirely. She was sure, from experience, that the bread would have the consistency of cardboard when chewed. Mom the Farmer was the world's salvation; Mom the Cook could be its doom.

No one spoke after they sat down. No one took a bite either—not that the food was a great attraction. Thorny hated the smirks she saw on Leif and Huan. They were anticipating the festivities.

"Thorny, from your call, something is wrong that you need to talk about, and you wanted your father here, which he is now, but you haven't said what it is, hardly a word, really, since yesterday," Penny said when it seemed they would sit around the table in silence until the food cooled and needed to be put in the refrigerator for another day. "Do you need to talk more about the past several days, or did something new happen? What's wrong?"

"Wrong?" Thorny's brain began to bubble. She hated the way her mother did that. "What could be wrong? I always call like I did yesterday when everything is just fine." The twin smirks across the table were very annoying.

"Your mother is not suggesting everything is fine," Hiep said. "We know it's not. But we talked about what went on before. I think we understand that. If we're going to deal with what is happening now, we need to know the specifics."

Specifics. Good old analyze-each-problem Dad. And there was half the issue right there. Thorny fought to keep her bearings. Mom's mind was in a thousand different places because, just like the previous day and all of this day, she was in her save-the-world mode. Dad was in save-Mom-from-the-world mode, which was how he usually operated, which Thorny supposed was actually a nice thing, and she would like it if someone had a save-Thorny-from-the-world mode, which reminded her that someone might actually have thought that way, but she had gone and fucked it up. As usual. Her brain was now smoldering, threatening to burst into flames.

The whole story poured out—the one she had so carefully hedged to this point—of the kids at school, and what they said when she went in there, and what they said would happen at the Demos. She managed to leave out Dani. There was plenty that she did say. "I'm fucked," Thorny finished. "Fucked up and fucked. The Demos will be a disaster. You know how the Demos goes. I heard all about what they're going to say about Fernando."

"The Demos can be managed," Penny said. "People shoot their mouths off. That doesn't mean anything comes of it. We will manage it."

"You didn't do such a great job the last time it was about you." Thorny threw down the gauntlet in front of her mother. "I still hear about it at school, and it's been years."

"You're right. I didn't." Penny was gripping the tabletop with both hands. "I made mistakes. I won't this time. I will be sure to manage it."

"Great. Just fucking great. You'll manage it. And even if you manage it, where does that leave me?"

"With the chance to make your own decisions," Hiep said. "You will be able to decide what you want to do. I promise that decision will be yours. Think about what you want, what you want to do."

"You have my promise as well," Penny added.

"I have no clue." Each word was a piece of sour lemon she bit off. "I have zero friends. Everyone hates me."

"What about Regan?" Penny asked. "She shared a hab with you all last term, and she's your habmate again this term. She must get along with you."

"Yeah. One person on the whole goddamn planet. And she only likes me because her mom is friends with you."

"Well . . ." Penny pursed her lips. "I wouldn't say 'friends,' exactly.

She's had a lot of questions about her farm, and I've always tried to help. And I do understand about feeling you don't have a lot of friends. I never really had any when I was growing up either, so I do know how it feels."

"Thanks a lot, Mom. Another wonderful trait I've inherited."

Hiep put a hand on Penny's arm, then leaned forward across the table. "Dani likes you. I am sure of that."

"Past tense." Thorny felt her face freeze. "I fucked that up real good." She could not stop herself. A detailed description of the awful mess with Dani followed, everything she had said, which had been the true impetus for her to make the call to her parents. The twin smirks across the table were becoming smiles.

Hiep kept his voice low. "Possibly so, but not necessarily. It may be fixable. It is important to pay attention to your people skills."

"You're the one to talk about people skills, Dad. Your people skill is killing them."

"Thorny's people skill is annoying them," Leif said with a lively tone.

Thorny glared across the table at what were now twin four-teen-year-old grins. It was too much. Her brain reached critical mass.

"You are absolutely fucking impossible!" She threw her arms in the air as she stood up. That knocked her chair over. It fell against the appliances behind her with a clatter. "All of you!" She tried to storm out of the eating area, but that was difficult because she had to pick her way past the other chairs and past the grins that turned to watch her. She did make a point of stomping through the front room on her way to the entrance to their sleeping quarters. What she wanted to do was slam that door so that it rattled in the walls and possibly broke off. This was an interior inter-unit hab door, however. It slid closed. Quietly.

DANIJEL

THE REMAINDER OF THE DAY AFTER HE LEFT THORNY AND MOST OF THE ONE THAT followed passed with Danijel in a daze. He went where he was supposed to go, sat in front of streams and vids he was supposed to study, answered the questions the computer fired at him—albeit with a far higher frequency of wrong answers than usual, which prompted a discussion with Gordon—but all of it was more like dream sequences than like real life. He was sufficiently distracted that even Kojo asked him if he was okay when they were in the hab together.

Life was untethered from reality. He had spent so long daydreaming about Thorny. Then fate had conjured up a scenario too bizarre even for a fantasy, and that had brought them together. It was the way, he thought, love was supposed to be: sudden, white-hot, and most of all, enduring. Then, in the space of one short conversation, he had lost it all.

Did that mean it had never been real? Was what he thought was love nothing more than a boy and a girl in a strange situation with no one to turn to except each other? Did she look back on those few days and chide herself for her involvement with someone so completely unsuitable, unattractive, and—basically—worthless as Danijel Petrovic? No one, he was quite sure, had ever felt the depth of despair into which he had sunk.

He spent the entire duration of a calculus stream trying to think of what he should do about Thorny. The differential equations on the screen were unhelpful. Should he think of some way to apologize? But what, precisely, was he apologizing for? He could not find the right words to put around the thought.

He supposed he could go over to her and say *I'm sorry if I was a jerk, but I didn't mean to be and I really love you,* but he doubted that would work. It did not sound very good even in the privacy of a one-person workroom with math on-screen. Even if he were going to try such a line, he did not know how he could *spontaneously* run into her to do it.

With all the talk among the students about Thorny's role in Fernando's death and their speculation about what the Demos would do when it met—now only a day away—Thorny had vanished from the school completely. He could, naturally, go over to her hab, but she would probably tell him not to come in, and this wasn't a conversation to have over a speaker or a phone.

He could not ask anyone for help. Kojo was useless. He could hardly ask his father. He did not have any truly close friends; certainly no one who might have insight into his dilemma and who, at the same time, would not turn it into mockery to spread around the school. As for anyone else, if he wanted a string of bland and useless suggestions, he could ask the computer.

It was in this mood, with his mind whirling in unending and non-productive circles, that he walked from the school building to his hab. It was on the late side for dinner, but he was not very hungry anyway. He stopped short as soon as he cleared the entryway into the front room. Kojo was not in evidence. Instead, it was Hiep who sat casually in one of the chairs.

"Kojo isn't here," Hiep said. "I thought we should have a private talk."

Danijel tried to gulp in a throat suddenly gone dry. The scene in which a boy had to have a "private talk" with a girl's father was an old trope of Earth vids and books. He had never heard of it happening for real in Saint Peterstown or the valley. It could not be happening. Except it was. And this father was a killer.

"What do we need to talk about?" The words came out in a croak.

"I understand you had a difficult conversation yesterday with my daughter." Hiep had a way of making the blandest, most banal comment terrifying.

Danijel looked for signs that would indicate his impending death. Saw none. Told himself that did not mean there was no risk. "I'm sorry about that." He would apologize to Hiep. Apologizing was the right route to take. "I didn't mean for that to happen."

"Those sorts of conversations will happen." Hiep's tone could have gone with a statement about the frequency of rainstorms on Heaven. "I would like to know if you are serious about your relationship with Thorny."

A hammer blow between Danijel's eyes would have been a tap in comparison to the way those words hit him. Was he serious about Thorny? Was he serious, knowing the temper and the storms that were part of her? "I . . . ah . . . yes . . . if I still have one . . . I mean . . . actually . . . I am serious." Danijel knew he sounded like an idiot, but he could not say the words more smoothly.

"Thorny will get angry. You need to understand that. You know about the heavy bag at the gym."

Danijel nodded. He thought of how he felt when he was with her. He thought of how miserable he felt without her. Yes, he would take the bad times; he wanted all of the time with her. "I do understand," he said.

"Understand that the tempest will blow up and blow over," Hiep said. "While the storm is raging, Thorny may say whatever comes into her head. When she is cool, however, you should know that Thorny will not lie to you. She does not lie unless her anger has a grip on her. Never lie to her. She will need support at the Demos tomorrow. Please be there."

"I will," Danijel said.

"Then I have said what I need to say." Smoothly, like a snake uncoiling, Hiep rose from the chair and left the hab.

Danijel stood in the empty front room, trying to figure out what had just happened.

Ajit

It was all of a day and a half before the first person he wanted, Chloe DiMasi, arrived in response to the message Cam had carried. That was plenty of time to worry—about whether she would come, whether Cam had really conveyed it, and whether he should have arranged the other conversation first—but the delay brought some advantages as well.

Cam stopped by to talk multiple times, conversations that showed sympathies that lay with Ajit. He brought news of the talk in town—the actual person-to-person talk—and not all of that talk, or so Cam said, was against Ajit. Under the surface, plenty of people in town had a dislike of Penny and a fear of Hiep that had solidified over the years. The talk about Thorny and Fernando amplified all of it. Ajit had intended to play on those feelings, albeit in a different way, but it was good to know they were still there for his present need.

Then there were the accommodations. Being kept shackled in

a stable stall did not help with grooming and the improvised toilet facilities were marginal for hygiene, but seeing this situation seemed to cement Cam's sympathies. Consequently, when Chloe did show up, Ajit was able to persuade Cam to let him meet with her in a separate part of the stable and use a real bathroom first.

"You look like shit" were Chloe's first words to him. "What is it you want?"

Ajit saw pity in her eyes. Pity was not the emotion he wanted to evoke, but if it was there and it gave him an advantage, he would take it.

"I've stayed in better hotels on Earth." Ajit made a show of brushing off his shirt and shorts with his hands, even though he had scrupulously cleaned up with damp towels in the bathroom beforehand. The chuckle from Chloe was what he wanted.

"It's not so much a matter of what I want," Ajit said. "The problem I wanted to talk about is that, in my current situation, I am going to have trouble helping you."

"What do you mean?" Her eyes narrowed.

"It's simple. You know how it is with the Demos. Once the meeting starts, anything goes. Absolutely anything. You know what's going to come up about your son, Dalton. We talked about that. You know what's being said about what happened to Fernando and about why our altrubber production is shot." Ajit had quite a bit of detail to transmit, and some of the talk Cam had supplied was good embellishment. Chloe blanched as he went through his recitation.

"Boy has shit for brains," she said when he finished.

Ajit studied her eyes, her stance. *Yes, and you would feed him to the sharks if that were the only question.* But that was not the way he was going to play his hand.

"I'm not going to argue the point," he said. "My point is to consider the Demos, the sorts of things we have all seen happen. You had nothing to do with what he did, but you are his mother, and your position includes responsibility for the altrubber production. There could be blowback to you, substantial blowback.

"Now, I know you have been very interested in my positions, and in the normal course of events, I would be able to help you with the situation your son has created for you. I said I would do that. What I have to tell you is that, in my present situation, I probably won't be able to help you. I'm sorry about that, but unless I get a lucky break, I won't have the position I need to do you any good."

Chloe's eyes squinted down further to narrow slits in puffy balloons of eyelid. "Okay. Suppose there was a way I could improve your chance of a lucky break."

By the time they were finished, Ajit knew this would be more than a lucky break. Chloe would do her part. He needed only one other piece. Fortunately, Chloe had left him enough time to take care of that as well. He sent a message to Cam, one that they had arranged. He did not care if anyone else read it, because it said only *Next*.

THE DEMOS

PENNY CAME OUT TO THE DOME WELL BEFORE SUNUP AND STOOD LOOKING AT the silent and still-empty structure. The Demos meeting would not begin until daybreak. They were well past the solstice, but the plan was to keep to solar time. She suspected—no, she knew—that chaos was in the offing with the sunrise. She would be in the center of the swirling chaos. She knew that too.

The solstice meeting, by virtue of being the only in-person assembly for the year and because of the effort required to come up from the valley, became a carnival as much as a political and business meeting. People brought their children if they had no one to watch them, and the children ran, shrieked, and played in the dome while the meeting and its oratory wore on. Meals were cooked and eaten, because with everyone having the right to speak, the meetings dragged on and no one wanted to miss a vote, a humiliation, or a fight.

This year was the first time a meeting had been postponed. The reasons for the postponement ensured that the attendance would be close to everyone who could possibly come. Major decisions were expected as well as plenty of entertainment.

·　　·　　·

IBIANA AND SONAL FOUND PENNY STANDING IN TOWN CIRCLE, EYES FIXED ON THE Community Dome, arms wrapped around herself, hands tucked into the sleeves of her cotton blouse.

"Why are you out here in the dark?" Sonal asked.

"Working to get my nerve up." Penny did not shift her gaze or her stance. "I never went to the theater as a kid on Earth, but I think it's the same way for an actor before they go onstage. Knowing they have to do everything perfectly. Wondering if they can. Wondering how the audience will react."

"You'll do fine," Sonal said. "You always do. I mean, after the times you were a kid in my Pioneer Youth—and okay, that last time maybe wasn't so great either."

Penny smiled a little at Sonal's attempts to minimize her screwups and gaffes. "There have been plenty of other times, more than I want to remember, like when we had the floods and they elected me again and I had to tell all of them what the food situation was."

"But you made it happen the way it needed to happen," Ibiana said. "Is the issue now your daughter? You're worried about her."

"Of course, and I can't let it show, certainly not to Thorny. That would make it worse. We did talk, for all the good that did." Penny still did not look at either of them. "I don't know how this is going to go. Not about Thorny, not about anything else we have to do.

"The one thing I have learned, though, in all the years of these meetings and all my mistakes, is to pay attention to what is happening, to listen, to watch people's body language, to feel the mood in there. Learning people is like learning math. I never liked math, but I figured out how to do it, figured out how to manipulate it." Penny unwrapped her arms and tried to smooth down her hair, a futile undertaking. "I can still shoot my mouth off, but I'm a lot more careful than I used to be. I do intend to change things. We need it."

"The problem is, as it always is, that there are essentially no rules." Sonal matched Penny's contemplation of the dome. "Anyone can stand up, be recognized, and say whatever they damn please. Or stand up and say it whether they're recognized or not. And propose anything. If somebody gets the mood of the crowd going, gets people behind them in the heat of the moment, the Demos can vote for whatever it wants, even if it doesn't make sense."

"*Vox populi, vox Dei.* 'The voice of the people is the voice of God.' Crazy way to run a planet." Penny did smile up at the clouds.

"Would you rather have one person in charge and making all the decisions, the way we had with Malachi?" Ibiana asked.

"I assume that's a rhetorical question," Penny said.

"Yes, but I have one that isn't," Ibiana responded. "Can we impose on you for a cup of your now-famous coffee? I think we could use some before this circus starts."

.   .   .   .

THE DOME WAS FILLING RAPIDLY AS REALITY AND TIFFANY, ALONG WITH GORDON and Poppy, shepherded their charges from the residence school across Town Circle to take their seats under the roof.

Once they were under the dome, Reality and Tiffany separated from Gordon, Poppy, and the students, all of whom were Heaveners. The Originals, the initial colonists, sat grouped by the ship they had come on, *Daredevil* or *Dauntless*. Therefore, Reality and Tiffany joined others who had once been the Pioneer Youth, even if they no longer resembled any kind of youth group. Those groups further sorted themselves between town-folk and valley-folk, dividing like bacteria.

Reality noted with a grimace that Miroslav, also a townie, maneuvered to sit as far away from her as possible while still staying within the group of townies from *Dauntless*. As the debate over equal shares had intensified, these subgroups further divided. Since Miroslav and Reality both aligned with work-for-reward rather than equals, they were both within that small sub-subgroup, which made it hard for him to put as much distance between them as he wanted to and made his effort to do so very obvious.

Reality sighed and looked away from Miroslav, away from the old Pioneer Youth and also away from the *Daredevil* Originals to where the students were seating themselves. The children, once they started residence school, always sat as a single group. The adult Heaveners now out of school had fissioned along the same lines as the Originals. She saw Gordon and Poppy wave to each other and then separate. The two of them had appeared much friendlier to each other since Gordon had driven the rover into gunfire as a decoy, but Gordon was a townie and Poppy was a valley-girl. That divide dominated in the Demos. Since this meeting would mark the first time the newly adult Heaveners would vote, the splits among them were obvious.

It occurred to Reality that if the human population of Heaven kept subdividing itself by more and more social, economic, and political schisms, eventually there would be a mass of political parties of one. Since she always felt solitary, it would be fine with her if the rest of them were forced to share her isolation. Reality hated the meetings of the Demos, hated them with a passion. They made her ashamed all over again at the way she had behaved in the early meetings after their arrival. Even if she tried to blank that shame out of her mind, the others would never let her forget it. This meeting would be worse than usual because they would need to vote on verdicts of guilt or innocence. Every minute of what she had done to help Malachi rig the votes he wanted would play through her mind. Miroslav would stare at her, which would make her want to proclaim herself guilty of whatever crime was being judged. No escape existed. Not for her.

·   ·   ·

CAM AND JESS LED THE THREE PRISONERS—WHAT OTHER WORD COULD DESCRIBE them?—into the dome. They were handcuffed into a single file, Northrup at the back end, Jones in the middle, and Mistry walking clumsily behind Cam because Jones's slow pace kept dragging his handcuffed arm back. They were taken to a table in front of the stands where the Demos sat, facing the dais of the town council. Normally, a defendant on trial by the Demos sat at a small desk in that position, but since there were three of them, a six-foot table had been put in place.

While they were being seated, Jacoby, Ibiana, and Sonal climbed the three steps to the dais and took their seats at the table there, Jacoby in the middle.

"Jacoby Grubb, mayor of Saint Peterstown. I'm going to declare this meeting of the Demos open, but before we start, I'm saying I'm resigning as mayor. You need to elect a new mayor."

The buzz of conversation that greeted Jacoby's announcement was muted because by this time most of the people knew it was coming. Guillermo Vargas stood up immediately from where he sat among the old Pioneer Youth who now lived in the valley.

"Guillermo Vargas of *Dauntless*, Original from the valley. I'm nominating Ajit Mistry to be mayor. I want justice for my son, and he is the only one who will give it to me."

The collective gasp that followed would have sucked the air out of the dome had it been enclosed.

"That means you're not going to resign just yet, Jacoby," Ajit said into the silence that followed. "I can't see how we can vote for mayor with me being accused of whatever I'm going to be accused of and no chance for the Demos to vote that I'm innocent." That started conversations all through the dome. It was as though, many people in the crowd said, Ajit knew the meeting would start this way.

Ajit managed to speak over the crowd noise. "And while we're at it, can we have these cuffs off? It's not as though there's any place for us to go." He yanked at the one connecting him to Jones, whose hands were in his lap, forcing Ajit to lean to that side.

"Well, ah—" Jacoby began.

"What is it going to be, Jacoby?" yelled someone from the back without standing up. "Sentence first, trial later? Or do it the right way?"

"Let's do it!" shouted another, and then there were more shouts from around the stands, with no one rising to be recognized.

"Do which?"

"Make a ruling, goddammit, Jacoby, you're still the fuckin' mayor!"

"All right, all right," said Jacoby. "Will you goddamn be quiet? I am so sick of this goddamn shit." The last was supposed to be a hiss only for Ibiana and Sonal, but the microphones in the table picked it up. The dome roared with laughter. "All right, goddamn you!" The speaker squealed as it carried Jacoby's voice over the background noise. "We'll do the trial first, then I resign, and I guess Ajit is nominated anyway and—"

"Could you tell the Demos and me what I'm charged with?" Ajit managed to project irritation. "And get this damned thing off!" He shook the cuff at Cam, who dutifully removed it.

"Ah yes," Jacoby said. "Ajit Mistry, Everett Jones, and Stephen Northrup, you are all charged with stealing the M8 rifles, attempted murder, an insurrection, and planning to take over Saint Peterstown. I can—"

"That's it? Good." Ajit stepped to the side of the defendants' table, facing the Demos more than the town council. "Ajit Mistry. Original from *Daredevil*. I'll speak first, and that will save the Demos a lot of time. I assume I can go ahead." That was a statement, not a question, and no one contradicted him.

The dirty T-shirt and shorts with sandals were far from the elegant attire he had worn on Earth when he faced down trouble in his casino or when he faced first investors and then the courts after his chicanery had been discovered, but he spoke with the same assured crispness he had then. It was as though he had taken charge of the proceedings.

"First, about the rifles. Sure, we took them, but that's not stealing, because those rifles are the property of the Demos of Saint Peterstown, and we have as much right to them as anyone. Sure, Vo Hiep locked them away after Malachi tried to set up a dictatorship, but that doesn't make them his. Or yours!" He jabbed a finger in Jacoby's direction.

"We have as much right to them as anybody does. If you want to charge Everett with breaking a couple of locks, I suppose you can, but that hardly seems worth it." He glared at the town council, then turned the glare on the Demos.

The dome went quiet save for a pair of four-year-olds who were having a skipping race up and down the steps of one of the aisles.

"So much for the rifles. Now, about attempted murder. That was self-defense, that's what it was, and that was my right. Vo Hiep took a rifle—took one before we did, if you still want to talk about stealing.

I had every reason to believe he would try to kill *me*. He knew I was going to be nominated for mayor and I support this town and the equals, which he does *not*.

"And I intend as mayor to prosecute his daughter for the killing of Fernando Vargas, which he intended to prevent. So, I knew he would try to kill *me*, and he is one of the Sicarii—and Originals know what that means.

"In fact, the only one killed was Oscar Gradison, and that was by Vo. I am sorry that Gordon Durham-Pole was *almost* hurt, we thought it was Vo, but Gordon was *not* hurt. No harm, no foul, as Americans on Earth used to say. As for insurrection, that never happened. Oh, wait! One candidate has been locked up to keep him from being mayor. *Me!*

"So, you see, we all agree on the facts. It is the reasons behind the facts that matter, and I have given you those. Anything else is a conspiracy, and you know who would be behind that." His eyes searched the crowded dome until he found Penny. Plenty of other eyes went the same way.

That was when Chloe stood up. "Chloe DiMasi, Original, *Daredevil*." The lighting in the dome emphasized the sweat on her face and the bags under her eyes. She was recognized. "What Ajit says is true. He spoke to me because he knew I support the town and equal shares. He told me that he feared for his life, that Hiep would kill him if he opposed Penny being mayor again.

"I didn't believe him at first, but now it's obvious. We know what Hiep will do. And Ajit had decided to stand up against Penny anyway. And that's the truth." Her descent into her seat was more of a collapse, but the crowd's focus was already back to Ajit.

"I think we know what the story is!" Ajit shouted. "So, what does the Demos say? Let's vote and have it over with."

•　　•　　•

From where he sat among the Heavener townies, Danijel watched in amazement as Ajit's oration went on. He could feel the mood of the crowd shift, not so much among the students around him, but elsewhere he could hear people agreeing with Ajit, saying Ajit had been wronged. Once Chloe had her say, the comments were no longer subdued. A scuffle in the back rows led to punches being thrown and then two men were on the ground grappling, with a ring of small children screaming at them to keep fighting while parents tried to pull the children away.

He's going to get away with it, Danijel thought. *It's not possible, but somehow it is. Even if Hiep or Penny stand up, I don't think this crowd is going to listen to them.*

Then one person did stand up, shove his way past seated people to an aisle, and walk down to the floor between the dais and the Demos.

"Gordon Durham-Pole. Heavener and townie, but I'm a Heavener more than anything else. I wish to speak before any vote."

"You are recognized, Gordon," Ibiana said when it appeared that Jacoby had lost the power of speech. "You have the floor."

"Thank you. I was the one in the rover that was shot up." He lifted his arms, then let them slap against his sides. "As you can see, no damage. I know what was going on because Everett Jones recruited me for their plan. Yes, they thought Vo Hiep would kill them." Gordon paused.

Danijel's heart sank. How could Gordon say this after what had happened? Could someone have bribed him?

"So they were going to kill him first," Gordon continued. "Self-defense? I leave that to you. What I do know is about insurrection. They were going to come here and have you under their guns while you voted to make sure you voted the way they wanted. I'd call that insurrection." His voice rose into a sudden shout. "What about you? What does the Demos say?"

A murmur started in the crowd. It rose to the level of a roar. Ajit gaped at Gordon, then started to snarl. "You traitorous—"

Gordon raised his fists. "Any time, asshole."

"Call the vote!" came a yell from the back row of the stands. "Call the vote!" Many shouts followed.

·   ·   ·

The Demos voted that the three were guilty of conspiracy to take over the government of Saint Peterstown and of being negligent in their use of the rifles, but that did not stop the commotion in the dome.

"The problem now is that we as the council have to decide on punishment for them." Ibiana leaned past Jacoby to speak in Sonal's direction, so the microphones picked up her words even though she kept her voice down.

"There's no good precedent. Malachi and the others with him were dead by the time we met. We didn't have to do anything about them," Sonal said. "And we didn't do anything to Reality."

People in the dome did not hesitate to contribute their own ideas at the tops of their voices.

"String 'em up from the dome rafters" and "Make 'em clean the stables for a year" and "Make Ajit mayor anyway" were some of the suggestions.

Ajit picked up on that last idea, waving his arms and screaming that he had been nominated for mayor so it was unfair to give him any sentence because that would influence votes.

"I told you I've had it," Jacoby said. "I don't want to be a clown in this circus. Not anymore. I'm resigning. Now! Elect a mayor and they can deal with this shit!"

"Fine!" Sonal slammed the flat of her hand on the table. The blow landed next to a tabletop microphone, setting off a boom that echoed from the roof followed by another earsplitting squeal from the speakers. That stilled the hubbub, and Sonal used it to shout, "I nominate Penny Panagiotidis! Come on down front, Penny!"

Penny stood up and picked her way a bit gingerly past knees and over feet to reach an aisle.

Her slow, careful movements led Ajit to point at her and say, "Penny, we know you're pregnant again. Do you really think you can handle the stress of being mayor now, or even the stress of this meeting?"

By the time he finished, Penny was standing in the aisle clear of everyone. She put her hands on her hips and grabbed the fabric of her pants to keep her hands in place. "Caterina Riario Sforza de' Medici took control of the fortress Castel Sant'Angelo in Rome with a sword on her belt when she was seven months pregnant. I think I can handle the likes of you."

It was doubtful anyone in the dome or listening on the network knew who Caterina Riario Sforza de' Medici was, nor did anyone bother to look her up. To know Penny was to expect non sequiturs. Laughter rose on all sides, but a lot of the laughs were directed at Ajit.

"Listen!" Ajit tried to compete with the laughing. "I am for the town. Always for the town. And I am for the equals. I will keep the equals. Ask Penny what she is going to do. When she opens her mouth, you never know what she is going to say."

Penny did not speak immediately. She walked down the steps and crossed the open space to stand in front of the dais and face the Demos. She found a moment, as she scanned the faces she knew, to marvel at the way the fear she used to feel when she had to speak in front of people had been replaced over time by a sense of excitement. She looked at the group of Heaveners from the valley to find Yong, who had ridden in that morning. Yong caught her eye, smiled, and offered a vigorous thumbs-up. Penny was glad for that extra measure of support. All the planning in the world gave no guarantee of what would actually happen now.

"What is important to know about the things I say is that they will make sense. That's what counts. Yes, we are going to have changes. Because we need to have them in order to survive. It's that simple. We can't keep having equal shares, because not everyone contributes equally to the community. Some people do more than others, and we need some people to do more than others.

"We need people to contribute to the maximum of their ability. They need to be paid for what they do. Otherwise, why should they do it? We won't leave anyone with nothing. There will be, call it a basic share, a minimum that everyone can have, but for more than that, compensation will be according to the work that is done."

"What about going south? Are you going to start that bullshit all over again?" That came from Maeve O'Brien, who had been in the Pioneer Youth with Penny. It made Penny feel as though she were back in the old days, when she had been mocked and disrespected by that very group of people.

What had changed was not the way Penny felt but the way she reacted. She had changed. "Yes," she said. "Because we can't stay forever just in the valley, and the town isn't viable without support. We need sources of metals, for one thing, real lumber for another, and resources for a larger population, because we can't stay static. Not if we're going to grow and survive. I am going to tell you: We can't survive in this part of Heaven without a technological civilization, but at the same time, we can't maintain a technological civilization here with only the valley and the town. It's that simple. There has to be change. If you don't want change, vote for Ajit, think of some good prayers, and hope he never wants to defend himself against you."

"Are there other nominations or others who want to speak?" asked Sonal. "If not, we should vote."

"Not so fast!" Guillermo was on his feet, and his voice carried. "I want an accounting for my son, and I want a judgment on your daughter, and I want it here and open. Will you promise that?"

"Yes," said Penny.

With that promise, moments later Penny was again the mayor of the only town on the planet. She stepped to the dais and replaced Jacoby at the council table.

"And now," Guillermo said as soon as Ibiana announced the tally, "in front of the Demos, do you keep your word?"

The tumult of the Community Dome was replaced again by a silence that made the wind sweeping through the open lattice sound loud. Even the smaller children who had been playing behind the last row of seats or wriggling on parents' laps quieted down. The question of what Penny would do was on every mind.

"I made a promise. I will keep it," Penny said. "A few matters to attend to first. You there"—she pointed at Mistry, Jones, and Northrup, "go sit on the floor by the framework until we decide what to do with you. If you leave, you get no food or supplements, so don't leave."

She looked back to the Demos. "Thorny, you need to come down and sit at this table." With an open hand, she indicated the table where the three men had been sitting.

Thorny, a stunned look on her face, did as she was told.

"Ibiana and Sonal will run the inquiry," Penny said. "I will not participate. That should be satisfactory."

"It most certainly is not." Guillermo had remained standing through the vote and its conclusion. He was still on his feet, an upthrust crag among the crowd, with people craning their heads to stare at him. "Those two were on your council when you were mayor before, and Sonal Davis, I remember she favored you when we first met as Pioneer Youth on Earth. No way the two of them will be fair. Ask the Demos what we think about that. See what you learn."

Penny let out a little sigh. Her fingers played with each other for a few seconds on top of the table. "I hear you." If Penny was surprised, she did not show it. "Then we will change the council as well. Ibiana, Sonal, I will need your resignations now."

Neither one seemed to quite believe what was happening, but they did as Penny asked.

When that was done, Penny straightened in her chair. "I said we need changes. The first change will be that Heaveners need to start taking responsibility and accountability. I want Gordon Durham-Pole as vice-mayor and Poppy Merriwether as secretary. Town and valley. Figure it out." No actor in a play had delivered their lines with greater passion. "What does the Demos say?"

.   .   .

Danijel thought his nerves were going to develop a bad case of whiplash. Like all the juniors and seniors and, for that matter, everyone in the dome, he stared at Gordon and Poppy when they stood after Penny called them out.

He heard the shouts from the Originals. "They're nothing but kids" was the nicest one.

"I was twenty-two when you elected me mayor the first time, and you should remember how young a twenty-two I was." Penny kept her voice hard, and her hands were still on the tabletop. "If you are Pioneer Youth Originals, you know. As for these two, they are responsible for our juniors and seniors now. They know everyone involved in this matter, and I will teach them how to manage our affairs. It's time for them to grow up."

"One's town, one's valley! How's that going to work?"

"I said figure it out." Penny's voice could have been cut from ice. "Heaveners are going to live here long after all the Originals are gone. They better figure it out."

"And what about equal shares?" The question came from the cluster of townie *Daredevil* Originals.

"I told you exactly what we need to do, and we are going to do it."

Danijel struggled to understand how Penny could be so cool in front of the unruly crowd. He would freeze if he had to stand down there.

"We will provide the basics for everyone; what I said will be basic shares. We can do that. Beyond that minimum, though, it has to be up to the person and what they do. Maybe we need to have money here. We'll figure it out. Now, what does the Demos say about my plan and council?"

If there were ever two people poleaxed by the same blow, they were Gordon and Poppy as they walked uncertainly to the dais and took their places to either side of Penny. Danijel did not think Ibiana and Sonal looked much better.

What was going to happen to Thorny now? That was the thought that pushed its way back to the front of Danijel's mind. How could Penny sit there and say that Gordon and Poppy would handle the case? He supposed that Penny had no real choice and that this was the best she could do, but how could she look so calm? He scanned the dome and found Hiep, who was not seated at all but standing near the framework of the dome's supporting structure, not far from where Mistry and his two henchmen were seated.

Neither Hiep's face nor his posture betrayed any tension. Danijel had learned that was typical; he did not think it reflected what might be inside the man's head. Hiep did not have a rifle, but he did have a sheathed knife at his belt, the same knife Danijel remembered him wearing out in the wild.

Danijel fastened on the knife, worn as casually as a phone in a pouch. What would happen if someone made the wrong move with Thorny? Which brought him back to Thorny, who was so alone at that table. She needed someone with her. She needed *him*. Hiep had told him to support her. How? Penny's words, *Figure it out*, banged in his head.

The proceeding began with Dr. Song coming down to stand at the side of Thorny's table and speak to the council about what she had found. She could not say for sure what had killed Fernando. That was what she said. There was no poison she could find. He had not taken a blow to the head that could have killed him. He had fallen face down, but with his head landing on one of his arms. The fall should not have killed him. She had learned only long after he was dead about what he had been inhaling, but she could not find any evidence that the compound had done it either.

"If he inhaled that chemical that night, yes, he could have had an allergic reaction, an anaphylactic reaction, but I can't prove it. I do think it is the most likely explanation. This was not due to trauma." When she finished, she did not go back to her seat but remained standing by the dais.

"Hershel Northrup, Original, *Daredevil*." While Dr. Song was speaking, Northrup and Mistry had been engaged in rapid-fire whispers. Now Northrup stood where the three had been seated, off to the side. "I assume I still have the right to speak."

Hiep looked at him, one hand on his belt near his knife, but did not move. No one gainsaid Northrup's assumption.

"The doc says there was no trauma, but I've heard there was blood in Fernando's head when they did the autopsy. Practitioner Yuki, would you speak?"

Yuki gave a fierce shake of her head. She did not stand up. That led to shouts of "Speak, Yuki, speak" that ran all through the crowd. It took less than a minute of that before Yuki was on her feet, visibly shaking. The death grip she had on her braid seemed likely to tear it from her head.

With a voice shaking as badly as the rest of her, Yuki told the story of the postmortem, of the blood she had seen, of the explanation from Jing dismissing it and the fact that Jing had excluded her from the examination of the brain.

"I stand by what I said," Jing said. "I am the only one here with the expertise to interpret the findings."

"I am not doubting our doctor's expertise, but I am wondering if she has taken a side in this matter," Northrup said. The glare he received from Jing should have made him hope that he never needed a doctor's services in the future, but he did not back down. "Maybe we should hear from the boys and girls who actually saw what happened and then, maybe, the Demos would like to revisit some votes, starting with the vote for mayor."

That led to the parade of Dalton and his group. They were each brought down to where Dr. Song had stood, and one by one, they gave their stories. They were all variations on one theme:

They had been outside the hydroponics facility when Thorny had appeared unexpectedly out of the dark. She had rushed to Fernando and kissed him. Then, suddenly, she shoved him away and hit him. When Fernando fell, they panicked and ran, but they did see Thorny take his phone. Each of them was vehement that Fernando had inhaled nothing, not that night. Nobody had been inhaling that night. They had waited for Fernando to come back, expected him to come back, had done nothing else until Kojo told them Dani went out. The implication of what had killed Fernando was obvious even if left unsaid.

Thorny seemed to squeeze into a tighter and tighter ball with each rendition. Danijel worried about the pressure building inside her head.

"Thorny, is that what happened? What actually happened?" Poppy made the question a gentle one.

Thorny's response was anything but gentle. Her head snapped up, her eyes blazed. "If you mean, did I go out there and did I kiss him, yeah, I did that, fool that I was." The snarl in her voice was unmistakable. "Regan told me that was the price of getting some of that juice Dalton had. So, yeah, I did. But he wouldn't stop. He wouldn't stop. And he had his hands . . .

"I wouldn't let him and I pushed him away and he jumped back at me and I hit him when he jumped at me. Once. And he went down. And I didn't take his fucking phone! But all of them"—she swung her arm around to encompass Dalton's group—"they were yelling for him to do me, to fuck me. That's what was going on!"

Immediately, Dalton and the others were screaming denials. No one had said any such thing. Danijel saw Hiep's fingers caress the hilt of his knife.

In the middle of the chaotic shouting, it was a minute before anyone noticed Jorge on his feet, demanding to be recognized. When he was finally able to speak, he said, "There is a lie here. I'm in the system. I have access, and at times like this, these chips are really convenient. Four of you kids"—he pointed at Dalton's group—"were calling his phone. Every fifteen minutes until about the time Dani was out there. So you weren't waiting for him. You knew something was wrong. His phone doesn't show on the system at all now. Where is it?"

"Maybe someone did make a call, and we forgot about it. We told you, she took it, probably dropped it out in the wild." Ethan started to point at Thorny but then pulled his hand back to his ribs and said nothing else.

Something clicked in Danijel's mind. He remembered Hiep's words to him: Thorny doesn't lie. He remembered other things from that night, ones that did not match up. He bolted to his feet. "Danijel Petrovic. Heavener. I need to speak! I need to speak!" All eyes went to him.

From the council table, Gordon said, "You found Fernando's body, but you weren't out there during any of . . . this."

"That is correct. But someone is lying, and it isn't Thorny."

"Go ahead then and speak."

The seconds it took Gordon to tell him to speak gave Danijel time to lose his nerve and regain it several times over. The weight of the stares from Dalton and the others was crushing. Despite a mouth as dry as overbaked clay, he managed to start. "I went out there because Regan called me. She said Thorny wasn't in their hab. She was afraid Thorny had gone out to Dalton's group and was worried something was wrong. That's what she said, and that's why I went.

"But you just heard Thorny say that Regan had told her kissing Fernando was the price for that stuff Dalton had. And after I came back from the South, Regan told me that Thorny had gone out there to screw Fernando, that she saw Thorny kiss Fernando. So, Regan lied to me that night. She knew where Thorny was, and she was out there watching. If Regan's lying about that much, she's probably lying about why Thorny went. I'll believe Thorny about that and about the phone. She doesn't lie.

"And that means the rest of you assholes are lying too. You all set a trap for her. This is your doing, starting with Dalton and Ethan, you and your friends. Mr. Vargas, what they did is why Fernando died."

Danijel wondered if he sounded convincing. He did not think he spoke with the assurance Penny or Jorge did. What had sounded so good in his head sounded lame when he said it. What mattered in front of the Demos was whether people believed what you said. That was all that mattered.

His words found a mark.

"Wait a minute!" The scream came from Ethan, hand clamped to his side. He rounded on Dalton. "You told me, and you told Fernando, that you had it all set up. That Thorny was going to do it because she wanted those visions, and she didn't care if we watched. You told me!"

"I didn't do it!" Dalton yelled back. "It was all Regan's fuckin' idea!"

"You fucking asshole!" Regan was standing in the student section, middle finger hoisted in the air, shouting as loudly as she could. "You were all cheering for him to fuck her!"

"But it was your idea, wasn't it?" Sonia moved in front of the others, somehow managing to speak while chewing so furiously on the insides of her cheeks that she might carve a hole in them. "This time I believe Dalton. I know how you like to get high. I helped you. You talked to me about how you hated having to be Thorny's habmate, but you had to do it to help your mother suck up to Old Lady Penny. You said you'd get even someday, and I'm sure I'm not the only girl you told."

"Fuck you too!" Regan now had the middle fingers of both hands extended.

"Yes!" Dalton shouted. "Regan came to me. She told me it was all arranged, that Thorny jumped at the idea. I gave her some stuff as a bonus. I can prove that!"

Sonia pointed a finger at Regan, biting her lip hard enough to start it bleeding. "When Ferdy didn't answer our calls, Regan, you told me that you'd call Dani, so he'd go out there. You said Ferdy probably got up, was pissed we left, and went to his hab and wouldn't answer our calls to spook us. That's what you said!

"So, Dani would be out there like an idiot and we could have a good laugh at him chasing Thorny. I mean we all know he can't keep his eyes off her and he thinks nobody sees that. And if something really was wrong with Ferdy, he'd be the one out there, not us!"

"Then you hid in our living quarters when Dani came over. Because Dani said Ferdy was dead!" Screaming and crying all at the same time, Dalton's face twisted into a caricature of itself.

"Enough! That's enough!" Song Jing had climbed the steps to the dais and was close enough to the microphones for her voice to dominate the dome. "The whole lot of you are disgusting. What it is, is that all of you connived at having Thorny raped. There's no other word for it. And when Fernando went down, you didn't call for help and you didn't even try to help him yourselves, because you were afraid that what you were doing—what you were really doing—would come out. Penny, I am going to ask you. What should we do with them?"

Other than a couple of crying young children, the dome hushed as Penny leaned forward. "If it was simply about how I feel, I'd build a gallows." She paused while everyone absorbed her last word. "This isn't like the situation with Reality years ago. She said she was wrong in front of the entire Demos and she came to me privately afterward to say she'd make amends by taking care of all the kids that were coming.

All this group is thinking of is how to hide what they are and what they did.

"However, we are too few to eliminate people, and we can't afford to have people who don't work." She drummed her fingers on the table; the sound amplified through the speakers. "I'll tell you what. We have land south of the Happy River that needs to be cleared and bridges that need to be built. They can do that work and get whatever we decide a basic share is. That's all they get for however long we decide. The Demos can vote on that."

"In a minute." Jing held up a hand. "I need to finish." She walked down the steps from the dais and over to where Thorny was still sitting. "This is about what happened to Fernando. Thorny, you did say you hit him."

"Yeah. I did. Only once." Wariness colored her voice.

"Show me how you hit him, where you hit him. Show it on me."

Thorny stood up. She extended her fist slowly until the front two knuckles touched Jing's chest a little left of center. "That's the best I can do to show you. It was dark. He was jumping at me."

"That's fine," Jing said. "I think that's the answer. We all know how hard Thorny can hit. I've seen her demonstration on Klaus's concrete. And she said Fernando was coming at her. I think, put together, that's enough force. If you hit someone directly over the heart, hit hard enough and that hit happens at just the right time in the heart's electrical cycle, it can stop the heart. It's called commotio cordis."

She turned a withering look on Dalton and the others standing with him. "Again, if you had called for help, if you had done CPR, he could have survived. You are responsible as well."

"You said she killed my son!" Guillermo was into an aisle, running down the stairs as he spoke. "You proved she did it!"

The scrape as Hiep's knife cleared its sheath froze Guillermo at the bottom of the stairs and brought a gasp from the crowd.

"Dad! Stop it!" Thorny shouted.

·   ·   ·

THORNY HAD SPENT ALMOST ALL OF A SLEEPLESS NIGHT THINKING ABOUT WHAT SHE wanted to do, what she should do. In fact, she knew the answers from the moment she set her mind to the question, but she kept turning over and over in her head whether she should say what she'd decided because of how it might sound, what people would think. First her father and then her mother had said they would support whatever decision she made. When those people made promises, they kept them. She should know. She had known them all her life! Why should they trust any decision she made? She doubted she had given them any reason to do so, but they had promised. That also meant they expected her to make a decision, and she did know what she wanted.

Then she sat at the table in front of the Demos. There was no question any longer what people thought of her. In a way, that was liberating, even empowering. She no longer needed to care what others thought. Well, there was one, but she had slammed that door shut herself. She shook off that thought. It was not worth grasping after impossibilities. The only problem that remained as she sat there was how to make herself speak. And then her father had drawn that knife.

After her shout, Hiep went completely still. The remaining distance between him and Guillermo was great enough to be safe. Unless he threw the knife. Guillermo groped with one foot for the stair behind him so that he could back up without turning around. Instead, he fell on his ass. He looked silly, but no one laughed.

With one swift move, Hiep slammed the knife back into its sheath. The snap as the guard hit the rim of the sheath was loud in the dome. The tension in the dome grew thicker, as though the turgid air itself were solidifying to the point that it would take that knife to cut through it. The time to speak had come, and she knew it.

"All right, all right!" Thorny found her voice again. "If you can stop prosecuting me for a few minutes, I have something to say."

The crowd looked to Penny for direction but did not receive any. "She is my daughter, so it is not for me to rule." Penny gestured instead to Gordon and Poppy. "Do you recognize her to speak?"

"What do we do?" Gordon kept his voice soft and his head turned from the Demos in the hope that his indecision was not obvious.

"Recognize her," Poppy hissed.

When Gordon did, it was like a weight being lifted from Thorny. She looked up at Poppy and Gordon on the dais. Then she turned around and looked at the Demos in their semicircles of seats that rose high above her head. It made her feel small. That would not do.

Leif chose that brief interlude to stand on his seat, wave his arms, and shout, "You tell 'em Thorny! You tell 'em!" He jumped up and down on the seat while waving his arms to make certain he was seen and heard.

That pissed her off enough to trigger action, but somehow she did not lose control. She swung a leg up onto the table where she had been seated and pulled herself up. She stood up on top of the table and faced the Demos that way. The table wobbled once as she found her balance. The thought flashed through her mind that she would look ridiculous if the table collapsed under her. She told herself not to care. She had no time for it.

"Okay, okay. Thorny Odyssey Panagiotidis. Heavener. I'm going to tell you a few things. First, you heard my mother say we need to end equal shares and to figure out how to move beyond the town and the valley. You need to listen to her! If she says we need to expand, then we need to do it. My mother is the most annoying human on the planet, but she is always right. Well, almost always. Well . . . never mind. That was the first thing.

"The other thing is about Fernando. Yes, I punched him. I hit him because he came at me again after I pushed him away. I did it to keep him off me and to keep his hands away from me. Dr. Song says that punch actually stopped his heart and she is the doctor and knows this stuff, which means that he died because I hit him. So that means I killed him. I'd call that self-defense, but maybe not everybody thinks that way. Maybe you think I brought it on myself. You can vote on it as the Demos, but however it comes out, I don't think the voting is going to change anyone's mind about what they believe. But I have a proposal."

She had to stop for breath at that point. Her chest was on fire; it felt like she had not breathed since she started to talk. It struck her, as she pulled air in, that no one used that break to start talking. No one took the floor from her. Her eyes darted around. She saw her mother's eyes on her. What was in her mother's mind? Mom was in her saving-humanity mode. That was probably a good thing, Thorny thought, because they needed Mom to do that. She checked her father. No sign of what he was thinking, but she knew he would do whatever it took to protect her and Mom and any of the other kids. Could she do what she had to do, what she had decided to do? *Do it, Thorny. You've thought about it long enough.*

Hiep nodded to her, his eyes never moving from her face. *He knows, doesn't he, knows even without my saying a word. They both know.* She noticed that she had brought her hands together in front of her, fingers interlaced. She thought that looked silly, looked weak. She wrenched them apart, stood straight with her fists at her sides.

"Here is what I think should be done: I'm going away from here. For two years. You can call it pioneering or you can call it exile. Whichever suits you. But I will go. I'm going to take supplies, and I'll go to that place I went to, call it South of Heaven. That name could fit a number of ways. Two years. If I can make it on my own down there, well, there's your proof that we can live elsewhere on Heaven. It's a big land open to us. If I can't . . . well . . . survive, then I guess some of you can feel vindicated."

"Are you saying you want us to vote on this?" Poppy asked.

"Yes!" Thorny was not sure if the table was wobbling or if it was her.

"We need a second." That was Gordon.

"Wait! I have an amendment!" Danijel clambered over a row of seats and the people in them, then shoved his way past obstructing legs to reach the aisle. From there, he ran down to the front, where Thorny was standing on the table. He climbed onto the table as well, took one of her hands in his, and raised their linked hands high.

"Danijel Petrovic. Heavener. My amendment is . . . I'm going with her!"

She turned to him with her face up. "I had a dream you would come with me, but I could never ask for that." In response, he kissed her in front of practically the entire human population of the planet.

The Community Dome resounded with a mixture of clapping and laughter, punctuated by squeals from the younger ones. In the midst of that, no one noticed the woman who had walked down to stand next to the table, facing the council, until she put her hand in the air and shouted, "Reality Busby. Pioneer Youth. *Dauntless*. I wish to speak!"

After Reality was recognized, she turned to face the Demos. "All of you know who I am. You know who I *was*. I have spent twenty years trying to atone for who I was and what I did, but the fact is that, except for a few, you are not ready to forgive me. So I'm done. I can't do any more. I'm going with Thorny and Danijel."

At that, the Community Dome did fill with a babble of voices. Everyone, it seemed, was talking at once. Gordon and Poppy looked first at each other in bewilderment, then at Penny. Penny grew a soft, sad smile. She gave each of them a pat on the shoulder.

Penny chipped in, made certain the microphones were on and at maximum. "The Demos will come to order!" Her voice boomed through the dome and across the people gathered there. All other talk trailed off. "Penny Panagiotidis, mayor of Saint Peterstown," she said. "We have an amended motion in front of us. I will offer a further amendment. That we provide proper provisions for all those who are going to South of Heaven and that if there are others who wish to join them, we will make provision for them. Do we have a second?"

"Seconded." Hiep did not need a microphone.

Penny drew herself up straight, her fingertips resting lightly on the tabletop. "What does the Demos say?"

CODA

The tumult and the shouting dies;
The Captains and the Kings depart:

Rudyard Kipling, "Recessional"

WINTER HY 23
SOUTH OF HEAVEN

THE LAST GLOW OF THE WINTER SUN HAD FADED FROM THE HORIZON. NONE OF the moons were up. The sky was lit only by star-spangled veils of multicolored auroras. Their light shimmered on the white webs that draped the lower branches of the trees and fell across the bushes.

On the hill overlooking the bend in the river, Danijel and Thorny stood in front of their log cabin. They had built a much bigger one since their return, and the original now served for their animals. Yellow light from the fireplace flickered through a window, and smoke curled from the chimney. It was cool enough in the winter in South of Heaven that heat was desirable, and it was better to save the electricity from the photovoltaic panels for other purposes. Besides, a fire in the hearth made the place more homey.

Past the cabin, off their hill and among the trees, another spark of light was visible. That was Reality's tiny cabin. Farther off, unseen in the darkness, were the homes of two other couples. Together, the four houses made up the community of South of Heaven. More people would come in the spring. Good land lay in every direction. Their community would grow.

"I think we've got the work done," Thorny said.

"For now." Danijel laughed. "The work is never done."

"I know. Sometimes I think I've sentenced us to a lifetime at hard labor."

"But together. That's what counts." He reached a hand out to her.

Thorny took his hand in hers. Two smiling faces turned up to gaze at the stars above Heaven.

DRAMATIS PERSONAE

ORIGINALS AND THEIR SHIPS

SAINT PETERSTOWN

REALITY BUSBY—Head of the residence school, *Dauntless*

CAM—Public safety officer and co-manager of the stable, *Daredevil*

CHLOE DIMASI—Director of printing and cell foundries, former scammer, *Daredevil*

OSCAR GRADISON—*Daredevil*

JACOBY GRUBB—Mayor of Saint Peterstown, *Daredevil*

VANESSA HUGGINS—Ibiana's partner, formerly ran an escort service, *Daredevil*

EVERETT JONES—Head of Saint Peterstown IT, a former thief, *Daredevil*

ATHENA MARKOPOULUS—*Dauntless*

AJIT MISTRY—Candidate for mayor, former casino manager and fraud, *Daredevil*

HERSHEL NORTHRUP—Vague about former dealings, probably in the street drug trade, *Daredevil*

IBIANA OWUSU—Vice-mayor of Saint Peterstown, Vanessa's partner, a former swindler, *Daredevil*

MIROSLAV PETROVIC—Town engineer, *Dauntless*

YUKI WATANABE—Practitioner, trained as a nurse, *Dauntless*

HAPPY VALLEY

DONNA BILLINGSLY—Farmer, Guillermo's wife, and Fernando's mother, *Dauntless*

Sonal Davis—Secretary of Saint Peterstown and Klaus's partner, *Dauntless*

Klaus Koch—Entrepreneur, farmer, and Sonal's partner, *Dauntless*

Maeve O'Brien—Farmer, *Dauntless*

Jorge Olivares—Former junior pilot of *Dauntless*, IT specialist, and Jing's husband

Penelope (Penny) Panagiotidis—Farmer, Hiep's wife, and former mayor, *Dauntless*

Song Jing MD—Former ship physician of *Dauntless*, physician of Saint Peterstown, and Jorge's wife

Guillermo Vargas—Farmer, Donna's husband, and Fernando's father, *Dauntless*

Vo Hiep—Farmer, Penny's husband, and former mercenary, *Daredevil*

HEAVENERS

TOWN

Ethan Cappelletti—Dalton's habmate

Gordon Durham-Pole—Residence school proctor for seniors

Sonia Janasch—One of Dalton's group

Regan Mulders—Thorny's habmate

Kojo Owusu—Ibiana and Vanessa's son and Danijel's habmate

Danijel Petrovic—Miroslav's son

Fernando Vargas—Guillermo's son

Dalton Watkins—Chloe's son

HAPPY VALLEY

Jordan Longfellow—Day laborer

Poppy Merriwether—Residence school proctor for juniors

Thorny Odyssey Panagiotidis—Penny's daughter and second child

Yong Panagiotidis—Penny's daughter and eldest child

Leif and Huan Vo—Penny's twin sons

ABOUT THE AUTHOR

COLIN ALEXANDER IS A WRITER OF SCIENCE FICTION AND FANTASY. HE HAS HAD A career as a physician, biochemist, and medical researcher. He now lives in Maine with his wife, where he also studies and teaches taekwondo.

I hope you have enjoyed the story of the colonists on the planet Heaven, whom we first met in *Murder Under Another Sun*. (What happened to Leif after he went back to Earth is detailed in *The Lucky Starman* and subsequent books in the series.) I will write other stories in the Leif the Lucky universe, some involving characters who met Leif along the timeline of the series, but the next book will be set in the universe of the Interstellar Reach. This will again follow the adventures of Saoirse Kenneally, picking up her tale a dozen years after the conclusion of *Complicated: The Interstellar Life and Times of Saoirse Kenneally*. Come along for a wicked ride.

BRICKS AND STONES™

Find Colin Alexander on the web at:
www.afictionado.com
www.facebook.com/ColinAlexanderAuthor
www.goodreads.com/colinalexander